D1582388

no
such
thing
as
perfect

no
such
thing
as
perfect

Emma Hughes

CENTURY

1 3 5 7 9 10 8 6 4 2

Century
20 Vauxhall Bridge Road
London SW1V 2SA

Century is part of the Penguin Random House group of companies
whose addresses can be found at global.penguinrandomhouse.com.

Penguin
Random House
UK

Copyright © Emma Hughes 2021

Emma Hughes has asserted her right to be identified as the author of this
Work in accordance with the Copyright, Designs and Patents Act 1988.

First published in Great Britain by Century in 2021

www.penguin.co.uk

A CIP catalogue record for this book is available from the British Library.

Hardback ISBN 9781529125818
Trade Paperback ISBN 9781529125832

Typeset in 12/15.5 pt Palatino LT Std
by Integra Software Services Pvt. Ltd, Pondicherry

Printed and bound in Great Britain by Clays Ltd, Elcograf S.p.A.

The authorised representative in the EEA is Penguin Random House Ireland,
Morrison Chambers, 32 Nassau Street, Dublin DO2 YH68

Penguin Random House is committed to a sustainable future for
our business, our readers and our planet. This book is made from
Forest Stewardship Council® certified paper.

MIX
Paper from
responsible sources
FSC
www.fsc.org   FSC® C018179

For my family

perfect (adjective): very suitable; as good as it could possibly be; without faults

In maths, something that is easily divided

PRESS RELEASE
EMBARGOED UNTIL 7 JUNE

NEXT-GENERATION MATCHMAKER CUPID IS ON A DATA-DRIVEN MISSION TO REINVENT DATING

It's one of life's biggest mysteries, isn't it? The spark, the chemistry, the thing that makes two people fall in love – and stay there. It's elusive and impossible to define. Right?

We don't think so. We're Cupid, a new kind of match-making service launching later this year, offering you a data-driven way of finding love. Imagine someone looking inside your head and discovering what really makes you tick, then using those insights to match you with someone that's perfect for you – and vice versa.

What makes us different from every other app on the market?

Well, we're not actually an app. We don't need to be. We're like that friend you always wanted to have who's great at matchmaking – except instead of knowing half a dozen single people, we've got millions of them.

The problem with existing dating apps is that all they've got to go on is what their users choose to tell them: the things they think they're looking for in a partner, their interests and hobbies, their hopes for the future. But people don't always know what's going to make them happy – and

3

even if they do, they might find it difficult to be honest about it for all sorts of reasons.

Here at Cupid, we're going to be doing things differently. No more fruitless swiping, no more conversations that begin promisingly and end up going nowhere. Instead, we'll be starting from scratch with the most reliable guide to the real you that there is: what you do online when nobody else is watching.

We've partnered with carefully chosen data-brokerage companies to create the largest and most detailed database of people looking for a relationship ever built, based on their internet search histories. Think of it as the world's most comprehensive psychometric test. You might not be fully aware of what your digital activities say about you, but you don't need to be – that's what we're here for.

How much will it cost? Well, we want to be available to everyone, not just a privileged few. So we're operating on a pay-what-you-can basis. We're happy to give you a steer on a suggested donation, but there's no minimum – and no money changes hands until we've lined up a match for you. Of course, if you're in a position to give more generously and you want to help us reach more people, we're certainly not going to send you away.

It might sound complicated, but it's actually beautifully simple. Give us your likes, your clicks, your dwell times and your most-watched videos – and we'll give you the love of your life.

Chapter 1

algorithm (noun): a set of instructions for solving a problem

The doughnut on Laura's desk in the *Bugle* office was monstrously large, glazed half an inch thick and pebble-dashed with peanuts. Raspberry jam oozed from a hole in its side. It looked, she thought, like a cartoon asteroid – or one of the pictures that might come up if you did a search for 'the Black Death'.

Inge, the Sunday magazine's features editor and Laura's manager, turned around and gave her a smile that was strangely bright for nine o'clock on a Monday morning. Her eyes were fixed on a point behind Laura's left shoulder – which was odd, Laura thought, because they were friends as well as colleagues, and she'd never noticed Inge doing that before. Also, Laura was standing in front of a totally blank wall.

'They were giving them away at Old Street this morning,' Inge said, the words tumbling out on top of each other. 'I remembered how much you liked doughnuts when we did that tasting! That was a great day, wasn't it? We ate so much! So funny!'

Something was wrong. As she took off her coat and dumped it on one of the dozens of empty chairs that littered the newsroom after the past few months' redundancies, Laura noticed Inge watching her closely – the expression on her face reminded her of the way Harrison, her parents' ageing collie, looked at her whenever he'd ripped one of his toys apart. She found herself picturing Inge sitting on the carpet, surrounded by fluff, holding a squeaker in her mouth.

The phone rang before Laura had even switched on her computer.

'Laura, *hi!* It's Poppy from the People Team!' The voice on the other end was simultaneously perky and abrasive – and just like that, all the morning's confusing pieces came suddenly and sickeningly together. 'We were wondering if you had a second to pop upstairs? I've got Glenn from Aero-dynamica here and he'd like to have a little chat. Only if you're not too busy!'

'I'm *never* too busy for you, Poppy,' Laura said. She re-placed the handset, pocketed her own phone and picked up the brand new, businesslike notepad she'd already decided she'd take with her when this call arrived. She'd known it was coming, but as she stood up, she realised that right until a second ago she'd still been clinging onto the hope that she might somehow slip through the net and be saved. All the way to the lift she could feel Inge staring at her, buffeting her back with pity.

***

The man waiting for Laura in the corner office where people got hired and fired was at least five years younger than her, with a pink, shiny face. As she opened the door Glenn leaped up and stuck out his hand for her to shake. He had bristly hair that reminded her of a kiwi fruit.

'Laura Morrison!' he said, cheerfully crunching her fingers. 'Good weekend? Get up to much? Watch the game? Old what's-his-name had a shocker, didn't he?' He let her hand drop. 'Right! Well. Let's get started, shall we? Take a pew.'

There was a window behind him – Laura could see her reflection in it, distorted by the tint on the glass and the lighting. It made her shoulder-length hair, which was quite a nice sort of coppery colour on a good day, a worrying shade of magenta, and her greeny-brown eyes were terrified-looking dots. Glenn settled back into his chair, unclipped the binder in front of him and pulled out a stack of printed flashcards. As Laura lowered herself into the chair opposite his she saw that sections had been italicised in a way that immediately made her think of the service sheet at a funeral. She positioned the notepad squarely in front of her so that it acted like a shield.

Glenn cleared his throat self-importantly.

'As you may be aware, Bugle Media Group is streamlining its operations,' he began. There was a pause while he shuffled a new card to the top of the stack. 'It's brought in the consultancy company I work for, Aerodynamica, to conduct a review of the business. One of the areas where potential cost savings have been identified is the weekend magazines …'

Is this how Glenn would break up with you? Laura wondered. By stealth? She imagined him reaching for her hand across a table in All Bar One on a Tuesday night and telling her he knew they'd always be in each other's lives, then ordering a nacho platter for them to share. She watched his lips move, fighting a rising tide of panic. She'd always lived from month to month on her overdraft; her savings account had £20 in it. She'd only been at the *Bugle*'s Sunday magazine for three years, which meant she'd be leaving with very little if they did get rid of her. It could be months before she found another job in journalism – if she managed to find anything at all.

'... so on behalf of Bugle Media Group, Aerodynamica will spend the next sixteen weeks assessing your role and the value that you add to the organisation,' Glenn continued, his face getting pinker as he tried to avoid looking at her. 'This is part of our work to, er, future-proof the company.'

He gave his tie an anxious little tug. He looked so young, Laura thought. Maybe this was his first job. Maybe he still dreamed of joining a band, or breeding rare sheep, or sailing around the world by himself. A small part of her felt sorry for a small part of him.

Glenn cleared his throat again, then ploughed ahead, flipping through the cards. 'At the end of the four-month consultation period you will be notified in writing of the outcome,' he went on. 'You will be pleased to hear that no input is required from yourself.' He realised he'd run out of cards and stopped talking abruptly.

'Does that, um, all sound OK?' he said after a pause.

'Great,' Laura said heavily. 'Really excellent, actually. Thank you.'

Glenn, who was clearly as unfamiliar with sarcasm as he was with the flashcards, looked relieved. 'Great!' he echoed. 'Nice one!'

Her knees clicked as she stood up. It wasn't even half-past nine, but Laura found herself wondering how long it would take Inge to notice if she curled up on the floor of a toilet cubicle and went to sleep.

'I bet you have a busy day ahead of you,' she said to fill the silence.

'Yeah, absolutely!' Glenn nodded enthusiastically as he walked her to the door. 'But they're the best kind, aren't they? Stops the day dragging. Keeps you on your toes!'

He laughed and tugged at his tie again. It was printed, Laura noticed, with tiny sailing boats.

***

Back in the corridor people were shuffling out of the morning news conference. Everyone looked grim and hunched, like they were walking into the wind. Laura realised, too late, that she'd left her notepad behind in the meeting room. She hovered uncertainly: she really didn't want to go back to her desk, but she wasn't sure what else she could do. Without her job, who would she even be? It felt like the sole marker of adulthood she'd ever managed to hang onto successfully, even though she was still, at the age of twenty-nine, only an editorial assistant.

The *Bugle*'s Saturday magazine was the one everybody read: it was big and glossy and always had a blockbusting celebrity interview on the cover. The Sunday one, which was smaller and printed on paper that stained your fingers, came tucked inside the golf section, so it went straight into most people's bins. But Laura had loved everything about it when she'd arrived: the fact it rolled up small enough to fit into a pocket; how they pieced it together like a jigsaw as a team over the course of the week; the way the ideas they talked about in their Monday meetings slowly became real and solid, until you could reach out and touch them on the newsstand the following weekend.

'Laura! Hey!' Femi, one of the graduate trainees, raced up to her. He was the most enthusiastic twenty-one-year-old she'd ever met. In fact, she thought, watching him zipping towards her in his slightly too big suit, he was probably the most enthusiastic *person* she'd ever met, full stop. He'd done English at Oxford and an internship at the *New York Times*, before getting a scholarship to study journalism at City University. He spent his weekends freelancing for up-and-coming websites, in between leading a youth a cappella group and driving his grandparents to and from church. He'd applied to do his placement in News, but he'd taken to being moored in the windless harbour of Features cheerfully, applying himself to writing gift guides and lis-ticles with a thoroughness that put the rest of them to shame. He was always so cheerfully keen, volunteering for errands and making them all endless rounds of unasked-for tea. Laura was meant to be showing him the ropes, but the idea that she could teach him anything – except maybe the trick to getting two Twixes out of the canteen vending machine when you'd only paid for one – was preposterous. She forced herself to smile.

'Hi, Femi,' she said, desperately trying to sound normal. 'Everything OK?'

'There's someone in reception for you – they've been trying your desk phone but you weren't answering,' he announced breathlessly. 'I said I'd come and find you.'

'Really? That's funny, I'm not expecting anyone. Did you see who it was?'

Femi shrugged. 'A guy. Steve someone?'

Laura's stomach tightened. 'Oh, shit,' she muttered; Femi's eyes widened. 'It's Walker, my old flatmate. That's his surname, Steve's his first name. Everyone used to just call him Walker but nobody does now apart from me …' She could hear herself babbling. 'He's meant to be drop-ping off some of my stuff that he took when we all moved out,' she went on, trying to pull herself together. 'He's a teacher and he's taking a school trip to the Canal Museum later. I completely forgot it was today.'

It was a sign of how much her meeting with Glenn had shaken her, she thought as she watched Femi bouncing away again, that she really had blanked out Walker's visit: for the past week the thought of it had kept her awake at night.

Walker had moved out of their old flat just off Holloway Road four months ago, to live in a shiny new-build place in Hammersmith with their other flatmate Sasha, who for the past eight months had also been his girlfriend. He and

Laura had grown up in the same Berkshire town – they'd actually been to the same sixth-form college, although they hadn't spoken until they bumped into each other at a Christmas party after they'd both left university – and for a few months in their early twenties they'd been a couple too. Her feelings about the whole situation were, to put it mildly, complicated. She'd been the one who'd broken up with him all those years ago and although Sasha wore jazzy leggings and put bee pollen on her porridge and played adult rounders, she was basically a very nice person it was impossible to hate. But Laura missed Walker and how close they'd been, more than she wanted to admit. While they'd been living together, people she'd just met would quite often think he was her boyfriend when she mentioned him, and sometimes she'd let them. Then Sasha had come into his life and Laura had to stop doing that.

Walker was standing in reception with his back to her, chatting to one of the security guards. He was wearing one of the suits he'd had to buy when he started working as a music teacher and holding a bundle of her blistered plastic spatulas – she'd watched him putting them into his box when they were packing and hadn't said anything, thinking that him taking them might be a good excuse for them to meet up. His strawberry-blond hair was sticking up in tufts – although he was nearly thirty it still resisted all his efforts to brush it into a grown-up shape.

Laura stood still as she watched him running a hand through it: she'd have given anything to tell him what had just happened with Glenn, but that felt impossible. The only real contact they had now was playing Words With Friends. Before Sasha moved in they'd played the Scrabble-a-like game constantly, messaging each other from their own rooms late at night between turns – Laura had been able to hear him through the wall punching the air and exclaiming whenever he bagged a double-score tile. But once he and Sasha got together, games that would once have taken an hour started to stretch to days, then weeks. Even the app's name, Words With *Friends,* seemed to be mocking Laura now. She'd invited him to a new game at the weekend, but the word she'd played – WINKED – was still alone on the board.

'Walker? Hi!' she called. He turned around, holding her things like a bunch of flowers.

'Special delivery.' He grinned. Was she imagining it, or did he look slightly nervous about seeing her too? She stayed where she was, worried that if he got too close he'd be able to sense her feelings.

'Honestly, you could have just posted these,' she said, sticking out her hand to take the spatulas from him. 'So! How's life in the Wild West?'

'Good! We've got a barbecue on the terrace now.' He was smiling broadly; any nerves there had been seemed to have gone now he was talking about his new life. His happiness felt oppressive, like the more of it he had, the less of it there would be for her.

'And how's Sash?' she asked, secretly hoping he might say something like *she's run away with the British Gas engineer.* 'All good?'

Walker's face broke into an even bigger smile. 'Yeah, great,' he said. 'We've signed up to do the Colour Run next month. You know, the one where they chuck paint at you as you go round?'

Sasha had moved to London from Melbourne two years ago and she was still enthusiastic about every novelty activity the city had to offer; whether it was pub golf or a ghost tour of the East End, she was up for it. Walker had always scoffed at all that stuff, just like Laura. But that was before the creaking floorboards and the wine glasses mysteriously appearing on the drying rack overnight. She felt a quick, sharp stab of grief and reflexively touched her phone through her pocket. He wasn't dead, she reminded herself – he'd just moved in with his girlfriend, which was a perfectly normal thing to do. He and Laura could still be in each other's lives. They both just had to make a bit more of an effort.

'It's your turn, by the way,' she said. Walker looked confused.

'What?'

'On Words With Friends.' Her face was burning – he clearly had no idea what she was talking about, which meant he obviously wasn't thinking about her that much. 'I just got thirty points for "winked".'

Walker's eyes crinkled as he smiled. 'Did you now?' he said teasingly and for a moment everything felt almost normal again. 'Alright. Challenge accepted.'

He took a step forward and it looked for a second like he was about to hug her. Then he stopped himself and converted the movement into a matey pat on the shoulder.

'Let's do something soon in real life?' he said. 'Please?'

Laura nodded, not trusting herself to speak. As she watched him loping across the polished floor towards the revolving doors she gripped the spatulas tightly.

***

The doughnut was still where she'd left it, sweating slightly under the office lighting. Laura couldn't remember a time when she'd felt less hungry. She sat down and took her phone out. The Flat 8A Eden Grove group chat, which had been at the top of her WhatsApp for four years, was now six up from the bottom, below a marketing text from Pizza Mario Bros offering her free dough sticks. She hadn't realised how many messages they'd all sent every day – the others who'd come and gone, but always her and Walker, the fixed points around which the third flatmates had moved like satellites – until they'd permanently dried up.

Instead of going into WhatsApp she opened Tinder and started flipping aimlessly through its digital brochure of faces. *No, maybe, hmm, no, definitely not, no, no, no.* It was the stickiest of all the apps, demanding a surprising degree of elbow-grease. Sometimes it felt as though it really didn't want you to swipe left and say no to anyone. Not that it especially mattered what you did: it was all basically random anyway. She'd long since lost faith in the idea that you could find out anything useful about someone just from looking at photos of them. The emotional aftermath of a fruitless session was unpleasant, like a sugar crash, but there was still something soothing about the act itself – on some level it made you feel like you were at least doing *something* to change your life. She sighed and squeezed the doughnut; a glob of jam leaked onto her desk.

'It's horrible.' Inge was behind her, carrying a coffee from the canteen. She handed Laura her paper napkin. 'I'm so sorry.'

Laura tried to wipe the mess up. 'It's the thought that counts,' she said, smearing jam around the desk. 'Thanks for getting it for me.'

'No, I meant …' Inge sighed. 'Look, obviously I'm your manager, but you can always talk to me about things outside work too. I mean, you just lost your flat – and now you might lose your job too, which of course makes it all so much worse. You must be feeling terrible.'

'Well, I am now,' Laura said, dropping the napkin into the bin. Sometimes Inge's directness, although it was kindly meant, was hard to take. (There had been one time, while they were in the toilets getting ready for the Christmas party, when Laura had asked if her jumpsuit made her thighs look chunky. Inge had put her head on one side, as though she was considering the viability of some architectural plans, then said, 'Yes – but then, they *are* chunky, so I think it's OK.')

'Sorry. You know what I mean.' She gave Laura an encouraging smile. 'Anyway, nothing's definite yet. Four months is a long time. Anything could happen. You might get an incredible scoop! They'd be idiots to let you go.' She glanced over Laura's head and rolled her eyes. 'Speaking of which ...'

Laura looked up and saw Phil Castle, the main paper's features editor – universally known as Bouncy – bowling towards them. He was holding an iced pastry in one hand and a big brown envelope in the other.

'Morning, girls!' he boomed. 'Inge, I haven't forgotten you need a designer to cover Asha's honeymoon in August – I've had a chat with Gardens and they might be able to spare Adrian a couple of mornings a week to help you with your pages. Apparently, he's blooming marvellous! Ha ha!' He took a step towards Laura; Bouncy always stood close enough to you that you could smell the stale coffee on his breath. 'Everything alright, Lonely Hearts? You look a bit glum.'

'We've just had some bad news, Phil,' Inge said, sitting down at her computer and making a point of turning away from him.

'Ah, yes, of course.' He drew a finger of the bun-holding hand across his throat, leaving a snail trail of icing behind. 'Well, look, nothing's been decided. I'm sure you'll make the cut, Laura. Anyway – I've brought you something that'll cheer you up. Art were updating the features gallery in the boardroom yesterday and I got them to do me an extra one of these. Close your eyes and hold out your hands.'

Laura reluctantly complied; Bouncy had been at the *Bugle* for almost as long as she'd been alive and he had the ear of everyone on the management team – she couldn't afford to make an enemy of him, especially not now. He placed the brown envelope on her palms.

'Well, aren't you going to open it?' he said. Laura, who already knew what it was, wondered for a fraction of a second if she was going to be sick.

When the redundancies had started happening a couple of months earlier she'd manically pitched all kinds of crazy features to everyone in the building – she knew that as an editorial assistant she was considered disposable and had hoped that if she stayed visible and looked busy she'd be safe. *We're looking for stuff that's a bit more PERSONAL*, Bouncy had replied to her suggestion for a piece on urban beekeepers. *Got anything?* Laura had started to reply, apologising profusely for the fact that she hadn't. And then, suddenly, she realised that she had.

She'd been going on dates for exactly ten years. Her romantic career had started at nineteen with an excruciating night of speed dating in Manchester's Union Bar during Freshers' Week (she'd ticked the wrong box and ended up going to the Jodrell Bank Observatory with a second-year astrophysicist who picked his nose on the bus there), progressing through stints on some earnest, question-heavy dating sites and briefly deviating into DM slides when Twitter launched, before finally ending up where it was now, shaped by hungover Sunday-evening-swiping and a cycle of interest, expectation and varying degrees of disappointment.

There had been half a dozen or so sabbaticals – three months here, six months there – when a *thing* had turned into a *Thing* and she'd found herself swapping singledom for life as half of a couple, complete with Sunday brunches, trips to the Barbican or Kew Gardens and, once, a long weekend in Paris. But none of the relationships had stuck in the way they seemed to for other people. Something always seemed to go wrong: they'd have a stupid fight that would blow up, or she'd wake up one morning and realise that she'd stopped fancying them, or they'd announce they were moving to Kansas to study wild turkeys (that was a thing that had actually happened). She never understood why things turned out like that for her – only that they did, like clockwork.

As time went on she'd started feeling more and more embarrassed about the way her instincts just seemed to be *off* and that she couldn't make anything last – even the end of things that she'd been iffy about felt like a failure, a shameful reflection on her capacity to love and be loved. The more she thought about it, the more bewildered she felt. *How did you do it?* she found herself wanting to ask couples. *How did you know?* In her darker moments, she wondered whether there was something about the whole business that she just wasn't cut out for. But by writing her dating disasters down, she told herself, she'd be able to reclaim them – so that's what she'd pitched to Bouncy. She'd envisaged it as being a fun but insightful piece – an unapologetic dispatch from the romantic frontlines. When she'd filed it, she'd smiled properly for the first time in weeks.

This is GREAT, Bouncy had emailed four minutes later, suddenly very enthusiastic. *We're going to shoot some pics of you so we can give it some more space – Tuesday morning OK? Don't worry about clothes, we'll sort all that.* She got to the studio to find a rack of white dresses waiting for her. The picture that ended up as the feature's opener – the one she was holding in her hands now, glued to thick card – was of her in the biggest of these, hugging her knees while the stylist tried to fix the heating. She looked sad and panicky; defeated, deflated, drowning in fabric. Back in the newsroom, someone had painstakingly cut her out and Photoshopped her onto the bottom of a giant Snakes and Ladders board.

Hours spent on the sofa swiping, dates who disappear, wedding bells a distant dream ... the introduction looming over her had read. *As she hurtles towards her thirtieth birthday, Laura Morrison is one of a growing number of twenty-something women who keep finding themselves ...*

BACK TO SQUARE ONE

The issue had come out six weeks ago, and it had been bad enough for Laura when it was on sale. But now it was on the *Bugle*'s website it kept popping up on Twitter; every time it appeared there she was in the picture, the official meringue-shaped mascot of romantic failure and disappointment. Whenever she thought about it, a queasy feeling of shame smothered her like an oil-slick.

Bouncy was studying her. 'I believe it's customary to thank people when they give you a present,' he said sulkily. 'It was your first feature in the main paper, Laura – I thought you'd like a little souvenir.'

She tried to look appropriately grateful and found she couldn't; her face had done enough pretending for one day. 'It's just ... you made me look like I'm wearing a wedding dress,' she said.

Bouncy scoffed. 'Everyone loved it – that issue flew off the shelves. And for what it's worth, the present Mrs Castle thought it was a lovely photo of you.'

'I've long suspected Mrs Castle might need her eyes testing,' Inge muttered.

Bouncy chortled. 'When you've quite finished, Inge, we're running a nice little piece on Swedish baking – buns, buns, more buns! I thought you might want to run your eyes over it, seeing as it's your part of the world.'

'I'm from Denmark,' Inge said, turning around and folding her arms. Bouncy waved a hand airily.

'Same difference. You all leap about in the snow starkers, don't you?' He glanced at his watch. 'Well, I can't stand around here all day chatting. Catch you later, girls! Be good!'

'Do you think he knows we hate him?' Laura asked as they watched him go.

'I think being Bouncy is a lot like being dead,' Inge said. 'It's hardest for other people.'

Laura stuffed the envelope down the side of her desk. Over the course of the morning her inbox had filled up with press releases: one for a £300 face cream made with real gold, another about a restaurant in Barking serving pizzas for dogs, an invitation to go wild boar watching in the New Forest. When she'd started the job she'd answered each unsolicited PR pitch she received, thanking them for getting in touch and politely explaining why it wasn't quite right for the *Bugle's* Sunday magazine. Now she just got rid of them, hacking through the digital undergrowth. There was also one from Asha the designer's maid of honour, Zoe, about Asha's upcoming hen party – it had the subject line *LAST FLING BEFORE THE RING* and was asking them all to transfer £25 to cover 'snacks and balloons'. Laura deleted that too.

She was nearing the top of her inbox when a new email appeared. The subject was *FOREVER STARTS HERE*.

She clicked on it.

> *Laura, hi.*
> *We hope you'll forgive the direct approach – we sent you our press release a couple of weeks ago, but we wanted to follow up with something a bit more personal. That's how we like to do things!*

We're Cupid. We're a new kind of dating service, one that's powered by your digital footprint.

We really loved the piece you wrote recently – if it's not a weird thing to say, we think you sound like our kind of person. And we've had an idea that we'd like to run past you.

Although we're not officially launching until later this year, we'd like to offer you the chance to be the very first person to trial our service – and to write about your experience. Obviously, there'd be no charge.

Have a think and give us a call. We reckon this could be the start of something really beautiful.

Love,

The Cupid Team

Laura stared at the email for a long time. The words stared back at her, unblinking. She took her finger off the track pad, hesitated, then replaced it, moved the cursor quickly over to the bin icon and clicked. The email disappeared with a hollow clang.

Chapter 2

relation (noun): *a set of ordered pairs and their outcome*

For the whole of the six years they'd been living at 42 Stony-brook Street, Laura's older sister Jamie and her husband Whit's front door had been painted in an expensive minty colour called Arsenic. But a couple of days ago a man in overalls had come to re-do it – Laura had no idea why; the old door had still looked startlingly new, just like the rest of the house – and now it was more of a mossy shade. (Bile? Mulch? Cholera?) As she trudged up the path and dug in her bag for her borrowed key she could smell the lingering fumes. It was barely five o'clock – she'd pretended she had period pains as an excuse to go home early and Inge had pretended to believe her.

Stonybrook Street was one of half a dozen doppelgängers that joined Clapham Common to the main road. It always made Laura think of a model train set: two rows of houses frozen beneath blankets of ivy and logoed scaffolding. There was rarely anybody on the pavement and never any traffic, not even during rush hour. At night it was so quiet that it was possible to imagine you had actually died. (Laura did, fairly regularly.) Like her old flat on Eden Grove, 42 Stonybrook Street was part of a Victorian terrace – but that was where the similarities ended. While Laura, Walker and Sasha had been squashed into a basement with one bathroom between them, Laura's sister and brother-in-law owned the entire house and had recently, for no clear reason, converted the loft. It wasn't, Laura thought uncharitably, like they needed more space.

Once she'd unlocked the door she crouched on the front step and poked the letterbox (antique brass, bought at an auction) open. Through it she could hear the Beach Boys and someone whistling a completely different tune over the top. Her heart sank: she'd forgotten that both of them had taken the day off for one of their impromptu long weekends. She pulled her shoes off, nudged the door ajar very carefully and tiptoed inside.

The hallway smelled of clean linen and the lavender oil diffuser on the table. Shoes in hand, Laura inched past the room with the big TV that Whit and Jamie had referred to as the 'family room' when they moved in (they didn't call it anything now), trying not to make any noise – she'd been keeping her distance from people all day, wanting to be alone with her thoughts. Now she was desperate just to get into bed with Netflix and a packet of chocolate digestives.

She'd almost made it to the foot of the stairs when one of the floorboards (oak, heaved back from a salvage yard and reconditioned) creaked traitorously. She froze. Then the door to the kitchen opened and Whit appeared. He was wearing an apron printed with cartoon ducks in chefs' hats.

'Hey, kid!' he bellowed. 'You're back early! Jamie's just showering – wanna give me a hand?'

Laura really liked her sister's husband, even though he wasn't, as her dad put it, the sharpest crayon in the box.

That was exactly why she didn't want to talk to him; she was worried that if she did, Whit would be so nice and well-meaning that she'd probably start crying and then wouldn't be able to stop. She dropped her shoes into the wicker magazine basket on top of *Condé Nast Traveller* and followed him reluctantly into the kitchen. It was an open-plan one with an island in the middle – the catalogue it had been bought from showed people standing around it laughing and eating nuts, but Jamie thought nuts made a mess, so there were never any of those around.

On the worktop was a shopping list in Whit's handwriting, four browned chicken thighs ready to go into the pan that was bubbling away on the hob and a saucer of bread-crumbs. Laura would never have told anyone this – being forced to move in with your sister at the age of twenty-nine because your flatmates had binned you and you hadn't been able to find anywhere else to live was embarrassing enough – but she was secretly grateful for the love and warmth that standing on the edge of these domestic scenes allowed her to soak up. The atmosphere was so different here from the tense one on Hazel Close in Bracknell that she and Jamie had grown up in. The house was also about three times the size of their childhood home and luxuriously warm, like a hotel – their parents' place had always been chilly by design, to save money. Overhead the waterfall shower roared.

Whit handed Laura a bag of salad and a big bowl to tip it into. He poured her a glass of wine. 'Good day?' he asked, turning the extractor fan on before she could answer. Her brother-in-law, who was the grandson of Canada's sixth-biggest maple syrup producer, was a senior associate at a law firm, just like her sister. (Laura found it quite hard to imagine him being senior to anything, except for maybe a filing cabinet.) She quickly lifted the lid off the pan, hoping that would let her get away without answering.

'Smells nice,' she said, inhaling the steam. Whit beamed.

'Oh, it's just a little Italian thing I've been working on,' he said, giving the sauce a stir. A bubble burst, splattering his apron with red. 'I got the idea for it when we were in Umbria – we went to this great place where they served this dish called Hunter's Stew.' He looked over at his shopping list and frowned. 'Wish I could ask him when the olives are supposed to go in.'

'Who?'

'Hunter.'

Laura looked at him to see if he was joking. He wasn't. 'I don't . . .' she began, before thinking better of it. 'I mean, I'm sure it doesn't matter. He'd probably say you should just do whatever feels right.'

Whit's face, which had been briefly clouded with concern, settled back into its usual happy shape. Sometimes, Laura thought, it was like being related to an Etch-a-Sketch.

The showering had stopped. Footsteps crossed the bedroom floor above them and came down the stairs.

'Ah, the lady of the house!' Whit announced.

Jamie padded into the kitchen with her hair in a towel and kissed his cheek, totally bypassing Laura, who found herself reflecting, for the millionth time, on just how unlikely they were as a couple: Whit, who was so gentle and uncomplicated, and Jamie, who was – well, neither of those things.

Jamie, at thirty-eight, was the extra parent Laura had never had – and never asked for. Jamie had been nine when Laura arrived and was twelve in her earliest memories, with a drawer full of *Blue Peter* badges and an imitation-leather briefcase she insisted on taking to school. Laura had always assumed there would come a time when she'd catch Jamie up and finally feel like an adult around her – or at least, when Jamie would start treating her like one. She was still waiting.

We do love each other, Laura had said to Walker, back when they first met. *I'm just not sure we like each other very much. Or, you know, at all.*

Today Jamie was wearing a pristine white shirt and cornflower blue cropped trousers made from a special material that never needed ironing. Laura couldn't think back to a time when her sister hadn't looked this way – like a perpetually pissed off Kate Middleton. Laura had never been allowed into Jamie's wardrobe, but she imagined everything hanging up arranged in complete outfits.

'I'm glad you're here,' she said, staring pointedly at Laura's wine glass, which was hovering just above the worktop. 'I was going to email you.'

'Why? I live with you.'

'That isn't *quite* how I would put it.' Jamie grabbed a coaster and thrust it under the glass. 'You're staying with us.'

'And paying you rent.'

'We agreed you'd pay a nominal sum to help you focus on finding a more permanent solution, yes. But I'd hardly call it rent.'

'What exactly would you call the money someone pays their own sister so they can sleep on an inflatable mattress?'

'It's a very nice air bed, Laura. Anyway, we talked about why you can't have the spare room. We need it.'

'Yes, for your friends – all six of them.' Laura picked her glass up again and moved it back onto the wood; Jamie winced. 'They definitely need somewhere to sleep after trekking from Parsons Green to Clapham for one of your Ottolenghi specials.'

This was what always happened: Jamie treated her like a child, so Laura behaved like one, and on it went. Jamie sighed heavily and closed her eyes. Laura imagined her counting to ten in her head, using some kind of corporate mindfulness technique.

'I was going to email because I wanted to talk to you about our barbecue,' she said, very slowly.

'What about it?'

'Well, the dress code is semi-formal. I thought you'd want to know that.'

There was a half-eaten packet of sea salt and cider vinegar crisps lying on the worktop, fastened neatly with a wooden clothes peg. Laura reached around Jamie and grabbed them.

'Sorry, go on,' she said, shoving four in her mouth at once. 'I only yawn when I'm really interested.'

Jamie rolled her eyes. 'All I'm trying to say is that it's going to be smart and it would be nice if you were smart too. OK?'

She spoke like a newsreader now, Laura thought – all the edges had been sanded off her voice over the years, as part of her ongoing project to remake herself. Laura ate some more crisps, revelling in the obnoxious noise they made.

'Did you invite Mum and Dad?' she said.

Jamie stiffened and Laura, who knew exactly what she was thinking, experienced a surge of sour pride at having scored a hit. It made her feel a strange kind of closeness to her sister.

'I'm sure they already have plans.'

'You don't know that.' *Crunch crunch.* Pause. *Crunch.* 'You should invite them.'

Jamie closed her eyes again, did some more of the silent counting, then folded her arms.

'I'm not going to do that.'

'Why not?'

'Because I don't want to,' she said. 'And I don't have to, because I'm an adult.' She started unloading the dish-washer. 'When you become one maybe you'll understand.'

Whit, who'd been quietly stoning olives, caught Laura's eye. *Please*, he seemed to be imploring her. She glanced at the table – it was, she noticed, only laid for two. An unlit candle stood expectantly between the two placemats.

'Well, I'm meeting someone in a bit,' she said, draining her wine glass and grabbing the crisps. 'I probably ought to get going.' Jamie turned, eyebrows raised, and gave her a searching look.

'Someone?'

'It's not a date, if that's what you're wondering.'

'Pity,' Jamie said tartly.

***

'I think I'm going to frame it,' Lil said.

She and Laura were in the biscuit-icing cafe in Herne Hill, which stayed open late in the summer. Dora, Lil's daughter, was sitting opposite them, earnestly decorating a gingerbread man – and her clothes – with the contents of several piping bags. They were reading her first end-of-year school report.

> NAME: *Dora Cho*
> YEAR: *Reception*
> *Dora is five going on thirty-five! She's always the first to put her hand up and she's a real little go-getter. It's lovely that she's so sure of herself, but we think it might be nice if she worked on letting the other children (especially the boys!) have a turn now and then ...*

Laura put it back in the envelope. 'Well, I'd hire her,' she said. Lil did her throaty laugh, which made all her hoop earrings jangle. She looked exactly how Laura remembered her the first time she'd spotted her in the *Bugle* office

27

almost three years ago, letting a door slam in Bouncy's face: dark hair piled haphazardly on top of her head, an off-the-shoulder top tucked into jeans that were buckled with a Dolly Parton-ish belt, expertly applied red lipstick and flicky eyeliner.

They hadn't been as close as they were now when Lil was on the *Bugle*'s Beauty desk – she'd still been in the eye of the new-parenthood storm and Laura was so comfortable in her flat with Walker that she hadn't really felt the need to deepen their connection. But a couple of months before Laura moved in with Jamie, Lil had left to become the chief copywriter for a make-up brand. They'd got back in touch on Instagram and started messaging every day; and now Laura was only living a bus ride away, they were seeing a lot more of each other. They were such different people: Laura hated talking about her feelings and had never met a can she couldn't kick down the road, while Lil was all about having it out with people, right here, right now. But they made each other laugh and, although she didn't want it to mean as much to her as it did, Lil was Laura's only single friend – and that really mattered.

The soft-voiced waitress who'd set up the table for them brought over their drinks: lemonades for Laura and Lil and a child-sized pretend cappuccino with mini marshmallows floating in the milk. She crouched down, beaming at Dora, who was covering the gingerbread man in squiggles of red.

'What have we got here, angel?' she asked.

'Blood!' Dora yelled, smacking the piping bag. Icing spurted all over the table.

'She's very into *Game of Thrones*,' Laura said, flicking a splodge of icing off her top. The waitress backed away slowly, like a hiker who'd just come across a bear in a clearing.

'I didn't tell you about Andreas!' Lil fished an ice cube out of her glass and crunched on it. She and Dora's dad had split up the day after her third birthday (the soft-play party had been booked for six months and the deposit was non-refundable). 'He's got a new girlfriend. She works for Lululemon, if you can believe that.'

Laura raised her eyebrows. Andreas was a cheerfully overweight animator who had once eaten an entire ten-person trifle by himself.

'Have you met her?'

'No, but she sent me an email last week asking for my blessing and saying she hoped we could all "move forwards in love and reflection". Then she invited me to come and watch her do yoga in the window of the Regent Street store.'

'Did you go?'

'Obviously.' In went another ice cube. 'It was pretty impressive, actually. She did this thing where she put her legs behind her ears and hopped around on her hands. I'm amazed Andreas isn't on crutches.'

Laura remembered Jamie telling her that Lil could get away with 'being crude' because she was beautiful. The implication, Laura had felt, was that she wasn't, and there-fore couldn't.

'Walker came to the office today,' she said, looking down at the table. 'He had to drop off my spatulas.'

Lil repositioned a kirby grip. 'Just him? No Ms Motiv-ator? I thought they were joined at the hip.' She snapped one of the legs off one of Dora's abandoned gingerbread men and took a bite. 'I still can't get my head around it – if you'd asked me nine months ago who the least likely per-son in the universe for Walker to end up with was, I'd have said a PE teacher who still unironically watches *Sex and the City* when she's getting ready to go out.'

Lil had been personally affronted by Walker's transformation from scatty musician into a faculty member at Holmworth Park Academy who actually had opinions on things like garden furniture and parking restrictions. *I managed to get married and have a kid without turning into a boring bastard*, she'd said once, thumping the table in the pub for emphasis. *People ought to get fined for it – a fiver in a jar every time they bring up baby-led weaning or Peppa sodding Pig.*

Laura tried to laugh, but it felt like there was something heavy sitting on her chest. 'It was the first time I'd seen him since we all moved out and it really brought it all back,' she said, not looking at Lil. 'I never thought I'd miss the Piccadilly line, but ...' She shrugged helplessly. 'I do.'

'Why don't you treat yourself to a trip?' Lil joked, putting an arm around her. 'Go round the Heathrow loop a few times, make a day of it.' She cocked her head. 'Look, this is none of my business, but are you completely sure you don't still have ...' She lowered her voice. 'You know. *Feelings*. For Walker.'

Laura looked away – she always felt like Lil could see straight through her – and shook her head. 'I just feel so ... alone now.' She snapped off the gingerbread man's other leg. 'I think the *Bugle*'s going to make me redundant,' she went on, biting into it. 'I found out today that they're going to be assessing my performance for the next four months. They got a guy in a novelty tie to break the news. Nice touch, right?'

'Seriously?' Lil shook her head. 'Fuck – I'm sorry. You're still at your sister's, aren't you?' Laura nodded. 'Well, that's something. At least it's better than sharing a room with small fry here. Less chance of waking up with someone dribbling on you. Or worse.'

Lil had actually been through a divorce, Laura reminded herself, plus the sale of her old flat and the negotiations over how Dora was going to split her time. When she compared her problems to all that, they felt so small and adolescent. What did she really have to complain about? Thinking that didn't make the pain go away, though. In fact, it made it worse – it just magnified her feelings of being hopelessly stuck in life's starting blocks while everyone else was sprinting away from her.

Dora leaned across the table and tugged at her sleeve.

'Laura,' she said insistently, peering up at her from under her dark, heavy fringe. 'Laura, look now.'

She was holding up one of the little pots of silver balls she'd been given to press into the icing. She grinned, pausing for dramatic effect, then dropped it. Laura watched as its contents scattered and rolled away across the floor.

***

Laura misjudged how long the journey back would take her – she could imagine Jamie's face if she turned up while the two of them were spooning into their pots of cheesecake, so she got off the bus early and walked across the Common, killing time. It had been four months since she'd heaved her boxes into an Uber and said goodbye to Eden Grove, but she was still trying to get used to it here: nothing about her new routine felt normal yet. She paused near the bandstand to step out of her flip-flops and scrunch her toes into the cool grass in the way she'd read somewhere cured jetlag. It was easy to laugh at the Bugaboos here and the middle-aged men who puffed past in brand new wireless headphones like they were the first people ever to have trained for a marathon, but she was growing to like it at sunset – there was a sweet, fresh smell to the earth that she'd never noticed in London before. She checked the time again: it wasn't even eight yet. The rest of the evening stretched ahead of her blankly.

The only free bench she could find was next to a bin – a run of warm evenings had turned it into a Vesuvius of pizza boxes, orbited by flies. She sat down at the end, took the packet of crisps out of her bag and unrolled it. It was nearly empty, so she licked her finger and used it to transfer crushed remnants to her mouth, piece by piece. It was slow work, which she liked; as long as she was doing this the rest could wait.

'You only get three of them in your life,' a teenage girl lying on the grass in front of her was saying. She and her friend were sharing cheesy chips from a Styrofoam container.

'Three what?' The friend was inspecting her fork. Her blonde hair was twisted into two little buns; every so often she would huff a loose strand out of her face.

'Loves,' the first girl said. 'It's such a *massive* thing, your body can only handle it so many times. Then it just kind of … runs out.' She flipped herself over onto her front and stared at the bin's halo of droning insects. 'You know – like bees. How they die when they sting you.'

Her friend snorted. Then she pulled her fork back like a catapult and pinged its load at the first girl. In the split second it took the chips to hit their target Laura was ambushed by a memory of when she and Walker had visited Stonybrook Street three years earlier. Jamie had deliberately left the wine they'd brought on the side, still in its plastic bag, so Laura had swiped it as they were leaving and they'd swigged it on the grass out here. Then they'd shared his headphones and drunkenly sung along to 'Bohemian Rhapsody', with him doing the high parts and her doing the low ones. She felt a lump forming in her throat. She got her phone out and opened Words With Friends to see if he'd taken his turn yet. He hadn't – WINKED was still there, all by itself. As she clicked out an advert popped up.

HOW ABOUT TRYING SOLO CHALLENGE? it yelled above a graphic inviting her to play against a cartoon computer. *IT'S FUN!*

How much more of this could she take? She found herself going into her work emails. There in the deleted items, above a reminder to enrol on an e-learning module called 'Everything You Ever Wanted to Know About Cloud Storage (But Were Too Afraid to Ask)', was the email from Cupid. Its final sentence stood out tantalisingly against the brightness of the screen, offering the promise of a new life.

We reckon this could be the start of something really beautiful.

Chapter 3

variable (noun): *an expression that can be assigned any of a set of values*

'Right, I've been having a look at that contract they sent you,' Inge said briskly down the phone line. It was a week later and Laura was across the street from Cupid's office, a co-working space called Double Negative Studios near the south side of Tower Bridge. Inge had gone into one of the *Bugle*'s empty conference rooms to call her; the speaker made it sound like she was ringing from the bottom of the sea.

'So you're agreeing to date whoever they match you with for twelve weeks and provide Cupid with press coverage at the end of that period, plus shoot some kind of promotional video for them,' Inge continued. 'That's all fine in principle, but if for whatever reason you don't fulfil your side of the bargain there's quite a lot of heavy-sounding stuff here about them going after you for "compensation", which I'm guessing means money. I don't know to what extent that's actually enforceable – I'd have to check with our legal department – but I'd rather not find out once you've signed up. I think with something like this, Laura, where there are so many unknowns … What I'm trying to say is, you can pull the plug on it today if you want to, OK? I know Bouncy's keen but you don't have to go through with it.'

'I do though, don't I?' Laura said, trying to keep her voice down. 'You saw his email. It's basically the only thing standing between me and a P45.' Glenn from Aerodynamica had been making his way around the desks, taking notes on their activities. How would it look if she backed out of a big feature that had already gone on the forward planner? That was what she'd been telling herself on the way here, anyway. But deep down, she knew that wasn't the only reason she was lurking here in her lucky polka-dot skirt. 'And I mean, it might …'

She stopped herself. One of the things she'd always liked about Inge was that she never grilled colleagues about their love lives. *Look, I was single for a long time*, she'd said during the first out-of-work drink they'd ever had, a month after Laura had started at the *Bugle*. *If you've got good news, you'll tell me. If you haven't, you aren't going to want to talk about it, are you?* Inge, she knew, thought of Laura as someone who swam against the social tide, sharing her bafflement at made-for-Instagram proposals and stork-confetti-strewn baby showers. Laura *was* genuinely bemused by all that stuff – but it didn't mean she wanted a life without love. Secretly, she'd been hoping that this whole thing might actually work: that the Cupid team would sift through the life she led online, find some vital key to her personality that she'd missed and use it to get her off the merry-go-round of disappointment that she'd been on for so long.

'I should go in,' she said quickly. 'I'll message you when I'm on my way back, OK?'

'I'd take your time if I were you,' Inge said. 'We're all being forced to listen to the staff choir singing Ed Sheeran in the lobby at four. The beatings will continue until morale improves.'

She rang off. Laura closed her eyes and rolled her shoulders until they crunched, trying to get some of the tension out of them. Then she opened her inbox to check the address – the email Bouncy had sent in reply to her pitch was still at the top.

> *L to the M! LOVE this. Human interest! Let's do it exactly like you've said – you get them to fix you up with a bloke, give us the inside story on that (and him, ha ha ha), few quotes from the founders, boom, done. Working headline 'HOW DATA SAVED ME FROM BAD DATES'. We could make the pics futuristic too, get some lasers involved – project a microchip onto your face maybe?*

That made her feel precisely zero per cent better. She went back to her home screen and flicked through her apps until she got to the cluster that was euphemistically entitled 'Social'. Tinder. Hinge. Bumble. She covered them with her finger, trying to conjure a world where she never needed to think of a witty opener again, or block someone who'd sent her forty-six dick pics in one hour, or self-righteously delete all the apps before reinstalling them a week later when it turned out that the real world wasn't overflowing with nice, normal, available people after all.

Double Negative Studios was on the ground floor of a warehouse that had once been a camera factory. There was nobody in reception apart from a girl in dungarees sitting cross-legged on a stool, reading an arty-looking magazine. Her tangerine hair was poking out from under a knitted bobble hat and she was wearing a badge that read 'Vibe Leader'. She didn't move when Laura arrived.

'Um, hi,' Laura said. Her voice bounced off the concrete walls; the whole place was unsettlingly quiet. 'I'm meant to be meeting Anoushka? From Cupid?'

The girl squinted at Laura. Then she pulled a tablet out from between the pages of her magazine and swiped through a series of screens, humming to herself.

'OK,' she said, giving the screen a tap. Then she went back to reading.

Laura stood there feeling a thousand years old.

'Should I ...' She looked around the room. None of the furniture had been obviously designed as seating, but there was a sort of big, squashy Lego brick in the corner that looked reasonably safe. The girl nodded without looking up.

Laura went and sat on the brick. She was at one end of a long corridor lined with glass-walled offices, like square fishbowls. In one a group of people were sitting in a circle on the floor with their eyes closed. The one directly across from it was empty, but the floor was covered in glitter. There was a blackboard positioned near the door, on which someone had written BE MORE UNICORN.

The girl on the stool called out to her.

'Do you want a juice?' She had a croaky voice, like the host of one of the true-crime podcasts Jamie listened to in the bath. 'We've got carrot and parsley or charcoal lemonade.'

Laura saw there was a clear plastic mini-fridge against the wall next to the girl, full of bottles. They were all filled with murky-looking liquid, like something you'd pour out of the bottom of a bin.

'Um, lemonade, please.'

'Good call,' the girl said, in a way that indicated she felt it was anything but. She opened the fridge with her foot, then hopped off the stool, got a bottle out and lobbed it across the room at Laura, who caught it awkwardly. She opened it and took a wary sip; it tasted even more disgusting than it looked. She put it on the floor and got her phone out. She was about to take a picture of it to send to Lil when she heard footsteps coming towards her – a chirpy *squeak squeak squeak* against the industrial rubber flooring.

'Laura! Hey, *you*!'

A very pretty, olive-skinned woman in a sundress and shimmery silver boots bounced out from behind a pillar and dragged Laura off the Lego brick. With her hair in a topknot, it was impossible to tell how old she was – she could have been twenty-one or forty-one – but she looked like she slept for twelve hours a night and never had to eat her toast at the bus stop because she'd forgotten to set her alarm.

'It's me, Anoushka! We've been emailing!' Cupid's head of marketing came in for a hug, crushing Laura's forehead into her collarbones. She smelled sweet and warm, like caramel wafers and freshly tumble-dried towels, and her voice was stridently posh. 'Did you find it OK? Which way did you come?' She gave Laura a final choking squeeze, then released her.

'Call me Nush, by the way,' she said, absent-mindedly fingering the material of Laura's shirt. 'Everyone does. This is lovely – blue is *such* a great colour on you!' She beamed. 'Come on,' she said, taking hold of Laura's arm. 'Let's give you the tour.'

She walked Laura to the other end of the corridor and back again. It was ferociously air conditioned. 'That's the tour!' she announced with a tinkling laugh. 'Only a couple of the offices are ours right now. We're a pretty small team at the moment, but we're on track to double in size by the end of the year. That is, if you give us a glowing write-up.'

She laughed again and dug Laura in the ribs. 'Kidding, kidding. Fancy a drink?'

'I've just had one of the lemonades,' Laura said, glancing back nervously at the bottle.

'Oh, how grim – then you'll *definitely* want something stronger.' Nush looped her arm through Laura's and steered her towards the doors. 'There's a place that's just opened around the corner called Sink or Swim. It's in the building where they made the *Titanic*'s navigational instruments – isn't that great?'

The glass box directly to their left was the busiest of all. There were at least a dozen young, cool-looking people in there, all clustered around a single screen. There was clearly a lot of animated discussion going on about something – Laura strained to hear but the glass was too thick for her to make anything out.

At the back of the group was a man with several days' worth of stubble and his arms crossed, surveying the scene. His brown hair was tied back in a knot at the nape of his neck and he had on a pair of ironic Clark Kent glasses, plus a grey zip-up hoodie and the kind of dark-wash jeans that Laura knew came from Japan and cost several hundred pounds. He was half smiling, as though somebody had just told him a joke and he was still deciding whether he thought it was funny.

'Who are they?' Laura asked, craning her neck to try and see what he was looking at. Light from the window was falling onto the screen, obscuring whatever was on it. She imagined her personality – all her hopes and fears and the things she'd never told anyone – spliced up there for everyone to see. Would it be like the pie chart she got from her bank at the end of every month showing her what she'd spent her money on? Except instead of things like coffee and Oyster card top-ups it would be … what exactly?

'Oh, that's Data,' Nush said. 'They crunch the numbers. Or they build the models that crunch the numbers, anyway. We recruited most of them from e-commerce sites – Amazon, Asos, that kind of thing.' She grinned. 'Of course, finding someone a life partner is a *bit* more complicated than helping them buy a toaster, but the underlying principles are actually pretty similar.'

She took a step towards Laura and lowered her voice. 'I'm not supposed to say anything, but they're fine-tuning your match right now …'

Laura remembered all the dates she'd been on when it had been painfully obvious in the first five minutes that nothing was ever, *ever* going to happen and felt herself going cold with panic.

'What if we hate each other?' she asked, trying to keep it out of her voice. 'Do I get another one? Can I swap?'

Nush laughed lightly. 'Look, let's cross that bridge if we come to it,' she said, giving Laura's shoulder a firm little scrunch. 'Obviously the *last* thing we'd want is for you to feel that way. But between you and me, I honestly don't think it's going to be a problem. Now, how about we grab that drink and chat about your feature?'

Just then the man with the glasses glanced up and his eyes met Laura's. He stared at her and she felt a jolt of something go through her – not because she recognised him, but because it was so obvious that he recognised her. He grinned. Nush, who'd already marched off, stopped and gave her a quizzical smile.

'What are you thinking, Lois Lane?'

'Nothing,' Laura said, turning away quickly. As she trotted to catch up with Nush she glanced over her shoulder. The man with the glasses had turned back to the screen.

***

Whoever designed Sink or Swim had really leaned into the *Titanic* theme. There were portholes instead of windows and the tables were all at a slant, to create the effect of a descent to the ocean floor.

'Isn't it brilliant here?' Nush sighed, once she'd parcelled them both into a velvet booth; a waiter was hovering, ready to take their orders. 'They do really great food, too – mostly fish.'

Laura scanned the cocktail list, which gave her flash-backs to the last time she'd sat opposite a stranger in a bar (he'd been a barista; she'd ordered two espresso martinis and been up for most of the night with chest pains; he'd messaged her the next morning to say he thought their en-ergies 'vibrated on different frequencies'). She attempted to locate the cocktail with the least offensive name; there was one with a tincture of iron in it called The Hull Shebang.

'Um, a White Star Line for me, please,' she said. The waiter whisked the menus away, saluted them both again and glided back to the bar.

'I want to know everything about you!' Nush exclaimed as soon as he'd gone. Laura felt like a butterfly being pinned to a board by a very forceful child.

'I thought you already did? I mean … isn't that the whole point?'

'Don't be *silly*,' Nush laughed. 'We're not *psychic* or any-thing. Obviously we've got a lot of data on you …' She pulled a tablet out of her bag, flicked the screen on, called up a document and started reading off it. 'So we know, for instance, that on a Saturday night six weeks ago you spent eighteen minutes looking at online guides to losing half a stone in a fortnight, then you watched that video of the guy from *Spider-Man* lip-synching to "Umbrella" eight times in a row.'

The blood rushed to Laura's face. 'That really isn't what my Saturdays are normally like,' she said quickly, realising before the words had even left her mouth that it was pointless protesting – Nush knew the truth and so did everyone else at Cupid. 'Jesus, you seriously have that much detail about everything I've been doing online? That's ... I don't even understand how that's even possible.'

Nush smiled. 'Oh, it's easy-peasy. Let's say you're ... well, we can use another real-life example. OK, so at the start of February you were looking for rooms in flats on SpareRoom in north London for less than six hundred and fifty a month including bills. When you did that search, a record of it was sold to something called a data broker – have you heard of them?' Laura shook her head, now even more unnerved. 'They're just companies that buy up your entire browser history and turn it into a profile of you. So that SpareRoom search suggested you were at a transitional stage in your life, that you weren't a high earner ...'

'Does the profile have my actual name on it? And a photo?' Laura felt dazed: *just* companies that buy up your entire browser history? Nush was talking about that like it was a completely normal thing. And maybe it was. But that wasn't how it felt.

'Hah! No photo. And not your name, just an ID number,' Nush said smoothly, breezing straight past her discomfort. 'But they're easy to de-anonymise.' She saw Laura's shocked expression and waved a hand airily. 'It's totally fine, everyone does it. Anyway, most of the profiles get bought by retailers who want to sell you things in a targeted way – if they know what makes you tick, they can press your buttons much more effectively, right? But we decided to do something we think could actually change the world for the better.' She stroked the tablet's screen thoughtfully, like it was a living creature. '*Anyway*, the point is, we have a lot of really valuable insights into your behaviour that we can feed into the matchmaking model. But the more we understand about you, the more we can help you. Human intuition is still a really big part of that, which is why we're going to have these face-to-face chats with all our members. Our big thing here at Cupid is honesty – we call it radical transparency.'

'Right.' A bit of the table's veneer had come loose; Laura picked at it, trying to relax. It was all so much to take in. And she was starting to realise just how much of her activity online she was ashamed of. Like the poems about being fine by yourself that she googled when she was feeling especially low. Or all the times she'd called up Walker and Sasha's new address on Street View and zoomed right in on their flat, torturing herself by looking at the matching deckchairs right next to each other on the balcony. She couldn't stop thinking about the people clustered around the monitor in the Cupid office – she imagined herself running back, bursting into the room and finding there, on the screen, a final answer to the question she'd spent so many hours turning over and over in the darkness. *Why can't I do this?*

'Well, where do you want to start?' she said. She felt so stiff compared to Nush; an awkward teenager yanking her skirt down on the fringes of a disco.

'Ooh, I don't know – how about uni? You're a journalist, you must have studied English, right?'

'Um, yeah. Medieval literature. I did my dissertation on King Arthur. Knights, round tables, swords in stones – that kind of thing.'

Nush clapped her hands in delight. Her nails were painted a pale glittery green that sparkled when she moved. (*Be more unicorn*, Laura thought, running a finger over her own unadorned ones and feeling deeply unexciting.)

'No way! That's one of my favourite love stories! So *romantic.*'

'You know, it's funny – they …' Laura stopped, alarmed; Nush had picked up her tablet again and was tapping away on it. She glanced up and gave one of her dazzling smiles.

'Just taking some notes!' she chirped, still tapping. 'I can stop if it makes you uncomfortable?'

Laura tried to remember the last time she'd been the focus of so much attention; in her mind's eye she saw the stylist zipping her into the not-wedding dress at the shoot. 'It's fine,' she said. 'Do whatever you need to.'

'Fab!' More tapping. 'OK, let's talk about your *relationship history.*' Nush gave the phrase a kind of transatlantic s*cha-wing*. 'I jotted down a few things from your article – which we all *loved*, by the way – and obviously you filled out that questionnaire for us.' She paused and looked up, locking eyes with Laura. 'But I'm sure there must be gaps, because it seems like your longest relationship was only about six months? Did we miss something?'

Laura swallowed. When she was eight she and Jamie and their parents had gone on a camping trip to Brittany – it was actually the last holiday they'd ever go on together – and one morning her towel and pyjamas had blown off their hook while she was in the shower block and ended up in the next field. She'd had to walk across the entire campsite with a bathmat wrapped three-quarters of the way around her, wanting to curl up in the mud and die every time the wind exposed another inch of goose-pimpled skin. This felt like that – only worse.

'No, that's right,' she said eventually. 'I mean, I've had lots of, you know, *things* …' She forced out a laugh. 'What is it – half of all marriages end in divorce? I don't know, I just …' She was starting to panic – her thoughts were stubbornly refusing to get themselves together into something

44

that sounded plausible. 'I was never the kind of little girl who doodled wedding dresses in their diary or anything like that. My sister says I'm missing a chip.' She ground to a halt, defeated.

Nush laced her fingers together thoughtfully and rested her chin on their tips.

'You know what?' she said quietly. 'It doesn't matter how long you take to get there – all that matters is that you get there eventually, right? And I think it's great that you're trying to make some changes.' She leaned across and squeezed Laura's hand. 'It's brave. I mean that.'

Their drinks arrived. Nush's was on fire, like a Christmas pudding. Laura's had a huge, jagged ice cube poking out of it.

'It's an iceberg!' the waiter said. He put the glass down on the table; it immediately started to slide down the slope towards the floor.

'Yeah, you have to keep a hand on it,' Nush said, blowing her drink out daintily. 'OK, so – how about your family? Do you get on with them?'

Her head spinning, Laura pictured Jamie in her corner office, sharpening the pencils in her desk-tidy to a uniform length. Then she thought about her parents, who'd be eating lunch around now – her mum at the dining table surrounded by a fortress of magazines, her dad standing up in the kitchen with something microwaved. The silence would be thick enough to spread on toast.

'Well, I'm living with my sister and her husband at the moment,' she said, which wasn't untrue, but also neatly skated over most of the actual facts of her life.

Nush raised an eyebrow. 'Oh, how come?' She sipped her drink. 'Oh, *of course* – your flatmates got together, didn't they? I remember from your article.' She cocked her head sympathetically. 'Shit. How was that? Weird?'

'I ...' Laura took a big gulp of her cocktail; it tasted like something you'd put down a blocked sink. 'It was a bit weird,' she conceded.

'Mmm, when you're single your friends are kind of everything to you, aren't they?' Nush said, her voice honeyed with sympathy. 'You really depend on them – emotionally and practically. It's so difficult when their lives move on and yours doesn't.'

The Pity Committee, Lil called it: when someone did the oh-no-poor-you thing with their face, then asked you whether you'd ever tried Online Dating. But Laura wanted to give Nush the benefit of the doubt – maybe she hadn't meant it like that. She had picked up her tablet again: the screensaver, Laura saw, was a photo of a huge, square-jawed man in a polo shirt that barely contained his python-sized arms. Nush was balanced on his knees like a tea set, throwing her head back and laughing.

'That's Ched,' she said, smiling adoringly at the picture. 'My boyfriend. We met when I was in the States – he's still there, but Cupid have been *so* amazing about letting me work remotely when I go to visit him. He's going to apply for a job over here later this year.'

Laura stared at the photo of the two of them, trying desperately to think of something to say. Ched's neck was noticeably wider than his head. Nush sighed happily.

'To be honest with you, he's the reason I left my old job and came here,' she continued. 'I just want other people to have what I have, you know? To be happy.'

Laura felt her fingers tighten around her glass. 'I am happy,' she said.

Nush reached across and gave her other hand a little squeeze. 'Of *course* you are,' she said. 'But you could be happier, couldn't you? I mean, we all could, right?'

It was hard to imagine Nush being much happier, Laura thought – she was practically levitating out of her seat. But difficult as it was to admit, she had a point. Nush was watching her intently.

'What does happiness look like to you, Laura?' she asked. 'How do you want to *feel* in a relationship?'

'I ...' Nush's eyes were boring into her. 'I feel ... I don't know, like a bit of an odd one out, I suppose,' she began hesitantly; she wasn't even sure she wanted to be saying this out loud but she couldn't stop herself. 'I'm always second-guessing myself.' She swallowed. 'So I think I'd like to feel ...'

A tinkling sound was coming from Nush's bag. She held up one finger.

'Hold that thought for two secs, OK?' Nush said, fishing her phone out. She stared at the glowing screen, a tiny frown furrowing her forehead. Then, all of a sudden, her face lit up.

'Wow,' she said. 'That was quick.' Nush swivelled excitedly in her seat. 'The guys back in the office just pinged me. They've found him.'

'Who?'

'Your match, silly! He's called ...' she scrolled and scrolled some more '... Adam.' She paused, then looked across at Laura, her eyes glittering.

'It's such a shame you're not called Eve.'

***

Laura Morrison
To: Anoushka De Souza
Re: Hello!
Tuesday 19 June, 9:15

Hi Nush!

Really nice to meet you yesterday!

I meant to say, I'd love to interview someone from the technical side of the business for my piece about how Cupid's matchmaking model works – maybe someone from the Data team, who you pointed out when we were in the office? We could do face to face or over the phone, whichever works best.

Looking forward to hearing more about my match Adam! Feels so strange typing that . . .

L x

Anoushka De Souza
To: Laura Morrison
Re: Hello!
Tuesday 19 June, 12:51

Ahh, babe, we were just talking about you over lunch!!! Your ears must have been burning lol. All good stuff don't worry!!!

We want to make sure you feel TOTALLY supported throughout this process, so we've decided that I'm going to call you every week to check in and see how you're getting on. Not like a formal thing so please don't stress!!! Just a nice natter about how you're feeling.

Re Data, sounds good! They're slammed atm but let me have a chat now and see what I can do. Sit tight!!!

Xxx

Laura Morrison
To: Anoushka De Souza
Re: Just checking . . .
Thursday 21 June, 9:10

Hi Nush!

Me again! Just wanted to see if you'd heard back from Data about me interviewing someone? Sorry, I know you're really busy!

   L x

PS – honestly no need to call me, I'm sure everything will be totally fine! But thank you!

Anoushka De Souza
To: Laura Morrison
Re: Just checking …
Thursday 21 June, 18:02

INSANE day here, babe, sorry! Nothing from Data yet but we've got loads of time until you'll be sitting down to write the piece, right? – which is great!!! I'll keep you posted, I promise.

   Ahh, I nearly forgot, Adam's made you a teeny tiny video introducing himself! I'll send it over to you tomorrow. I've told him you'll do one too but NO PRESSURE, it's literally just a quick hi and bye. But maybe have a think about what you'd like to say to him and what you'll wear, stuff like that.

   Ahhh, this is all SO EXCITING!!!

   PS – nice try getting out of my calls babe ;)

Chapter 4

match (noun): *something that harmonises with another*

Laura and Inge watched the file downloading at Laura's computer. Patrick from IT Help was at Inge's desk, trying to get hers back online. Like everything else at the paper, the office's internet connection was unstable – a week ago the entire thing had been crashed by someone trying to upload a video of a twerking cat to the @BugleDaily Twitter account.

'Nervous?' Inge asked.

'Nope.'

'You look nervous.'

'Well, I'm not,' Laura lied. Actually, her stomach was pitching and rolling; the whole situation felt suddenly, terrifyingly real. Inge prised a cheese twist – her regular Friday treat – out of the packet between them and stuck it in her mouth like a cigar.

'I don't know why they haven't just sent you a photo,' she said, chewing thoughtfully. 'This feels so … audition-y.'

'You need to see someone in motion,' Laura said, repeating what Nush had told her over the phone at lunch.

She'd been surprising herself by doing that a lot over the four days since her visit to Cupid's office: reaching for Nush's words whenever anyone had quizzed her about what she was doing and why she was doing it. Her formulations were all so neat and convincing – they were a bit cringey, but producing them was strangely satisfying, like whipping a perfectly risen cake out of the oven.

Inge took another twist and waved it at Laura, who shook her head. She offered it to Patrick, who took it from her wordlessly. He was frowning in the style of someone trying to defuse a bomb in the final minutes of a film. The file was 96 per cent downloaded now. Laura swallowed; her mouth was sandpapery.

'So what have they actually told you about him?' Inge went on, leaning back in her chair. 'What if he has terrible breath? Or posts on conspiracy theory forums? Surely they'll let you bail out if you hate each other? I mean, three months of dating could feel like a *long* time.'

'It's to give us a chance to connect on a deeper level.' Laura heard herself parroting Nush again, but inside she was in turmoil. Sitting through a few tense drinks on a blind date with a total stranger was bad enough – she found it horribly easy to imagine the awfulness of realising early on that Adam just wasn't into her and still having to tough it out for twelve weeks. And even if they *did* both hate each other as Inge was suggesting, there was no way she could back out. There was a bank of redundancy-emptied desks in her eyeline – some looked like nobody had ever sat at them, but others were still littered with pens and scrunched-up bits of paper, as though the person who'd worked there had just popped out to buy a sandwich.

Finally the file bounced into the dock; Inge reached across Laura and clicked on it. There was an agonising, endless second of stillness and then a face – Adam's *actual* face, Laura thought, as she gripped the edge of her chair – filled the screen.

'There he is,' Inge said. 'Mr Perfect. Huh. Not bad.'

Laura took him in piece by piece, cautiously circling the fact that this was *him*, this was *it*. He was handsome and looked, from what she could see of his broad shoulders, like he had a gym membership he actually used. His neat, dark hair was slightly grey above his ears, which suited him, as did the little crinkles at the corners of his brown eyes. He was wearing a smart navy blue suit and an open-necked shirt the colour of a summer sky – it looked like he'd only just taken his tie off.

'Wow,' he said. 'This is …'

He had a nice voice – soft, Scottish, the kind that would make you feel reassured about the roundabout you were hurtling towards if it came out of a SatNav. He paused and ran a hand through his hair, composing himself. Laura felt her scalp prickle involuntarily.

'Um, hello,' he said into the lens. 'Hello, Laura.'

'Hello,' Laura said automatically. For a split second she wondered whether Adam had somehow managed to hear her through a rip in the space-time continuum, because he looked straight at her and smiled. A little dimple appeared by each corner of his mouth.

'So, I'm Adam Fraser,' he said. 'But you knew that already, I guess. I'm thirty-four – getting on for thirty-five, just between you and me. I'm from Edinburgh and I've been here in London for …' He totted it up in his head. 'Thirteen years. Nearly fourteen. I work in green energy. I've been with the same company the whole time I've been here, basically – they're a really nice bunch and the hours aren't so bad. And outside work … I mean, I like all the normal things, you know? I play a bit of rugby at the weekends – there's a gang of us here who've known each other since we were kids. Most of them have kids of their own now!'

Laura quickly thought back to the yellow duffel coat she'd bought online for Dora's birthday at the start of the year and all the new baby cards she'd made on Moonpig. Was that one of the reasons they'd been matched? Because they both felt like they were lagging behind their friends? She forced herself to focus on Adam again – he was smiling ruefully.

'Hmm, so there's that,' he went on. 'What else? I like cooking and I'm ...'

'... just as happy on the sofa with a glass of wine as he is in a nice restaurant,' Inge cut in. 'What? OK, I'm not the target audience, but I know his type.' She pressed pause and turned to Patrick. 'What do you think?'

Patrick, who was making a point of only looking at Inge's screen, allowed himself to be coaxed into turning around. 'He seems ... pleasant?' he ventured.

'Can we just watch it?' Laura pleaded. As the words were leaving her mouth she looked up and her heart sank – Bouncy, outlandishly sunburned from a week in Spain, was barrelling towards them, chewing the last of something.

'Is that him?' He peered at the screen. 'God, he's good-looking, isn't he?' He turned to Laura. 'What do you reckon, Meals For One? Think you could love him?' He chortled. 'Not that you have to go that far – you could just have sex with him. Joke! That was a joke! Don't tell HR!' He leaned forward; Laura got a blast of tuna mayonnaise. 'Although to be honest, it would help if you did. Narrative *thrust* and all that.'

'Ignore him, Laura,' Inge said, fixing Bouncy with a smile that could have frozen lava. 'It's been so long since he enjoyed the love of a woman that he's forgotten what it actually involves.'

'While we're on that subject, how's your gal pal, Inge?' Bouncy asked, waggling his eyebrows. 'I enjoyed chatting to her at the summer party.'

'I'd call you a pig, Phil,' Inge said. 'But they're very intelligent, sensitive creatures.'

'Oink!' Bouncy grinned at them; he never seemed to think Inge was being serious. 'Oh, Laura – I was chatting to the bigwigs upstairs about you in the planning meeting this morning and they're really *interested* in this piece, if you catch my drift. Pull it off and you might just escape the axe!'

The three of them watched him walk away in silence.

'That wasn't as bad as I was expecting,' Inge said. Laura goggled at her. 'No, not Bouncy – your new boyfriend. I don't think he's going to murder you, anyway.'

'He's cute,' Laura said slowly. 'And very ... different.' She'd never really thought of herself as having a type (although she'd always been secretly partial to nice eyes and hands) but looking over her back catalogue, she couldn't see anyone in it who was quite this – well, *wholesome*. She remembered what Nush had said to her as she'd hugged her goodbye after their drink. *You'll know it's good because it won't feel like anything that came before.* It certainly sounded like something that ought to be true. Didn't it?

Patrick got to his feet, triumphant. 'We're all done here,' he said to Inge. 'Just need you to log back in.'

'Oh, my password's there,' she said, pointing at a Post-It stuck to her hard drive. Patrick blinked slowly, as though he couldn't quite believe what he was seeing. Then his face darkened.

'You should *never* have it written down like that,' he hissed. 'It's *extremely* insecure.' He yanked the Post-It off the desk. 'Do you want to do this or shall I?' he said. Inge looked at him blankly.

'Do what?'

Staring at her, Patrick tore the Post-It into pieces and let them flutter dramatically onto the carpet. Nobody spoke for a long time.

'All right, well – thanks, Patrick. I'd, er, better make tracks,' Inge said finally. She started piling things into her bag: her laptop, proofs, the last of the cheese straws. She turned to Laura. 'Lia's doing tacos at mine tonight. There'll be plenty to go around if you don't have plans?'

Inge and her girlfriend, a freelance picture editor she'd actually met at the *Bugle* (*We found love in a hopeless place*, she liked to joke), had only been together for just over a year, but Laura could tell, looking at them and feeling the familiar combination of awe and envy, that it was the real thing.

'I'd love to, but it's my parents' fortieth wedding anniversary,' she said reluctantly. 'Someone my mum works for gave them tickets for *Jersey Boys* – I said I'd have something to eat with them beforehand and my sister's got plans, so I really have to go.' She sighed. 'Not that Jamie would have gone anyway – she doesn't really like spending time with them. Or, you know, me.'

Inge whistled. 'Forty years,' she said. 'What an achievement.'

Laura imagined her parents on the 16.42 to London, arguing viciously over the position of the arm rest. Once, when they'd been going up to visit her dad's sister in Windermere, the two of them had such a terrible fight that her mum had actually got off the train at Warrington and stayed there for six hours. *Never get married, Laura,* her dad had said under his breath as they watched her marching down the platform. She'd pretended not to hear.

'That's certainly one way of looking at it,' she said.

Inge smiled serenely. 'Relationships always make me think of rugs,' she said. 'You flip one over and it's such an ugly mess, all those scraggy bits. But as soon as you turn it the right way it all makes sense, you know?' She zipped her bag up. 'Or something like that. Thanks again for all your help, Patrick.'

Still scowling, Patrick stooped to pick up the Post-It fragments, then marched off with them in the direction of the shredder.

Once she was alone Laura leaned her chair back as far as it would go and folded her hands behind her head. Adam's face was still on her screen in front of her, frozen where they'd left him. She almost felt embarrassed to be looking straight at him, like she was spying on someone.

'Look what I've got ...'

Femi was behind her, holding a plate with the remains of a chocolate caterpillar cake on it. 'It's Richard's birthday,' he said, offering her the tail piece. 'They left this behind when they went for drinks and I'm the only one from that bank of desks who's still here, so ...'

Laura took it gratefully; all the adrenaline that had been coursing through her earlier had ebbed away and she was suddenly incredibly hungry.

'Is that him?' Femi said, looking at the screen. 'That guy you're being set up with?'

'That's him.' Laura bit into the caterpillar's tail, soothed by the familiar crack of the chocolate, then the squish of the buttercream and the bounce of the sponge. 'Oh, I don't know, Femi. I mean, look at him ...' She pointed at Adam. His eyes were closed and he had his mouth open, but he was still extremely handsome. 'I've never imagined I'd have a chance with someone who looks like that. That's not me fishing for a compliment or anything, I'm just being ... realistic.'

She shrugged, then looked away, embarrassed. Out of the corner of her eye she could see Femi tactfully busying himself straightening the caterpillar's face. Once he'd finished he cleared his throat.

'You said they basically have all the single people in the country on their books, right? They've got access to the same massive data sets that advertisers do – that's how they've been able to find you someone before they've even officially launched?'

'Apparently.' Nush still hadn't come back to her about interviewing someone from the Data team. It just didn't seem possible that they'd been able to comb through the search histories of everyone in the country – and yet, here she was, looking at the evidence that they'd done exactly that.

'Well, that means they could have chosen anyone for you, doesn't it?' Femi went on. 'And they chose him. So ...' He put his head on one side, considering Adam. 'Anyway, he doesn't seem like one of those good-looking guys who's really into himself,' he said. 'He looks ... decent. Solid.'

Laura took another bite of the cake. *Solid*, she thought as she chewed. As desirable qualities in a partner went, she had to admit that it had never been top of her list. But then, how far had her list got her? It was time to give something new a try.

'He does, doesn't he?' she said.

***

Laura's mum, who did book-keeping for local businesses from Jamie's old bedroom, had wanted to go out for a meal before the show to celebrate their wedding anniversary. Her dad, who was the head of sales for a company that produced tractor parts, had wanted to bring sandwiches.

Laura had suggested they meet in the coffee shop next to the theatre. It was a compromise, which meant they were both annoyed – but that was better, Laura thought as she half-ran from the Tube, than one of them winning. She saw her role as being to monitor and adjust each side of the scales to stop the whole apparatus toppling over.

She found them inside, by a table with a tray of food on it. They were each clutching a side, as though they were about to start a tug-of-war with it. Her mum took one hand off it to wave to her, shimmery nails winking under the lights. Her dad, who was wearing a jacket and tie that had clearly been picked out for him (and a pair of hiking boots that clearly hadn't), gave her one of his little nods. Neither of them was smiling.

'Why don't I get these?' Laura said, kissing them both on the cheek and prising the tray off them. Her mum frowned.

'You don't have to do that, love,' she said, reaching over to tuck a loose bit of Laura's hair behind her ear. 'We were just saying that you ...'

Her dad cut in. 'You're a good soul,' he said to Laura. 'We appreciate that, don't we, Shelley?' The two of them glared at each other. The currents of feeling lapped un-pleasantly around Laura – the tide of the evening was already starting to turn.

'You sit down and relax,' she said, practically pushing them into their seats. 'It's your wedding anniversary!'

As soon as she was across the room Laura let go of the breath she'd been holding in, then grabbed a wrap, a packet of crisps and a bar of chocolate, and took everything up to a till.

'Thirty-seven pounds sixty, please,' the cashier said. Laura put the chocolate back and then the wrap. She could see her parents out of the corner of her eye, sitting like a pair of mismatched bookends. Jamie, with her cheekbones and long legs, had her mum's face and her dad's height. Laura had somehow ended up with the exact opposite combination. (It was fine; Jamie had weird thumbs and still couldn't ride a bike.) Her parents had grown up implausibly near each other: her mum in Birkenhead and her dad up the coast in a village near Preston, which, according to a faded article from the *Blackpool Gazette* that he'd hung in the toilet, was home to more shire horses than people. He played his roots up, she played hers down, and each of them thought less of the other for doing it.

When she got back to the table Laura strategically positioned herself in the seat between them. 'How about this weather!' she said in an overly cheerful voice, laying out their food for them and opening her crisps carefully. 'Hottest July since 1973!' When they were in this kind of mood with each other, which seemed to be more often than not nowadays, if you wanted to avoid escalating the situation the best policy was to keep things light and not make any sudden movements.

Her dad had already peeled his sandwich apart and was regarding it with intense suspicion. Her mum, pointedly ignoring him, gave Laura a worried look.

'Is that all you're having?' she asked. Laura could imagine her cajoling the holidaymakers she'd looked after before she'd got married – she'd been a Monarch Airlines stewardess, dressed like Jackie O in a suit and pillbox hat that matched the plane's livery – in exactly the same way.

'I'm honestly not that hungry,' she said unconvincingly. Her mum put a hand on her arm and gave it a light pat.

'You know we're here if you want to have a natter about having to leave your flat, don't you?' The pat became a squeeze. 'It's not good to keep this kind of stuff all to yourself, love. I know you were happy there with Walker and that nice Australian girl. Sheila, wasn't it?'

'If she wants to talk to us about what happened, she will,' Laura's dad said, biting into his sandwich. 'I reckon she'd rather drill a hole in her own skull.'

'How's Harrison?' Laura asked at lightning speed. Both of her parents, she was relieved to see, softened visibly – the dog was guaranteed neutral territory.

'Oh, he's a big silly,' her dad said. 'The other day he ate a bag of self-raising flour. Can you believe that?' He chuckled. 'He's lucky he didn't turn into a scone.'

'It took most of a morning to clear up,' her mum said, but she was smiling again. She looked around the room, nodding approvingly at the velvet armchairs and tealights.

'Well, this is nice, isn't it?' she said. 'Very civilised.' She turned to Laura's dad. 'Are you enjoying your sandwich, Jim?'

'It's almost exactly like one I'd make for myself,' he said. 'Only half the size and twice the price.'

Laura's mum's smile didn't waver. 'Jim,' she said through her teeth. 'If you keep this up, I'm going to give your ticket to Laura – and don't think I won't, because I will. You can sit here by yourself for the rest of the evening grousing about how expensive everything is. OK?'

She stood up, scooped up her handbag and strode off to the bathroom. Laura's dad stared at a poster on the opposite wall advertising a multicoloured drink called a Mermaid Frappé.

'Jamie OK, is she?' he eventually asked, not looking at Laura. Laura, who wasn't looking at him either, shrugged non-committally. She felt a surge of resentment – why did Jamie always snatch a get-out-of-jail-free card? Why did she never have to do this? The answer, of course, was that she'd left home to go to university and had basically never come back, not even in the holidays. By removing herself from the situation, she'd left Laura no choice but to step in as referee.

'They're actually having a barbecue next Sunday afternoon,' she said. 'I told her to invite you both.' Her dad took a deep breath and raised his eyes to meet hers; he looked like he was about to take a run at something. Laura was suddenly seized by a scary urge to clamp a hand over his mouth.

'Look, I ...' he began. He stopped, swallowed; whatever it was he'd been about to say, he'd thought better of it. 'Let me give you something for the food,' he said, fishing out his wallet and busying himself with it.

'Dad, no – I want to do this for you both, it's ... What's that?' In amongst the receipts and tattered business cards belonging to feed merchants and agricultural supply stores was a flash of neon pink plastic.

'Oh, it's called an Art Pass.' He quickly thumbed past it. 'Gets me into all sorts of places for free, apparently. Galleries, museums ... Your mum gave it to me this morning. Said she thought I ought to ...' he coughed '... broaden my horizons.'

Laura couldn't look at him. 'Well, I think that's really nice,' she lied. 'What did you get her?' Her dad looked slightly embarrassed.

'I didn't think we were doing presents,' he said.

They sat in silence. A young, brutally attractive couple drinking Mermaid Frappés stared at them for a couple of seconds with detached curiosity, then went back to their phones. Laura could imagine exactly what had happened that morning: the jumble of resentment and longing her mum had packaged up along with the Art Pass, her dad's total inability to spot and separate out the strands of feeling, much less deal with them in the way she was still, after all this time, hoping he'd somehow be able to. She inserted herself into the scene, next to an oblivious Harrison – in her mind's eye she saw herself putting a hand underneath the rug in front of the electric fire and worrying fruitlessly at the tangles.

When her mum reappeared her lipstick had been carefully applied and she was carrying a pair of plastic cocktail shakers filled with fruit salad. Her smile was bright and breakable.

'I got us these to share!' she said, putting them down on the table. 'I thought they were fun. Aren't they fun?'

***

All the lights were out at Stonybrook Street. Jamie had left a note for Laura on the kitchen worktop.

OUT TIL LATE. SCALLOPS IN THE FRIDGE. DON'T EAT THEM.

Whit had drawn two smiling stick figures in the corner. She left it where it was and trudged upstairs in the dark.

Her temporary bedroom was at the top of the house. Before she'd got there it had been Whit's home office and the first thing she saw when she opened her eyes each morning was the spine of one of his MBA textbooks urging her to *Get To Yes*. Before that – before the acupuncture and the injections and the dozens of stubbornly singular blue lines on test sticks that had been talked about constantly, and then not talked about at all – it had been something that might one day have become a baby's bedroom. The walls were painted a soft, sunny yellow. When she was putting her clothes away on the first night Laura had found a little cuddly elephant with a price tag still on it at the back of a drawer. She'd gone straight downstairs and wrapped her arms around Jamie, who'd brushed her off like an insect. *What?* she kept saying. *What?*

Laura flicked Whit's desk lamp on and got under the duvet with all her clothes on. She lay there for a while, listening to the noises the house made at night: the purr of the boiler, the creak of shifting timbers overhead. It was comforting to feel something that could pass for life humming through the place. Her phone was next to her in her bag – and on it, in her inbox, was the video of Adam. She stuck an arm out from under the duvet and dug around. She'd get Inge to help with the actual video first thing on Monday, but maybe a practice run would be a good idea. She held the phone over her head and switched it onto voice record.

'Hi, Adam!' she began. Then she took her finger off the screen and played it back. *Hi, Adam!* Too peppy: she sounded like she was trying to sell him car insurance. She tried again.

'Hi – Adam.'

'Adam, hi.'

'Adam? Hi!'

She wondered where he was right now: on his way home from the gym, maybe, hair still slightly damp from the shower? Or working late, tired but cheerful, and looking forward to a weekend of pub roasts and misty pitches? She smiled and picked her phone up again.

'I'm excited about meeting you, Adam,' she heard herself saying – and realised that she meant it.

Chapter 5

model (noun): a mathematical representation of a real-world process

It was coming up for six on the hottest day of the year so far and Laura's dress was sticking unpleasantly to her back. It was a blue gingham one with a swishy skirt that she'd bought at lunch in a panic after spending the morning sweating through her shirt. She felt ridiculous, like a sheep-less Little Bo Peep. There was no shade on the South Bank and the still air was ripe with the queasy smell of candy floss and fried onions. She always forgot how much she hated this bit – the long hours before a first date when you couldn't think about anything else.

It was the Monday following her meeting at Cupid and she was in the queue for the London Eye – Nush had booked her and Adam tickets – behind a group of American teenagers in Harry Potter capes. A boy with the beginnings of a beard gave her a prod with his wand.

'Do you want one?' he asked, offering her a chocolate frog from a paper bag.

Laura hesitated. She ought to talk to him, she told herself – get some practice before she had to speak to Adam, whose video she'd been studying. Every time she thought about what was about to happen, she wanted to duck under the rope and run. When she'd woken up that morning the novel feeling of purpose and direction that she'd had ever since Nush had confirmed the details of their date on Saturday (everyone at Cupid seemed to work on the weekends) had evaporated. Instead, she felt like she was strapped to a rocket. Why was she doing this? It was completely insane. They might hate each other on sight – and then what? And to make things worse, Bouncy had ordered her to get a selfie of the two of them for her feature. *Can't stretch to a photographer this time, I'm afraid, Tinder Surprise*, he'd told her at lunchtime as he bowled past with his panino. *Still, nice excuse to cosy up to him, eh? Eh?*

She took a frog. 'Thanks!' she said to the boy. 'Er, how many galleons do I owe you?'

'It's cool.' He sniggered. 'You can just show me your Snitch sometime.'

'Jordan!' The man at the front of the group, who was wearing a Sorting Hat, looked over his Tube map. 'You apologise to the lady or I'm pouring your Butterbeers down the toilet when we get back to the hostel.'

Jordan leered at her. 'Sorry, *miss*,' he said. Laura briefly considered a withering reply, but she wasn't up to it; she felt like she was in fancy dress. Instead she got her phone out to tell Lil what had happened and saw she'd missed a call from Nush. She gulped. Nush seemed to have a sixth sense that meant she made her check-in calls at the worst possible times – the last had come when Laura was trying to get a burned crumpet out of Jamie and Whit's toaster. And every time she'd talked breezily about the sheer volume of data Cupid had on Laura, without ever actually spelling out what exactly they knew, or what they'd deduced from it. It was all a bit unnerving.

'Who's excited?' Nush trilled when Laura called her back.

'Erm ... me?' She could feel the frog melting in her fist.

'Yeah, you are! Woo! Anyway, just a *super* quick call to let you know we've got you a fast-track ticket, so you don't need to wait in line – you can go straight to the front! How good is that?'

Laura's heart sank. There were at least a hundred people in front of her, shuffling slowly towards the platform where the Eye's pods would scoop them up. The sight of them all – a human buffer between her and whatever was about to happen – had been deeply reassuring. 'It's fine,' she said. 'I actually really like queues!'

'You're killing me, Laura!' Nush hooted. 'I meant to say, Adam messaged me at lunch when he got your video to say he thought it was hilarious. We both did. The bit when you came out from behind the plants – RIP me!' She lowered her voice. 'I shouldn't really be telling you this, but he said you were cute too.'

'He said that?' 'Cute' wasn't a word she could imagine someone who looked like Adam using about her – or one she'd ever have applied to herself. Still, she couldn't help feeling a tiny bit pleased.

'Don't say anything to him! Forget I told you! *Aaaaany-way*, the other bit of *massive* news is that we pulled a few strings and you guys get your own pod.'

'So it'll just be ... us?' A new rivulet of sweat sprang up on Laura's chest. The pods were massive, easily big enough for twenty – and the two of them would be rattling around inside one like loose oranges in the bottom of a shopping trolley. It was hard to think of anything more awkward.

'Exactly! We wanted you to really be able to get to know each other. No distractions.' Nush was chewing gum; Laura could hear the snappy little clicks. 'Ahh, I have *such* a good feeling about tonight! Seriously, your match percentage is insane – like, one of the highest we've ever seen. The guys here couldn't believe it. You're like Romeo and Juliet!'

'But they didn't ...' She needed to try to be enthusiastic, she reminded herself, even if she wasn't feeling it. When she'd signed her contract with Cupid she'd promised that she'd go into the process 'with an open mind and an open heart'. She pictured Nush's iridescent nails, then Bouncy's sausagey hands and finally the fingers of Glenn from Aerodynamica, scrabbling at a locked box in her chest.

'Well, I'll let you know how it goes!' she said, trying to echo Nush's carefree tone.

'You'd better!' Nush tinkled. 'Or else!'

She hung up. Laura took the phone away from her ear and saw with a jolt that Walker had finally played his turn on Words With Friends. There was a DOOM hanging helpfully off the end of her WINKED now. She put her phone away, closed her eyes and let herself drift back to the night the two of them had met. The memory called to her like a comfortable bed at the end of a long day. She'd just spend a minute in the past, she told herself. Then she'd snap out of it and get on with her future.

***

Every December, Holly Nash, who Laura had known since they were eleven years old, had thrown a Christmas party. The previous ones had been at her parents' place while they'd been on their annual cruise to the Canary Islands: aged fifteen Laura had thrown up in the Jacuzzi; aged seventeen she'd lost her virginity to Holly's cousin Robin in the guest bedroom. But this year it had happened in the house – the whole *house*, Laura had thought in disbelief as she'd wandered around it with a plastic cup of mulled wine – that Holly and her fiancé Matt had just bought on the edge of Bracknell. Like Laura, Holly had only been twenty-one. How did their lives look so different?

Holly had got an office job at the start of her gap year. It was meant to be temporary, but not long afterwards she'd met Matt on a night out – he was ten years older, an estate agent with a zippy Mini – and after a few months of dinner dates and weekends away, the idea of living in halls and stumbling through Freshers' Week lost its appeal. Tonight she and Matt were dressed up as Mr and Mrs Claus, Holly in a red minidress, him kissing her through his bushy fake beard until she squealed. He called her *angel* and *sweets*. Nobody, Laura had realised with a twinge of longing as she'd watched them play-fighting under the mistletoe earlier, had ever called her anything like that in her life.

It was nearly nine. She'd arrived at eight and spent the past hour in perpetual motion around the lounge and kitchen, like a shark trying not to sink, dodging questions from Holly and Matt's friends in their loafers and bodycon dresses. Where was she living now she'd graduated? What about a job? Was she seeing anyone? What was her *Plan*? She'd known it would be like this, but it had been that or sitting in front of the TV with her parents. Now she was on Holly and Matt's cushion-strewn bed, wondering whether the pub she'd been working in since June would let her go and do a three-hour shift if she phoned them. It felt as though everyone downstairs had been given some kind of instruction manual for life that she'd completely missed out on.

The door creaked open. She leaped to her feet, racking her brains for an excuse, and saw a guy she vaguely recognised. He had tufty strawberry-blond hair and started guiltily when he saw her.

'God, sorry,' he said, backing away. 'I didn't realise ...' His clothes looked strangely out of time: baggy jeans, a faded Metallica t-shirt, a single beaded bracelet, like he'd teleported in from the nineties – they suited him though, she thought. His eyes under his shaggy fringe were a gentle green.

'It's fine, I'm not supposed to be in here either,' she said quickly, still trying to place him. 'But there's only so much Michael Bublé you can take, right?' He threw back his head and laughed – he was holding a can of Dr Pepper. 'Not drinking through the pain?' she went on. 'That's pretty brave.'

He pulled a set of keys out of his jeans. 'I'm driving,' he said, giving them a little shake. 'But I wish I wasn't. To be honest, I wasn't even going to come tonight, but I thought I should ...' He pulled a face. 'You know. Make an effort. That's what my mum keeps saying to me. I just moved back here from Liverpool. I was at music school there.'

The fob had a guitar pick attached to it. Now she knew where she'd last seen him. 'We went to college together, didn't we?' she said. 'You were in the same year as Holly and me. You're Steve ...'

'Walker.' He gave her a little wave with the key hand, sending the bracelet down his freckled arm. 'Just Walker.' He put his head on one side. 'And you're Laura Morrison, right? You used to write stuff for that paper we had. You reviewed the band I was in when we played at the Corn Exchange.'

It was all coming back to her now: him sitting on the steps outside the college's main building playing his guitar on a hot June afternoon, a girlfriend in an oversized man's t-shirt on the step above him, her eyes closed and her fingers raking through his shaggy hair. Laura found herself thinking about Matt's pet names for Holly. What would Walker call her? she wondered. Not *angel* or *sweets*. *Babe*, maybe. She could imagine that. The thought made the blood rush to her face.

Walker was looking around the bedroom. Laura watched his eyes rest on the huge holiday photo collage, Holly's dressing table with its flashbulb-ringed mirror, a cupboard door slightly ajar to reveal suits and dresses still in plastic bags from the dry cleaner. They'd given Laura something like vertigo, a sensation of dizzying distance.

'Makes you feel like you're from another planet, doesn't it?' he said, touching the transparent wrap on one of Matt's jackets like he'd read her mind. 'I don't even own a suit.'

'I don't either.' She shuffled along the bed in the hope he might sit down next to her – she didn't want him to go. 'Maybe we're from the same planet?'

'Planet Suitless.' He let the plastic drop and gave her a conspiratorial smile. 'Maybe we are,' he said. 'Maybe we are ...'

***

She saw Adam before he saw her. He was just a few metres ahead of her, next to the steps that led up to the departure platform, holding a bunch of flowers in brown paper wrapping. He was broader around the shoulders and taller than she'd thought he would be, even though she'd gathered, from the crib-sheet Nush had sent over, that he was 6'3" (she'd also listed his shoe size – twelve – and the fact he was a Sagittarius). He had the same dark-chocolate eyes, just-brushed hair and navy blue suit she remembered from the clip. He was scanning the crowd for her. She quickly turned her back to him and pretended to be absorbed in her phone, hoping he'd spot her and come over. She hated the thought of their eyes meeting and her having to make her way to where he was standing while they were forced to look at each other, the tension of the moment like an elastic stretched to snapping point. Her heart was racing.

A few seconds later, she heard his voice coming from in front of her.

'Laura?'

'Hi!' She glanced up, feigning surprise. He looked just like he did in the video, just as handsome and approach-able – but she still flinched at the three-dimensional reality of him. Before, he'd just been an idea, one she could take out whenever she wanted to feel a certain way, then put away again. She couldn't put him away now – this was it.

'Have you been waiting long?'

'Only just got here!' It was exactly the sort of thing she'd said on dozens of normal blind dates in the past – but, of course, nothing about this was normal. And he was so good-looking, it was throwing her totally off balance. She had no idea what to do with her hands – right now they were almost level with her shoulders, like she was about to break into a dance routine.

'Ah, great.' His voice really was lovely: soft but deep. 'These are for you,' he said, holding out the flowers. Laura was reaching to take them when her stomach plummeted – he was staring, she realised, at the melted brown mess covering her palm. She'd been so distracted that she'd com-pletely forgotten about it.

'It's a chocolate frog,' she said, wiping it on her dress in a panic and leaving a skid mark on the fabric. 'Was a chocolate frog. Somebody gave it to me in the queue earlier.' She looked back at the line; Jordan, who was staring at her, waved and then poked his tongue against the inside of his cheek, making it bulge grotesquely. Adam looked slightly alarmed.

Before she could say anything else, a man in a shirt with the Eye motif stitched on the pocket, bustled over. 'VIPs?' he asked, herding them up the steps. 'You're up next!' A pod was coming towards them, full of people. The doors swung open with a whoosh as it neared the platform and the passengers poured out onto the steps – a couple with their fingers interlaced hung back, nuzzling. Laura, acutely conscious of Adam standing next to her, looked away.

A high-ponytailed woman in the same uniform appeared. 'These are for you,' she barked, presenting them with two slightly sticky plastic champagne flutes. 'Have a great flight!' She hustled them into the now-vacant pod. The doors slammed shut and they were alone. *Oh, god.*

Adam inspected their surroundings as they started to gain height – Laura wondered if he was the sort of person who took a lot of photos of their hire car before they drove it away. She took a bigger gulp of her drink than she'd meant to and started coughing. It was tooth-achingly sweet, but she was relieved to have it in her hand. It was very warm in the pod.

Adam cleared his throat. 'So apparently this is the hottest July since 1973,' he said, not quite looking at her.

'Yes! Whewf!' She fanned herself with the flowers. Adam waited politely for her to finish.

'Nush was saying you work near Kings Cross,' he said. 'Which, er, way did you come?'

'Victoria, then Jubilee.' Where could she take the conversation from here? Beneath them the train tracks unspooled from Charing Cross.

'Did you know it only takes thirty-one minutes to get from one end of the Victoria line to the other?' she offered.

'I didn't know that,' Adam said. 'My goodness.'

The pod inched upwards. It felt like they'd barely moved since the last time she looked. How long were they going to be on here, Laura wondered – half an hour? Longer? Were they actually going backwards? The minutes they had left stretched agonisingly ahead, horrifying in their blankness. What were they going to say to each other? She found herself thinking back to all the internet rabbit-holes she'd fallen down: CCTV footage of the Hampton Court ghost, Wikipedia's Unusual Deaths page, an entire Reddit thread devoted to photographs of dogs dressed as bees. What did they say about her? And, even more worryingly, what did they say about Adam if that was why they'd been matched? She scanned down her body, reminding herself to stand up straight, hold her stomach in and tilt her chin up so it didn't do the unattractive squashy thing she'd seen it do in photos. She glanced at Adam, who was tapping the rail around the bottom of the pod with the toe of one well-polished work shoe.

'Have you been on this before?' he asked her.

'It's my first time, actually.' She gave him a wink. 'Be gentle!' Adam looked at her as though she'd flipped her skirt over her head. She sat down.

'I'm sorry,' she said. 'This is all so ...'

'Bizarre?' His expression softened. 'It is bizarre. Signing up for this without having met each other ...' His eyes widened, as though he was only now taking in the full implications of what they'd agreed to. Then he smiled at her and his dimples popped. 'But lots of good things are bizarre at first, aren't they?'

'Snorkelling,' Laura suggested. 'Cheese with fruit in it.' He laughed and sat down next to her.

'Exactly.' The distance between them, which had felt so vast a second ago, seemed to shrink. It was all going to be OK, Laura told herself. Cupid had done the sums. All she had to do was relax and the rest would take care of itself. She tucked the flowers carefully into her bag.

'Why don't you tell me about your job?' she said. 'It sounds amazing – I wish I was making a difference like you are.' Adam looked pleased; she felt pleased that he was pleased.

'Well ...' He cleared his throat. 'At the moment I'm overseeing projects in the wind division – turbines, basically ...'

'I love them!' Laura blurted out. Adam blinked.

'You love wind turbines?'

'I just think they're very underrated.' She crossed and uncrossed her legs. 'As a source of energy, I mean.'

'You're right! They get such a bad name for being eye-sores, but they're the future, you know? Anyway, I work with the teams who are looking at prospective sites, helping them identify all the potential issues and find ways around them.' He took a measured sip of his drink. 'It's all about expecting the unexpected.'

Laura pictured him on a blustery spit of sand with an Ordnance Survey map flapping around his face. She populated it with grateful-looking seals and gave him a cameo on *Blue Planet*.

'Ah, so you play it safe for a living,' she said with a grin, trying to sound playful. 'Don't you ever … go wild?'

A faint blush crept up his neck. 'Maybe I do,' he said, giving her a look; she was terrible at reading signals but it struck her as a plausibly flirtatious one. 'Sometimes.'

They were nearly at the highest point of the wheel now. The blue sky above them was cloudless, full of promise.

'Have you ever wondered what would happen if the Eye rolled away?' she asked, patting the pod's wall.

Adam tilted his head, looking bemused. The connection she'd felt between them a second before seemed to have evaporated. Her heart sank.

'You know what?' he said, giving her a shy smile, 'I hadn't thought about that – but I reckon it wouldn't actually get that far. We're in a natural depression here, there's nowhere really for it to go.'

This was good, she told herself. It was a good start. She moved a fraction closer to him.

'Well,' she said, smiling back, 'I don't know about you, but I've already learned something new today.'

***

So far, Laura was cautiously counting the date a success. They'd made it all the way around without any more silences. As they were stepping out of the pod Adam had suggested they get a drink in one of the South Bank Centre bars. She'd been worried that he wouldn't want to, but then she'd remembered that she didn't have to be – whatever happened tonight there was definitely going to be a second date and a third ...

They were at the top of the steps leading up to Waterloo Bridge when she was suddenly hit by the left-your-wallet-on-the-bus feeling.

'Oh, god, I totally forgot.' Adam glanced back at her – he was a fast walker – looking concerned. 'I promised I'd get a selfie of us on the London Eye to go in the piece.'

Adam stopped too. 'Well, why don't we take one here?' he suggested, giving her a smile. 'The view's almost as good, right?'

'Are you sure?' She busied herself getting her phone out of her bag, glad to have something to do with her hands – she felt like a starstruck fan asking for a photo with a celebrity. 'Sorry, I ...'

'It's no bother, Laura.' Before she could say anything else he'd walked back over to her and arranged himself at her side. Her head came up to just above his shoulder and he had a clean, soapy smell, like he'd recently got out of the shower. They were almost but not quite touching. It was the closest they'd been to each other so far and the sudden intimacy was startling – but nice, she thought, trying to relax into it as she held her phone out, wiggling it around to get them both in the frame. It was definitely nice to be so close to someone like him. Her heart was racing.

'Ah, sorry, it's tricky with me being taller,' Adam said, putting his arm around her shoulder and leaning down.

The line had been crossed and there was no going back: now they were *actually* touching. The phone wobbled in her hand – it was still so hot, probably in the high twenties, and the thought of sweating on him was mortifying. She could tell he was keeping his arm tensed so he wouldn't put too much weight on her – *solid*, she imagined Femi saying.

'Say cheese!' she cried. Neither of them actually said it. She tapped the shutter with her thumb, then stepped to the side and called the picture up in her gallery. He looked exactly like he did in real life, good-natured and handsome. There was an easy smile on his face, but hers was frozen in a rictus grin and her nose was shiny. One of her ears was poking through her hair too, *Lord of the Rings* elfstyle. She wanted to take another one so they'd look less mismatched, but she couldn't bring herself to ask. Adam had taken a respectful step away; he was leaning on the rail behind them now, looking back towards the station.

'All good?' he asked her. She nodded quickly. He smiled, narrowing his eyes against the sun. 'I actually used to walk over this bridge every evening after work,' he said. 'Six of us from uni had this place in Kennington, right by the Oval. After we . . .' He corrected himself. 'After *I* moved out into the place I'm in now, I actually really missed it. I still see the guys a fair bit, but it's different, you know?' He stopped and turned back to Laura. 'When you're younger you think you'll always have everyone, don't you?' he said. 'You don't know . . .'

They were the same, Laura thought, a giant swell of feeling catching her off guard.

'I know what you mean,' she said quietly. 'Come on – let's get that drink.'

The bar was a big, echoing place where the staff were all dressed like Star Trek characters, the customers were all wearing suits and the cocktails all cost twenty pounds. As they ordered Laura felt like an interloper – she kept expecting to feel the manager's hand on her shoulder. But Adam was smiling at her, so she smiled back.

'Have you eaten?' His gaze settled, just for a second, on the chocolate smudge on her dress, before he realised what he'd done and looked away politely. She clapped a hand over it.

'Oh, I'm not super hungry,' she said, not wanting him to think she was the kind of person who habitually grazed in the queues for London landmarks (she definitely was). He looked a tiny bit disappointed; she quickly backtracked. 'But if you are then let's get something! I can always eat!'

'Hah. Me too.' He smiled. He took the food menu out of its holder and opened it – she watched him running a finger methodically down the 'Snacks' section at the top. 'Why don't we get some chips?'

'Great!'

'Great.' He looked across at her. 'Regular or sweet potato?'

Laura hesitated, trying to decode his expression. He must have a preference and she wanted hers to match his. If she had to guess she'd have said he was a sweet potato guy – that tended to go with being sporty, didn't it? Maybe he ordered burgers without the bun, she thought, trying not to feel sad about that.

'Sweet potato ... ?' she ventured. His expression stayed the same; she tried again. 'Or regular? I'm easy!'

'Yeah, let's go for regular.' He closed the menu and put it back carefully in its holder. 'Sweet potato ones are just never that nice, are they?'

'Like eating wet cardboard.' He laughed and she felt a little more of the tension starting to ebb away. 'That must be one of the things they matched us on,' she added. 'Snack compatibility.'

Adam nodded, considering this. 'I suppose they can figure that out, can't they? From looking at what food photos
you've liked on social media.' He shook his head in wonder. 'Crazy. I still can't get my head around the whole Cupid
thing, can you? I'm not going to lie – when I got that email
from Nush out of the blue, I nearly didn't reply.'

'Well, I'm very glad you did,' Laura said, instantly regretting it – was that too forward? Was there even such a
thing when you knew you were contracted to see each
other again? 'So, er, what exactly did she say?' Laura asked
quickly.

A waitress was hovering with a sleek steel jug; Adam
gave her a confident little nod – he was obviously used to
these sorts of fancy places – and she filled their water
glasses.

'She just told me what they were doing, said it looked
from their initial profiling of me based on the information they had as though we'd get on, and did I want them
to dig into my personal data a bit more?' He picked up
his glass and she watched his throat move as he drank.
He noticed and stopped; she blushed and looked away.
'Once I'd got over the shock, I figured I might as well.
I've got no idea how she knew I'd had a break-up, though.
I'm not on Twitter or Instagram and I barely use Facebook . . .'

'Had you been buying a lot of ice cream online?'

'I'm actually not a big . . .' He stopped. 'Oh, god, sorry –
that was a joke, wasn't it?' He smiled then and did a
self-effacing shrug. 'Can you tell I'm out of practice?'

Laura made herself laugh. 'You've not been single for
very long then?'

Adam shook his head. 'Nearly ten months.' He looked
away. 'It's funny, actually,' he said, in a way that made her
think whatever was coming had about as much comic

potential as a recently amputated limb, 'I was meant to be getting married this week.'

One of his cuffs, she noticed, had a loose thread hanging from it. He'd wound it around the little finger on his opposite hand as he was talking, turning the skin surrounding it a livid red, then white.

'We were at the cake tasting. We'd narrowed it down to coffee and one of those ones where the icing changes colour as you go up, you know?' The thread tightened, cutting into his finger. 'We were talking about which one to go for when she stood up and went: *I'm sorry, I can't do this*. I thought she meant picking a flavour, but she was actually talking about marrying me. We met through work – she's a geologist – and we were still in the same office at that point, which made things … tricky. She's got a new job with another energy company now.' He laughed; it sounded forced. 'Anyway, I didn't come here tonight to talk about all that. And it feels good to be …' He nudged his little finger against Laura's, then let it rest there. 'You know. Moving on.'

His touch sent a little prickle of electricity through her. As she stared at their hands, feeling surreally distanced from it all, like she was watching herself on TV, she realised that someone was calling her. She grabbed her phone and was hit by a second jolt – a queasy one this time – when she saw the name on the screen. Her mum had taken to WhatsApp enthusiastically (*lovely weather here 2day* 😎 🌴 🍸 *hottest day of the year so far apparently* 🥵 🔥 🌞 *i know they say u shouldn't tan but remember every1 looks better with a bit of colour love from mum x x x*) and never phoned her now – the only other time Laura could remember her calling was when Harrison had chased an ice-cream van onto the dual carriageway. Something terrible must have happened.

'Er, sorry – back in a second,' she said to Adam, scrambling out of her chair. She could feel his puzzlement at her sudden disappearing act as she hurried across the room.

The bathroom she ducked into was being redecorated: the tiles had been prised off the splashbacks, exposing the scuffed-looking concrete beneath.

'Mum? Is everything OK?'

'Hi, love!' Her mum's voice was too loud and bright. Laura could hear boozed-up chatter in the background – and more distantly, the honk of a saxophone.

'Mum, where are you?' There was something else too: the faint click of a lighter. 'Are you … smoking?'

'I'm at the Pizza Express Jazz Club!' She inhaled; Laura imagined her jetting smoke out of her mouth in the way she always used to when she had a glass of wine in her hand, before she'd given up. 'Just having a drink with a friend.'

'Um, OK.' Something wasn't right – but whatever it was, Laura decided, she didn't want to know about it tonight. She couldn't face it – and anyway, she needed to concentrate on making a good impression on Adam. 'Well, I'm having a drink with a friend too, so …'

'You're alright, aren't you, love?' her mum blurted out. 'I know you've had a hard time, but things are getting better now, aren't they? And work's fine, isn't it?'

Laura put her free palm against the concrete. 'Yup, it's fine,' she said, trying to identify each individual bump and dip. The roughness was uncomfortable but that was good, it gave her something immediate to think about. 'I'll give you a call at the weekend, OK, Mum?'

'Love …' her mum began. But Laura had already taken the phone away from her ear. The only thing worse than being around her parents was not being around them – at least when she was actually there she could keep an eye on them, mediate, stop any petty bickering escalating. But when it was just the two of them, with no buffer, the cracks in their relationship became great yawning crevasses. Right now, she had a sense of something creaking ominously. She made a fist and pressed her knuckles hard into the wall.

***

When Laura came out of the bathroom the setting sun was streaking the darkening river gold. As she made her way back to Adam, she watched a tugboat chugging past and wondered how many of them were still out there, all trying to get home before the light went. The thought made her feel suddenly cold and lonely. The bar was busy now, humming: every seat was taken and all the tables seemed to be occupied by people in pairs, symmetrical and self-contained.

Adam had pushed his chair back so he had a better view of the water and propped one foot on the opposite knee. Their drinks and the chips had arrived and he'd laid out two paper napkins: one for her and one for him. She stopped, got her phone out and took a picture of the sunset, then racked her brains for a suitable caption – Nush had followed her on Instagram that morning and Laura knew she was being watched.

New beginnings, she typed. She posted it, then dropped her phone back into her bag and made her way over to the table. Adam heard her coming and turned around.

'You OK?' He looked anxious suddenly.

'Oh, fine.' She sat down, smoothing her dress out to try to look more together. 'Just family stuff.'

'Ah, phew.' There was a pen lying on the table with its cap off; he leaned over and clicked it back on, not quite looking at her. 'I thought maybe you'd got a friend to call you with a fake emergency so you could get out of here ...' He tailed off. The napkin in front of her was still folded into a triangle, but Laura noticed that his was flat on the table, unfolded – she could see a faint outline of black ink showing through the paper. Before she could stop herself, she'd picked it up and turned it over. On the other side there was a little pen sketch of the view in front of them, with the buildings on the far bank of the river mapped out in deft, precise strokes. There was the boat she'd seen. It was like something from a picture book.

'What's all this?' She looked up at Adam. He was blushing.

'Oh, nothing.' He shook his head self-deprecatingly. 'Just a silly doodle. I do them sometimes when it's just me.' He picked up the napkin and folded it in two. 'It's been just me quite a lot lately.'

He was looking straight ahead at the sun sinking into the water. She'd never in a million years have had him down as artistic. And if she'd been wrong about that ... what else was in there? He clearly had hidden depths.

'Adam, this is really good,' she said softly. 'You're really good.'

'Thanks.' He turned back to her and smiled. The napkin was still in his hand. 'I thought about going to art college after I left school, but ...' He shrugged, then held it out to her. 'You can keep it, if you like. But don't feel you have to.'

'I'd love to.' As she took it she let her fingers rest against his, just for a second. Their eyes met and they smiled at each other. Laura felt warmth spreading through her as she moved her hand away.

'Hey, listen,' she said, reaching for a chip. 'What are you doing next weekend?'

***

Adam:

Hey, did you get home ok?

Laura:

Hi!

I did thanks

You?

Adam:

Yeah easy journey – straight onto a train
  and then it's just one stop, happy days

Laura:

Ah great!

Adam:

Might get a takeaway

Laura:

Ah sorry I totally missed this!

Was having a shower

What did you go for?

Adam:

Hey no worries!
Just made pasta in the end
I should get some sleep

Laura:

Yeah me too!

Adam:

Looking forward to Sunday

Laura:

Can't wait!

Night

Adam:

Sweet dreams Laura xx

Chapter 6

convolution (noun): an operation that multiplies an input with a filter

Jamie's friends Pip and Fergus, who'd been the first to arrive at the barbecue, were leaning over the tray Laura was holding. She shifted her weight from foot to foot – her wedges were making her feel like she was on stilts, but the long 1970s-style dress she'd borrowed from Lil made them a necessity.

'Ooh … and what's *this* one?' Fergus asked, pointing at one of the little pastry cups Jamie had spent the morning assembling with tweezers. He jabbed it, knocking it into its neighbour.

'It's fox,' Laura said – the two of them had quizzed her at length about every single canapé and she was starting to lose patience. She had formed a strong and immediate dislike of Fergus, who apparently earned eye-watering sums of money from insuring boats but had turned up clutching a bottle of wine whose peeling label suggested it had done the rounds of every party in south-west London.

'What?'

'Lox. You know. Like in New York.' It was actually beef.

'Gosh,' Fergus said. 'What fun!' He picked it up and swallowed it whole, python-style.

'Laura! Hello, *you*!' A pregnant blonde woman in a flowery wrap dress was waving at her from across the garden, towing behind her a very tall man wearing linen trousers that were slightly too short for him. 'It's me – Caz! We met at Jamie and Whit's wedding. You remember my husband Rory, of course.'

'Um, of course.' Laura kissed her on the cheek, holding the tray out of the way. 'Congratulations!' she added, noticing Caz cupping her bump.

'Oh, you're sweet,' she said, stroking it. 'Number three, so no big surprises – but it's still such a special time. We're loving it, aren't we, Rory?'

'We're loving it,' Rory confirmed.

Caz looked over to the other side of the grass, where Whit and a circle of frowning men in chinos were ministering to a barely smoking barbecue. 'Can you believe it's been five years since their big day? Now, let me see – you were with . . .' She clicked her fingers. 'Ohhhh, yes, I remember now – you'd just stopped seeing a bloke and there was a bit of a hoo-ha about where you were going to sit, wasn't there?' Her face assumed an expression of infinite sympathy; Laura clocked Caz stealing a glance at her left hand. 'Is there someone special on the scene these days?'

'There is, actually,' Laura said, with a speed that surprised her. 'His name's Adam. He's coming today.'

Caz perked up instantly. 'Oh, good for you!' She beamed. 'Lovely!'

Right now, Laura reflected, Adam was Schrödinger's plus-one: both here and not here, invisible but filling the space with his presence. She hated herself a bit for enjoying it so much, but it was such a relief to be able to shut down

Pity Committee conversations by summoning him up. It had been just over a week since they'd first met. Although they hadn't actually seen each other in that time they'd kept up a flow of messages. They mostly talked about work and stuff on TV, but the messages' content felt less important than the fact they were there – every time she saw his name on her phone's screen she felt a little more solid, a little more of a functioning adult. It was like being on holiday from herself.

'I should go and see if Jamie needs some help,' she said, but Caz had already turned away to whisper to Rory, who gave her a hostage's smile. Laura weaved her way across the grass past people she vaguely recognised – Jamie's colleagues, a few neighbours, a red-faced delegation from Whit's squash club – all standing placidly in twos like animals waiting to board Noah's Ark.

Jamie was alone in the kitchen, cremating an aubergine over the hob. She was wearing a dress that was identical to Caz's and her hair had been blown out into huge, bouncy flicks by a woman who'd come to the house with a suitcase of rollers at 6 a.m. Jamie kept touching them, as if she was worried they might fall off. Whenever Laura saw her with her friends she seemed slightly on edge – scared, maybe, that something would slip and they'd realise how different her childhood had been to theirs.

'How is everyone?' Jamie asked without turning around. Laura dumped the tray in the sink and helped herself to a miniature Taiwanese steamed bun from the dish next to her.

'Oh, you know. Obsessed with Inheritance Tax. Wearing a lot of Boden. These look really good, by the way.'

'You are extraordinarily tedious.' Jamie slapped the bun out of Laura's hand. 'Anyway, where's your new boyfriend? Why isn't he here yet?'

'He's on his way. And he's not my boyfriend.' She allowed herself a slightly smug smile. 'Yet.'

The aubergine was starting to smoke. Jamie switched the gas off and dumped it into the blender, where several others were already lying in a steaming heap. 'Run me through this again,' she said, briskly spooning in some tahini. 'A company that's bought records of everybody's online behaviour appeared out of nowhere and announced that they'd help you find a relationship. Now you're going out with the person they set you up with so you can write a feature about it?'

'That's not the *only* reason I'm doing it,' Laura said defensively. 'He's lovely *and* he cares about climate change.' Seeing that Jamie was unmoved, she got her phone out of her pocket, called up the photo of Adam's napkin sketch that she'd taken to show to Lil and everyone at work – the real thing was on the table by her bed – and waved it at Jamie. 'And he drew this. Isn't it good?'

Jamie gave the screen a cursory glance, then leaned across and switched the blender on, obliterating the aubergines in seconds.

'And what happens if you break up? Sorry, *when* you break up.'

Laura grabbed two buns and defiantly stuffed them both into her mouth. 'We're not going to,' she said, chomping. 'They've matched us really carefully. It's groundbreaking technology.'

Jamie stared at her as she cranked the blender's speed up. 'You don't actually believe that, do you?' she said. 'I mean, it's obviously nonsense. Love isn't a science.'

Laura swallowed. 'Actually . . .' she began. But before she could finish the sentence her phone lit up – Lil was video-calling her.

'Have you got the dress on? Let me see!' Lil hollered. She was sitting cross-legged on her living- room floor, surrounded by a small army of Dora's soft toys – the one nearest her, a cuddly panda, had toppled over drunkenly onto its side. She was inexplicably wearing blue lipstick and pink glittery eyeshadow. Laura dutifully held her phone at arm's length so Lil could see her dress.

'What do you think?' she asked, doing a shimmy.

Lil wolf-whistled. 'You look HOT. You know if you stand with the light behind you it goes a bit see-through, right? Use that information as you see fit …'

'Thanks for the tip.' Laura grinned. Jamie tutted under her breath, then marched over to get something out of the fridge. She and Lil had only met once, at Laura's birthday drinks the year before, and it hadn't gone well: Lil had led the entire pub in a karaoke rendition of 'She Hates Me' by Puddle of Mudd while Jamie stared in open-mouthed horror at Whit, who'd joined in.

'Hi, Jamie!' Lil called out to her. 'Your hair looks fucking great! Love the curls!'

Jamie paused for a second in view of the screen, holding a metal tray of skewered prawns.

'Thank you, Lillian,' she said stiffly, before clacking away again. Laura waited until she was out of the shot before pulling a knowing face at Lil.

'Strong look at your end today,' she said, pointing in the direction of Lil's Technicolor make-up.

Lil laughed. 'Dora did it. I'd better go, actually – she's covering her entire face in Mac highlighter as we speak … Let me know how it goes, yeah? Tell *ADAM* I say hi!'

She ended the call. Laura stared at the blank screen, suddenly nervous now that Lil's buoyant presence had vanished. She'd gone home from the South Bank feeling like she and Adam had made a good start, but what if that had just been the alcohol? What if they ran out of things to talk about today? That happened sometime on second dates, which this technically was. She was wondering whether she ought to brush her teeth again when a message from him appeared. *Outside*, it read. And then, in a second one, an *x*. Laura took a deep breath and pressed her lips together.

'He's here,' she said to Jamie, who was painting the prawns in marinade with a pastry brush.

'I see,' Jamie said, without turning around. 'Well, you'd better go and let him in, hadn't you?'

As Laura walked down the hall she could see Adam silhouetted on the other side of the frosted-glass panels. When she opened the door he was standing expectantly on the step. He had a bottle of wine in a gift bag and a pair of sunglasses clipped into the pocket of the bodywarmer he was wearing over his shirt.

'Made it!' he said, which was obvious really, but Laura forgave him because he looked just as handsome as she'd remembered and for the first time in her life she wasn't going to have to face one of Jamie's awful parties alone. He went to kiss her on the cheek; she moved too and their faces collided. They sprang apart, embarrassed, then tried again. This time they managed it.

'You look really nice,' Adam said, pulling back and clearing his throat. 'That's a great dress.'

Laura realised there was a shaft of sunlight just to her left. Remembering what Lil had said, she stepped into it and watched as Adam's eyes drifted gratifyingly down the flimsy fabric. She spun on her wedges.

'Oh, this old thing?' she said, giving him a smile over her shoulder and setting off back down the hall. 'Come on – drinks are this way.' She was actually starting to enjoy herself.

Whit, who was doing his best impression of a Mr Whippy van in a white shirt and pale blue trousers, had joined Jamie in the kitchen. Laura hovered in the doorway with Adam next to her.

'Guys, this is Adam, my ...' She hesitated. Obviously they'd only been on one date so far, but they'd already agreed to keep seeing each other for the rest of the summer when they signed their Cupid contracts – so what was he? What were they? *Were* they even a 'they' yet? Whit bounded forwards before she could finish.

'Whittaker,' he said, shaking Adam's hand vigorously. 'Call me Whit, everybody does. And this is my wife Jamie – everybody calls her boss!'

Adam handed her the wine and kissed her on the cheek. 'Lovely to meet you, Jamie,' he said. 'I've heard lots about you – all good things, obviously.'

'I seriously doubt that,' Jamie said, giving him an appraising once-over. As she watched her sister taking in his neat hair and regular features, the perfectly ironed shirt and the bodywarmer, Laura realised she was holding her breath. Jamie had never liked anyone while her sister was going out with them (Walker had become a saint in retrospect, but mostly, Laura suspected, because *she'd* broken up with *him*). She wasn't sure why she still felt the need to present them to her sister like prize-contender marrows. She slipped over to the sink where the bottles were cooling and poured herself a tumbler of vodka, topping it up with just enough tomato juice to turn it red.

'You know, Jamie and I actually met online too,' Whit said. 'Years ago, back when it all got going. Let me see, I was ... SingleLawyer, that's right. Pretty self-explanatory. And Jamie was ... Oh! I remember! You were Mysterious-Girl, weren't you, sweetheart?' He pulled her into a hug.

'*Whit,*' Jamie muttered, wriggling a bit. '*Please.*'

'Well, I always thought it was a great song,' Adam said. 'And I'm told he was robbed on *I'm A Celebrity.*' Inside,

Laura punched the air in triumph – he was handling them both so well.

'Thank you, Adam – you're welcome here any time,' Jamie said in a noticeably warmer voice. 'Now, let's get you a drink.' She freed herself from Whit and raised her eyebrows at him – he leaped into action, uncorking a bottle. He was standing behind Adam; as he was pouring the wine out, he turned to Laura and gave her a huge and unsubtle thumbs up. She rolled her eyes, trying not to smile.

'Well, cheers,' he said, passing Adam the glass. 'Here's to …'

The doorbell went. Jamie's head snapped around.

'I thought everyone was here?'

'I'll get it,' Laura said quickly, snatching up her glass.

She was fully expecting to open the door to an unaccounted-for clone of Pip or Fergus. It took her a second to realise she was staring at her dad, who was swaying slightly and brandishing his Art Pass.

'I've been at the London Transport Museum!' he announced. 'You get in free if you've got one of these. Magic, eh?' He peered over Laura's shoulder. 'Well, are you going to let me in or not?'

Whit, Jamie and Adam were standing around the island in the middle of the kitchen, deep in conversation.

'That's a great oven you've got there,' Adam was saying. 'Very energy-efficient. And if you're looking for something …'

Jamie was nodding and smiling; as she turned around Laura felt like she was watching a vase wobbling on the edge of a shelf right before it toppled off and smashed into a million pieces.

'Adam's just been telling us …' She ground to a halt. 'Dad? What the … what are you doing here?'

'Did you know they used to run steam trains on the District line?' Laura's dad said cheerfully. 'They went all the way to Windsor. Incredible.' He helped himself to a couple of loaded potato skins from the tray Whit had been about to take outside. 'Now, I don't want you to think I've been *drinking to excess*, girls,' he said, crunching through them. 'I just had a couple of Singhas with my lunch at what's-its-name – Mamawag? Nice place. Noodles were a bit wet, mind.' He swallowed, then squinted at Adam; Laura fought the overwhelming urge to stand in front of him, shield him from whatever was coming. 'This your new bloke, love? You kept it very quiet.'

Adam cleared his throat. 'I'm Adam,' he said, very politely, sticking out a hand. 'Laura was telling me you work in agricultural sales, Mr Morrison. That must be interesting, especially at the moment.'

'I'd agree with you,' Laura's dad said, clapping him on the shoulder, apparently unaware of the outstretched hand; Laura winced. 'But then we'd both be wrong.' He laughed as he picked up the ceramic fruit bowl off the worktop and turned it over, looking for a price tag. 'This must have cost you a bit, Whit.'

'*I* paid for it,' Jamie snapped. 'And, yes, it did. May I talk to you for a second, please, Laura? *Alone.*'

Her sister half-dragged her into the walk-in store cupboard. The jars lining the shelves all had labels on them that Whit had made with a special gun; the one on the quinoa read *KEENWAH*.

'Why have you done this?' Jamie hissed.

'I didn't do anything!'

'Then how did he know we were having a party? Why has he pitched up here *today* having a midlife fucking crisis?' Jamie pressed her fingers into her temples, rubbing them in angry little circles. 'May I just remind you that we're not obliged to put a roof over your head?'

Outside, someone popped a cork; Laura heard whoops and cheers echoing around the garden. She wondered whether she ought to apologise, then felt the familiar unedifying urge to double down.

'I read somewhere that it's technically possible for full siblings not to share any DNA at all,' she said. 'I think that's really interesting, don't you?'

Jamie crossly straightened a tin of anchovies. 'I find that very easy to believe,' she said.

Here they were again. Same old script, same old cues. And it couldn't just be the age gap: Lil's half-brother was eighteen years older than her with *a grandchild* and they weren't like this with each other. Laura sighed.

'Look, I'm sorry, OK?' She tried to sound conciliatory. 'It just popped out when I was with them the other night. It's not a disaster – he's fine really, they both are. He'll behave.'

'I wish I shared your confidence,' Jamie said bitterly. She shook her head. 'Adam's coping well. I have to say, he's exceeded my expectations.'

Jamie actually smiled at her then – only for a fraction of a second, a tiny sunbeam of approval. But it was enough.

'Science one, Jamie nil,' Laura said triumphantly.

When they came out of the store cupboard Whit was showing Adam and Laura's dad what all the KitchenAid attachments did.

'And this is a dough hook,' he was saying earnestly, like a presenter on the shopping channel. 'Makes the best focaccia!'

'Do you bake, Mr Morrison?' Adam asked.

'Call me Jim,' Laura's dad said. 'I've actually just bought one of those Jamie Oliver ...'

'Dad, why are you here?' Jamie demanded. He froze.

'I ...' He inhaled, then let all the air out in a ragged huff. 'Well – here's the thing. Your mum ...'

The phone rang. Jamie snatched it off its cradle.

'Hello?' Her cheeks, which had been flushed with stress all day, suddenly went white. 'Yes, he's here. Mum, what's going on ... What? When did this happen? Are you ... ?' She paused; Laura could hear crying at the other end. Adam was staring at the floor. 'Mum, stop. I'm not ... No, I didn't say that. Look, I'm going to call you back tonight, OK? I really can't speak now.'

Jamie hung up. 'That was her,' she said, turning back to face them all. Her voice was even more carefully modulated than usual. 'She says you're having some "time apart". Is that true?'

Laura's dad picked up the KitchenAid's paddle. 'She's gone to stay with a friend,' he said, turning it over and over in his hands. 'Someone she used to fly with, apparently.'

Laura's blood ran cold. She pictured the Pizza Express Jazz Club, which she imagined to be packed with late-middle-aged couples who were probably less than an hour away from having full sex. Then she looked across at her dad, his shoulders slumped and his eyes downcast, and felt the familiar, awful tightening in her chest – except this time it was even worse, because there was a witness.

'Why don't Adam and I take these outside?' she blurted out, grabbing the nearest tray, which was covered in mince-filled lettuce cups. She needed to get him as far away from all of them as possible. Adam followed her silently into the garden.

They didn't talk as they walked across the lawn to the table with the food on it. Now they were alone she couldn't even look at him; she felt like she was drowning in shame. What must he be thinking about her, having just seen all of that? That she was emotionally damaged, probably – and definitely not someone you'd want to be contractually obliged to get to know better.

'Laura, I'm sorry,' Adam said quietly behind her. 'Are you alright?'

She nodded, not trusting herself to speak. They kept walking.

'Jamie's nice,' Adam said eventually.

She stopped and glanced back at him. 'You're joking.'

'I mean it. Do you not get on?'

'She's my favourite person.' One of her wedges had started to sink into the lawn. 'Apart from every other person I've ever met.'

Adam frowned; he clearly thought she was being serious. Laura yanked her heel out of the grass, nearly losing her balance. He put a hand on her arm to steady her and she tried to focus on the warmth of his touch. 'You OK?' he asked solicitously.

'Totally fine.' She straightened up and forced herself to smile at him; if she wanted to avoid frightening him off, she thought, the best bet was to downplay the whole thing. 'It's happened before, actually – Mum left when we were younger. She ran away with one of Jamie's teachers, if you can believe that!' Adam looked horrified and Laura realised she'd made a mistake trying to make a joke of it. 'I mean, she came back after a week,' she added, trying to regain the ground she'd lost. 'Less than a week, actually. Six days. And they sorted it out.' He still didn't look convinced. 'It isn't a big deal, is what I'm trying to say. I'm OK. Really.'

***

From the moment Laura had seen her mum and Mr McManus drinking Campari in the garden that Friday afternoon, she'd known. Not just that something was going to happen – that had been obvious to her, although she had only been nine so she hadn't had the words for what exactly *it* was – but that the two of them were, in some fundamental way, the same sort of person. Glamorous. Adventurous.

'You're back early, love!' her mum called out from the other side of the rockery. 'I thought you were going to have tea at Becky's?'

'She got a bug in her eye and had to go to the hospital,' Laura said, distractedly rubbing the skin under the neck of her itchy school jumper. She assessed the man sitting at the patio table. He was about ten years younger than her mum, had dark, curly hair and very white teeth.

'Who are you?' she asked him.

Mr McManus – *hello there, Laura, your mum's told me all about you* – put his Campari down and stood up to introduce himself, shaking her hand as though she was a grown-up. He taught Jamie French at college, he explained, but he was actually Italian; his mum's parents had run an ice-cream parlour in a Scottish seaside resort. Did Laura like ice cream? She did, but she told him she didn't.

'Are you here to see Jamie?' she asked him warily, unable to put her finger on what it was about this friendly, nice-looking man that she really didn't like. 'She's not here. She has trampolining on Fridays.'

'Ah, no – your mum and I have been talking about me giving her some adult Italian lessons,' Mr McManus said, smiling at her. He patted her mum's arm easily. 'She's already pretty good!'

'*Grazie*, Carlo!' Her mum's cheeks were pink like she'd just run for a bus. She took a dainty sip of her drink. 'If I got better at Italian we could go on holiday to Italy and eat lots of pizza, love,' she said to Laura, her eyes big and bright. 'You'd like that, wouldn't you?'

Trips to hot countries, Laura knew, were in the same category for her dad as bottled water and putting the heating on before December: an unnecessary extravagance. That summer they'd gone camping in the New Forest – it had rained every day and her mum had cried on the last night when the gas had run out while they were trying to cook their sausages.

'I'm going to watch *Neighbours* now,' Laura said, turning to go back inside. She wasn't meant to watch any TV until she'd finished all her homework, but neither of them tried to stop her.

The Italian lessons happened every Monday night at Mr McManus's flat, which was in a swanky new development near the station. Their mum would change out of the crisp blouse and skirt she wore to do her accounting work into what Laura thought of as her holiday clothes: loose white linen trousers with strappy gold sandals underneath. When she came back she was always in a sparkly mood, singing snatches of songs, hugging Laura and Jamie and covering them with kisses.

Let those who God has joined together ... That was what the priest had said to her and Jamie's cousin Lisa at her wedding the summer before. A priest had also said that to her parents at their own wedding – in the one photo she'd seen, her dad was beaming in his brown flared suit, and her mum had a big bunch of flowers held over the bump that would become Jamie. It meant that God had decided you were supposed to be together forever. But what if God had got it wrong?

***

By three o'clock Laura was back in the kitchen, piping cream into profiteroles (if you did it too early, Jamie had told her sternly, they went soggy). She'd volunteered for the job: as long as her hands were moving, she felt OK. But if she stopped, even for a second, a torrent of disturbing images rushed in to fill the space. Her mum chinking glasses with a faceless man, wearing the fruity Nina Ricci perfume she saved for best. Her dad, alone in a darkening house with Harrison whimpering to be let out.

Miraculously, Adam didn't seem to have been spooked by the chaos – in fact, he was being an even more perfect guest than he had been before, topping up everyone's glasses and laughing when Whit showed him his favourite YouTube video of raccoons trashing a picnic. Laura put down the piping bag and watched through the open French windows: Adam was standing in the middle of a group with his sunglasses on and his sleeves rolled up, exposing his tanned, strong-looking forearms. He'd got his phone out and was showing Laura's dad how to use emojis.

'What about this one?' her dad was saying, peering at the screen. 'Does that have a meaning?' Without his glasses on he looked soft and vulnerable – a turtle blinking in the sunlight.

'The aubergine?' Adam coughed. 'Best not to use it, actually. Just to be on the safe side'

'I'm old enough to remember when these were called hieroglyphs,' Laura's dad said. Everybody laughed good-naturedly. Jamie, who was picking up discarded paper plates, stopped and looked at him, then shook her head dismissively.

Whit came out of the utility room, carrying a tray of ice-cream sandwiches – Jamie had been up until midnight moving scoops of homemade raspberry ripple to a baking tray with a toothpick so they could harden up.

'Hey, kid,' he said to Laura. It was the first time they'd spoken since her dad had arrived and he couldn't meet her eye. 'Look, I'm sorry about your parents. It's rough.'

'They'll be OK.' Laura stuck the nozzle of the piping bag into another pastry puff and squeezed hard. 'They always sort it out.'

Whit looked like he was about to say something, but he thought better of it; he was someone who always liked to look on the bright side. 'Adam's a great guy,' he said cheerfully. 'He just kind of fits in, doesn't he?'

Laura looked back at Adam, who happened to glance over his shoulder at exactly the same time. As their eyes met his face broke into an easy smile. She smiled back at him, trying to imagine what it would be like if her love life was actually something she could rest her weight against, rather than a thing she had to carry the weight of. Perhaps that was another reason they'd been matched – he was steady and reliable enough to take it. But which bit of her online behaviour had tipped Cupid off about her dysfunctional family? She made a mental note to ask the Data team, if Nush ever allowed her to speak to them.

Whit slapped her on the back. 'Come on,' he said. 'Let's get these out before they melt.'

The party was starting to thin out. Laura found Adam by the dying barbecue, talking to Caz and her five-year-old son, who was small and pale with huge, watery blue eyes.

'What's your name?' Adam asked, crouching down so they were the same height.

The little boy chewed his lip. 'Kael,' he said.

'Like ... the vegetable?'

'It's actually a very ancient Gaelic word,' interjected Caz. 'It means "mighty warrior".'

'My mistake,' Adam said. 'It's a lovely name.'

Kael tugged at his sleeve. 'I hid my Paw Patrol lookout tower in a bush. Can we go and find it?'

'You bet.' Adam winked at him. 'Maybe we can hit the buffet afterwards, eh?'

Kael's eyes widened in excitement. He grabbed Adam's hand and hauled him off in the direction of the food.

'Keep him away from the desserts, please!' Caz called after them. 'We're trying out an exclusionary diet for his eczema. He can have a little bit of dark chocolate as long as it's raw and sugar-free, but dairy is *poison*.' She shook her head, then turned to Laura. 'Is that your man?' she whispered. 'He's a *natural*! Haven't you done well?' She gazed mistily at Adam, who was on his hands and knees in front of the rhododendrons, with Kael directing him. 'I wouldn't hang about if I were you, Laura. You think you've got all the time in the world, but biologically speaking you're already running out of road ...' She put a hand on her bump and patted it. 'I mean, look at the problems poor Jamie's had.'

There was a soft, wet thump behind them. They turned around. There was Whit, holding out the tray. There was one ice-cream sandwich missing; it had rolled off and splattered on the grass. Next to him was Jamie.

Caz's cheeks caught fire. 'I just remembered I left Kael's antihistamines in the car!' she said, kissing the air next to Jamie's face as she rushed past. 'Wonderful food, darling – I wish I could cook like you. You're so *clever*.'

Jamie didn't look at her or say anything. She took a paper napkin off the tray, crouched down and started scrubbing at her espadrilles, which were streaked with red and white. The skin showing through her centre parting looked jarringly naked.

'I'm going upstairs to change these,' she said to Whit in her normal, businesslike voice. She glanced over at her and Laura's dad, who was alone by the barbecue, prodding its embers with a pair of tongs. 'And when I come down, I want him gone – I can't deal with him right now. OK?'

Whit was staring at the smears on the grass. He nodded. Jamie stood up and unshowily linked the fingers of her empty hand with his.

'Thank you,' she whispered, squeezing. Then she scrunched the napkin in her other fist and walked purposefully back to the house. Just before she disappeared inside, Laura saw her stop in front of the glass and drag a thumb under her left eye, then her right.

Adam was over by the food table, watching Kael, who was wrist-deep in the tiramisu, squeaking like a bat. Laura took hold of Adam's hand and dragged him behind the shed.

'Let's go,' she said urgently. He looked startled.

'What, right now?'

'Right now.' She squeezed his fingers, just like Jamie had a second ago with Whit's. 'Please.'

'Where?'

'To yours?'

'I mean ... if that's what you really want.' He reached for her other hand. It felt like they were making some kind of vow to each other – Laura tried not to think about that. She tried not to think at all.

'It's what I really want.' She stretched up to kiss him properly for the first time, pushing her body to his. After a second's hesitation, he put his hands on her waist and kissed her back, pressing her gently against the side of the shed.

Chapter 7

distribute (verb): to multiply out the parts of an expression

The first thing Laura noticed when she woke up was that there was nothing in Adam's bedroom. Unlike her room at Jamie and Whit's, which was strewn with piles of books and shoes, it was disconcertingly empty. There were no pictures, or shelves, or even flat surfaces – all of the storage was built into the walls. (She had a vague memory of going around slapping them the night before, trying to work out where the hidden panels were.) The second was that the lack of things in the room extended to Adam himself – the other side of the bed was empty.

She rubbed her gritty eyes and sat up. The carpet was the colour of fresh cream – there was nothing on it apart from her phone, which was sticking out from under the cushion she'd dropped onto it to stop it lighting up, and the bottle of wine she'd insisted on opening when they'd got in and then insisted they bring through to the bedroom when they ... She groaned, letting herself collapse backwards onto the pillow. There was a lipstick smudge on the duvet cover where she'd had it pulled up against her face in the night.

Next door in the kitchen – which was coming back to her now, the Nutribullet and neat rows of supplements like something out of a *Men's Health* spread – the kettle beeped. Laura flipped the duvet over so the smudge was hidden and arranged herself under it. She lay there listening to Adam moving around. He'd told her he'd bought this flat with his ex (Beth? Becca? She couldn't remember, but it had definitely made her think of *Little House on the Prairie*), but there was no trace of her anywhere in it – or, to be honest, of him. It felt like a show home, or one of those CGI images the *Bugle* ran in its property pages of developments that hadn't actually been built yet.

The momentum they'd built up behind the shed had powered her through the Uber ride back to his flat. They'd sat close together in the back of their getaway car, her leg against his and his fingers tracing slow circles on her knee. The next thing she could properly remember was the two of them positioned slightly apart on his pale grey, L-shaped sofa with the wine, lapsing in and out of silence – now they were actually here, neither of them seemed to know what to say. She'd suggested some music as an icebreaker and had settled on an early 2000s chillout album from his CD collection (he *was* five years older than her). Once it was playing she'd gone back and kneeled flirtatiously on the floor in front of him.

So, she'd said, running her hands over his legs. *What else do you like? Apart from Morcheeba.* He hadn't seemed to know where to look. *Oh, you know*, he'd said, stroking her hair. *All the usual stuff.* She'd tried not to look disappointed – she'd been hoping for something unexpected and personal, something that would light up the flickering connection between them like his drawing in the bar had.

Rather than saying anything else she'd stretched up to kiss him, letting the song wash over her. He'd drawn her up onto the sofa so she was straddling him and she'd lowered her head so she could kiss along his jawline, enjoying the way that made him tighten his grip on her hips. She'd started unbuttoning his shirt and pressed her mouth to his ear; he'd groaned. His body had felt exactly how she'd expected him to: smooth, solid, straightforwardly responsive. After that, they didn't speak for a while.

Blinking herself back into the room, she stuck an arm out from under the duvet and retrieved her phone. There were five missed calls from her mum: the three she'd ignored the night before, and two new ones. There was a voicemail message too, and a WhatsApp: *love it's me please can we speak this has been hard 4 me 2 u and Jamie r my world call me when u get this pls love from mum x x x*. She cleared all of them and dropped it back onto the floor.

She heard footsteps, then the soft whoosh of the door brushing the carpet. She shut her eyes again, pretending to be asleep. When she opened them Adam was in the doorway, wearing his dark blue work trousers – oh, god, it was Monday, she'd completely forgotten – and a belt but no shirt, holding a mug with KEEP CALM AND HAVE A BREW printed on it.

'You're up!' he said brightly, holding out the mug. The design was a bit cringey, but Laura tried to look past it and concentrate on his broad shoulders and tanned, well-muscled arms instead. It was always such a high-stakes thing, unwrapping a new person for the first time, but she'd enjoyed undressing him, even if his body had made her feel a bit self-conscious about her own at first. Not that he'd seemed to have any complaints – he'd breathed, *God, you're gorgeous*, as she pulled her dress over her head.

Now, she took the mug and propped herself up on her elbows, the duvet tucked under her arms like a TV character before the watershed. Adam cautiously sat down at the foot of the bed. 'How did you sleep?' he asked.

'Great!' She'd actually spent most of the night curled up uncomfortably in a corner of the bed, trying not to wake him up. 'You?'

'Yeah, great.' He looked out of the window. 'Look, last night was ... I wouldn't normally – you know. So soon after meeting someone.'

'Me neither!' In fact, she and Walker had ended up having sex in his car in a National Trust car park the night they met. 'But, you know – when it feels right ...'

'Exactly.' Adam looked relieved. 'Anyway, it's just coming up for eight – do you want a quick shower?'

Before she could answer he kneeled down, opened one of the drawers under the bed and got out a white towel rolled into a swanky hotel sausage. As Laura put the mug down on the bedside table and reached a hand out to take it the duvet started to slip. A smile flickered across Adam's face before he quickly looked away.

'Sorry, I'll leave you to it,' he said, getting up. He was blushing. It was obvious he was thinking about what had happened the night before – and that he knew she was thinking about it too. She was suddenly very aware of the insistent throb of her pulse.

'Wait, I ...' She pretended to be giving him a searching look. 'You've got something on you. Come here a second.'

Adam looked down, confused. 'What?'

She tucked her thumbs into the waistband of his trousers, letting the duvet fall, and looked up at him. 'Oh, just ... these.' He laughed and tilted his head back, letting her pull him down on top of her.

'What time do you have to be at work?' she asked, reaching for his belt.

'Nine.' He put a hand over hers, guiding it. 'I'll be late. I'm never late.'

She unbuckled it and moved on to his zip, tracing her fingers downwards – he breathed in sharply. 'Just this once?'

He kicked the duvet out from between them and ran a hand down her thigh. 'Just this once.'

***

She took her phone into the bathroom with her afterwards. It had a heated floor and every reflective surface gleamed. She winced as she was confronted with her slept-on hair and mugshot expression over and over again in the chrome taps, the towel rail, the two mirrored cupboards above the sink. Lil had messaged her.

> Lil:
> *What's another way of saying smooth?*
>
> Laura:
> *If you want me to help with your Hinge answers you can just ask*
>
> Lil:
> *VERY FUNNY*
> *Doing the blurb for ANOTHER exfoliator* $z^z{}_z{}^z{}_z{}^z$
> *How was the party?*

She pressed each of the cupboards in turn, popping them open.

> Laura:
> *Bad*

> *I'll tell you later*
> *Stayed at Adam's*

The first cupboard was empty and there wasn't much in the second one: a razor and a stack of blades, something called Facial Fuel in a silver tub, ibuprofen. Three identical, untouched tubes of toothpaste. The now-open box of Durex (Extra Safe), down by two.

> Lil:
> *!!!*
> *What's his place like*
> *Does he have more than one towel*
> *That's very important*
> *Unrelatedly*
> *We've just been sent the dress code for Asha's hen*
> *It's . . .*
> *'Like A Virgin'*
> *I LONG FOR DEATH*

There was something else in there, hidden right at the back. A bottle of perfume. Laura took it out and unscrewed the top. It had an old-fashioned glass stopper, the kind you were meant to dab on your wrists. She sniffed – dew-drops on grass, meadow flowers – then rubbed some on her skin.

***

They left the flat to set off to their separate offices, fingers threaded together. The forecast had said it was going to be another hot day but the sun was still shrouded in hazy mist. Laura shivered in Lil's floaty dress, which she'd obviously had to put on again, and the flip flops she'd stuffed into her bag as they were leaving Stonybrook Street – she felt like she had a giant neon sign above her head flashing WALK OF SHAME. Adam lived at the eastern end of Bermondsey, in a block of half a dozen apartments that butted into a small park. The night before there had been a group of people sitting in a circle under the trees, cooking sausages on a foil barbecue and passing a joint around. One of them had a guitar and he kept playing the opening notes of 'Layla' over and over again. Adam had pulled a face. *Somebody really needs to cut that grass*, he'd said, unlocking the front door. Laura had lingered.

'Paradise Street,' she said now, pointing to the sign. 'Nice.' Adam nodded.

'That was one of the reasons we bought this place, actually. Bella – that's my ex – said you could never be unhappy living somewhere with a name like that. I guess she was wrong.' He grimaced. 'It's been a bit of a nightmare taking over the mortgage to be honest, but it was that or sell up and I just couldn't face it.'

Laura pretended to be running her fingers through her hair so she could surreptitiously sniff the wrist that wasn't touching his. She thought of the empty left-hand cupboard and imagined it full of shampoo and body cream and make-up brushes. Then she imagined Adam coming across the bottle of perfume somewhere and unstoppering it like she had, breathing in the scent of Bella. Choosing to keep it. She swallowed. That wasn't a thought she wanted to be having right now.

'Busy day?' he asked her. 'We've got our team offsite next week, so I'm trying to crack on with as much ...'

Her hangover was creeping up on her again and Laura felt herself zoning out, her mind drifting to coffee and breakfast. Once they got to know each other properly, she thought, it would be better – they wouldn't have to make small talk like this.

They'd reached the Tube. Adam stopped and turned to her, letting go of her hand.

'Well, I'm heading down here ...'

'I'm going this way!' She was pointing in the opposite direction; it had been a reflex, like flinching when you touched a hot pan. Adam frowned.

'To the river?'

'I just fancy a walk – blow the cobwebs away!' A flicker of disappointment passed across his face. She reached for his hand again quickly, wanting to make up for it.

'It's great, isn't it?' she said, giving it a squeeze. 'Knowing we're going to see each other again. Not having to go through all that who's-going-to-text-first stuff.'

'Hah! That's very true.' He smiled, then bent down and gave her a kiss on the lips. 'Well ...' he said when he straightened up. 'Thank you for last night, Laura. It was really nice.'

She watched him as he crossed the road and merged with the crowd heading into the station. There *was* something restful about not having to spend the day staring anxiously at her screen. But it was strange too, everything already being so settled, and she had to admit that she felt a bit flat – she didn't have any of the butterflies in her stomach that she normally would have at the start of a promising new romance. Halfway down the station steps Adam stopped, turned around and raised his hand. She waved back. Once he'd disappeared she got her phone out – before she'd even unlocked it the screen lit up with an incoming call.

'Sorry, sorry, I know it's *disgustingly* early!' Nush sounded very awake; Laura imagined her starting the day at sunrise with lemon-infused hot water on a roof terrace, probably in Notting Hill. 'But I'm *dying* to know how yesterday went! Adam said he was meeting your family! This is *huge*, babe!'

'It went ... well.' There was a low brick wall just behind her; Laura sat down. 'I stayed the night at his actually.'

'Oh em *GEE*,' Nush squealed. 'You guys! How are you feeling?'

'Good!' She tried again. 'Really good. It's just ...'

'What's up, babe?'

Radical transparency, she reminded herself. That was what she'd signed up for with Cupid. 'Honestly, it's nothing massive,' she began tentatively. 'It's just that this whole situation still feels a bit ... I don't know. Strange. Like something's missing.' Her free hand moved to the bit below her ribs where the butterflies normally were. 'And feelings are important, aren't they?'

'Oh, *absolutely*,' Nush purred. 'But you can't always trust them. They're not objective, you know?' She paused. 'Put it this way – if your feelings had been right in the past, we wouldn't be having this conversation right now, would we?'

'What do you mean?'

'Well, you wouldn't still be single!' She laughed. 'I mean, you've always thought your intuition was a bit iffy, haven't you? We're here to help you move into a more ... functional dating space.' Another pause. When she spoke again her voice had an edge to it. 'What was that thing your sister said? About you missing a chip?'

It was like a time-lag on a Skype call. Laura heard exactly what Nush had said, but for a couple of seconds she didn't feel anything. Then a cold queasiness flooded her, followed by a scorching rush of shame.

'Are you there, babe?'

'I'm here,' Laura said flatly. It was as though Nush had found her sorest spot, stuck one of her holographic nails into it and twisted. Deliberately. There was a copy of Sunday's *Bugle* further down the wall next to a kebab with a fork still sticking out of it. The wind was ruffling the pages – then a gust blew it open and there was that week's magazine tucked into the midsection. As she stared at the cover lines she'd helped to write Laura felt the humiliation morphing into annoyance. Maybe she *had* gone to Cupid hoping they could help her, but that didn't mean she was going to let herself be pushed around. She was still a journalist and this was still her job. She cleared her throat.

'I'm glad you called actually, Nush,' she began, trying to sound businesslike. 'I was really hoping we could fix up a time for me to chat to someone from Data about how Cupid works. Do you think one of the team might have any time to speak to me this week?'

'Ahh, I was going to message you about this later!' Nush's voice was back to normal now; pumpkin spice-sweet. 'So we've been chatting and we think it's best if you ping your questions for them over to me in an email – I'll pass them on to someone from that side of the business and then they can pull something together for me to brief you with. Sound OK?'

Laura set her jaw; this time she wasn't going to let Nush fob her off. 'Why don't I just have a quick chat to them myself?' she suggested. 'Save you the bother of going between us. It won't take long.'

'No, this way's better,' Nush said firmly. 'They're sweet and *so* good at what they do, but not the greatest communicators, you know? Trust me. Anyway, I've got to run – love to Adam! Kiss kiss!'

She rang off. Laura took the phone away from her ear. A scraggy pigeon had landed on the wall and started pecking at the kebab container, its orange eyes flashing. She watched it for a bit as it attacked the chips, then opened her phone's browser. Because it hadn't officially launched yet, Cupid's website was still a skeleton – there was just its name on the front page and a drop-down with two options, *WHAT WE*

ARE and *WHO WE ARE*. She clicked on the second and started scrolling through the team pictures. Nush was near the top, wearing thick, matte lipstick and a septum ring. Underneath her was the man with the glasses she'd seen in the office, looking a little like Jesus, if Jesus went to Burning Man and kept CBD gummies in his desk drawer.

Dr Cass Bryant, Data Science Lead.

Laura tapped on it and a box of text unfolded.

Cass came to Cupid after supercharging the recommendation engines at several globally successful e-commerce sites in both the UK and the USA. He has a PhD from the University of Berkeley in California, co-authored What's Next For Big Data Analytics? *and was on* Wired's *most recent list of 100 Under-35s to Watch in Tech.*

Laura closed the window and typed Cupid's office address into Citymapper, her pulse starting to race. Twenty-five minutes on foot, it said. She checked the time. It was 9.33 now – and nobody, she remembered Nush saying, got in before ten o'clock. She gathered up Lil's dress and started walking.

***

The street was still deserted when she got there. The only place that looked open was Sink or Swim. The same waiter was there, wearing a lifejacket and mopping the floor.

'Ahoy!' he called out when he saw her. 'Drink?'

'Just a Coke, please. Um, can I sit over there?' She pointed to the row of portholes at the front of the room. The waiter nodded enthusiastically.

'Absolutely! Watch the floor – we had a flood last night.'

Laura sat on a stool in front of the middle porthole, got her phone out and saw that Sasha had tagged her in a photo. It was a Timehop one of the three of them from exactly one year earlier, about six months after Sasha had moved in: they were at the bar in the Malaysian restaurant that had just opened down the road from 8a, steaming bowls of laksa lined up in front of them. Walker was in the middle, grinning, with his arms around both of them. Sasha's head was resting on his shoulder in a way that Laura hadn't even noticed at the time but which now felt like a violin striking up in a horror movie. *Good times with two of my faves!* Sasha had written underneath, with the hashtag #whatadifferenceayearmakes. Laura liked it, unliked it, then liked it again. She really needed to just mute both of them, she thought, knowing full well that she wouldn't. Nush's words were reverberating around her head. *We're here to help you move into a more functional dating space.*

The street was starting to get busier now. A pair of men in Lycra were folding their bikes outside the Double Negative Studios and a woman with a precision bob dyed to look like a sunset was walking up the steps while checking two separate phones. Behind her another woman, who had bleached hair and was wearing a denim pinafore, was carrying a cardboard food-delivery box with VEGAN- ISED printed on its side. Cupid, Laura had read, let its employees set their own hours and take as much holiday as they wanted. She watched people swiping themselves into the building. Did they look happier than everyone she worked with? Or just as unhappy, but in a different way?

The waiter appeared with her Coke. He'd poured it into a cocktail glass and stuck an orange slice optimistically on the rim.

'I've just remembered, it's our first birthday party next week!' he said; Laura noticed a glacé cherry bobbing in her glass. 'You should come – we're hiring a paddling pool.'

'You don't think this is all a bit . . .' Something – someone – walking past outside caught her eye. It was him: the man she'd made eye contact with when Nush was showing her around and whose face she'd seen on her phone's screen earlier that morning. 'Um, never mind.'

She yanked a fiver out of her wallet, dropped it on the counter in front of her and sprinted for the door.

'Bon voyage!' the waiter called after her.

Cass was a couple of buildings away, walking towards Cupid's office. He was wearing head-to-toe black: black t-shirt tucked into black jeans tucked into black eight-eye boots, with a black rucksack slung over one shoulder.

'Hey!' Laura yelled. He kept walking. 'Hello! Excuse me! Cass!'

He stopped and turned around. He was holding a re-usable coffee cup with a thick band of cork around the middle.

'Oh, hey,' he said casually. He had a lazy West Coast accent and was watching her approach with dispassionate curiosity. She felt wrong-footed by all of it. She'd been so focused on tracking him down that she hadn't actually worked out what her opening line was going to be.

'I've been looking for you,' she said. He took a sip of his coffee.

'This must be what they call investigative journalism . . .' He had a geometric line drawing inked on the inside of his right arm, she couldn't help but notice. 'Well, you found me. How can I help?'

'I'd like to interview you,' Laura said. 'For my piece.' The breeze was toying with the hem of her dress and she noticed Cass's eyes straying to it just for a second like Adam's had the day before – she gave the fabric a swift whack like she was swatting a wasp. 'Look, it's really important that I understand how Cupid's matchmaking model works. And right now, I don't.'

'I mean, that's not really surprising.'

'What isn't?'

'That you don't understand it.' He smiled. 'No offence – it's pretty high-level stuff. No fun for anyone apart from the likes of me.'

He was shorter than Adam – 5′10″, maybe. Everything about him was infuriating, from his stupid boots to his stupid man-bun, which he'd tied up with an elastic band. Laura imagined grabbing fistfuls of his t-shirt and shaking him. The strength of the feeling was unnerving.

Cass drained his coffee. He was clearly trying not to laugh, which annoyed her even more.

'Look, I'm not supposed to talk to journalists – none of us are.' He shrugged. 'I'm really sorry. But if you send Nush some questions she'll pass them on to me and I'll give her some pointers. Is that OK?' He wedged the cup into a pocket on the side of his rucksack. 'Have a great day, Laura.'

Laura watched him silently as he walked up the steps, swiped his pass on the reader by the door and disappeared into the building.

'Wanker,' she muttered.

Chapter 8

vector (noun): *something that has both magnitude and direction*

'Hey, I realised today,' Adam said casually to Laura, who was chopping coriander. 'It's been exactly a month, hasn't it? Since our first date.' He opened his microwave and took a steaming pack of rice out of it.

In the weeks following that first night at his flat, the two of them had fallen into a routine: every Wednesday and Sunday they'd eat dinner at his and watch something on Netflix, then she'd stay over. The novelty value of sleeping in a non-inflatable bed still hadn't worn off. They had sex in the mornings because Adam wasn't keen on late nights; he'd nudge her awake when his radio alarm blared into life on the dot of seven. She liked watching him striding to the shower naked afterwards, thinking about how many people would kill to be waking up next to someone who looked like him. (Sometimes she wondered whether that was actually the best bit of the entire process.) It was easy to forget that there was a clock ticking away in the background, counting down the days until their allotted three months with Cupid were up. After that they wouldn't be obliged to stay together, but Adam seemed perfectly happy with how things were between them. And as Laura nudged the leaves neatly to the edge of the chopping board – she was a much tidier cook in his kitchen – she felt that she was too.

She couldn't lie – she still had moments when she couldn't quite see why they'd been matched. Adam was an early riser even at the weekends; she liked to sleep in until lunchtime. He found routine and order reassuring, whereas she silently chafed against them. But there were plenty of overlaps too. Well, maybe not plenty, but certainly enough to be getting on with. They both, for instance, loved pizza (although Adam only let himself have it once a week as a treat) and saying hello to other people's dogs in the street. And the weekend before they'd been on a lovely cycle ride together all the way around Hyde Park. He had his own bike, a sleek racing model that he spent hours maintaining. She'd had to hire a clunky Santander one, but he'd been really sweet about setting it up for her and had even presented her with a bright pink cycling helmet as they were leaving his flat. She hadn't asked whose it was.

'So it has,' she said, nodding and scooping up a handful of coriander. 'Good old Cupid, eh?'

'Good old Cupid.' He carefully divided the rice between two bowls, then took the lid off the pan on the hob and served out the curry that had been heating through. He always did five days' worth of cooking on Sunday evenings – when he'd first told her that, she'd found the idea of planning exactly what you were going to eat for the entire week a bit depressing, but then she'd remembered she didn't even have her own fridge and reconsidered.

'Well, happy one-month anniversary, I guess!' she said, showering the bowls with green and watching it settle. 'Go us!'

'It's mensaversary, actually,' Adam said, leaning in to kiss her cheek as he picked up the bowls to carry them to the table. 'The anni bit in anniversary means "year". So you can't have one for just months.'

She felt a flash of irritation at the correction. Then her eyes alighted on his hands, which were one of her favourite things about him, and it evaporated. She got her phone out of her pocket and saw that Walker had WhatsApped her out of the blue.

> Walker:
> *Evening stranger . . .*
> *Saw on Insta you were in Hyde Park the other day*
> *Me and Sash were playing Ultimate Frisbee there!*
> *Wish you'd said*
> *We could have teamed up!*

It was funny, she thought as she scanned the message preview – a couple of months ago, seeing the words 'Sash' and 'Ultimate Frisbee' in the same sentence would have made her see red. But now that she had Adam, it barely annoyed her at all. She was clearly growing as a person.

'One second,' she said to him, swiping the notification back up and opening the camera. 'Keep your hands like that?'

He stayed obligingly still while she took the photo, a smile tugging at the corners of his mouth. 'Are you posting that? Does that mean we're Instagram official now?'

'Maybe.' She smiled back at him as she typed a cryptic – but hopefully not *too* cryptic – caption. *The best dinners are the ones someone makes for you.* 'You don't mind, do you?'

'Of course not.' He watched as she tapped *Share* and it went up. 'So are we . . .'

'Are we what?' She looked up at him playfully, making her eyebrows dance. He turned away to put the bowls down on their respective place mats – he laid the table here every night, she'd discovered, even when it was just him. She had her own napkin ring now: a circlet of brushed chrome, like a spare car part.

'Well, if we're Instagram official, are we officially official too?' He turned back to her and put his hands on her waist, like they were about to dance. 'Boyfriend and girlfriend, I mean.'

Laura imagined herself at the top of a mountain, brushing the snow off her boots, surveying the distance she'd climbed to the summit. Wasn't this everything she'd always wanted?

'Yes, I think so,' she said, turning her face up to his and closing her eyes. They kissed and she felt like she was enveloped in a warm bubble. When she looked back at her phone two new notifications had popped up. @nushofcourse had liked the post and commented on it – a single emoji, staring out at them from the screen.

👀

Laura shook her head, smiling. 'God, she's everywhere.' She clicked through to Nush's profile and tilted the screen to show Adam the latest picture of her and Ched. They were in a swimming pool this time – he was holding her out of the water above his head, like the *Dirty Dancing* lake scene. She snorted. Adam gave her a quizzical look.

'Oh, come on,' she said, nudging him to try to get him to join in. 'Look at them. He's called *Ched*.'

'Well, as long as they're happy,' Adam said evenly, not taking the bait. 'Good for them, eh?'

He sat down, tucked his napkin into his jumper – it was a pale blue merino wool one; he clearly didn't want to run the risk of getting anything on it – and picked up his fork.

'Speaking of Nush,' Laura said, shaking hers out, 'does she keep phoning you too? I get a call once a week "checking in" ...'

'Mmhm,' Adam nodded, chewing; he wasn't the sort of person who spoke with his mouth full.

'What do you and her talk about?'

He swallowed. 'Just about how everything's going, really. Nothing much.'

'I'm nothing much, am I? Cheers, pal.' She pulled a mocking face. He looked slightly pained.

'Come on, I didn't mean it like that, Laura.'

'I'm kidding.' Sometimes she'd make a joke and he wouldn't laugh until she'd flagged up that it was a joke. 'She finally emailed some answers back to those questions I sent her about how Cupid's matchmaking model actually works,' she said, changing tack. 'Took her long enough.'

Adam looked up at her. 'Oh, yes? Did you get what you needed?'

She shrugged. 'Not really – it was basically just the stuff from their press release. There wasn't any new detail.' She forked up some rice. 'I find it odd that she's so cagey about it, don't you? Surely they want all the *Bugle*'s readers to know exactly how clever they are?'

'Well, maybe they're just worried about competitors stealing their ideas.' Adam gave her bowl a concerned glance. 'Hey, your dinner's getting cold.'

***

'You should wear heels more often – they're very slimming,' Jamie said that Saturday, putting her trowel down and inspecting Laura's outfit. 'Where are you going this afternoon?'

They were outside on the decking; Jamie had spent the afternoon digging up the tubs, ready to re-plant them with flowers approved by *House & Garden*. There was a copy next to her, open at a feature on tobacco plants, and a plastic tray of identical trumpet-shaped ones on the bench.

'It's Asha from work's hen.' Laura crouched down on the grass, hugging her knees. It reminded her of being seven and allowed to sit on the end of Jamie's bed (as long as she didn't speak or make any noise) while she revised for her GCSEs. Since the barbecue Laura had been gentler with her elder sister, trying to give her the benefit of the doubt – and Jamie, to her surprise, had reciprocated. How long the truce would last, Laura wasn't sure. But for now, it was a relief to feel like they really were on the same team.

'Oh, yes?'

'We're doing archery.'

'Give me strength. When I had mine we didn't have any of these ridiculous activities.'

'Not even cave painting?'

Jamie pulled a face. 'How's Adam?' she asked. 'You've been seeing each other for ... what? Four weeks now? You know you can bring him here whenever you like, don't you?'

Laura stuck her hand in the bag of topsoil and squeezed its contents, like one of the branded stress-balls they were always being given at the *Bugle*. She felt reluctant to take that step, and she wasn't quite sure why.

'I want to ... take things slowly,' she said. 'Thanks, though.'

Jamie nodded. 'Sensible. You need to get to know each other properly.' She yanked a plant out of the tray. 'It took me ages to warm up to Whit – I thought he was a total idiot when I first met him.'

On cue, Whit strode out into the garden with the phone to his ear.

'Jim!' he was bellowing into it. 'Everyone's here – hold on, I'm putting you on speaker.' He pressed a button and held it out. Laura looked at Jamie, whose jaw was clenched. She imagined them side by side with their backs against the door of an overflowing cupboard, trying to keep it shut.

'HELLO JAMIE,' their dad's voice blasted out of the handset. 'HELLO LAURA.'

'You don't need to shout, Dad,' Jamie said. 'We're not on an oil rig, we can hear you.'

'How're you doing, Jim?' Whit asked. 'Everything OK down there?'

'Oh, you know. Can't complain.' There was clearly something he wanted to say, but he wasn't saying it. Thank god for Whit, Laura thought, watching him nodding at the handset. He could keep a conversation going with a rock.

'How's Harrison, Dad?' she asked, raising her voice so he could hear her.

'Well, it's actually him I'm calling about.' There was a worryingly long pause. 'I've got a lot of work trips coming up, see, and I can't take him with me. But I can't leave him at home, now that ...' He coughed. 'Now. So I was thinking ...'

'We'll take him!' Whit cut in. 'It'll be fun!' Jamie froze, the plant still dangling from her hand.

'Whit, *no.*' She grabbed the phone. 'Dad, it's me. I'm sorry, but this isn't going to work. We're both out of the house from seven until extremely late and Laura's never in during the week. Who do you think's going to walk him?'

'I'll take him out first thing and we'll get a walker to come at lunchtime or something,' Whit said, easing the phone out of her hand. 'Come on, sweetheart – he's an old boy, he's no trouble.'

'He is a *lot* of trouble. Remember the time he used a chair to get into the fridge?'

Whit chuckled. 'That was funny,' he said. 'He's really smart.'

'Compared to some humans, yes.' She snatched the phone back. 'Dad, why can't Mum have him for a bit?'

There was an excruciating silence. Laura could picture her dad in the armchair he'd worn shiny over the years, listening to the ticking of the carriage clock above the fire, suddenly much too loud. She couldn't picture her mum. Although the blankness where she should have been was unsettling, the alternative was far worse. She was staying with the nameless person from her flying days somewhere in south London, she'd said – not far from Gatwick. She and Laura still hadn't spoken (Laura had actually blocked her calls) but they'd messaged a bit. *please come 2 visit love*, the last one had read, *we're only twenty mins from Victoria.* That *we* had bothered her so much that she'd ended up deleting the entire thread. Would you use it to refer to yourself and someone else if the two of you were just friends? Her mum was an eager reader of romantic novels – surely she knew what *we* implied?

'Jim, it's fine,' Whit said. 'We'll take care of it. You go easy now, OK?' He hung up and turned to Jamie. 'What?'

Jamie rammed the plant into the tub. 'He's *embarrassing*,' she said, thumping the soil down over its roots. 'He's an *embarrassing dog*.'

***

Harrison had come into their lives when Laura was twenty-one and Jamie had just turned thirty, during the Sunday lunch their mum had organised for Jamie's birthday. It was nearly two o'clock: their dad, who'd spent the morning on the company's stand at an agricultural show, was supposed to have been back by one, but nobody had heard from him. There was a leg of lamb going dry in the oven and gravy growing a skin in the china jug that only came out on special occasions.

'Look, let's just start,' their mum said darkly, putting a dish of roast potatoes on the table and checking her watch again. 'His can go in the microwave when he turns up. *If* he turns up.'

Walker, who'd been Laura's boyfriend for twelve and a half weeks at that point, was next to her, sitting up very straight in a t-shirt and jeans he'd ironed especially. She'd stayed with him at his mum's the night before – he'd brought her toast in bed like he always did and kissed her eyelids to wake her up – and she'd asked him to come to the lunch for moral support. She'd thought someone else being there might make her parents behave themselves. But that clearly wasn't how it was going to go, and she was mortified that he was going to witness it. One of the bands he was in was going on tour in three weeks' time, he'd been telling Jamie.

'What did you say they were called again?' Jamie asked him. They'd never met before and Walker was wilting.

'The Velveeta Incident,' he said, looking at his plate.

'They're really good,' Laura added loyally, hoping he couldn't tell she was bitterly regretting inviting him along and exposing him to her family.

Jamie wrinkled her nose and took a gold-capped lipgloss out of her bag. It was a huge, squashy, caramel-coloured leather one that she'd had to join a year-long waiting list to buy – she kept touching it, as though she expected it to disappear.

A thump on the window made them all jump. It was Laura's dad, waving to them from the garden. He was grinning and looked out of breath.

'Sorry I'm late!' he announced when Laura lifted the catch. He addressed Jamie and Walker over her shoulder. 'Happy birthday, love. Afternoon, Mr Tambourine Man.' He was bubbling over with something; a warning shot went off in the pit of Laura's stomach. 'I've got a surprise in the car.'

'For me?' Suddenly Jamie was fourteen again, her hair crimped, gleefully unwrapping a padded and padlocked diary on Christmas Day.

'For everyone!' He vanished. When he came through the front door a few minutes later he was carrying his coat, a bunch of petrol-station flowers and a black and white collie puppy.

Laura's mum stared at the dog in silent horror.

'Jim, this is a joke, isn't it?' she said finally. 'Please tell me this is a joke.'

'Frank at Harrison Tractors was selling him.' Laura's dad ruffled the dog's enormous ears; he had a placid but watchful expression. 'Eighteen weeks old – he's from a long line of champion herders. His granddad won the national trials twice.' He handed Jamie the flowers, like an afterthought.

'And what's he going to herd, Jim?' Their mum's voice was rising. 'When was the last time you saw a sheep around here?'

'How do you get the potatoes like that, Mrs Morrison?' Walker asked diplomatically, skewering one with his fork. 'They're so crispy!' His parents had split up when he was eight, but they were good friends now, he said: they watered each other's plants and went to the cinema together once a month. When he talked about them (which wasn't very often) he looked happy and untroubled. It gave Laura the feeling that, rather than both of them being from Planet Suitless, she was an alien – and he wasn't.

'Ah, they're very adaptable, collies. He'll be fine with a couple of walks a day.' Laura's dad lowered the puppy onto the floor; he stayed where he'd been put, looking up at his new flock with his head cocked. 'And you work at home, so he'll have company, won't he?'

Under the table, Walker squeezed Laura's hand.

'Yes! I *work* at home. I have a *job*, Jim – I can't just drop everything to clean up after a dog.' Their mum's voice was breaking. 'I can't believe you've done this. How long do they live for? Ten years? Fifteen?'

She started to cry. Jamie's jaw was clenched and her nails were digging into the plastic wrap around the flowers. In a minute, Laura thought, her chair would screech on the floor as she scraped it back, before storming out and getting on a train to London.

Their dad had been watching their mum with his arms folded.

'Well, that's nice, isn't it?' he said. He'd wanted to say something different, Laura could tell, maybe even apologise, but it had curdled and come out all wrong. 'He's only been here five minutes and you're already wishing him dead.'

The puppy had started batting at the tassels on Jamie's bag. Laura quickly scooped him up and put him on her lap. He yawned, paddling his paws against her jeans, and closed his eyes. She felt for the steadying thump of his heart beneath his fur. Walker squeezed her hand again. She didn't squeeze back. Her blood ran cold as she imagined the two of them fighting exactly like this – determined to see the worst in each other, deliberately setting out to wound. Even though they'd never actually had an argument, it felt horribly inevitable. Her parents must have been like them once, she thought – and look at them now.

They left before dessert; Laura had invented someone's birthday drinks in the pub. But as soon as she and Walker were outside by his car, she started to feel like she was suffocating. It wasn't just her family she was suddenly desperate to get away from – it was him too.

'I'm going to go for a walk,' she said. Her chest was tight and her voice didn't sound like hers. Walker put his arm around her.

'Good idea – I'll come with you,' he said. She shrugged him off.

'Please.' She took a step away from him and crossed her arms. 'I really just … want to be alone right now. OK?'

She watched him driving away, his shoulders hunched. It was horrible to see him looking so bewildered, but she felt like somehow she was avoiding something much, much worse.

Over the next few weeks the feeling that their relationship was inevitably going to end in disaster grew stronger. She started squirming out of his arms when he was asleep; the more he pulled her close, the more she found herself pushing him away. She could see he was hurt and confused but she couldn't stop.

She was meant to go and stay with him in Bristol when his band went on tour, but she kept putting off booking her train ticket until it was too expensive for her to go. They argued about it for a week, then she called him from the pub's car park and told him she thought it was going to be too difficult for them to keep seeing each other. She crouched down on the gravel and cried, hugging her knees, as soon as she put the phone down. But it was a relief, too. The whole time they'd been together she'd felt as though she'd been carrying around something fragile that she was terrified of breaking. Now that it had broken – now that *she'd* broken it – she didn't have to worry about that happening anymore.

***

'I'd like you to take a moment to reflect on the fact that you're about to be initiated into a practice dating back to the very dawn of human history,' said Thor, who was leading the archery workshop. He adjusted the bronze torc on his left arm, pushing it higher on his massive bicep. 'Right! Any questions?'

Asha, who was wearing a glittery sash with *FUTURE MRS GEORGIADIS* printed on it, raised her hand.

'Have you got a charger?' She held up her phone. 'I'm on one per cent.'

Thor sighed. 'Behind the bar,' he said wearily. 'You can unplug mine.'

It was four o'clock in the afternoon and they were facing a target in the basement of a club on Shaftesbury Avenue. Thor – whose real name was Gareth – was a personal trainer at Fitness First on Tottenham Court Road, who topped up his salary by teaching groups of women how to use historic longbows. He was wearing a brown leather kilt, a matching vest and a lot of aftershave.

'So, let me get this straight,' Laura said to Zoe, Asha's best friend from school, who'd gone full 'Like A Virgin'-era Madonna in long white lace gloves and a looped string of pearls (everyone else had ignored the dress code). 'We're finishing here at six, then going to Shoreditch for street food, then ...' she peered at the paper itinerary Zoe had instructed them all to print out in advance '... coming back here?'

'That's right!' Zoe chirped. 'It's an electro-swing night. We're on the guest list!'

'Look, I really don't want to tread on anybody's toes here ...' Laura tried to keep the exasperation out of her voice '... but wouldn't it make more sense for us to have dinner somewhere a bit ... closer?'

'But Asha's wanted to go to Street Eats for ages,' Zoe said, sounding peeved. 'There's a Las Vegas theme this weekend. It'll be really fun!'

'Oh, well, that's OK then!' Lil said sarcastically. 'If there's a Las Vegas theme it makes perfect sense for us to schlep all the way over to the other side of London for some ten-pound tacos!'

Asha was getting the barman to mix her a margarita. He was holding the tequila bottle over the shaker and she was urging him on like someone watching a horse race. Thor looked worried.

'While we're waiting for the bride-to-be, which one of you would like to go first?' He turned to Laura. 'Fair maiden?' He held out one of his hubcap-sized hands and she let him heave her to her feet.

'I'll come with you,' Lil said. 'If I stay over there, I won't be responsible for my actions.'

Thor led them over to the target. His kit bag was in front of it. 'Choose your weapon,' he said solemnly. There was only one bow. Laura took it out. It was heavier than it looked.

'OK, so you've got your handle here,' Thor said, posing her with it like an action figure. 'Keep your arm out really straight – that's it. Imagine the wood is part of you. These bits are called the limbs and this is where the arrow goes.' He loaded it up, then turned Laura so she was facing the target. 'So what I need you to do now is put a foot on either side of this line *here*, then you just have to put two fingers *here* and pull your arm back ...'

'How are things with Adam?' Lil asked.

'Really great!' Laura let go of the arrow. It shot into the air at an angle, arcing up towards the mirrorball hanging from the ceiling, before clattering to the floor a metre away from the target.

'Failure is a delay, not a defeat,' Thor said, handing her another arrow. Lil gave her a searching look.

'And how are *things*?'

Laura slotted the arrow into the bow and pulled her arm back. 'Fine!'

'Don't bowl me over with your enthusiasm ...'

'No, they're good! Honestly! It's just ...' Her eyes drifted to the table in the corner, which had a plate of sausage rolls on it. She lowered the bow and turned back to Lil. 'You know when they put those out earlier, and everyone stood around going *oh, no, after you*, and nobody was actually having anything?'

Lil frowned. 'Are you the sausage rolls in this scenario? Or is Adam?'

Laura forced herself to laugh and turned away; she was suddenly finding it hard to look at Lil. 'Oh, I don't know – I guess it's always a bit awkward at first with a new person, isn't it?' She handed Lil the bow and they swapped places. 'I'm probably just being stupid.'

Lil loaded an arrow, waving away Thor's offers of help.

'If you like him and he likes you, it'll sort itself out.' She pulled the bow taut and let go with a twang. Laura watched as the arrow rocketed towards the centre of the target. Lil punched the air in triumph.

'Anyway, there's no such thing as perfect,' she said, handing the bow back to Laura with a wink.

***

Street Eats had taken over the bottom of a disused multi-storey car park just off Curtain Road. Someone had tipped dozens of bags of sand over the pavement outside it – a nod to the desert around Las Vegas. It had probably looked quite good at the start of the night, but now it was peppered with bent cigarette butts and the tarmac underneath was starting to show through in places. As a woman dressed up like the Statue of Liberty scanned the QR codes on their tickets Laura noticed a bulldog in an Aran jumper eyeing up a virgin patch of sand. Its owner was on the phone, looking the other way.

Inside there were trucks selling mac-and-cheese pots and alcoholic milkshakes and people in sequinned costumes wandering around trying to get everyone in the mood to spend, but the whole place basically looked the same as it did in its ordinary life: the neon signs lit up the greasy puddles of rainwater that had collected in the dips in the floor and the roulette tables wobbled on the concrete.

'If I'd wanted to eat my dinner standing up in a horrifically noisy room I'd have stayed at home with my daughter,' Lil said, cupping her hand around Laura's ear to make herself heard over the blaring music. 'Can we just go once Thor's back with our chips? Ash has had about six of those gin slushie things already, she isn't going to notice.'

Everyone else was over by the slot machines – the two of them had peeled off with Thor after Asha had dragged him along from the workshop. Laura was looking at her phone, trying to put words to the unsettled feeling she'd had ever since Adam had messaged her a few minutes earlier. He'd sent her a photo of him with his sister, her husband and their chubby-cheeked baby son. They were all in matching Scotland rugby shirts and he was holding the little boy on his lap. *Future winger!* he'd written.

'What do you think a "Roulette Burger" is?' she asked, quickly turning back to the list of food traders they'd been given by the Statue of Liberty when she let them in. Lil snorted.

'One in six of them isn't cooked? Fuck knows. Oh, thank god, here's the chips.'

Thor had emerged from the crowd with a Styrofoam box, holding a bundle of plastic cutlery aloft like he'd just yanked it out of a stone.

'So you all know each other from working at a newspaper?' he said to Lil as he munched a chip. 'That's so cool! I write too actually. Poems mostly – I'm really into exploring ancient ideas of masculinity. Maybe you could take a look at them?'

'Gosh, I'd love to, but I have to be really careful about the amount of reading I do,' Lil said, grabbing a fistful of greasy potato chunks. 'I have, er, carpal tunnel.' She stared meaningfully at Laura. 'We should really try to find the bride-to-be, shouldn't we, Morrison? Make sure she's not spent all the honeymoon money?'

'You guys go ahead,' Laura said; she felt bad about leaving Lil with Thor and his terrible poems, but suddenly really wanted to be alone. 'I'll be there in a second. I've just got to … do a thing quickly.'

She watched them being swallowed up by the crowd. Maybe everyone arranging their burgers into pyramids and posing by the Vegas sign was just grimly collecting experiences because they thought they should, rather than actually enjoying them. Or maybe they weren't and she was the oddity. She'd hoped that having a proper boyfriend would make her feel less isolated, more connected to the world around her – but right now, she just felt like she was on the wrong side of a thick pane of glass.

She got out her phone and opened her chat with Adam. He'd last been online three minutes ago, she noticed. She decided to message him.

Laura:
Can I ask you something?

Adam:
Hey!
Sure
Ask away

Laura:
Do you ever feel like the odd one out?

Adam:
What do you mean?

Laura:
You know
Like you're on the outside looking in
Wondering how the hell everyone's doing it all

Adam:
I think maybe you've had a few too many cocktails

She scrolled up and tapped on the photo of him again. There he was: her handsome boyfriend, who always bought the *Big Issue* and never forgot to turn off lights when he left rooms, surrounded by his happy, uncomplicated family. She experimentally closed one eye and then the other, shuttling between them like the optician had asked her to the last time she'd gone in for a test, trying to get the answer right. *Which is better – one or two? One? Or two? Or neither?*

Laura:
Hah
Yeah maybe
Hope you're having fun
Say hi to your nephew from me

She dropped her phone back into her bag and scanned the room. She'd head towards the gaming tables, she decided, where the crowd was a bit thinner and she'd be able to hear herself think. Everyone was dressed up and drinking from plastic flutes, waiting for the evening's promises to come good. She watched the wheels spinning for a while until she clocked that a security guard was eyeballing her – Whit, who was a strikingly unsuccessful member of a poker league, had stories about people who teamed up to scam casinos by signalling to each other. She backed away from the table without looking where she was going and smacked straight into someone walking towards the bar.

'Oh my god, I'm so ...' she began, spinning around. Then all the pieces of the person in front of her – tied-back hair, trendy jeans, zip-up hoodie – clicked into place and she realised exactly who she was looking at. It was Cass, holding a box of food in one hand and a neon pink can of beer in the other.

'Laura?' He took a step back, looking startled. 'What are you doing here?'

'Well, I'm on a hen,' she said, enjoying having the upper hand this time. 'What's your excuse?'

He wasn't wearing his glasses tonight – his eyes, she noticed, were a very pale, clear blue. He actually wasn't bad-looking, she caught herself thinking: sort of intense, with good stubble and cheekbones. Still annoying, obvi-ously. But in the abstract, not unattractive.

'Oh, it's someone from work's birthday,' he said, recover-ing his composure. 'Everyone else is in the queue for the ribs, but I'm vegan, so ...' He gestured at the box he was holding. 'I get these. Textured soy protein bites in uniden-tifiable spicy sauce. Yum.'

Laura grinned in spite of herself. 'You're not missing out, to be honest,' she said, warming to him slightly. 'I think the buffalo wings I just had came from a pigeon.'

He laughed. 'Hey, look, Laura,' he began. 'Since you're here … I've been feeling really bad about the other day. They're being so tight about everything ahead of the launch.' He gave her an apologetic smile. 'I'm sorry that I wasn't more helpful when we ran into each other. And that we had to go through Nush. I totally get why you'd want to actually speak to someone in person about the technical stuff before you write your article – you're just doing your job.'

Was it an American thing, all this unbroken eye contact? She wanted to look away, but she also didn't.

'You're forgiven,' she said, a little stiffly. 'Thank you.'

'OK, great.' He smiled at her again and she let herself smile back, feeling slightly more relaxed with him now. He opened his can of beer with a hiss.

'So, anyway – I was thinking,' he said, slowly twisting the ring-pull. 'Well, if you wanted to talk about how it all works over a coffee … I'm working late a lot at the moment, but I could find some time next week – maybe Wednesday. Why don't I give you my number? We don't have to say anything to Nush right now. Or, you know, ever.'

Her chat with Adam was still on her screen; Laura quickly clicked it away as she gave Cass her phone, then checked herself. Why had she just done that? He of all people knew exactly who Adam was. She watched his fingers flying across the glass.

'I've never met a Cass before,' she said, feeling like she ought to fill the silence. 'Is it short for something?'

'Cassidy. Like Butch.' He shook his head ruefully. 'It's like my parents wanted me to have a terrible time in high school.'

Laura took her phone back. It was hard to imagine him being uncool. 'I can see how that might have been quite … challenging.'

'Oh, it gets worse,' Cass said with relish. 'I was the founding member of the chess club. And there were no other members.' They both laughed. 'I'm guessing that's your friends I just saw over on the slots,' he said, taking a swig of his beer. 'How's that working out for them?'

Laura looked over to where he was gesturing; Asha was at the centre of a huddle, pounding one of the machines with her fist.

'From the looks of things, not brilliantly. But you're bound to lose on them, aren't you?'

'Not necessarily. I mean, they always win in the end. But you can definitely still turn the way they're built to your advantage.'

Laura rolled her eyes. 'Tell me your secrets, Dr Bryant,' she said. 'Please.'

He grinned. 'OK, so they're all made in one of two ways: they either give you lots of small wins but almost never pay out in a big way, or very few small ones and the occasional massive one – they call it low volatility versus high volatility.'

'Which is the better bet?'

He shrugged. 'It depends. But put it this way: if my friends had spent a long time playing a particular machine and it hadn't paid out anything yet, I'd be thinking that was the one to try my luck with.'

'I'll bear that in mind,' Laura said. They looked at each other; the silence stretched on for a beat too long and she felt something zip through the air between them. She put her phone away to give her hands something to do.

'Anyway, I'll message you,' she said quickly. 'About coffee.'

'I'll look forward to it.' He smiled.

As she walked away she found herself idly wondering if he was watching her. She wanted to turn around, but stopped herself.

When she got to the slots Asha, who had a slushie in one hand and a fiver in the other, was trying to teach Thor the swing routine she and her fiancé had been learning for their first dance. Every time she moved, her drink sloshed down his back.

'That was the world's longest toilet break,' Lil said when Laura squeezed in next to her. 'Thanks for leaving me in the trench to get shelled.'

'Sorry, I …' It would be too complicated to explain everything, she decided. 'Just bumped into someone. What's my share of our millions?'

Lil held up her empty chip box. 'Nobody's won anything yet, unless you count the actual five pence I just found in here that had been through the fryer.'

There was nobody on the machine. Laura got her wallet out – there was a single pound coin in there between two cards, glinting in the light. 'Can I have a go?' she asked.

Lil shrugged. 'Sure, but I wouldn't get your hopes up. I reckon we've got about as much chance of hitting the jackpot as Thor has of getting out of this place alive.'

Laura got onto the stool in front of the machine and woke it up. It felt surprisingly solid, like something that really might drop a hundred pounds into your lap. She pushed her coin into the slot, listening as it ricocheted around the innards, then tapped the screen to start a new game. *TANGERINE DREAM*, the machine announced, and rows of cartoony fruits appeared. She'd thought there would be a big lever on the side that you pulled dramatically, but there wasn't – just an ordinary, scuffed-looking plastic button. She hesitated for a couple of seconds, like she used to when she was making a wish before blowing out the candles on a birthday cake. Then she pressed it.

The rows whirred into life. For a few seconds, all she could see was a rainbow blur. Then, gradually, it started to resolve itself into shapes as they slowed down.

Two lemons and an apple. A tangerine, a cherry and a pear. A tangerine, a lemon and another tangerine. Three tangerines.

JACKPOT! flashed across the screen. *JACKPOT! JACK-POT! JACKPOT!*

Chapter 9

clipping (noun): a way of handling outliers

'Can I ask you something?' Laura whispered to Adam.

It was the Monday night – their normal Sunday date hadn't happened because she'd been too hungover from Asha's hen – and they were lying in his bed with the lights out. He slept on his front in his boxers and a white t-shirt; he took a clean one out of the drawer every day, she'd noticed. She was on her side facing him in her pants, running a finger lightly up and down his spine. She liked touching him like this in the darkness. It stripped everything else away.

He didn't say anything. She shuffled a little closer to him.

'Would you draw me?'

He made a noise that was somewhere between a laugh and a groan. 'Laura, it's half-past eleven,' he mumbled sleepily. 'I've got the board meeting tomorrow, I need to get some rest ...'

'Now *now*, obviously.' She stretched over to kiss the nape of his neck. 'But would you?'

'Would I what?'

'Draw me.' She wriggled out of her pants and whooshed them around her head, then chucked them across the room. 'Like one of your French girls?'

Adam stuck an arm out. 'I'll something-else you in a second if you're not careful,' he said in a jokily exasperated voice, draping it across her and pulling her into him. She pressed herself against him, but they were obviously in very different moods – the kiss he planted on her forehead felt like a full stop.

'To be continued tomorrow morning,' he said firmly, detaching her. 'And, yes, I will draw you if you'd like me to. Goodnight, Laura.'

He arranged himself on his front again, hugging the pillow. She lay on her back listening to his breathing settle, watching headlights from outside dance tantalisingly across the ceiling.

***

'OK, wait, I saved the best for last,' Whit said, ducking behind the sofa. It was Wednesday, a few days later. Laura was eating toast for breakfast on the living-room carpet, surrounded by the things he'd bought for Harrison: two paw-printed bath towels, a knotted rope, a plastic bagel that squeaked when you squeezed it and a kilo of organic dog biscuits shaped like bones.

'Ready?' There was the high-pitched whirr of a motor and a toy sheep on wheels skidded out from behind the curtains. Whit popped up again, holding a remote control.

'Isn't it great?' He was practically hopping from foot to foot with excitement – he'd even arranged to work from home for the day to settle Harrison in, he'd told Laura. 'I got it from the US, express shipping. He can chase it!'

Jamie, who was gaffer-taping the cord from the lamp to the skirting board on the other side of the room to chew-proof it, rolled her eyes. Whit looked like a balloon that had just been popped.

'It's just a bit of fun, sweetheart,' he said. He parallel-parked the sheep carefully next to the coffee table. 'I want him to like it here.'

'And I want a house that isn't full of plastic crap.'

'Yeah, well, it's my house too,' Whit said quietly. He sent the sheep into the hallway and followed it out, his shoulders hunched. Jamie huffed and tore off another strip of tape with her teeth. The room had suddenly become several degrees colder; Laura crammed her crusts into her mouth, feeling like a teenager again, and reached for her phone. As she unlocked the screen she noticed an Instagram notification. She tapped it and saw she had a new follower – someone called @SeaShell. Whoever it was had no profile photo and had only posted once, the day before: a photo of a pair of feet in familiar purple trainers, geotagged to Farthing Downs, near Croydon.

just thinking xxx, the caption read.

As she zoomed in on the shoes her heart flip-flopped. The last time she'd seen them they'd been on her parents' doormat. Shell was short for Shelley. It was from her mum. The toast stuck in her throat.

'They're here!' Whit hollered from the front door. Laura flicked the screen off and scrambled to her feet, gulping painfully to force her breakfast down. Jamie's knees cracked as she stood up.

Their dad's scuffed and dented old Land Rover was pulling into a space on the other side of the street. The three of them watched tensely from the step as he switched the engine off, got out, went round to the other side of the car and opened the passenger door like a chauffeur.

Harrison hopped out of the footwell into the road. Laura's heart swelled as she took in his shaggy outline and the way one of his front legs jarred as he landed. He was nine now, and although his dark eyes were as bright as ever there was no denying the fact he was getting on. Harrison shook himself, making his tags jangle, then sat down on the tarmac, assessing his surroundings.

'I just want it on record,' Jamie said, 'that I think this is a terrible idea.'

In collie terms, Harrison was a failure. He didn't seem to have any interest in livestock, and his agility career had come to an end after he lay down in the plastic tunnel during the Berkshire Canine Club's summer show and went to sleep. The only sheepdog-like thing he did seem to enjoy was herding his humans: on the rare occasions when all the Morrisons took him out for a walk he'd circle them constantly, butting their knees with his nose when they didn't take the hint, forcing them all together. He generally reserved his energies for occasional but spectacular acts of destruction, like unwrapping all of the Christmas presents one year, or eating £75 in cash.

Now, he looked both ways ('Told you he was smart,' Whit said, slipping an arm around Jamie), then crossed the road, jumped up onto the pavement and nudged the gate open. Laura ran down the path to meet him and he picked up his pace, panting happily. She crouched to hug him, squashing her face into the downy fur above his collar. He smelled strange – like a fruit salad. She looked up; her dad was fidgeting with his car keys. There was a full bin bag in his other hand.

'I had to give him a bath with your mum's shampoo,' he said, not making eye contact. 'I don't know where she put his stuff. I'm going to get her to write it down for me when she gets back.'

'Good idea.' The two of them still hadn't talked about any of it – he wasn't a chatty sort at the best of times, which had made it easy to avoid the subject. Laura superstitiously touched her phone in her pocket. It felt like a grenade: she'd clicked out of Instagram but the photo would still be there when she went back into it.

Harrison got up, ambled the rest of the way up the path and plonked himself down in front of Whit.

'Hey, buddy!' Whit scruffed his fur up and tickled him vigorously behind the ears; Harrison stared up at him adoringly, thumping his bushy, white-tipped tail on the path with pleasure. Satisfied, he moved on to Jamie, who'd been watching everything with her arms folded.

'Yes, hello,' she said, giving him a cursory pat. He stayed where he was, his head cocked. 'What do you want?' He rolled over onto his back and stuck his legs in the air, whirring them around.

'OK, fine,' Jamie said, getting onto her knees. 'I'll rub your tummy. Happy now?'

Harrison made a noise like a car backfiring, stood up and wandered into the house, making straight for the living room. There was a loud squeak as he found the bagel.

'Here's his bed.' Laura's dad held out the bin bag. 'His bowls are in there too. Oh, and he has his, er, supplements twice a day with his food.'

'Oh, for god's sake.' Jamie took the bag reluctantly. 'Does he also have a meditation app?'

'They're in a little plastic bag, you can't miss them. Just make sure he takes them, OK?' Their dad checked his watch; he seemed preoccupied. 'Better get going, the A1's going to be murder. Thanks again, girls.' He patted them both distractedly on their respective shoulders.

Whit chased after Harrison, leaving Jamie and Laura alone on the step. They watched their dad getting back in the car and driving away in silence. Laura kept her hand on her phone, sealing its contents in her palm.

'That was the first time,' Jamie said as the Land Rover turned the corner.

'What?'

'The first time he's thanked us for doing this.' She shook her head; she'd put her foundation on but hadn't had time to do the rest of her make-up; without it she looked much softer, younger. More easily hurt. 'So he shouldn't have said "again".'

'You're such a lawyer. Keeping tabs on everything.' Jamie was an expert cataloguer of grudges, forever raking them into piles for easy access. She remembered everything. It wasn't always bad: even when they'd barely been speaking from one month to the next she'd never forgotten her sister's birthday (the card inevitably arrived two days early) and she'd taken the loofah out of the bathroom before Laura moved in because she knew she had an irrational phobia of them.

'WHO'S A GOOD BOY?' Whit's voice foghorned from inside. 'YOU'RE A GOOD BOY! YES, YOU ARE!'

'Somebody has to in this house,' Jamie said sardonically.

Back indoors, Laura decided to make herself another coffee, even though she'd woken up feeling inexplicably twitchy. As she stuffed a pod into Jamie and Whit's machine and topped up the milk-frother she caught herself picking anxiously at a loose thread of skin at the edge of her thumb-nail with her index finger.

She and Cass had arranged to meet at six in Kings Cross to talk about how Cupid worked; ever since they'd fixed the time she'd felt on edge. She was only talking to some-one for a feature, she reminded herself as the coffee machine whirred into life. It really wasn't a big deal. She'd done it dozens of times before. So why hadn't she told Inge? Why, when Adam had asked her if she wanted to do something tonight, had she said she was going to the cinema? Why – she stuck one of Jamie's spotty Emma Bridgewater mugs under the spout just in time to catch the stream of hot coffee – had she googled Cass so many times that her browser was now auto-suggesting his name every time she typed a capital C? (She made a mental note to clear her history before she left for work, just in case Cupid still had access to it somehow – the thought of him knowing she'd been looking him up was mortifying.) She felt totally unprepared for their discussion.

She took her coffee through to the living room, where Whit was having a tug-of-war with Harrison.

'Um, Whit?' He looked up; he and Harrison wore exactly the same expression on their faces. 'You were a Maths minor in college, weren't you?'

'Sure was!' He gave the rope another tug; Harrison growled delightedly. 'Major in ice hockey!'

'Have you still got your books?'

'Yeah, I think so.' He let go and Harrison shot backwards; he looked surprised when he landed, like someone had pulled his chair away as a prank. 'Good effort, buddy! Check upstairs on the shelf in your room.'

As she blew on her coffee, she realised she was actually quite looking forward to getting up to speed for their interview by spending her lunch break reading about algebra. She quickly took a photo of Harrison and sent it to Adam.

***

'Right, folks!' Bouncy barged into the planning meeting ten minutes late, kicking the door of the conference room shut behind him. Laura, Inge, Femi and Izzy, the other

Features graduate trainee, were sitting around the table, ready to brainstorm the special feelgood pages that the *Bugle* produced every August Bank Holiday. It had always been one of the dates in the editorial calendar Laura looked forward to: the year before, she'd written a piece about people who went swimming with their pets that had gone viral. Her phone lighting up with Twitter notifications of people retweeting it had been a perfect distraction from Walker and Sasha's burgeoning romance. Today, though, her heart wasn't in it. And it wasn't just the now-familiar dread that settled over her as soon as she walked into the office – she still felt twitchy, like she'd done something awful and was about to be found out. That second coffee had definitely been a mistake.

'We've got sixteen pages this time, so let's make the most of them, eh?' Bouncy went on. He sat on the edge of the table and pointed at Femi. 'Big man! What have you got for us?'

Femi opened a document on his laptop; out of the corner of her eye Laura could see a neatly formatted page of notes and diagrams.

'OK, so last year we broke down the list of things to do over the long weekend geographically,' he began. 'From looking at the September reader survey, the feedback we got was that overall people found it useful, but that it didn't make an impression on them visually. So I was thinking we could do it as an A to Z this time. That gives us a lot more scope for ...'

'Great, great,' Bouncy cut in. 'I really want to get a cool mix of activities in. Cutting edge. Some more urban stuff. What are you and the guys into these days?'

'Sorry?' Femi blinked.

'How about day trips?' Izzy blurted out.

'Boring!' Bouncy mimed a yawn. 'First rule of lifestyle journalism, Iz, is that you've got to shake it up.' He clicked his fingers. 'How about ... day ships?'

Izzy started dutifully scribbling in her notebook. She looked up. 'Um ... what ... are they, exactly?'

Bouncy shrugged. 'I dunno – ships you can go and see in a day? We don't need to get too hung up on the details at this stage.'

'Last-minute weekends away?' Laura suggested. Bouncy nodded enthusiastically.

'Like it, like it. Prince Charming whisking you off some-where, is he?' He pulled a paper napkin from the canteen out of his pocket and blew his nose into it. 'Laura finally got a boyfriend, everyone. They had to get a super-computer involved, but still! Ha ha ha!'

'We're not doing anything,' Laura said. Everyone was looking at her. 'I'm, er, dog sitting.' Adam had actually been sharing runs he thought they could do together over the long weekend on Strava. She'd responded with smileys – she always seemed to get distracted before she could reply properly.

'Dogs!' Bouncy thumped the table. 'Brilliant, let's get some dogs in the mix. Readers love 'em. We could use that great photo of the mutt eating an ice cream.'

'You mean, the same one we used last year?' Inge asked. 'And the year before that?'

'Exactly!' He tapped his nose. 'That'll have been three hundred and sixty-five days ago by the time it comes out, Inge – they'll all have forgotten by then. Are you going to remember this meeting in a year's time?'

'I think I will, actually,' Inge said tersely. 'I think we all will.'

Twenty minutes later they were back at their desks; Bouncy had cut the meeting short after Tony Eddison-Jones, the racing correspondent, banged on the glass and mouthed PUB at him. It was coming up to five-thirty; Laura topped up her lipstick and pinched her cheeks. The nervy fizzing in her stomach had started up again.

'You off? I'll walk out with you,' Inge said, shutting her inbox down. 'Lia and I are looking at a house tonight – our viewing's not until seven but if I stay in here a second longer I'm going to set fire to something.' She looked over Laura's shoulder. 'I think someone's waving at you.'

Laura turned around and saw Glenn bounding towards her like a long-lost friend.

'Hey! Lizzy!' He was wearing a different tie, she noticed; this one was covered in palm trees. 'How's tricks?'

'It's Laura,' she said. Glenn slapped his forehead.

'God, what an idiot! I've had so many meetings here, you've all kind of blurred into one. No offence!' He was grinning from ear to ear. 'Anyway, I'd love to chat, but I'd better dash – I'm off on holiday tonight. Bali for two weeks! Won't lie, it wasn't cheap, but you can't take it with you, can you?'

'Who was that?' Inge asked as they watched him strolling towards the lift. 'He can't work here, he looks too happy.' Laura started putting her jacket on.

'One of the Horsemen of the Apocalypse.' She changed her mind and took it off again; nothing felt right today, everything was either too much or not enough. 'You know. Aerodynamica.'

'Well, that's a good sign! He wouldn't have come over if they were going to get rid of you, would he?'

'Lizzy will be relieved.' Laura hefted her bag onto her shoulder. It was groaning with Whit's maths textbooks – she'd spent a full hour poring over them, her Tupperware of lunchtime pasta going cold in front of her. Inge gave her an awkward pat on the back like she was winding a baby.

'Well, I still think no news is good news.' She glanced at the bag. 'Where are you taking those?'

Laura hesitated, the words she knew she ought to be saying ticker-taping through her mind. *I'm meeting Cupid's head of data for a coffee. He's going to tell me about how their matchmaking model works. I think it'll make the piece much stronger, don't you?*

'Oh, just back to the library,' she said instead.

***

Cass had asked her to meet him at a new cafe in Coal Drops Yard. She took the shortcut across Granary Square, picking her way around the dancing water jets and the tables of people having after-work pints in the sunshine; they were a week into August now, and the crowds had thinned out because everyone seemed to be on holiday. Adam had already been away with his friends in June, to Mallorca, and even in normal years she'd been too disorganised and strapped for cash to manage anything more than a long weekend somewhere. Now, with the threat of redundancy hanging over her head, even that felt impossible. And who would she go with? Walker was obviously off the cards, Lil had Dora to think about, and she still wasn't sure her and Adam were at that stage. As she made her way down the ramp into the yard she wondered if Cass was going anywhere, and her pulse suddenly felt skittish. Just an interview, she reminded herself. That's all this is. No big deal.

The cafe was down one of the side streets, opposite a record store. When she walked in Cass was already there at a table in the corner, eating a cup of charcoal-coloured soft serve with popcorn stuck in it. The glasses were back, along with a white t-shirt like the one he'd been wearing the first time she'd seen him and the jeans he'd had on the second. She made her way over to him with the books clutched to her chest. He looked tanned, as though he'd been out in the sun all weekend.

'The death throes of late capitalism,' he said, holding the cup up in a mock toast. He scooped out the last of its contents and dropped it into the recycling bin behind him. 'Tasty, though.'

Laura squeezed herself into the seat opposite him and dumped the books down on the Formica. As soon as they landed she regretted getting them out – she'd had the idea that they might impress Cass and make him take her more seriously, which seemed ridiculous now. It wasn't a big table and the shape was awkward; she was extremely aware of the proximity of his knees to hers underneath it.

'Someone's been prepping.' He picked up the top one from the pile and turned it over. 'Vuong and McConnell's *Abstract Algebra, Part One*. Call me a contrarian, but I just don't think they hit their stride until Part Three.'

'I prefer their early work,' Laura said. He laughed gratifyingly as he put the book back.

'So, I was having a little snoop around the *Bugle*'s website before you got here,' he said casually. 'I've been reading your stuff – you're a really good writer.'

'Stalker.' She pulled a face, but she could feel her cheeks glowing with pleasure. Her parents had stopped buying the paper a long time ago, Jamie thought what she did for a living was ridiculous and, as far as she knew, Adam hadn't read anything she'd written. He'd certainly never complimented her on her work. She looked up at the ceiling.

'Um, which ones did you read?' she said, trying to sound blasé. 'Just out of interest.'

Cass got his phone out and opened a new browser window. She watched him tap the top of it and start scrolling through a list that came up.

'Have you *bookmarked* my articles? Wow, you really are stalking me.' She'd never normally have teased a near-stranger like this, but there was something about him that invited it – everything about him was so nonchalant, she couldn't imagine any of her jokes landing badly.

He grinned. 'Just keeping them somewhere safe. I mean, you never know when you might need to look up ...' he adjusted his glasses '... a guide to London's most extra burgers. Wow, that one actually has the fries inside it. Impressive.'

'That was May's most-read article online, I'll have you know.' She whacked his foot with hers.

'I liked it!' Cass protested, gently kicking her back; her toes prickled disconcertingly inside her shoes. 'It's funny. You're funny.'

He really did have very unusual eyes, Laura thought. And nice hands. She gulped.

'Anyway, what about you?' she asked quickly. 'Where were you working before Cupid?'

Cass yawned and stretched. 'Netflix, actually. Weirdly, the work was almost identical to what I'm doing now – except we were optimising for subscription payments, rather than long-term relationships.'

'It sounds so romantic when you put it like that.'

'Well, everything's optimised for something these days,' Cass said. He gestured at the room. 'Like this place – it's optimised for Instagrammability. Natural light, marble tabletops, cute little cakes that look good in pictures ... Seems to be working, too.'

He glanced across at the couple next to them: a man with a Viking beard was standing up, taking a photo of an elaborately knotted cinnamon bun on a plate. The man opposite him, who was wearing a denim jacket covered in patches, was doing the same thing. They kept smiling shyly at each other. 'I reckon that's a first date,' Cass said, leaning in towards her and lowering his voice. 'Good choice of venue. Casual, but not too casual. Nice vibe. Unintimidating.'

Laura shook her head, enjoying the feeling of being co-conspirators with him, even though she knew this was a million miles away from what they were actually meant to be talking about. 'Second date,' she whispered. 'At least. Look at how the bearded guy is touching the other one's arm – there's at least a date's worth of intimacy there.'

'How charmingly old-fashioned of you,' Cass said. She dared herself to hold his gaze, allowing herself to imagine what he'd be like on a first date, really trying not to think about Adam's fingers nudging hers across a table.

'Oh, you'd be straight in there from the get-go, would you?' she teased him. 'One bun, that's all it takes? Americans, honestly ...'

He raised his eyebrows. 'Are you asking if I'd have sex with someone on a first date? Probably not – but you never know. I'm not big into rules.' He leaned back easily in his chair. 'How about you, Laura Morrison?'

'How about me what?'

'Well, would you?'

'Absolutely not,' Laura said mock-indignantly. 'Date three at the earliest.'

'I'll bear that in mind,' Cass said, nodding thoughtfully, head tilted to one side. His eyes twinkled. 'For our records, I mean.'

Stop this, Laura told herself. *Now*.

'So!' she said, slapping the table harder than she'd meant to. 'Cupid's matchmaking model! Tell me everything!'

'Right! That's what we're here to talk about, isn't it?' He gestured to the pile of books. 'You're actually not going to need any of these – this whole area isn't so much maths as ...'

Suddenly his phone, which was face down on the table, lit up in a blue halo. He turned it over and looked at the flashing screen for a couple of seconds, weighing something up.

'Argh, I have to take this,' he said apologetically, standing up. 'Don't go anywhere, OK?'

Laura waited until the door had swung shut behind him, got her phone out to message Lil, then decided against it.

'I've always wanted to live in a lighthouse,' the bearded man next to her was saying, clearly trying to give CPR to a dying conversation. The other man yawned and started unravelling the cinnamon bun. Whatever number of date they were on, Laura thought, there wasn't going to be another. She felt a twinge of regret; she'd got quite invested in their budding relationship.

She opened *Abstract Algebra* and started looking through it, her eyes drifting over the dense text without really taking any of it in. She flipped past incomprehensible equations and diagrams, dense spider's webs of letters and numbers. This stuff was running everyone's lives now (especially hers, she thought with a flicker of discomfort), whirring away beneath every online transaction and interaction, making predictions and decisions. The tiny percentage of people who understood it wielded so much power – but like almost everyone, she trusted them to do the right thing with it. What choice did you have? You couldn't disconnect everything. There were arrows everywhere in the book, flying across the pages, hemming things in.

'I'll be testing you on that later.'

Cass had come back in without her noticing; he was standing in front of her next to the table, his hips at her eye level. She looked up at him: he'd only been gone for a couple of minutes but his reappearance felt like the sun coming out from behind clouds.

'And what happens when I pass?' she said, feeling herself being drawn back in. He raised an eyebrow.

'If you pass.' He glanced down at the book. 'I mean, you're holding it the right way up, that's a good start ...'

She pulled a playfully mocking face at him. 'Are you always this much of a dick to journalists?'

'Only the ones I like,' Cass said. They looked at each other – Laura imagined she was on a tightrope, tiptoeing forwards, trying not to topple off. Then it snapped.

'Look, something's just come up,' he said, waving his phone. 'I have to head off, I'm afraid – I'm really sorry, I know we didn't get through any of your questions.'

'Of course! I'd better go too, actually.' She felt like she'd been unplugged. 'We could ... catch up another time?' She tried to keep her voice light, casual, uninvested. Cass nodded, smiling.

'I'd like that.' He took his jacket off the back of the chair and started putting it on. Laura watched as his t-shirt rode up, exposing the buckle of his belt and a couple of inches of skin. She spotted the beginning of another inked line-drawing running up his side and looked away quickly. 'It's actually really nice, chatting to people about this stuff. I don't get to do it very often.'

They left the cafe together and headed for the exit from the yard.

'Have you got far to go?' she asked, trying to keep the conversation going. He shook his head.

'Not at all – I live here.' He pointed through the arch at the canal. 'Down there, actually.'

'You live on one of those?' Laura stared at the water, trying to imagine him on one of the painted narrowboats moored along the banks, bobbing serenely in the evening light. 'Wow. I had you down as the featureless white box type.'

'I'll take that as a compliment.' He smiled. 'See you soon, Laura.' His eyes were always on her for a fraction too long. Then he turned to walk away.

The second he'd turned the corner she felt like someone had shaken her awake from a dream. She got her phone out to check for Tube disruptions and noticed that Adam had sent her a picture. It was another sketch – and even before it had fully downloaded, she recognised the outline of her hair from her Facebook profile photo. He'd drawn her, just like he'd said he would. Guilty heat crept up the back of her neck. She was suddenly desperate to hear his voice, to be reassured that she hadn't somehow caused him to evaporate. She called him.

'Laura?' He picked up on the third ring, sounding startled. 'Is everything OK?'

'Fine!' His first impulse was to worry about her – now she felt even worse. 'Er, why wouldn't it be?'

'Just checking. I don't think you've ever called me before ...' He cleared his throat in what struck her as a rather formal way. 'So – how are things?'

'I just wanted to tell you how much I loved the picture,' she said in a rush. 'You're so sweet to have drawn it. It looks exactly like me.'

'You turned out pretty well, I think.' There was a faint hissing in the background – something cooking. Laura cast her mind back to the meal planner. Stir fry, that was it. Chicken, broccoli and peppers. Four portions' worth.

'What are you going to see?'

'What?'

'You're at the cinema tonight, right?'

'Yes!' she agreed guiltily; she'd totally forgotten the lie she'd told him. 'Um, an old one – I can't remember the name. It was Lil's choice. She's just arrived, actually, I'd better go.'

'Ah, no worries. Oh, before I forget, that uni reunion I was meant to be going to the weekend after next just got cancelled – shall we book in another bike ride? The weather looks good, although you do have to take these long-range forecasts with a pinch of salt ...'

'I'd love that,' Laura said quickly, even though she'd never made plans that far ahead in her life and felt like she'd only just recovered from their last cycling trip. She could actually hear him smiling – she pictured his dimples and the solid set of his jaw, willing the details to ground her.

***

As she unlocked the front door of 42 Stonybrook Street, Laura heard a familiar voice coming from inside, like nails down a blackboard.

'... Xanthe's just so excited about starting at The Willows in September, isn't she, Rory? She just felt completely at home there on the open day. Instead of having assembly in the mornings, the children all meditate together – isn't that wonderful? So nurturing ...'

Jamie and Whit were sitting at the kitchen table, hemmed in by artfully torn balls of mozzarella and sliced figs. (Had Jamie actually studied this stuff? Laura wondered. Were all her Saturdays between the ages of twenty-one and thirty spent taking notes in Waitrose?) Opposite them, smiling like plaster saints, were Caz and Rory. A feeling of heavy, bone-deep dread settled over Laura – but she wasn't going to be able to escape, they'd already seen her.

'Laura! Come and join us!' Caz cooed, patting the bench next to her. 'We were just talking about you and your lovely man! When do we get to see him again?'

Laura looked at Jamie, who looked down at the table. She'd done her hair again: it was in the kind of waves that magazines described as 'relaxed' or 'beachy', but which Laura knew took her sister nearly an hour to achieve with tongs. She imagined Jamie carefully curling each strand, trying to shrink what Caz had said at the barbecue with every twist, until it was just a nasty smudge, like a smear on a windscreen. She wanted to move Caz and her elder-flower pressé out of the way and put her arms around her sister, but obviously that was impossible – Jamie didn't even like hugs when nobody was watching.

'I'm not really hungry,' Laura said. 'I think I'm just going to go to bed. Thanks, though.'

Upstairs, she found Harrison lying across her inflatable mattress, snoring. Her mum had banned him from the bedroom after he chewed up a pair of her slippers; since she'd gone the rules had clearly been relaxed.

'Shift up,' Laura said. He opened one eye and gave her a baleful stare but allowed himself to be heaved onto the other half of the bed. She got in next to him and lay down on her side so she could feel the rise and fall of his breathing against her back. The first drawing Adam had done was still on her bedside table, in her eyeline. She stared at it, willing herself back to the night they'd met, but she kept drifting away from the memory and re-playing her conversation with Cass instead. She sighed heavily and rolled over; Harrison made a disgruntled rumbling noise.

She thought about Inge, wondering how her viewing had gone. By selling her flat in London Fields, which she'd bought before the artisan bakeries moved in, and Lia's draughty studio in Queens Park, which she'd inherited from an uncle who painted celebrity portraits, they could afford a two-bedroomed place in Zone 2. Inge spent her lunch breaks looking at PDFs from estate agents now. Sometimes she asked Laura what she thought about dual-aspect windows or decking; it felt like being asked for her opinion on getting to the moon.

Next to her, Harrison squirmed, making the mattress squeak. Before the room had come up at Walker's Laura had lived in two other dingy, impersonal shared flats where the rent and bills had been exactly half of what she was earning each month. She didn't want to go back to that, but there was no way she could afford to live by herself. Especially not if she was going to lose her job.

She opened the photo of Adam with his nephew again and set it as her phone background. She stared at his kind, handsome face without blinking until her eyes started to swim and everything else blurred. To form a habit, she'd read once, you needed to do something sixty-six times. She pressed the power button again and again, watching as the picture flashed up and disappeared, trying to force it right to the front of her mind, until she fell asleep. She dreamed of greenish water lapping around her feet.

Chapter 10

perplexity (noun): a measure of how accurately a model is accomplishing its task

'What do you think about long hair on men?' Laura asked Inge – it was coming up for 5.30 on Friday and that week's magazine had gone to print, so they were both tidying their desks. 'Not, like, super long. Just below chin length.'

It had been over a week since their meeting in the cafe and Cass still hadn't messaged her. She hadn't messaged him either, but she'd kept her phone next to her keyboard, waiting for the WhatsApp notification to appear. Every time one popped up her stomach lurched. Every time it wasn't him her heart sank. She'd found herself bringing up things that were vaguely to do with him just so she could talk around the subject.

Inge pulled a bottle of turmeric latte shower gel she'd been sent by a PR company out of her top drawer. 'You're asking the wrong person,' she said, running her fingers through her cropped hair as she squinted at the bottle's label. 'I'm not sure "Golden Showers" is the name I'd have chosen for this particular product … Do you want it? It's brand new.'

'Tempting, but I think I'll pass.' Laura was picking ancient grit out of an open tin of Vaseline. Inge had already moved on to her bottom drawer.

'Ha!' she cried, producing what looked like a thick USB cable. 'This brings back memories …' She started winding it around her fingers, smiling. 'This is from my undercover journalism days. It's a wire! When I started here I worked on the cash for access story, can you believe it? That was back when people bought newspapers and we actually had the money to do proper investigations.' She finished looping the wire and leaned over to push it into the side pocket of Laura's handbag. 'Here you go – you have it. My days of sneaking around hotel bars are over, I think. But perhaps yours are ahead of you.'

'Hah. I think not.' Laura put the Vaseline tin down and started collecting lint-covered loose paperclips. It was just a crush, that was all, she told herself. A daft, meaningless crush, the kind that had always kept her ticking over during stretches of romantic nothingness, like snacking between meals.

Inge gave her foot a nudge under the desk.

'I think we've got a situation developing over there,' she said. 'Bless them. Don't be obvious, OK?'

Laura looked. Femi and Izzy were over by the ancient printer, waiting for something to come out (which wasn't, no matter how you spun it, a two-person job). They were facing each other with the toes of their shoes almost touching, smiling like they were both in on a secret. They were almost the same height – a bit like her and Cass, Laura thought, before she could slam on the brakes. She forced herself to stop and run through a list of Adam's best qualities, like a mantra. *Kind, thoughtful, looks good naked, saves trees*, she repeated silently. *Kind, thoughtful, looks good naked, saves trees …*

'That thing must have some kind of electromagnetic field,' Inge went on, turning back to her screen. 'Lia and I used to talk in the printer queue when she was here. I only asked her out because we'd been standing there for about twenty minutes and I'd run out of things to say.' She smiled to herself. 'Are you and Adam doing anything this weekend? I've just seen the forecast – the weather's going to be beautiful.'

Laura watched as Femi took a stack of A4 paper from the output tray and handed it to Izzy, who took it like it was a box of chocolates.

'I think we're going for a bike ride tomorrow – then on Sunday we're having a picnic,' she said. 'On, er, Hampstead Heath.' In fact, they hadn't made any plans for Sunday – but now she'd said it, she found that she liked the idea of doing something so quintessentially romantic. It would be fun, she decided, to be one of them. Half of a pair. Someone who'd cracked love's code. The thought drew level with all the confusing Cass stuff, then started to overtake it. *Just a crush*, Laura told herself again. It didn't mean that she and Adam weren't right for each other. And like all crushes, it would pass.

Inge closed her drawer firmly. 'Well, if I were you, I'd go early,' she said. 'The world and his dog's going to be there.'

***

'He's been too quiet.' Jamie was staring at Harrison, who was sunbathing next to the barbecue. 'He must be building up to something. Are you sure you want to take him?'

'It'll be fine,' Laura said unconvincingly, transferring the now insane-seeming selection of items she'd bought after work that evening to the fridge: two pots of garlic olives, a pack of sausage rolls and a barely solid wedge of French cheese, which already smelled like it might be able to make its own way to Hampstead Heath. Why hadn't she got strawberries and that bread you were meant to tear apart and share romantically with your significant other? Why had she decided in the supermarket to invite Lil and Dora, rather than just keeping it to her and Adam?

Jamie opened one of the kitchen island's built-in cupboards. 'I'm going to phone Mum tomorrow,' she said, pulling out a flowery Cath Kidston cool-bag. 'This has gone on for long enough. I can't stand being stuck in the middle of her and Dad – they need to sort it out. You haven't spoken to her, have you?' Before Laura could answer, her sister dumped the bag into her arms. 'You can borrow this on Sunday if you like, but I want it back, OK? My spare sunglasses are still somewhere in your room ...'

Laura pulled a face at her sister, but inside she was feeling horribly churned up. Jamie obviously didn't know about their mum's Instagram account. Although Laura was still blocking her calls she'd started checking it several times a day, half hoping to see a new post on the grid, half dreading it. That morning, finally, there'd been one: a patio that she'd never seen before photographed at sunset. *still thinking xxx*, the caption had read. As she combed the picture for clues – whoever's patio it was put Schweppes in their gin and was into ornamental stone frogs – she had to hack her way through the usual thicket of contradictory feelings. Wanting to know. Not wanting to know. Wanting it to end. Wanting the opposite.

'Nope,' she said. 'I haven't spoken to her. And your aspirational picnic container is safe with me, don't worry.'

Outside, Harrison did a slow barrel roll, coating himself in grass cuttings.

***

Laura and Adam's bike ride the next day got off to a bad start. Adam had suggested they meet at Waterloo station under the clock – by the time Laura got there at ten it was already twenty-seven degrees and the baking heat seemed to be seeping out of the ground. It was definitely too hot to be moving, but when she'd suggested to Adam that they just find somewhere shady by the river to sit and have a drink instead, he'd looked a bit shocked. *But I've been really looking forward to it*, he'd said sadly, and Laura had fought the urge to tell him that this was exactly why you shouldn't make plans so far ahead. Now, she was wobbling along the South Bank on a Santander bike. It had been the only one left in the dock, and as soon as they set off she'd realised why. Adam was zipping ahead of her along the cycle path, in a sporty t-shirt and leggings with a pair of shorts over the top.

'Keep up!' he called out cheerfully over his shoulder.

'This thing weighs as much as a car ...' Laura muttered angrily. The bike's gears got stuck between second and third and she swore again under her breath.

Adam signalled with his hand that he was pulling in, stopped and hopped off his bike next to the BFI. As Laura drew level with him, tomato-red and sweating, he glanced back at her chassis and frowned.

'Hmm, you've got one of the old models,' he said. 'The newer ones have a blue seat post and smaller wheels – they're a good five kilos lighter. See if you can grab one of them next time, you'll find it much easier.'

'I'll do that,' Laura said, gritting her teeth while she slowed down. The brakes squeaked as she stopped. Adam gave her an unperturbed smile, then whipped a portable pump out of his backpack and kneeled down to unscrew the inlet on his front tyre.

'You should really just get yourself a bike,' he said cheerfully as he started topping it up. 'Evans have some bargains at the moment – you could probably pick a really decent one up for less than a grand.'

Laura stared down at him, trying to stay upright. He wasn't being sarcastic, she realised – he just didn't see that as a lot to spend. He'd obviously never had to worry about money, whereas she couldn't remember a time when she hadn't. The anxiety had always been there, hissing faintly in the background like a broken radiator.

'I'm just an editorial assistant, remember? I definitely don't have that going spare,' she said with a hollow laugh.

Adam's forehead was furrowed. 'You could ask your parents?' he suggested. 'I'm sure they'd want to help you with something like that.'

'Are you being serious? My dad drives to the next town to get toothpaste ten pence cheaper than it is in the super- market . . .' The South Bank Centre was looming over them: Laura thought back to her and Adam's drink in the swanky bar that had put her on edge, how totally at ease he'd been while she was flushed with embarrassment. She'd always known that the two of them had had very different child- hoods – he'd mentioned the private school in Edinburgh he'd been to and family skiing holidays – but until now hadn't realised quite how little overlap there was. Or how unaware he seemed to be of that. It seemed incredible to her that Cupid would have waved something like that through. He still looked nonplussed by her reaction. Why was he forcing her to spell it out like this?

'Anyway, they definitely don't have a thousand pounds either,' she went on, sounding more defensive than she'd meant to. 'Not all of us grew up rolling in cash, you know.'

Adam looked crestfallen. He glanced away and started pumping the tyre again – she immediately felt a guilty squeeze of her heart. It wasn't his fault he didn't under- stand, she told herself. He was doing his best.

'Sorry, Adam,' she said quietly, getting off her bike, kicking its stabiliser down and taking a step towards him. 'That came out wrong. It's the heat, it's making me grumpy.'

He looked up and gave her a forgiving smile, then stood up and checked his Fitbit.

'Right! Shall we get going?' he said. 'I thought we could stop at Borough Market for a sandwich.'

They got back on their bikes and set off again, Adam in front, Laura trailing behind. The river to their left looked impossibly wide and calm and cool. As they rounded the corner under the Oxo Tower she found herself wondering if it joined up with the canal that flowed through Kings Cross – and if it did, how long it would take her to get there if she just jumped in, let the water close over her head and started swimming.

***

Sunday dawned even hotter. They were giving out free bottles of water at Clapham Junction and the tunnel underneath the station was like an oven.

'We should really get on, don't you think?' Adam said mildly.

He and Laura were on the Overground platform with Harrison sitting placidly between them – and although she couldn't put her finger on it, something about the whole situation still felt off. The rucksack Adam was wearing with a tightly rolled picnic blanket strapped to it like he was going on a hike, the way he kept checking his watch . . . She was suddenly finding it all quite annoying and didn't really know why. She looked down at Harrison, staring at the cool-bag, and remembered how he'd trotted along obediently next to Adam, making big soppy eyes at him. Dogs were very good judges of character, she reminded herself. Maybe she was still just in a bad mood from the day before.

'It doesn't leave until quarter-past – Lil said she was five minutes away,' Laura said, trying to keep the irritation out of her voice.

Adam looked doubtful. 'Yes, but that was eight minutes ago,' he said, glancing at his watch again. Laura shunted the cool-bag behind her out of Harrison's reach, forcing herself to keep quiet.

'Hi! Sorry! Sorry!' Lil was clattering up the stairs in high-heeled clogs and cotton dungarees, hauling Dora behind her. 'She wanted to wear her Elsa outfit but it was covered in shit. Not literally.' She launched herself at Adam and kissed him on both cheeks; he looked slightly taken aback. 'I'm Lil and this is Dora. Dora, say hi to Laura's friend Adam.'

Dora peered up at him. 'Where are Walker and Sasha?' she said, narrowing her eyes. 'For my birthday they came with Laura to the park, and that swan chased Walker, and then Sasha showed me how to do a cartwheel.'

'Walker and Sasha and Laura don't live in the same house now, sweetie,' Lil said, patting the top of her head. 'A bit like me and Dad, but ... different.' She grimaced at Adam. 'They've got zero filter at this age – the other day she poked a guy's stomach in the Co-op and asked when his baby was coming. Anyway, Laura was telling me you work in climate justice! Good on you!' She raised a fist. 'Divest now!'

'I don't exactly ...' Adam moved to hold his hand up for a high-five, then stopped. 'Oh, right – we're not doing that. Sorry.' He bumped the back of it tentatively against hers.

Had he always been this ... *stuffy*? Laura wondered.

Dora was still scrutinising him. 'Do you and Laura live in a house together now?'

'Not right now,' Adam said. He looked away and started adjusting one of the straps on his rucksack. 'Maybe one day.'

Lil caught Laura's eye and started blinking rapidly. This, Laura knew, meant: *What just happened???*

Dora, satisfied, turned her attention to Harrison, flinging her arms around his neck.

'Gently, Dora, he's old,' Lil said, putting a hand on her shoulder. 'That's it, say a nice hello.'

'He's not *that* old,' Laura protested. Adam was looking at his watch *again*.

'I really do think we should get on,' he said anxiously. 'We'll struggle to get seats at this rate.'

They managed to find two pairs that were practically opposite each other. Dora grabbed Adam's hand and dragged him into the seat next to hers, leaving Laura and Lil to sit together. The train had been shuttling up and down the line in the sun all morning and it was stiflingly hot – Harrison flopped down on the floor between the four of them and closed his eyes with a sigh. Dora wriggled out of her seat and lay down next to him.

'Dora Cho, stop cuddling him,' Lil said, giving Laura a sideways look. 'He's very tired and he needs to sleep.' She yawned. 'Like me.'

Dora sat up, scowling, took off her backpack and pulled out a chunky plastic caterpillar. It had glittery purple feelers and a zonked expression, like someone had shot it with a tranquilliser dart. She held it up to Adam.

'Will you help me?' she asked.

His face broke into a big, encouraging smile that exaggerated his dimples; he had such a nice face, Laura thought guiltily. How could she be sitting here thinking this stuff about him? She needed to snap out of it.

'Of course I will.' He took it, turning it over, looking for a switch. 'Um, what is it?'

'It's a Code-a-Pillar,' Lil said. 'The segments are all programmed and it's meant to go in different directions depending on how you stick them together. "Sequencing play", her teacher calls it. Apparently you're never too young to start thinking about getting a job at Google.'

The horsey-looking woman in cropped trousers and a cricket jumper sitting opposite them was watching closely, beaming at Dora. She leaned forward in her seat.

'What a *lovely* name!' she said to Lil. 'Cho … Do you mind me asking where you're from?'

Next to her, Laura felt Lil's shoulders stiffen. 'Surbiton, originally,' she said. 'But if you mean where's my family from, they're Korean.'

'Oh, how wonderful!' the woman exclaimed. She patted the knee of the man next to her. 'Well, we're very keen on dim sum, aren't we, Nigel? There's a lovely little place that's just opened around the corner from us. The owners are *delightful*.'

'That's nice,' Lil said, deadpan, getting her phone out. Laura, recognising her cue, reached for hers too.

Lil:
SIGH

Laura:
Urgh
Sorry

Lil:
Ffs
On a happier note
Adam's easy on the eye eh?
Good with children and animals

Laura:
He is!

Lil:
It's funny ...

Laura:
???

Lil:
I mean, he's SO not who I'd have picked out for you
But then
I married a guy who said he didn't want to be in the room
when I gave birth because he'd find it 'too upsetting to see me
like that'
So what do I know!

Adam, who'd just slotted the Code-a-Pillar's tail segment into the rest of its body, gave it back to Dora. When she put it on the floor of the carriage it bleeped, then skittered off in a circle, flashing red and green. She squealed and hugged Adam's leg; he laughed, placing a hand protectively on top of her head. Laura turned away.

They got off the train at Gospel Oak and caught the single-decker bus going up the east side of the Heath. Dora scrambled onto a seat and immediately started trying to get into the luggage rack; Lil was busy listening to a long voicemail, so Laura hoisted her onto her lap. The weight and warmth of her was always a shock; it catapulted Laura back to being eight or nine and being allowed to pick up their new neighbour's kitten, feeling its tiny body vibrating with life as she held it. She could sense Adam watching her.

As they pulled into the stop at the top of Merton Lane, Lil took her phone away from her ear, shaking her head.

'Guys, I'm sorry, I have to call Andreas – he was meant to sign this thing and he hasn't. Now the solicitor's on my case. Can you go on ahead with her? I'll catch you up.' She crouched down so she was at Dora's eye level. 'Sweetie, hold Laura's hand, OK? And Adam's. I'll come and find you in a minute.'

'OK,' Dora said, reaching for them both obligingly. They set off in a human chain with her between them. Every now and then she'd jump and swing in the air, letting them carry her. Adam caught Laura's eye and smiled.

'We've never talked about any of this stuff, have we?' he said, tilting his head towards Dora. 'Do you want … well, this?' His face coloured. 'In the future, I mean – not right now, obviously.'

A montage of images played out in Laura's mind. Lil, thirty-six weeks pregnant, painting her bump to look like a Tunnock's Teacake. Jamie phoning a babywear company at Christmas to complain about the catalogues she kept being sent, and the person on the other end not being able to find her on the database, and her shouting at them, then hanging up because she was crying. Joining the morning after pill queue outside Boots on a Sunday morning as a student. The time she and Walker had drunkenly uploaded photos of themselves to a face-merging website called BabyMaker. Harrison, oblivious to everything she was thinking, trotted along next to Adam, panting happily. The boating lake twinkled below them. The air was full of joyful shrieks being carried along by the breeze.

'Oh, I haven't really thought about it,' she said finally. 'I'm not even thirty yet. Loads of time, right?'

'Can I have an ice cream?' Dora butted in, pointing with her foot at the candy-striped truck parked ahead of them at the bottom of the hill. It was playing a tinkly tune; Harrison's ears twitched and Laura tightened her grip on his lead.

'Sure you can.' She got her wallet out, relieved to be off the hook. 'As long as you promise to let me have a lick, OK? Come on.'

Adam held them back. 'Shouldn't we check with Lil?' he said. 'Dora hasn't had her lunch yet ...'

Laura bristled. Why did he have to be so orderly about everything? Why couldn't he ever go with the flow? 'Her lunch is a couple of Babybels and some Wotsits,' she said tersely. 'It doesn't make much of a difference, does it?'

He shrugged, pointing to a shady patch of grass under a tree just ahead of them. 'Shall we just grab a space until she arrives?' he said, the picture of calm. It was exactly the same spot, Laura realised, that she'd been imagining when she'd been talking to Inge. The weather was perfect, the setting was perfect – but she could feel the familiar niggle of dissatisfaction starting up again. And the nicer Adam was to her, the stronger it got.

'I don't know,' she muttered as they made their way towards it. 'Maybe we should see what *Lil* says.'

Adam nudged her. 'Hey, don't be like that.' He unclipped the blanket and spread it out on the grass, carefully smoothing the wrinkles; Dora jumped onto it and started hopscotching along the checks. Laura let Harrison off the lead and began unpacking the cool-bag. The smell of the cheese was overpowering.

'Oh my god, what is that?' Adam turned around; he was holding a Swiss Army knife with the corkscrew bit out. 'It's like ...'

'... someone opened a coffin?'

'I was going to go with the changing room after a match – but, yeah, that works too,' he chuckled.

Laura allowed herself a little grin, feeling some of the tension ebbing away. She was making too much of a big deal out of this, she thought as she laid the rest of the food out. All couples got on each other's nerves sometimes. She lay back on her elbows and tilted her face up to the cloud-less sky so she could feel the sun on it. Harrison moseyed over and shuffled under her right arm – as she was raking a hand through his fur she spotted an exhausted-looking Lil coming towards them and waved her over.

'Everything OK?' she asked as her friend sat down. Lil unbuckled her clogs and kicked them off, massaging her feet.

'Ugh. It's just . . .' She hesitated and turned to Dora, who'd opened one of the tubs of olives and was swooshing her fingers in the oil. 'Sweetie, do you want to watch *Moana* on my phone for a bit?'

'Yeah!' She ferreted Lil's wireless headphones out of her bag and jammed them onto her head, leaving shiny smudges on the plastic. Lil passed her the phone and kissed her hair, lowering her voice.

'I get worried about what her takeaway is from all of this, you know? What are we teaching her about relation-ships, about families? I don't want her to grow up thinking this is what happens whenever you decide to build a life with someone.'

'I wouldn't stress too much about it – nobody in my fam-ily can stand each other and look how I turned out,' Laura said cheerfully, holding out a paper plate.

'You're kind of proving my point there, Morrison.' Laura smacked her with it. 'Ow! Adam, ignore me, Laura's com-pletely normal, no emotional issues at all from her parents' marriage. Anyway, tell me about you! How was your week?'

Adam, who'd been watching their back and forth with a benignly puzzled look on his face, was neatly slicing a saus-age roll in two. 'Oh, you know,' he said. 'Same old. And you? You used to work with Laura, didn't you?'

'At the *Bugle*, yeah. Otherwise known as hell's innermost circle.' He didn't laugh; Laura winced. 'But I'm with a make-up brand now,' Lil went on. 'The pay and the hours are much better – plus I get as many tubes of this bad boy as I want.' She pressed her red-painted lips together and made a noise like a cork popping.

'Right. Right.' Adam nodded slowly, trying to think of something else to say. 'Well, your make-up is very ... professional.'

'Thanks, Adam!' There was an edge creeping into Lil's voice; Adam clearly wasn't the only one who was finding the conversation hard work. But then, it was always a bit like this, Laura reminded herself, trying to keep her face diplomatically neutral. Your friends were one part of your life's Venn diagram, your partner was another. The main thing – sometimes the only thing – that they had in common was you. They didn't need to agree on everything.

'So ... have you ... got any nice holidays planned?' Lil ventured. Adam shook his head.

'Not for the rest of the summer, no.' He picked up the sausage roll halves and held them out for Laura and Lil. 'Me and the guys did a trip to Mallorca in early June.'

'That's where my parents met!' Laura chipped in, trying to help things along. 'They were on the same package holiday in 1979, if you can believe that.'

Lil looked incredulous. 'Seriously?' She sniffed her piece of sausage roll and frowned. 'I wouldn't have thought wet t-shirt contests were Jim's thing. Or maybe they are – still waters run deep ...'

Laura threw an olive at Lil and watched Adam flinch as it bounced off and landed on the blanket. Laura quickly rescued it. 'He was the only person under the age of forty in his village and he wanted to meet someone, so ...' she said, scrubbing at the oil it had left behind with a paper napkin. She remembered her dad telling her the story for the first time and getting the sense that, in spite of everything that had happened afterwards, it was still one of his happiest memories.

'Anyway, they had a holiday fling – he was really keen but Mum wasn't. She actually threw his number away at the airport.' Laura balled the napkin up in her hand and tossed it into the cool-bag, then inspected the sausage roll's pappy, pinkish interior. She'd never looked inside one before and now she really wished she hadn't. 'A couple of weeks after she got home she found out she was expecting Jamie, so she called his office and asked to speak to him. As soon as she told him she was pregnant he asked her to marry him ...' She closed her eyes and bit into the sausage roll; it took effort to chew and swallow it. 'That was it, really. She had to give up flying, which she was really gutted about. She loved that job.'

Adam was carving up another one. 'They can't have been completely unhappy all this time, though,' he said. 'I mean, they had you, didn't they?'

Laura shrugged. 'Jamie always says that she was an accident, but I was a mistake.' In fact, Jamie had only said it to her once, a long time ago, when they were arguing – Laura was the one who'd kept repeating it, turning it into a joke to try and take the sting out.

Lil raised her half of the sausage roll again. 'Well, here's to times having changed for the better,' she said. 'We're all still making mistakes, but we don't have to stick with them forever now. Progress!'

Next to them, some teenagers were kicking a football around. Adam looked doubtful.

'I do think we're all too quick to walk away from stuff as soon as it gets difficult, though,' he said. 'My parents have had their ups and downs, but they've worked through them because they love each other. Surely sticking can be good sometimes, can't it?'

'Well, that does *kind of* depend on what you're sticking to,' Lil said. The edge was back in her voice and Laura could tell Lil was annoyed; she felt like a cracker being pulled slowly in two different directions.

Harrison, meanwhile, had been watching the group passing the football with his ears back and his eyes narrowed. He got to his feet and started creeping through the long grass towards them, inching forwards almost silently, freezing whenever anyone looked in his direction.

'Um, what's he doing?' Adam asked Laura. 'Should he be doing that?'

Laura felt her hackles rising again. 'He just likes it when everyone's all together,' she said defensively. 'If people are too spread out he wants to herd them.'

Adam didn't look convinced. 'Didn't anybody ever train him ... not to?'

A girl in a playsuit with freckles and a halo of dark curls booted the ball down the hill in the direction of the lake. Harrison yelped and went charging after it, galloping unstoppably towards the water.

'Harrison, no!' Laura yelled, scrambling to her feet and sprinting down the hill after him. She watched as the ball landed in the water – and a second later, just before she could dive for his collar, the dog followed, belly-flopping into the lake with a massive splash. He looked delighted.

'I think you'll find pets aren't allowed in there,' a man walking past with a camera tripod called out pointedly. 'It's called the boating lake, not the *dogging* lake.'

'That word doesn't mean what you think it means,' Laura shouted after him, yanking a stick out of the bank and shaking it. 'Harrison, come on – Jamie's going to kill me.'

'Need this?'

This time, it was a woman's voice, one that she recognised. Laura looked up and saw Inge standing over her, gamely holding out a towel. Next to her was Lia in an old-fashioned bikini top with ruffles and a halterneck, shorts and star-shaped sunglasses. They were both laughing.

'I couldn't stop thinking about coming here after you mentioned it on Friday – we're going for a swim!' Inge watched Harrison paddling towards them. 'Looks like someone had the same idea ...'

'You two are lifesavers,' Laura puffed, taking the towel from them gratefully. Harrison allowed himself to be heaved out, nosing the ball onto the bank. As soon as he was upright he did a carwash shake, splattering the three of them, then sat down at Laura's feet, panting with the satisfaction of a job well done.

Adam was jogging down the hill.

'Sorry about him,' he puffed to Inge and Lia. 'We should have kept him on the lead.' Lia looked nonplussed.

'Why are you apologising? He's a dog, they do this stuff the whole time. My folks' poodle ripped the door off the garage once.'

Why are *you apologising?* Laura thought resentfully; something inside her was bubbling dangerously, threatening to boil over. Inge draped the towel over Harrison and turned to Adam.

'I recognise you from your Cupid video! I'm Inge – Laura and I work together. This is Lia, my girlfriend.'

Adam shook both their hands – they smiled in unison at his formality – then turned to Harrison. 'That was *bad*,' he said, wagging his finger. 'You can't just run off whenever you feel like it, alright? OK?' Harrison lowered his head and stared forlornly at the grass.

'Excuse me, he's *not* your dog,' Laura snapped, kneeling down and drying him off protectively. Harrison tucked his tail between his legs. Adam looked crestfallen.

'I only meant he could have hurt himself. Sorry, Laura.' He put a hand on her shoulder; she shrugged him off. She knew she was making a scene but she didn't care.

Inge and Lia exchanged a look.

'Right, we'll leave you to it!' Inge said. 'Really nice meeting you, Adam! See you on Monday, Laura. Don't worry about the towel – just bring it in whenever. I know where you live. Roughly.'

Laura waved them off with a tight smile, her gaze fixed on Inge's back as she and Lia set off up the hill, falling into step easily with each other, their fingers woven together. Inge said something to Lia, who laughed, then rested her head on Inge's shoulder.

Chapter 11

confusion matrix (noun): a visualisation of a model's
performance

The three of them got the train back alone – Lil had made
her excuses and taken Dora (who, oblivious to the atmosphere, had fallen asleep on the cool-bag) to Colindale to see
her uncle. Laura was standing slightly apart from Adam
on the platform with a soggy Harrison at her feet, holding
one of the bottles of water he'd got for them from the kiosk,
trying to pretend everything was back to normal. He'd said
he was sorry again, so had she, but she still felt off-kilter –
and deep down, she knew that had more to do with her
than anything he'd actually done.

A Clapham Junction train pulled in and she watched
the happy groups of people getting off, ready for an afternoon of fun. She and Adam boarded it in silence: as soon
as they sat down Harrison lay across their feet, pinning
them in place. Every time either of them moved he fixed
them with a basilisk stare.

She got her phone out and saw that Jamie had messaged her. It was a link to a news story about redundancies

at the *Bugle*. She bit the inside of her cheek as she started typing a reply.

> Laura:
> *Wow you really know how to brighten*
> *up a weekend!*

Jamie:
Is this going to affect you?

Laura still hadn't told Jamie anything about what was happening at work. Her sister, she was sure, would have zero sympathy – she'd probably just tick Laura off for not having three months' income saved up.

> Laura:
> *It's fine*
> *Don't worry*

As she pressed send she had a moment of relief before she was plunged into a grim picture of life after being made redundant. Carrying her box of office stuff back on the Tube. Spending the shapeless days applying for jobs that she knew she wouldn't really enjoy. Being rejected from them with template replies. Not having anything to talk to Lil about, or money to do things with her. Being forced to tell Jamie she couldn't actually pay her the rent right now and having to plead for a bit more time.

Jamie:
Is this why you're writing the feature?
To stop them getting rid of you?

'Fuck off, Jamie,' Laura muttered before she could stop herself; luckily Adam was absorbed in his own phone. She

prided herself on being able to decode all of her sister's little tells, like the way the skin around her ears mottled red
when she was angry. But it cut both ways – Jamie was just
as good at reading Laura.

Laura:
Don't you have an Ocado shop to be
unpacking or something?
I thought you liked Adam

Jamie:
I do
That isn't what I asked you

Adam finished whatever he'd been reading on his phone
and slotted it back into his pocket. Laura reached for his
hand and he accepted hers without hesitation. She needed
him, she reminded herself. There was no Plan B.

It was even hotter on the train home than it had been on
the way to Hampstead; the air in the carriage was oppressive. She started swiping through apps with her free hand,
looking for a distraction, and realised that it was still her
turn on Words With Friends with Walker – he'd last played
a word the evening of her and Adam's first date. She'd been
so caught up in everything since then that she'd never actually responded. She went into the game and saw she had a
Y on her deck: if she put it onto the end of his DOOM to
make DOOMY, she thought, she'd get all his points, plus
six for landing on a double letter tile. She dragged it over to
the square and dropped it.

He messaged her almost straight away.

Walker:
SO ANNOYING

Laura:

I know you are x

Walker:

Why do you always do that?
Piggyback off my words

Laura:

It's a perfectly legal move

Walker:

Yeah but it's really feeble
You're just taking the easy way out

Why was everyone getting at her today? He couldn't talk about taking the easy way out, she thought, bristling suddenly. She wasn't the one who'd thrown her entire personality in the bin to go out with the most basic person in the Northern Hemisphere. She let go of Adam's hand so she could type faster.

Laura:

Someone's grumpy
Things not going well in an escape room?
Or whatever bit of organised fun you're
doing today

Walker:

Don't be like that, Laur
I wasn't having a go

He was still typing, but Laura clicked out of the chat anyway, already regretting snapping at him but not knowing how she could try to fix it without making things even worse. When they'd lived together it hadn't felt like a big deal if they'd bickered on their phones – sooner or later they'd be in the kitchen at the same time and things would just naturally go back to normal. But Walker was on the other side of London now and things were never going to be normal for them again.

The Tannoy spat and crackled.

'We regret to inform all customers that this Clapham Junction service will now be terminating at Shepherd's Bush,' a tinny voice announced. 'Shepherd's Bush will be the next and final stop. All change, please.'

'Oh, excellent.' Laura tried to lighten her tone. 'How about a nice trip to Westfield?'

'Ha!' Adam squeezed her fingers. 'Honestly, if we can make it to the end of our lives without having to set foot in that place, I'll chalk it up as a success.' He got up, shouldering his rucksack, and strode towards the door. Laura followed him with Harrison at her heel.

'Please make sure that you have all your personal items with you,' the Tannoy voice instructed as they pulled into the station. 'Any unattended items will be disposed of.'

'That's you,' she said to Harrison as they got off the train. He leaned against her leg, trying to nudge her into line with Adam. His white bits were stained brown from the water and up close he smelled like compost. 'What do you reckon counts as an impersonal item?'

Adam wasn't listening. He'd finished his bottle of water and was scanning the platform. 'Can you see a recycling bin?'

'I think there's one down there . . .' She pointed at a green shape by the exit.

'Great.' He gave her an easy smile; it was like the past couple of hours had never happened. 'Back in a sec.'

She watched him walking away. 'Come on, then,' she said to Harrison, giving his lead a tug towards a bench. 'Might as well sit down.'

Harrison wouldn't move. He was staring at the crowd behind her around the entrance to the station, his ears twitching. Then he let out a joyful yelp and started straining at the lead.

'What is it?' She tried to look where he was looking; all she could see was a swell of shoppers weighed down by their purchases. 'Harrison, there's nothing ...'

An icy hand grabbed hold of her heart and squeezed it. There, carrying a John Lewis bag, was Sasha, in a pair of pink shorts that showed off her tanned legs and a scalloped white t-shirt. Next to her, holding a matching bag and wearing a Hawaiian shirt Laura hadn't seen before, was Walker. They were both staring in her direction.

'Laur!' Sasha called out. 'Oh my god! We were literally just talking about you! Walker was saying what a little terror you are on that word game!'

Harrison yelped again and started tugging Laura towards them. She allowed herself to be pulled down the platform, sweat springing up on her forehead.

'There he is,' Walker said, giving Harrison an extended tickling. Laura had an awful feeling he was trying to postpone having to touch her – he was always scrupulously careful not to be too familiar or tactile with her when Sasha was there. Finally he ran out of bits of dog to pet and straightened up, giving Laura a stiff hug.

'So, er, how are the spatulas settling into their new home?' he asked. She scanned his face for signs that he was angry with her after their exchange earlier, but he didn't seem to be – he just looked slightly uncomfortable, which was actually much worse.

'They're fine,' she mumbled. 'They say hi.' She accepted Sasha's warm embrace, both relieved and embarrassed by how nice the other woman was being to her. What on earth were they doing here?

'Sash's class gave her some vouchers at the end of term,' Walker said, as though he'd read her mind. He linked his hand with Sasha's in a stagey way that seemed to be for Laura's benefit. 'We thought we'd spend them on a juicer and some other bits for the flat. We're boring like that, aren't we?'

But he didn't look bored, Laura thought – he looked totally enchanted, just like he had been by everything Sasha had introduced him to. Tim Tams. Acupuncture. Her running club friends, who started coming back to 8A to use the shower before they all went to the pub together. Each thing knitted him more tightly into their shared world and took him further and further away.

'Can you believe I didn't have one before?' Sasha laughed. She started tracing a slow circle in Walker's palm with her finger. 'We miss you, don't we?' she said, addressing Laura but looking at Walker. Suddenly Laura couldn't stop thinking about the casual intimacy of their shoes all mixed up in the hallway, and their toothbrushes touching like they were sharing a secret, and the tealights she'd found around the bath one Sunday when she'd come back early from a weekend away. She wished a crack would open up in the platform and swallow her.

'I miss you guys too,' she managed to say. Harrison was straining on the lead again: Adam was coming towards them, minus the water bottle. She'd never felt happier to see him.

'This is Adam,' she announced when he got to them, awkwardly manoeuvring her free arm around his waist. 'My, er, boyfriend.'

Walker and Sasha both did *aaaah!* noises. They introduced themselves to Adam ('We're her old flatmates!') and he shook hands with them both, just like he had with Inge and Lia. Out of the corner of her eye Laura watched Walker's face. He clearly wasn't having the same difficulty fixing a smile to it that she'd had whenever he'd talked glowingly to her about Sasha in the early days. He really *was* smiling. What he actually looked, more than anything, was relieved. It made Laura feel ill.

'Why don't we have you guys round for dinner next week?' Sasha suggested. She nudged Walker. 'You could do that incredible curry you made, couldn't you?' Walker grinned proudly. When she'd first moved into 8A, Laura thought, pasta with ketchup and grated cheese stirred through it had been about the limits of his culinary repertoire.

'I'll have a look and send you some dates,' she said non-committally. 'Sounds fun!'

At Sasha's insistence they group-hugged when they said goodbye, with Harrison in the middle. All three of them were significantly taller than her and she was swallowed up by the huddle. Laura watched Walker and Sasha meandering down the platform towards the exit with their arms around each other's shoulders.

'Nice couple,' Adam said cheerfully. He pushed his hands into his pockets. 'So, I tried to find out when the next train's coming but the boards are all out. Must be the heat or something.'

'I'll check,' Laura said quickly. As she got her phone out, switched it back on again and opened the app she could feel him watching her.

'You OK?' he asked after a while, putting a hand on her shoulder. 'You look like you've seen a ghost.'

'Fine.' Her eyes had started to swim; she blinked the tears back as she scrolled through the list of station names. 'Just ... hay fever.'

'Yeah, the pollen's really bad this year.' He patted her back, as though she had hiccups, then took a breath. 'I keep meaning to say, my parents are here next weekend – they go to the Royal Academy Summer Exhibition every year, it's sort of a tradition. Anyway, we were going to have an early dinner together on Saturday ... and I was thinking, maybe you could come too? We wouldn't have to go to look at the art with them or anything like that. We could do something just the two of us afterwards.'

Walker had sent her a message. A single sentence, as stiff as his hug.

I'm really happy it's all worked out for you.

She swallowed; there was a dry, bitter taste in her mouth, like nail-varnish remover.

'I'd love to,' she said.

***

'Hey, listen to this,' Walker had called out from the living-room floor on a Friday evening four years earlier, picking up one of his guitars. He looked up at her and grinned, then barred a chord and started picking out a series of notes that trailed and wound their way around each other like climbing roses.

Laura had watched him from the doorway, wrapping her lanyard around her finger. This Walker was the one she liked best – the one who lost hours experimenting with riffs, who sometimes forgot to get dressed. For just over a month they'd been living together at 8A with Aoife, a surveyor who bought five microwave lasagne on a Monday and stoically ate her way through them for the rest of the week, for just over a month.

After their break-up Walker and Laura stayed friends on Facebook – Laura hadn't been able to bring herself to cut that final tie and Walker wasn't the type to delete anyone – and she'd watched as he moved to Liverpool, Bristol and then, finally, to London. She'd been sitting in a tiny, mould-speckled bedroom on the other side of the city that somehow cost half of what she took home from her temporary job uploading content to a DIY website each month, when she'd seen that he'd posted an advert for a spare room in his flat. It looked cosy and lived in. Before she had a chance to think better of it, she'd taken a deep breath and sent him a message asking if it was still available. They met for a drink in a pub behind Kings Cross and she was amazed by how easy seeing him again felt – he really seemed pleased that she'd got in touch. She gave her notice on the mouldy room there and then. He'd been doing some work as a teaching assistant at a school, but it was the holidays now, so he was around a lot during the day, sleeping or noodling around on one of his ever-expanding collection of instruments. She loved getting in from work and finding him there – it felt like coming home in a way that unlocking the front door of her parents' house after school never had.

'How was your day?' he asked her once he'd put the guitar down. 'Did the *Bugle* ever call you back about that job you had the interview for?'

'They did, actually.' Laura stepped out of her shoes; the carpet at 8A was a migrainous swirl of browns and oranges, but she was already attached to it, like everything else in the flat. 'Today. I didn't get it, but they gave my CV to someone at one of the magazines who needs cover and she wants me to go in. Her name's Inge.'

'Yes! Brilliant! Ahh, come here!' He got to his feet and pulled her into a hug; she closed her eyes and breathed in, feeling the tension of the day ebb away.

'I've got some news too,' Walker said. 'The school I was at last term wants to put me through teacher training.' She let him go – he was smiling fit to burst, his eyes were shining. 'The money's good and the kids are really sweet. I just want to be able to get on with my life, you know?'

'So you'll be a teacher full-time?' Laura felt like someone had rearranged all the furniture in the room without asking her what she thought about it – she liked the set-up exactly as it was right now and she didn't want anything to change. 'What about your music?'

He shrugged. 'I can still do gigs, if anyone wants me. And even if they don't, it's not like I'll be giving it up totally – Krish in IT has said I can join his band. They're pretty good.'

She was being a bad friend – she needed to stop it, she told herself, right now, before she spoiled his happy mood. 'Well, that's brilliant,' she said, forcing herself to mirror his smile. 'We should celebrate!'

They finished a pack of Kopparbergs on the sofa and started on another. Aoife came home, microwaved the day's lasagne and took it into her bedroom. There was a James Bond film on TV, the one where Roger Moore goes into space. He was kissing a woman in a nightdress when Walker put his arm around Laura's shoulders. It was a surprise – they'd been scrupulously friends-only since she'd moved in – but it felt warm and familiar and *good*. She leaned into him, closing her eyes. Their foreheads were almost touching when a sharp thought pierced the haze.

If she had him, she would lose him. If she didn't, then she couldn't.

She shuffled away. He gave her a gently quizzical look.

'I just don't want things to get messy,' she said quickly. 'Mess ...' she couldn't get it to make sense – and it wasn't just the alcohol. What she'd felt a second ago resisted being put into words '... is bad.'

Walker gave her an affectionate nudge. '*Ooh, mess is bad,*' he said, laughing. 'You sound like Jamie.' She put her bottle down and hit him with one of the sofa cushions.

'Well, we're *definitely* not having sex now,' she said. She drained her bottle. 'It's late. I should go to bed. You should too.'

The next morning Laura found a mug of coffee and a plate of toast outside her room. They didn't talk about any of it again until the night before Walker and Sasha moved out.

***

She and Harrison had been gone, Laura realised with dismay when she got back to Stonybrook Street, for less than four hours. The afternoon had compressed itself into a series of horrible GIFs: Lil's furiously folded arms, Adam shouting at Harrison, Walker and Sasha's his-and-hers John Lewis bags. She hovered on the step; she could see all the way through to the garden, where Jamie was lying face down on a towel in a pair of bikini bottoms, her fingers spread so she'd tan between them.

'Please, please be quiet,' Laura whispered to Harrison, taking his collar off so it wouldn't jangle. 'If she sees you like this we're both toast, OK? We need to get you into the bath.' Harrison, who'd been plodding and subdued ever since they'd got on the second train, let her shepherd him up the stairs.

The bathroom was a copy of the one from the hotel in the Maldives that Jamie and Whit had stayed in on their honeymoon. The tiles were sealed with a custom-mixed sky-blue grout and the outside of the roll-top bath was painted in a matching shade. Harrison watched Laura stolidly from the mat as she started filling it. When she moved to pick him up, he reversed towards the door.

'It would have been great if you'd decided you didn't like water a couple of hours ago, you know,' she said, cornering him and lifting him in. As she kneeled down to take the shower head off its perch she had a flashback to Sasha tracing the shape in Walker's palm. She put her head on the side of the bath and banged it half-heartedly against the enamel, trying to dislodge the image.

'Idiot,' she mumbled. 'Idiot, idiot, idiot.' Harrison sidled up to her and rested his muzzle on her hair. As she started washing him she could feel tears pricking at the back of her eyes; she tried to concentrate on sluicing away the grime, lifting each of his paws in turn so she could clean under them. There was something comforting about the way the water flattened his coat, smoothing out all the kinks and whirls in it.

She heard the floorboards creak – Whit was standing in the doorway, wearing a checked baseball cap.

'Hey, kid! You're home early!' He spotted Harrison, sitting in the now-murky water. 'What happened?'

'He jumped in one of the ponds,' Laura said, trying to block him from view as she switched the shower off. 'Don't tell Jamie.'

Whit mimed zipping his mouth shut. 'Scout's honour,' he said, tickling Harrison under his chin. 'What are we going to do with you, huh? Huh?' Harrison whirred his tail around like an outboard motor.

Whit had a short attention span; Laura expected him to zoom straight back out of the bathroom once he'd finished fussing over Harrison. But when she looked up again he was still hovering, trying not to look at her. Something was coming, she could feel it – and it wasn't anything good.

'So ... Jamie called your mum while you were out.' He started flicking the door handle; Laura fought the urge to stick her fingers in her ears. 'She said she really misses both her girls.'

'We miss her too.' She turned back to Harrison, hoping Whit would take the hint. But he stayed where he was, shifting his weight from foot to foot.

'She wants you to meet the friend she's staying with,' he went on. There was a long pause. 'It's, uh, a guy, apparently. If you catch my drift.'

Laura started frantically patting her pocket.

'Oh, I think someone's calling me,' she lied. 'Sorry.' Her heart was pounding. It wasn't hearing it that was the problem. It was knowing that someone else knew – the way that transformed it from being something she could turn away from if she needed to, into a thing that she'd be expected to think about, talk about, maybe even *do something* about.

'Cool, no worries!' Whit looked as relieved as she felt. 'Hey, I found this great Netflix documentary about the secret lives of bears – want to watch it with me later?'

'Sounds good! Thanks, Whit!' She dug her phone out; she didn't trust herself to turn around again. Adam had messaged her.

Hey, just booking somewhere for Saturday. Steak OK? xx

She sighed and all the irritation she'd felt on the station platform came flooding back. His message was so blandly cheerful: it was like the afternoon hadn't happened. And she knew that when they next met he'd be as polite as he had been on their first date. If opposites really did attract then she could see why Cupid's model had matched her with him – where she was full of doubts and questions about the world, he was totally certain. Her chaos (in theory) took the edge off his regimented life. But maybe – she circled the thought, not quite able to look directly at it – there was only so far you could go with someone who was so different from you.

She clicked out of the chat, back into her contacts. She found herself scrolling through them until she reached C – for Cass. His WhatsApp photo was of the canal (Adam's was the same as his LinkedIn picture). There had been a handful – fine, more than a handful – of times over the past week and a bit when she'd tapped on Cass's name and started writing him a message, before quickly deleting it and switching her phone off, as though he could somehow see her through her screen. This time, she didn't stop.

> Laura:
> *There's something I've been wondering*
> *You know Cupid's whole thing*
> *About predicting romantic chemistry*

Two grey ticks appeared. He'd switched his last-online time off, so she had no idea if he was even looking at his phone. She put hers on the toilet seat, facing upwards. She wouldn't look at it for at least five minutes, she told herself, squeezing shampoo between her palms and lathering Harrison's fur. She tried to concentrate on the task, but after about thirty seconds her eyes strayed back to the screen. The ticks had turned blue; her heart knocked against her ribs. *Online*, it said underneath his name. Now he was typing – and typing, and typing. She held her breath for what felt like a million years.

> Cass:
> *yes …*
> *(hello)*

Harrison snorted and shook himself, splattering the walls with foam.

'Sorry, sorry.' Laura quickly rinsed him off, then went back to her phone. Her heart was still thumping.

> Laura:
> *Well*
> *I mean*
> *It sounds great on paper*

> *Being able to work out exactly who'll like who*
> *But what about surprises?*

Cass:
what about them?

> Laura:
> *Well ... they're nice, aren't they?*
> *A good thing*
> *In relationships?*

She waited. He went offline, then came back online again. Nothing. Had she gone too far? It felt like that game she used to pester Jamie and her friends to let her play, the one with the mule you had to load up with guitars and frying pans without triggering the spring that made it buck everything off.

A message appeared, then another. Relief flooded her whole body; her toes, which she hadn't even realised she was tensing, unclenched.

Cass:
sometimes ...
i've been surprised by a few things recently

Quickly, before she had a chance to think better of it, she shuffled across the floor so she was behind Harrison, held her phone at arm's length and took a photo of them. He had water dripping from his ears and looked annoyed, but she looked quite nice under the circumstances, and she liked the idea of her face being on Cass's screen. She pressed send. A reply appeared almost instantly.

Cass:
*now that **was** a surprise*
very cute

Cass:
(the pup, obviously)

Laura grinned. She was racking her brains for a reply when another message from Adam popped up at the top of her screen.

Found a really good OpenTable deal
Three courses + a glass of wine for £24.99!

She swatted the notification away and went back to Cass.

Laura:
Your turn

Cass:
not sure about a dog
will ducks do?

A pixelated square appeared, the little circle within it spinning agonisingly slowly as it loaded. There was Cass, lying on the roof of his boat, shielding his eyes from the sun with one hand. She went into her gallery so she could zoom in, mapping his face: the bump on the bridge of his nose, the weekend's worth of stubble, the tiny depression of a healed-over piercing in his left ear.

Laura:
I thought you lot burst into flames if you
went out in the sun?

Cass:
ah, no, that's vampires, not software engineers
we're both nocturnal
but vampires are better dressed

anyway
i'm from california
sun-proof

She wasn't doing anything wrong, she told herself. They were just friends, having a fun conversation. Adam probably had friends he had fun conversations with too. It was fine.

Laura:
I like your boat

Cass:
thanks!

Cass:
i was thinking of taking her up past regent's park next saturday actually

Cass:
it's a really nice trip

Cass:
probably more fun if there are two of you

'You guys almost done?' Whit hollered from the other side of the door. 'I'm making nachos!' Laura dropped her phone on the mat and pulled the plug out.

Just friends, she told herself firmly. *Nothing wrong with that.*

'Two seconds!' she yelled. She yanked one of the towels off the rail and swaddled Harrison in it. His eyes stared accusingly out at her as she patted him dry.

Chapter 12

similarity metric (noun): a function that computes the alikeness of two things

'This is your fault,' Jamie said to Whit, tipping Harrison's untouched kibble back into the Tupperware box. Whit, who was plating up the pancakes he'd just made, stopped whistling.

'How is it my fault?'

'You keep feeding him stuff from the fridge. No, don't look at me like that – there was an untouched sachet of almond butter in there when I went to bed and I'm the only person in this house who eats them. Anyway, now he's got a taste for it and he doesn't want his actual food.'

Whit sprinkled the pancakes with blueberries, then opened the Tupperware and sniffed. 'Would you eat this junk? I wouldn't.' He crouched down by Harrison's spot on the floor and rubbed his stomach. 'Poor guy. Maybe we should get him to the vet.' Laura, who was sitting at the table painting her nails an uncharacteristic red to match her uncharacteristically short dress, could feel him trying his hardest not to look at her. 'He might have ... picked something up. From a pond. Or something.'

Harrison coughed like the heroine of a Victorian novel. Laura looked away. Although she didn't want to admit it, she was worried too. But that awareness was jostling un-successfully for space in her mind with the fact that in three hours' time she was going to be on Cass's boat. The closer it got, the harder it became to keep telling herself that her feelings about this were the same as they would be about any other summer day-trip. She dangled her un-painted hand for Harrison, who gave it an enthusiastic lick; she felt a tiny bit less bad.

Jamie sat down at the table with her coffee (black, two sugars; she always waited until nobody was watching to spoon them in). 'You're meeting Adam's family tonight, aren't you? Where are you going?'

'Just somewhere in Covent Garden.' When they'd seen each other on Wednesday he'd told her the restaurant's name, but she'd completely forgotten it. Right now the prospect of sitting down for a meal with his parents seemed remote and colourless. If she was being honest, she'd barely thought about the dinner all week.

Jamie was watching her. 'Are you excited?'

'Of course.' She quickly slicked more red onto her thumbnail. She could feel her sister's eyes boring into her.

'You don't look very excited.'

'Well, I am,' Laura snapped. 'What do you want me to do, cartwheels?'

'Ladies, please! Breakfast is served!' Whit put a plate of pancakes down in front of Laura with a flourish – he'd arranged strawberries on the top to make them look like smiley faces and dusted them with icing sugar. Once he'd put his own plate on the table he got his phone out and took a picture of it.

'You two go ahead,' he said, frowning as he tapped the screen. 'Just going to send this to Adam before I forget – he asked for my recipe.'

Laura froze with her mouth full. 'Wait, what?' she managed to get out. 'You're messaging Adam?' Jamie gave her a flinty *manners, please* look; Laura swallowed with difficulty. 'How do you even have his number?'

'Oh, he gave it to me at the barbecue,' Whit said breezily, putting his phone away again and sitting down between them. 'He's got mine too. We talk when there's a game on – you know, guy stuff.'

When Adam had come to Jamie and Whit's party, Laura had been so pleased by how they'd taken to him. The three of them getting along had made her feel like she was finally her older sister's equal. Suddenly, though, it felt horribly claustrophobic, like they were all hemming her in.

'Were you going to tell me you'd become pen pals?' she asked Whit. He looked slightly hurt.

'Would you rather we pretended he didn't exist?' Jamie asked her, letting her hand rest briefly on her husband's knee to show she was on his side.

Laura shook her head, silently admonishing herself. She hated to admit it, but Jamie was right – it was a nice thing for your family to keep in touch with your boyfriend. Obviously.

'Of course not,' she said quickly. 'It just feels like a bit of an ... escalation, that's all.'

Harrison's nose periscoped up from under the table.

'See,' Jamie said, watching him sniff the pancakes. 'He's fine. Everything's fine.'

***

Everyone in Camden was kissing. As Laura came out of the Tube and started walking up the High Street she felt like she was wading into a sea of couples, most of them teenagers in patterned neon cycling shorts with rainbow hair, tied into human knots outside Urban Outfitters and the Electric Ballroom. She reached for her phone to check the time and saw that she'd got two voicemails while she was underground. She quickly ducked into a doorway and called her answerphone.

'Hiiiii!' Hearing Nush's voice in her ear always made Laura tense up, but right now it felt like the other woman had actually jumped out at her from behind a bin; Laura instinctively checked over her shoulder to make absolutely sure Nush wasn't there. 'Happy Saturday, babe! Just thought we could have this week's check-in at some point today? Call me back! Love to Adam!'

Nush would be expecting her to ring back right away and it wouldn't go down well if she didn't. Although their chats had all been pleasant since the *functional dating space* one, the flash of cold steel she'd seen then was always there in the back of Laura's mind, making her uneasy. But she was already ten minutes late to meet Cass. Nush, she decided, was a problem that she could deal with tomorrow. She pressed three to delete the message. The next one started playing automatically.

'Love, it's me,' came her mum's voice. Laura instinctively moved the phone away from her ear – the rest of the message travelled through the air faintly to her, its edges dulled.

'Jamie and I had a chat yesterday and I was hoping you and me could too, if ... Anyway! I was saying to Jamie that I thought it would be nice if the four of us could meet up for a drink in town. Have a think. Lots of love. Bye now.'

Laura deleted the message. *The four of us.* She wanted it to be the three of them plus ... well, whoever he was. The man who drank Schweppes and was into ornamental stone frogs. She really didn't want any of that stuff leaking into her afternoon with Cass. Instead of calling her mum back she went into their WhatsApp chat and started recording a voice note.

'Hi, Mum!' She sounded fake-cheerful, like she was dialling into a Zoom call for work. She slid her thumb across the screen to cancel it and tried again. 'Hi, Mum – it's me. Listen, I … I'm busy all day but we could speak tomorrow? Or next week. I've got quite a lot on at the moment. But a drink sounds nice! I love you too. Bye.'

Laura screwed her eyes shut, balling her free hand into a fist. When she opened them again, she saw that one of the kissing couples had broken apart and were sharing a takeout pint of what looked like it might be cider.

Cider! She would buy some and drink it with Cass, she decided. It was the perfect weather for it.

She ducked into the off licence opposite and grabbed six stubby brown bottles, checking they were vegan-friendly before she took them up to the till – she seemed to have developed a superhuman memory for everything he'd told her about himself. She headed back outside with them clinking in a blue plastic bag and started walking, faster now. The bridge was just ahead of her and under that was the lock – she scanned the crowd twitchily for him as she crossed over onto the cobbles. There he was: sitting on a bollard across the water from her with the sleeves of his t-shirt rolled up to his shoulders in a concession to the weather. He waved; her insides flip-flopped.

'Ahoy!' he called out as she approached. She gave him a clumsy salute with the arm that was holding the bottle bag; they clanged as they crashed into each other

'I'm not even going to ask what you've got in there,' he said, getting to his feet. 'You look very summery. Love the red.'

'You too!' She gave her dress a self-conscious tug; he seemed about five thousand times more relaxed than she felt. He smiled and led her down the towpath.

'We're just here – I thought I'd spare you the locks so I brought her up this morning from St Pancras. That's my home mooring, but as long as I keep paying the rent on the space, I can pretty much take her wherever I like.' He smiled. 'I can never get over how peaceful it is – you know, there's actually a bit under the Caledonian Road that's so quiet people go there to fish. I love it there.'

There were multiple boats tied to every mooring – a kind of floating shed with tarpaulin for a roof was butting up against a massive, Art Deco-luxe barge with a recycling box on the deck full of empty champagne bottles. Some of the boats were so damp and mossy that they seemed to be cresting organic-ally out of the water like hump-backed whales; others looked like they'd only been sailed out of the showroom five minutes ago. Which camp would Cass be in? Laura wondered.

He stopped in front of a narrowboat and dug in his pocket for his keys. It was a surprisingly old-fashioned one, painted in fruit pastille red, forest green and sunshine yellow. There was an abbreviated deck at each end – the one at the back had a funny kind of wicker enclosure around it, like a deconstructed picnic hamper.

'This is her,' Cass said, unlocking a gate and jumping aboard. 'My one and only – I bought her last summer. Best money I've ever spent.' Laura tilted her head to read the name painted on the side.

'Did you seriously call your boat ... *Puddleduck*?'

He grinned, holding out a hand to her across the water. 'She came with the name – and I'm American, remember, I love all that old-timey shit. Mind the gap.'

He was waiting, beckoning her with a smile. Laura put her hand in his, supernaturally sensitive to the pressure of his fingers as they tightened around hers and the tension in his forearm as he pulled her towards him. Having a crush, she thought as she stepped across the gap, was a bit like being the kind of stoned that caused you to lose an entire afternoon staring at your own toes in the bath. Everything was suddenly so textured, so *interesting*.

'Welcome aboard,' Cass said, going over to the dashboard and starting to flick switches. She leaned against the wicker enclosure around the deck and watched as he turned another key in the ignition; she felt something rumbling into life underneath her feet.

'Two seconds, OK?' he called over his shoulder. 'The engine just needs to warm up.'

He disappeared into the body of the boat. Laura squinted after him into the darkness. There was a galley kitchen with a campfire kettle on the hob and a wood-burning stove with a chimney that poked up through the roof; Cass was looking for something in one of the cupboards. Further down she could make out a throw-covered sofa pushed against one wall, a chair and a table with a desktop Mac on it; against the other, right at the back, a tantalisingly open door leading to another cabin. There was no evidence of anybody else's presence.

'Where were you living before?' she called through the hatch, trying to memorise the scene so she could comb through it later for clues.

'Before before? Oakland, then San Francisco. Have you been?' Laura shook her head, feeling very unworldly. 'It's gone downhill. Honestly, my advice would be to just drink fifteen dollars' worth of cold brew in the Apple store and save yourself the fare.' He shut the cupboard and tossed her a bottle opener. 'I moved here a couple of years ago – for the weather, obviously.'

Laura's eyes strayed involuntarily over his shoulder to the cabin. The bed was unmade and the duvet was distractingly rucked up. She couldn't quite stop herself from imagining him waking up with it tangled around him, yawning, stretching lazily . . .

She was saved from that train of thought by her phone buzzing at her from under its swaddling in her bag. She dug it out: Lil.

'I've just watched Bouncy getting stuck in a revolving door,' she said as soon as Laura answered. (Lil had a habit of repeatedly ringing if you didn't pick up the first time; her record was fifteen missed calls over the course of a single trip to the cinema.) She was clearly about to launch into a story, which was good because it meant Laura wouldn't really have to say anything. She'd obviously have to tell Lil about this at some point – but tell her what exactly?

'*The* Bouncy?' she asked, playing for time. Cass was sitting on the narrow steps that led down into the body of the boat, watching her with an amused look on his face. She widened her eyes in warning, miming a cutting motion across her throat. He put his hand on the top of the open hatch door and started drumming his fingers audibly on it.

'No, the other terrible person with exactly the same nickname. He was coming out of the Streatham Homebase with this big bag of fertiliser and it got jammed in the gap – they had to slash it open to get him out and it went all over his shoes. He went *purple* – like Barney the fucking dinosaur or something. I was going to film it for you but I was laughing too much.'

'I'm imagining a whoopee cushion deflating,' Laura said distractedly, in a voice that felt like it was at least an octave higher than her normal one.

'Exactly!' There was a pause. 'Where are you? Sounds . . . splashy.'

'Camden.' Cass started rocking the hatch door cartoon-ishly on its hinges, making it squeak; the corners of his mouth were twitching. 'I'm, er, going to the dentist.'

'In *Camden*? You're not getting your teeth filed into fangs, are you, Morrison? I keep telling you, body modification might be having a moment but it's not a great long-term choice ...'

'Very funny,' Laura said. Cass got to his feet and crossed the deck, giving her a wry glance as he passed that made her stomach somersault. She watched as he crouched down to grab the mooring rope and started deftly unwinding it from the bollard. 'Look, I have to go.'

'OK, love you.' She could hear Dora's piping, insistent voice in the background. 'Small fry says she does as well.'

'Love you both too – I'll speak to you later.' Laura hung up, rodenty guilt gnawing at her. Cass was laughing.

'You really missed your calling as a spy, you know that?' he said, still working at the rope. He didn't seem especially interested in who she'd been talking to or why she'd lied about where she was, which was a huge relief. He chucked the rope over his shoulder and stood up. 'Ready to go?'

The boat started to drift towards the centre of the canal. As Cass navigated, Laura surreptitiously tried out various poses against the wicker – eventually she settled on one foot up against it. She got two of the ciders out of her bag and offered one to him. He shook his head.

'Moving this thing around is a bit like trying to get a bunch of trolleys across a parking lot. I'll have one when we're moored, though.'

The engine rumbled away under her feet. Her mind had gone totally blank. It felt impossible that she was actually here, with him – and that they had the whole afternoon together.

'So ...' she began, awkwardly patting the boat's flank. 'How many miles to the gallon do you get with this thing?'

Cass burst out laughing. 'Seriously?'

'What? What's so funny?'

'You're *painfully* British, you know that?' He grinned. 'You're a journalist – come on, ask me some hard-hitting questions. Get some more background for your piece.'

'I mean, if you're sure you can handle it ...' She had a bolstering gulp of cider. 'OK, fine. Well, you know all about my family from Cupid – why don't you tell me about yours?'

Cass shrugged. 'Honestly, there isn't much to tell,' he said, steering them away from the bank. 'I'm an only child and I don't have much to do with my folks. They got divorced when I was young and shuttled me between them after that – neither of them had what you'd call a fixed address. I was kind of ... camping a lot. For a while I was actually sleeping in a bath with a quilt over me because there weren't enough beds in my dad's girlfriend's place.' He swept an arm across the deck. 'Maybe that's why I like it on here. Water.'

They were passing the Pirate Castle; kayakers sculled past them, sleek as sharks. Laura thought about a miniature version of Cass curled up in a bathtub and felt her heart clench like a fist.

'God, I'm really sorry,' she said. She glanced across at him sympathetically, but he was smiling, no trace of pain on his face.

'Don't be – I'm incredibly well adjusted. See?' He crossed his eyes and laughed. What would it be like, Laura wondered enviously, to be the kind of person who could just leave the past behind them? No what-ifs, no regrets. She swigged, letting the liquid prickle at the inside of her mouth.

'I googled you,' she said, after swallowing most of it in one go. 'I read your PhD.'

'The whole thing?' Cass raised his eyebrows. 'Now who's the stalker?'

'Just the first page.' He was looking directly into her eyes and her face flushed – it felt like she'd lost all control of her body's thermostat. 'Did you like doing it?'

'Bits of it.' He nudged them to the left. 'And it means I get paid pretty well to do something I'd probably do for fun anyway, which is nice. Remind me what you studied?'

'Medieval stuff. I did my dissertation on King Arthur's court – Guinevere and Lancelot.' A group of people were doing paddleboard yoga to their left, positioned strategically in front of the graffiti on the bank to their right; a man was photographing them from a stepladder on the opposite one. *'JUST PRETEND I'M NOT HERE!'* he was bellowing.

'Ah, that's right – I remember Nush saying.' Cass gave a wry smile. 'They had a fling, didn't they?'

'They did.' Laura lifted the bottle to her lips, smiling back at him. 'It was fine for a bit, then it all got a bit … awkward.'

'I'm sure that's exactly the word Chaucer used to describe the situation.'

'Oh, *please*,' she said, rolling her eyes as she drank, 'Chaucer was *much* later.' The first cider, she realised, was already down to its foamy dregs; she opened the second, not wanting to break the spell. She honestly couldn't remember the last time she'd had an instant rapport like this with someone. 'Finally! Something you don't know about.'

'Well, enjoy it while it lasts,' Cass said, laughing as he steered them around a knot of weeds. A couple of seconds later they started gliding into the cool shadow of a tunnel and he went quiet. The bottle's label was damp in her hand;

she started picking at it nervously, waiting for him to break the silence.

'I guess Guinevere wasn't as happy with Arthur as everyone thought she was,' he said finally. The words echoed, bouncing off the bricks. 'Then Lancelot came along and he was – what? Good-looking? Charming?' She could just about make out a raised eyebrow. 'No, wait, I've got it – really funny.'

'A dickhead?' Laura said. Cass laughed easily. She pressed the cold bottle against her forearm to keep herself in check. Something was gathering speed between them and it was making her nervous, not because she wasn't enjoying it, but because she was. Far too much. She looked away pointlessly, from the dark into the dark.

They emerged from the tunnel into a wide pool, with the floating Chinese restaurant that was in all the London guidebooks to the left of them and tightly packed ranks of deserted houseboats on the right. There was no other traffic passing through and the towpath was empty.

'Hey, can I ask you something personal?' Cass said casually.

She shifted nervously. 'Um, sure,' she said, trying to match his tone. 'Go ahead.'

'So, Nush was saying you told her that you used to live with your ex.' He steered them towards the centre of the pool. 'What happened there?'

***

On their last night as a three in 8A before Walker and Sasha left for Hammersmith, Laura had picked her way past the cardboard boxes to escape for 'dinner' with Lil in the pub (a bottle of wine and a torn-open bag of crisps on the table between them).

'It's just a bit shitty, isn't it, them leaving you in the lurch?' Lil said, brimming both of their glasses; Andreas had Dora for the night. She turned the now-empty bottle of wine upside down and stuck it in the bucket like a head on a spike. 'On the upside, you're never going to have to look at that carpet again. Come on, let's get another one.'

They did and the conversation looped back to the beginning again. Laura went along with it. Being angry was fine, but she worried that how she was actually feeling deep down wasn't. Losing the happiest home she'd ever had, being downgraded from one of the main characters in Walker's life to an occasional walk-on part – it had all thrown her into a state of blind panic.

Walker was alone in the empty living room when she got back, lying on the sofa with a plate of chocolate-covered dates next to him. There were boxes everywhere, taped shut. Laura went straight to the sink and started running water into the Tupperware box the dates had come from to give her something to do.

'Where's Sash then?' she asked, going for a measured tone but landing on 'wild-eyed interrogator' – the wine, she already knew, had been a mistake.

'Gone for a run before bed.' He pinged the edge of the plate. 'Want some? They've got almond butter in the middle.'

'No, thanks.' She squirted too much washing-up liquid into the box and started attacking it with Sash's frog-shaped pot scrubber. Its bright green face stared up at her mockingly, fixed in a stupid grin. She put her thumb in the centre and pressed down, trying to bend it out of shape, but the plastic was too solid. Her feelings were whirlpooling violently.

'Hammersmith?' she exploded. 'Seriously?' She heard a violent creak from the sofa; her outburst had jolted Walker upright.

'Wow, OK. I mean, I know it's not really your vibe, Laur, but it's nice round there.' She heard him chewing – he'd popped another date into his mouth. 'And it's great being close to the river. Sash really likes the Boat Race.'

'Why can't she just watch it on TV?' Laura could hear her voice rising. The frog had slipped out of her grasp; she chased it around the suds-filled sink. 'West London's shit. You're going to hate it.'

Walker shrugged. 'It wasn't my first choice, but relationships are about compromise, aren't they?'

'It isn't a compromise if one of you just turns themself into the other one,' Laura practically spat. She knew she was being horrible and that she should go to bed, but right now she didn't care – the hateful words were forcing their way out of her mouth, demanding to be said.

There was a pause; she heard him shifting his weight from one end of the sofa to the other. 'Maybe you just don't know how to do it,' he said slowly, weighing each part of the sentence out very carefully.

Laura spun around to face him. 'Do what?'

'Compromise.' He was staring at her, his face set. 'I mean, you have no idea how it actually works because you've never done it.' He was so placid normally, so reluctant to bring anything to a head – she couldn't remember the last time she'd seen him looking like this.

'Excuse me?' She picked up the dripping box and waved it at him. 'I'm literally doing your washing up right now – what's that? A compromise!'

'You broke up with me because … what was it? I was going to be away a lot and the trains were too expensive?' Walker shook his head grimly. 'Then I thought maybe we could give it another go after you moved in here, but you didn't even want to hear about it ...'

'So that's what this is really about, is it? You're fucking me over because of all that?' Laura gulped – she was suddenly finding it hard to breathe – and without any warning a huge sob escaped from her mouth. 'Look, I'm sorry, I didn't ... that wasn't why I ...'

'Hey.' He jumped off the sofa and rushed over to her. 'Hey, come on. Don't be like that.' His expression softened as he pulled her into a hug. 'I'm sorry too,' he whispered, stroking her hair. 'It's ancient history.'

That made her cry even more, because it was true and there was a stupid part of her that wished it wasn't. What might have happened, she wondered, if she hadn't been so terrified of it all going wrong? What if she'd ignored that voice in her head telling her that no good could come of it and had just let things between them unfold, rather than breaking up with him before he went on tour? Maybe it wouldn't have worked out, but maybe it would. Maybe they'd have been a couple who went the distance. She'd never know – and now she was going to lose him anyway. She squeezed her eyes shut, letting the tears scald her cheeks. When she opened them he was looking down at her sadly. She moved to kiss him and he quickly put a hand in front of his face to stop her, as though he'd been expecting it. That was the bit she always came back to – the worst bit.

'Laur, don't,' he said quietly, as he gently disengaged himself from her.

***

They turned out of the pool and started drifting up the canal towards the zoo. This stretch of it felt different: shaded by drooping trees and sound-tracked by hoots and shrieks. Laura watched a coot sticking its head into the mackerel-shimmering water, frantically flapping its feet in the air as it dived for weeds. She glanced across at Cass; he was steering them quietly, eyes fixed on the horizon. He was the first person she'd told the whole story to – even Lil had got a cleaned-up version.

'Can I have a go?' Laura asked, even though the thought of actually being responsible for a thing this size made her palms damp – she just wanted to break the silence.

'Sure.' He stepped back from the tiller, making space for her. 'Remember that when you push it to the left, the boat goes right and vice versa, OK?'

'Thanks, Captain Haddock.' The tiller was heavy under her hand. She couldn't look at him.

'You think there's something wrong with me, don't you?' she said after a while. They were heading into a carpet of algae that was disturbingly thick and solid-looking. Cass was behind her, pulling a cider out of the bag.

'No,' he said evenly, popping it open. 'I definitely don't think that.' He was back in her field of vision now, leaning on the wicker.

'Well, Nush does,' she said, without looking round at him. 'My sister too, actually.' She tried to laugh, but it came out sounding strangled and fake. 'I guess everyone does! I mean, it's not normal to be twenty-nine and never to have had a long-term relationship, is it?' Now she'd started she couldn't seem to stop. 'Sometimes I feel like my life is so … I don't know. Small. When I look back it's just … Crumbs. Nothing solid. Nothing that's lasted. But whenever something looks like it might, I do something to screw it up. Or I don't do something and it gets fucked up anyway. I'm just completely clueless about what it actually means to be in love, to be honest with you. I've got no idea how anybody does it.'

Cass stepped forward. 'Let's park up for a bit,' he said gently, putting his hand back on the tiller, close to hers but not quite touching it. He steered them towards a metal loop on the bank and tied the boat to it. Once they were moored, he sat down on the deck with his legs crossed. She tried to do the same opposite him but ended up knocking over an empty bottle.

'Sorry,' she said, fumbling for it, still finding it almost impossible to look at him – she couldn't believe she'd just delivered that speech, to him of all people. 'I've had quite a lot of cider.'

'I should catch you up, in that case,' Cass said, smiling at her as he swigged his. He stuck his little finger out in a pantomime of politeness. 'Cheers.'

They sat quietly like that for a while, Laura letting the canal's sounds wash over her.

Cass was the first one to speak.

'You know, I saw *Hamlet* at the theatre the other night,' he said. 'He was having all the same problems as you.'

Laura couldn't help laughing. 'Was he really?'

'Yeah, he was.' Cass reached for another bottle of cider. 'I mean, he's stuck, right? He can't seem to move on with his life. Because ...'

'... a ghost told him to kill his uncle?' Laura raised her eyebrows.

'Not that bit. What I meant is, he's got this messed up family, the entire court's nuts and he's looked at them all and gone: *You know what? Thanks, but I think I'll pass on all this stuff.* But because he runs away from everything he misses out on a lot. Like Ophelia. Anyway, what I'm trying to say – not very well, clearly – is that nobody gets through life without getting hurt.'

It was like he'd taken everything, turned it over in his hands so he could see what it was made of and carefully given it back to her – only now it didn't feel hopeless. It actually felt almost ... hopeful.

'And that's all we've got time for, folks – take care of yourselves and each other,' Cass said with a grin, breaking the silence. Laura laughed again, but the shadows on the boat were getting longer and she realised it was getting late – far later than she'd meant to stay. She'd reached the stage of intoxication where the world had narrowed itself down to her immediate surroundings.

'OK, my turn to ask you a question,' she said, reaching behind her for another bottle.

'I'm an open book.' Cass spread his palms on his knees. 'By Shakespeare, obviously.'

She prised the cap off. 'You have access to almost everyone in the country, right?' she began tentatively. 'At Cupid, I mean.' He nodded. 'So what happens if someone comes to you and says, *OK, find me my perfect match* – and you do the search, but the person at the top of the list isn't ... actually single?'

'I was hired to create a model that matches single people with each other,' Cass said. 'That's the principle we built the whole thing around – trying to get it to do something else would be like driving a car down a runway and asking it to take off.' He shrugged. 'I mean, it learns as it goes, so I guess there's a chance it *might* throw up a kind of false positive early on – where somebody the data suggests is single actually isn't – but if that were to ...'

'But it happens in real life all the time, doesn't it?' Laura cut him off; she knew she was really playing with fire now but she couldn't stop herself. 'Someone might be with someone, but then they meet someone else they like more and ...'

Cass put his bottle down on the deck. 'And?' he said. 'What happens then?'

Outwardly, nothing had changed, but inside she was fizzing – like sherbet dissolving not on her tongue but everywhere. Her eyes alighted on the rolled-up sleeve of his t-shirt; she suddenly felt compelled to close the gap between them.

'I like what you've done here with the customisation,' she said, reaching out to touch it. 'A style expert as well as a theatre critic, I see.' She applied the tiniest amount of pressure – she could feel his skin through it and his steady pulse through that.

'Coding, but make it fashion.' Cass glanced down at her fingers on his arm. 'It would look good on you, I think.'

She drew her hand back and flicked her eyes down to the deck. Cass put his head on one side, studying her. Then, slowly and deliberately, he reached across and placed his hand over hers, interlacing their fingers.

'So, this isn't an invitation I extend to everyone who comes on a boat trip with me ...' he said quietly. 'But would you like to stay for dinner tonight?'

Even for a habitual sign-misreader like her, there was absolutely no ambiguity in his voice or his body language.

'I ...' She wondered if her heart had actually stopped.

'Look, I know this isn't exactly the plan,' he went on, his fingertips pressing gently against her knuckles. 'But I think about you, Laura. All the time.'

Every single muscle in her body was screaming at her to say yes. She let her fingers relax into his, just for a second – then, suddenly, she had an image of Adam waiting for her outside the restaurant. Tapping his foot anxiously on the kerb, scanning the Covent Garden crowds for her, getting increasingly worried. He'd never in a million years imagine she was with someone else.

'Fuck.' She abruptly pulled her hand away. 'Cass, I can't. Look, I'm sorry. I have to go. I have to be somewhere.'

She scrambled to her feet, snatched her bag off the deck and hurled herself onto the bank.

Chapter 13

exploding gradient problem (noun): *the tendency for gradients to become surprisingly steep*

Laura had always had her own personal sliding scale of lateness. Anything up to fifteen minutes was basically on time. Fifteen to twenty-five minutes was quite late and quite bad, and anything beyond that was very late and very bad. Right now, puffing through Covent Garden towards the restaurant, she could feel herself emerging from the far side of the final category into an entirely new and terrible one. You couldn't cut through the zoo if you didn't have a ticket, so she'd had to go all the way around its perimeter to get out of Regent's Park, being eyeballed by meerkats. Adam had booked dinner for six o'clock; by the time she'd got to the Tube it was already ten to. She'd known it was going to be impossible for her to get there even remotely on time, but that had been the least of her worries. She felt like she'd swallowed a grenade.

She could see the restaurant on the other side of the road, a fancy French place with curtained windows and a heavy front door. It was the sort of venue she'd have been uncomfortable in whatever the circumstances, but right now it felt impossibly daunting. She had no idea how she was going to make it through a single minute with Adam, let alone an entire dinner. He'd been calling her and she hadn't been able to bring herself to pick up. Surely what had just happened – or nearly happened; she was desperately clinging onto the technical difference – was written all over her face?

She stopped to get her breath back; whenever she drank in the middle of the day it seemed to slacken the world around her, making it soupy and hard to wade through. She dragged the back of her hand across her eyelids, which were itchy with sweat, and there he was behind them – Cass, his fingertips pressing against her knuckles. *I think about you, Laura. All the time.*

She checked the time on her phone and saw, with a sort of detached horror, that it was coming up for half-past six. Barely a second later the screen lit up with another incoming call. It was Nush – Laura had totally forgotten to ring her back. Her throat felt like an invisible hand was squeezing it. Nush was the last person in the universe she wanted to speak to right now, but her brain and her fingers didn't seem to be communicating very well. Before she could stop herself she'd answered.

'*There* you are,' Nush trilled. 'Got you! How are things, babe? What have you been up to today?'

Laura dug her nails hard into the palm of her phone-free hand, trying to erase the memory of how Cass's clear eyes had seen all the way through her.

'Oh, nothing really,' she babbled. 'I mean, just lots of stuff at home. Boring stuff.' A man in a Westminster City Council vest was sitting on the kerb next to a freshly painted double-yellow line, unwrapping a KitKat. 'I was, um, painting actually.'

'Nice!' There was a wet smack at the other end of the line, then a pop as a gum bubble burst. 'How's Adam? All good?'

'All good,' Laura repeated robotically. She could hear Nush's expectant breathing – she was obviously going to need a bit more than that if Laura wanted to get rid of her. 'I'm having dinner with his parents tonight,' she went on. 'First time! I'd really better go, actually ...'

'Go! Go!' Nush squealed. 'Ahh, I'm so pleased it's all going so well – not that I ever seriously thought it wouldn't, *obviously*, but ...' she paused ominously '... you know, sometimes people with low self-esteem can self-sabotage by derailing promising new relationships. And I'd hate that to happen to you, because you deserve to be happy! Anyway, I'll let you go! We're all right behind you! Kisses!'

She rang off. Laura peeled the phone away from her ear with clumsy hands. The *we* hung in the air – it had been enough to conjure Cass again, swigging casually from a bottle of cider this time. Laura closed her eyes and rolled her shoulders. Everything that had happened with him, she told herself firmly, she was leaving here, outside, in the past – where it belonged. And she'd worry about Nush later.

She saw Adam's back first: he was wearing a blazer. She tried to focus on it as she pushed the door open and shut everything else out, the way the life coach the *Bugle* had hired for Mental Health Awareness Week had showed them. *Describe something that you can see to yourself,* she'd cooed, while they tried not to imagine the dozens of emails piling up in their inboxes while they were away from their desks on compulsory relaxation training.

It's a very nice back, Laura thought. *A very nice back that belongs to Adam. Adam who is my boyfriend. My boyfriend who*

I definitely haven't cheated on. And who I'm definitely not going to cheat on.

His parents were sitting opposite him, facing the door. When they saw her they stood up in smiling unison.

'We were about to send out a search party!' Adam's dad announced. He gripped her hand. 'I'm Duncan. And you must be Laura!'

Looking at him, Laura had the eerie feeling that someone had pressed fast-forward on his son by thirty-five years. He had the same square jaw, brown eyes and healthy spots of pink on his cheeks – only his hair was iron grey all over, rather than just speckled with it like Adam's was, and his Scottish accent was slightly stronger. Her arm was spaghetti-limp.

'And I'm Diane,' Adam's mum said, tiptoeing forwards like a ballerina. 'We're so pleased to meet you, Laura.' She was tiny and dressed very neatly in pastels, with a fine gold chain sitting delicately above the neck of her cashmere cardigan. As she kissed her on both cheeks Laura had an image of Duncan proudly telling his friends that she 'hadn't let herself go'. (*No, stop it*, she told herself. These were nice people and she was going to have a nice time with them.)

'Great to meet you both!' Her voice didn't sound like hers. 'Sorry I'm so late!'

'What happened?' Adam asked her as she manoeuvred herself into the seat next to him; here they were, both being interviewed for the job of Mr and Mrs Fraser. He squeezed her hand; she forced herself to relax into it. 'Are you OK? I kept calling you ...'

'I was ... at the zoo.' If you were going to tell a lie, she'd found, it was safest to tell one that was almost the truth – but she still couldn't look at him while she was saying it.

'With Dora. She didn't want to leave the Insect House. She's very into ... bugs.'

'Now, this is your friend's little girl, isn't it?' Diane said, draping her napkin across her lap. 'Adam told us about your trip to Hampstead Heath – we're so looking forward to doing things like that with Euan when he's older.' She took a tiny sip of her sparkling water and smiled. 'That's Adam's sister's boy. Do your parents have any grandchildren, Laura?'

She shook her head; her mouth had gone dry. She felt like she was being buried up to her neck in wet sand.

'We've got to be at the Academy for seven-thirty, so we ordered your food for you,' Duncan said, summoning a waiter over. 'Adam said you eat everything. Yes, could we have the wine list? Laura, do you have any preference wine-wise?'

'As long as there's lots of it I'm happy!' she said, too loudly. Diane flinched. Laura glanced across at Duncan flipping purposefully through the list and tried to imagine her own dad doing the same thing in a place like this. It was impossible – she couldn't get the thought off the ground. She'd never even seen him drink wine. She picked up the bottle of water and was about to start pouring it into her glass when a waiter rushed over to do it for her. A flush of embarrassment crept up her neck.

'Now, you're from Hampshire, is that right?' Duncan said, peering over the top of the wine list at her. 'Some nice fishing spots around there. And the shooting's first class – though obviously it's not a patch on what we've got back home.'

'Oh, yeah. Of course.' The job-interview feeling was getting stronger and she was horribly conscious that everyone else at the table was stone-cold sober, unlike her. 'How about you guys?'

'Well, a few years back we moved out to East Lothian, to be a little closer to Muirfield, you know – for the golf,' Diane said. She leaned in conspiratorially. 'I shouldn't really tell you this, but Duncan's favourite to become the club's next Secretary.'

'Wow,' Laura said, hoping she sounded sufficiently impressed. Judging by Diane's tone this was a big deal, but she couldn't honestly say that she knew what it meant. Arranging the chairs before meetings? Making sure the biscuit tin was full? 'So he's an excellent typist, I assume?'

Diane blinked and Laura clocked her own misstep. 'Adam tells us you work for the *Bugle*, Laura,' she went on politely, performing surgery on her roll with the tip of the butter knife. 'That must be fascinating! Did you always want to be a writer?'

Laura nodded, trying to pull a piece off her own bread. It was the chewy kind that didn't tear easily. Her elbow hit one of her forks, which clattered off the side plate and onto the floor. God, these kinds of places were obstacle courses, she thought bitterly as she leaned down to grab it – they were built to trip up anyone who hadn't spent their whole life going to them. When she straightened up Adam was watching her with a puzzled expression on his face. Their eyes met, just for a second.

You're looking at me, she thought, straining to telepathically beam the words into his mind. *But can you really see me, Adam? Do you even want to?* He blinked – he was starting to look more put out than puzzled now. Nothing. The message wasn't getting through. Laura reluctantly turned back to Diane.

'When I did one of those careers quizzes in my last year at school it told me I should be a journalist,' she said. 'The other option it gave me was air traffic controller, but everyone got that so I thought I could probably ignore it.'

'Where did you go to school?' Duncan cut in. Laura bristled. People had been asking her that ever since her first day at university – what they actually wanted to know, she'd learned, was whether you were one of them.

'I didn't.' It came out snappier than she'd meant it to. 'I mean, I went to a school. But I didn't go to a *school*.'

A thick, fog-like silence blanketed the table.

'Excuse me for just a second,' Laura said, pushing her chair back.

***

The bathroom was all mirrors. They covered the walls, the fronts of the stalls and even the ceiling – everywhere Laura looked, there she was, pink from being out in the sun, still sweaty, her parting wonky where she'd tried to sort her hair out – and, yes, looking guilty as sin. She went into a cubicle and shut the door on herself.

People with low self-esteem can self-sabotage by derailing promising new relationships, Nush had said. Was that it? Was that why she was picking holes in everything Adam did and allowing her head to be turned by Cass? Was she just doing what she'd done with Walker all over again?

The pristine sinks gleamed at her as she walked out of the cubicle. She squared her shoulders in the mirror and took a deep breath. She was going to go back out there, she decided, stop being so negative and wow them. Really knock their socks off. They wouldn't know what had hit them.

***

She was nearly back at the table when she heard Diane – for such a softly spoken person her voice really carried.

Laura ducked behind a large potted plant so she could listen.

'Perhaps she's nervous,' she was saying sweetly to Duncan. 'She might not be used to places like this.'

The three of them had their heads together like a team at half-time discussing tactics. Adam was at the top of the triangle, facing his parents who sat on the opposite side of the table. He really did look just like Duncan, right down to the blazer and chinos, but there was something of Diane in him too, Laura thought – the politeness that kept everything nice and safe and bland. She could feel all the little shoots of resolve she'd been tending to in the bathroom starting to wither.

'You met her through some internet thing, didn't you?' Duncan asked Adam, who was looking down at the table-cloth. 'Well, if ...'

Laura didn't catch the rest of it; just then a waiter swept past her with a tray of plates balanced on the palm of one hand. He was weaving towards the table – *our table*, Laura thought, but it wouldn't stick; it felt even less like somewhere she had any kind of claim on now.

'Perfect timing!' Adam called out to her as she walked towards them. None of them had started eating yet – they were making a show of waiting for her, waving their manners in her face. Her glass had been topped up. Duncan had put a glossy Royal Academy brochure on the table and was leafing through it.

'We like to get the catalogue in advance so we know what to make a beeline for,' he said, picking up his cutlery and starting on his meat. 'I don't expect you had the chance to visit many of the big galleries when you were growing up, Laura?'

Laura looked down at her steak. She didn't actually have to say anything, she thought. She could just smile like she was doing now and then do something with her face that suggested she agreed with him. In fact, she could keep doing that for the rest of the meal – if she did, she'd almost certainly earn their grudging approval. She imagined them at the sinks in their hotel bathroom later, Diane taking her make-up off while Duncan flossed his teeth briskly, one of them saying to the other, *Well, it could have been worse.*

'Sorry?' she said, slicing; blood leaked out onto the plate, staining the mashed potato pink. 'I don't understand.'

Duncan smiled benignly. 'It's just that you weren't in a city,' he said, conveying a piece of meat to his mouth.

'Sometimes we got on trains to them.' Laura took a bite of her steak; it was delicious, obscenely so. 'In between drinking out of puddles and cleaning our teeth with twigs.' She arranged her face into a matching placid smile.

Adam pressed his leg against hers under the table, signalling a warning. She found she was quite enjoying the pressure of his tensed muscles against hers. The sensation of his touch had come unstuck from its meaning. She pressed back.

'The most extraordinary thing happened to us on the way here …' Diane began saying. The talk veered off into an actually not extraordinary at all story about trying to get a taxi on Marylebone High Street; Laura let them get on with it. She drank a lot of wine quickly. Adam, she noticed, was draining his glass much faster than he normally did too – usually he was only a couple of gulps in by the time she'd finished hers, but tonight he was matching her.

As soon as they finished eating the waiter whisked their plates away and replaced them with dessert menus. The conversation had moved on again and Adam was now talking about the beach near his parents' house, which was apparently very clean and home to several rare species of gull. The wind speeds, he was saying, were really something.

'Bella loved it there, didn't she, darling?' Diane said casually. She put her menu down. 'Would anyone like to share a chocolate mousse with me? I can never seem to manage a whole one!'

Duncan asked her something about where Jamie worked – she must have been too slow to reply (time was alternately crawling along and lurching forwards), because Adam answered for her.

'Ah, yes, a very well-respected firm,' Duncan was saying. 'And she's full-time there, is she? I suppose she can be, if they don't have children.'

Laura's eyes drifted towards the restaurant's glass front. She pictured something crashing through it, upending tables and scattering screaming diners.

'What do you mean?' she asked.

'Well, just that it's hard to have a high-powered career when you're a mother.' Duncan gave Diane's slender arm an approving pat. 'Diane made Adam and his sister a packed lunch every day, didn't you? And she never missed a sports match.' Diane's cheeks pinkened with pleasure.

'I actually think it would be Whit making the packed lunches,' Laura said, putting her menu down. 'In fact, I'm pretty sure he'd be doing most of the work at home – he's much better at all that stuff. And Jamie's definitely better at the law stuff.'

There was that infuriating, indulgent smile again; a teacher humouring a child who'd asked why you couldn't just print more money so everyone had enough. Laura knew she ought to leave it alone but she couldn't.

'I mean, they'd both be becoming parents, wouldn't they?' she pressed on. 'And they earn the same. In fact, Jamie earns a bit more. There's no reason for her to be the one who stops working – unless you think that childcare is

225

automatically the mother's responsibility. Which it shouldn't be, obviously.'

Duncan had been watching her with a bemused and slightly suspicious look on his face. There was a long, excruciating pause. Then he cleared his throat.

'Well!' he said. 'You're clearly a woman who knows her own mind!'

Laura emptied her glass. The dregs felt gritty in her mouth; she swallowed them anyway, then topped it up herself.

'Too fucking right, Duncan,' she said, giving him a wicked grin. Diane was staring at a plant in the corner of the room and all the colour had drained from Adam's face.

Just then the waiter appeared. 'Any dessert?' he asked, hovering expectantly. Diane made a show of looking at her watch.

'Goodness me, is that the time?' she said. 'We're going to miss the speeches!'

'Yes, we should really be off,' Duncan said, pointedly turning away from Laura. 'Just the bill, please.'

'You go,' Adam said. 'I'll get this.' They all stood up. None of them were really looking at her now.

'Really nice to meet you both!' she said loudly, knowing they wouldn't be able to ignore that; their social programming wouldn't let them.

'Uh, yes,' Duncan managed to say. 'Lovely.'

'Lovely!' echoed Diane, coolly kissing her cheek. 'Take care, Laura. Hope to see you again soon.'

She and Adam watched them leave the restaurant. Duncan held the door open for his wife; she scooted under his arm girlishly. Adam sighed and rubbed his eyes, then turned to Laura. *I'm not angry with you,* she imagined him saying. *I'm just disappointed.* The thought made her stifle a snort.

'Did you have to do that?'

'Do what?' She reached for her glass – a disapproving look flashed across his face before he could stop it.

'You know. Swear like that.' He was trying really hard to stay calm, she could tell, but she felt an overwhelming urge not to let him, to break through his polite, reasonable veneer and bring whatever this was to a head. 'There's really no need for it, is there?'

'Wow, I'm sorry – I hadn't realised we'd travelled back to Victorian times.' She pretended to be yanking a skirt down. 'Oh, no, my ankles are showing!'

'*Laura.*' Adam sounded exasperated. 'All I meant is, stuff like that upsets them. They're pretty traditional, you know? Old-fashioned.'

She stared him out. 'So that's where you get it from.'

He looked startled. 'What's that supposed to mean?'

'Well, I noticed you weren't exactly disagreeing with your dad when he was saying that women should spend their lives icing cupcakes.' Adam's face didn't move; she tried again. 'He's a bit of a dinosaur, isn't he?'

'Why are you being like this?' Adam demanded. 'Seriously, why?'

She frantically scrabbled around for something she could twist into a justification. 'How do you think I felt hearing about your romantic walks on the beach with Bella?'

She thought she saw him wince. He reached for his glass and drained it grimly in one go. Then he leaned across the table.

'You want to know what I think?' he said, lowering his voice. It was unsteady; like her, she realised, he was well on his way to a hangover. 'I think you're unbelievably immature.'

Laura put her hand on her glass. She ran her finger up and down its stem, feeling how fragile it was, how little it would take to destroy it. Then she tipped it over.

'Oops,' she said.

The wine flooded the tablecloth, drenching it in red and puddling around the side plates. Adam shoved his chair back to avoid it; his face was stony. Laura watched, mesmerised, as wine started to drip off the edge onto the floor. Their waiter rushed over with a roll of kitchen paper.

'Please don't worry, this happens all the time,' he said solicitously, dabbing at the stain. 'Would you like to finish your meal at another table?'

'No, I think we're all done here,' Adam said, staring at Laura. She couldn't remember the last time she'd seen anyone look so furious.

They paid in silence, Adam punching the numbers into the proffered card machine with a grimly resolute look on his face. They got up from the table and crossed the restaurant in silence, him marching ahead of her. She stayed a couple of steps behind him as they wound their way between the tables – she could actually feel the anger coming off him, shimmering like a heat haze.

The evening air was still warm outside and heavy with the smell of spilled drinks and cigarettes from the bar next door. Adam stopped and got out his phone to call an Uber. He was gripping it so tightly that his knuckles had gone white, Laura noticed. She felt like she'd got hold of a loose thread – and for reasons that still weren't totally clear to her, she really wanted to keep tugging it.

'Where are we going?' she asked him. He let out a hollow laugh.

'*We?*' He shook his head. 'Jesus, Laura. How can you ...?' He stopped himself; when he spoke again his voice was tightly measured. 'I need to cool off,' he said, putting his phone back in his pocket. 'My driver's a couple of minutes away, OK? We can talk tomorrow. I don't think it's a good idea for us to spend tonight together.'

She was close enough to him that she could watch the laboured rise and fall of his chest. Seeing him like this, struggling to keep control of his emotions, was doing something to her. In her mind she'd time-travelled back to his flat and the first night they'd spent together. She'd been trying to get under his skin, hoping that she'd uncover something that matched up to something in her. Something unexpected or complicated or *messy*. Something that would make her feel less alone. She'd never managed to find it – and with Cass, she hadn't had to try. It had just all been there, right from the start.

But maybe she'd been wrong about Adam, Laura thought now, taking a step in his direction and then another. Maybe there were parts of him she was only just starting to uncover. Parts that felt things deeply, that were surprising, that were intriguing. Parts that were worth digging a little deeper for.

'Sure about that?' she said quietly, looking up at him from under her eyelashes. Then she reached out and touched his chest. She felt his pulse speeding up.

'What are you doing?' he asked. She lifted her hand a couple of millimetres away from his shirt, giving him the space to move if he wanted to. He didn't. She slipped her fingers under the fabric, finding the skin beneath. His heart was racing.

'What does it look like I'm doing?'

He kissed her then, just like she'd known he would. His hands were firm on her shoulders and he turned her around and pressed her against the wall in the way he had at the barbecue behind the shed, only so much better. She dug her hands into the back pockets of his trousers and ground her hips against him, and he made a noise in the back of his throat that made her do it again, harder.

When they broke apart, Adam stared at her for a moment, his eyes wide with surprise and glazed with need. Laura slipped one of her hands underneath the back of his jacket and stood on tiptoes.

'They're digging up Waterloo, remember?' she murmured, moving his collar to one side so she could kiss his neck. 'It'll be quicker to get to Jamie and Whit's.' She slid the other hand downwards towards his belt. He inhaled sharply.

'Fine,' he said, gripping her wrist. 'Let's go.'

Chapter 14

converge (noun): to approach a finite limit

When Laura woke up, Adam was still asleep, lying on his front. The duvet was bunched around his legs, exposing his broad back. She watched the rise and fall of it for a while, newly appreciating the knots of muscle around his shoulders, the tan on the back of his neck, the two dips just below his hips like thumbprints in clay. She propped herself up on one elbow, feeling pleasantly achey. There were five small, darkening marks on his side where she'd been gripping him tightly. She rested her fingers against his skin, fitting them to the bruises. The exactness of it, she thought, was nice – glass-slipperish.

Adam woke up with a start.

'Jesus.' He rolled over; his eyes were screwed up with sleep. 'You scared me, I was dreaming.'

'Sorry.' She didn't want the feeling to evaporate. 'Go back to sleep.'

'I'm awake now.' He stuck a hand out, feeling around for his phone. Laura could see it out of the corner of her eye, next to Whit's ice skates and a plastic flag that read GO

231

GROUNDHOGS GO – a link in the trail of clothes and shoes snaking its way over the carpet. 'What time is it?'

'Eight. Still early.' She lay down next to him and pulled the duvet over them. They were both naked; she could feel the body heat coming off him. 'We don't have to get up just yet ...'

He moved away from her; the mattress, which had deflated slightly in the night, let out a sad sigh. 'I need to drink something,' he said, rolling off it and pulling his trousers on. He couldn't look her in the eye. The hangover she hadn't realised she had broke over her like a water balloon being burst.

He left the room, shutting the door behind him. Laura lay back down, her stomach churning, and started panning through the events of the night before. She remembered them wrapped up in each other in the taxi, him actually biting her neck (she touched the spot under her ear, which was still tender; yes, it had really happened). Taking his hand as they were going up the stairs and digging her nails into his palm. Him pushing her down onto the mattress and standing over her while he got undressed. The astonishingly sexy look on his face. Her pulling him on top of her before he'd even managed to get his shirt off. They hadn't said a word to each other the entire time. They hadn't needed to.

She heard footsteps – Adam's even, measured ones; she was suddenly beguiled by the specifics of anything particular to him – then silence. When he did eventually come back in she saw that he'd splashed water on his face.

'I'm sorry,' he said to her, in a stiff, giving-a-presentation-at-work voice. She sat up, pulling the duvet defensively around her. It was like being on a video-call where there was a time-lag – the words were all wrong, they weren't what he was meant to be saying at all.

'For what?'

'Last night.' He was still over on the other side of the room – standing about as far away from her as it was possible to be. 'I was angry and you were angry, and we'd both had a bit to drink, and I think it made us not ... ourselves.'

All of it came rushing back, flooding her brain like the wine drenching the tablecloth. Laura ran her finger across the duvet's bumpy surface, cringing as she mentally replayed the terrible dinner with his parents. When they'd finally broken apart in the early hours of the morning, exhausted, she'd told herself that what they'd just done had wiped the slate clean. But, of course, it hadn't.

'Forget about it,' she said. 'I said some pretty terrible stuff too ...'

Adam shook his head; he looked even more uncomfortable now.

'I didn't mean that.'

'What did you mean?'

He shot a glance at the mattress. 'You know. All of it. Before. And here.' His face was going red – he wasn't putting this on, she realised, her heart sinking; he really was ashamed of himself. 'I don't know ... I don't know what I was thinking. I've never been like that with anyone before.'

'Well, neither have I.' She shuffled cautiously towards him; the newfound confidence she'd felt in this, in *them*, when she'd woken up was ebbing away. 'But you shouldn't be embarrassed. I liked it.'

'Look, I think we both just got a bit carried away,' Adam insisted. He stared at various different things in the room, as though one of them might back him up. Then: 'I don't understand.'

'What?'

'Why you liked it. Being like that with each other. Angry and then ... you know.'

'I thought you liked it too.' She raised her eyebrows. 'It seemed like you did anyway.'

'That wasn't me.' He shook his head, like she'd just told him the sky was green. 'I don't find arguing with people a turn-on.'

Laura stared at him in disbelief. 'Could have fooled me,' she said.

There was a creak outside: Harrison appeared in the doorway with his squeaky bagel in his mouth. He looked at Laura, then at Adam, and reversed straight back out of the room again.

Adam had started picking up the rest of his clothes from the floor. 'I should go,' he said, grabbing his wallet from behind the bin; Laura remembered him hurling it there the night before. 'I'm meant to be meeting my parents for breakfast before they head to the airport.' The word *parents* hung in the air like a bad smell.

They got dressed in tense silence. As she watched him buttoning his shirt up to the neck she remembered moaning to Lil, with Dora fast asleep between them on the sofa, how boring it was that Walker and Sasha got a Dine In For Two meal every Sunday night and ate it together in front of whatever had just been released on Now TV. *I feel like he's … I don't know, putting it on,* she'd fumed, trying to keep her voice down. *Pretending to enjoy this shit.* Lil had shrugged. *Or maybe he was putting it on before,* she'd said, stroking Dora's hair. *Maybe this is who he really is.*

Once they were both dressed Laura followed Adam downstairs, trying to keep up – she always had trouble matching his pace, but this morning it really felt like he was trying to get away from her. She'd pulled on a jumper over last night's dress but still felt uncomfortably exposed.

Whit and Jamie were in the kitchen on their matching iPads, having waffles. The warm, sugary aroma, which she'd always been childishly excited by, was suddenly nau-seating to Laura.

'Adam!' Whit called out to him with his mouth full. 'Good to see you, buddy! Come and join us – plenty of batter in the fridge. Fix you a coffee?'

'I need to get going, I'm afraid,' Adam said, visibly uncom-fortable. 'Nice seeing you both.' He turned on his heel and started striding down the hallway. Laura went after him.

'Wait ...' she began as he opened the front door. Adam stopped.

'Last night ...' He turned around – his face was set. 'That isn't how I want things to be with us, OK?'

Laura couldn't face getting into it again – she was too hungover. And what was the point anyway? He'd made his feelings crystal clear. Whatever door had opened briefly between them was now locked shut. He looked a tiny bit happier as he bent down to kiss her.

When she came back into the kitchen Whit was doing the crossword.

'OK, seven across, mountain range in Africa,' he an-nounced. 'Pyramids? No, wait ...' He chewed the end of his pen. 'The pyramids aren't in Africa.'

'You two made a lot of noise when you came in last night,' Jamie said. The corners of her mouth were twitch-ing; she looked like she might actually be about to snigger. 'A *lot* of noise.'

'Don't, OK?' Laura snatched the half-eaten waffle off her plate and bit into it. 'Just don't.'

***

She made her way upstairs, head pounding, and started running the bath. The post-sex aches in her arms and legs felt different now as she got undressed – they were a mortifying reminder of how optimistic she'd woken up feeling, and how utterly wrong that had turned out to be.

The floorboards squeaked; the crack of light between the carpet and the bottom of the door disappeared. Harrison, she knew, would be lying across it like a draught excluder. *Keeping an eye on me*, Laura thought. She opened the bottle of foam without paying attention and ended up pouring most of it in – bubbles surged upwards, obliterating everything.

That isn't how I want things to be with us, OK?

When the bath was full she stuck a leg in the water and swore; it was scalding hot. She took the plug out and ran the cold tap for a bit, then sat on the edge of the bath with her feet in it, waiting for it to cool down. Suddenly the chirping of digital crickets echoed around the house, then Whit's voice started drifting up the stairs.

'Jim!' he was hollering; he'd taken his iPad out into the hall where the signal was better. 'Didn't know you used Facetime! I can't ... Ah, wait, I don't think you need to put it against your ear, buddy, you just stick it on the table in front of you ... That's it! Yup, loud and clear. How's it all going? Where are you?' There was a pause. 'Melton Mowbray – that's where they make the pies, right? Sounds pretty great! Save one for me!' Another pause, much longer this time. 'So you texted Shelley when? Right, right. Have you tried calling her?' This pause was the longest yet, heavy with unsaid things. 'Email's good, email works. Uh, Jamie's ... not here right now. She's at one of her classes. You know how she is! I'll tell her you called though.' Silence. 'Yup, he's fine – we love having him. We've found a great walker who takes him out for a couple of hours over lunch. I'll send you some photos when we all hit the Common later. OK, buddy. OK. Take care. Talk to you soon. Bye.'

'What was he saying?' Jamie's voice pierced the quiet.

'Oh, man.' Laura could hardly hear Whit now – he'd gone back into the kitchen. 'That was bleak.'

'What's happened? What's he done?'

'He's been messaging your mum and she hasn't been replying. I feel so bad for the guy. He has no idea.'

'She keeps badgering me about going for a drink with … I mean, I suppose he's her boyfriend? I don't know what the hell I'm going to do, Whit, she's putting me in such a difficult position. Not that that's anything new. God, what a mess.'

'Hey, you don't have to handle it all by yourself, remember? You've got me. And Laura.'

Jamie said something inaudible. Whit laughed. Laura looked at her feet, which were starting to poke through the dissolving bubbles, and imagined them taking her through a life with Adam. Forty years. Longer than she'd already lived. Maybe as long as she was going to live.

It happens all the time, doesn't it? Someone might be with someone, but then they meet someone else …

And?

An invisible force propelled her legs out of the bath. The next thing she knew she was crouched next to the toilet, vomiting waffle batter and red wine into it, her nose burning and her eyes streaming. She coughed, spat a final glob of magenta into the water, flushed and curled up on the floor, pressing her forehead against the cool porcelain foot under the bowl.

Ten minutes later she was dressed again and rushing down the stairs, out of the door.

***

She turned left at the end of Stonybrook Street and started walking fast. She didn't feel sick anymore but nothing around her seemed quite real. Clapham Common flashed past as though she was watching it from the window of a fast-moving car: the climbing frame, the netless football goals, the lone tree that had been bent double in a storm long before she'd got there. It was just after nine o'clock in the morning now. Dew was steaming off the grass and there was almost nobody about. She hurried towards the Tube, glad there were no witnesses to what she was doing – even though she wasn't sure what exactly that was. All she knew was that she needed to see Cass again. Right now.

She went to check the time of the next northbound train on her phone and saw she had sixteen new messages from Lil.

Lil:
So
You know that project manager I was really into at work who left?
Hot Ben?
Well
He DMd me yesterday!
After I posted that pic of the dinosaur cake
Didn't think it was my best work tbh
But anyway
We've been messaging loads
And we got talking about this linocut workshop
In a few weeks' time
He wants to come with me!
Andreas is on a silent yoga retreat
(I know)
So I was thinking . . .
Maybe you and Adam could watch Dora, if you're free?

Laura:
YES

EXCITING
I can do it
Not sure about Adam

Lil:
???

Laura:
Met his parents last night
It did not go well

Lil:
How not well are we talking
On a scale of one to ten
Ten being someone got arrested?

Laura:
9?
9.5?
His dad's awful
And his mum just sat there

Lil:
Hmm
Did you … make your feelings clear?

Laura:
A bit

Lil:
I see
Oh dear

Laura:
We had a big fight after they left
Then we came home and it got a bit intense
Like
Sex intense

Lil called her.

'Andreas and I went through this phase of trying to spice things up after Dora was born,' she said. 'Latex is a real bastard to get on and off. You're meant to completely cover yourself with talcum powder before you start, to stop it sticking, but this one time we ran out and had to use cornflour. It was like a really dark Mary Berry outtake.'

'Thank you for that lovely visual,' Laura said, sitting down heavily on the railing that divided the grass from the pavement. Hearing Lil's voice had brought her abruptly back down to earth. Her resolve was starting to falter.

'You're welcome! Was it fun? The sex bit, I mean. Not the dinner. That sounds bad.'

'I thought it was ...' Laura tailed off, remembering Adam's fingers closing around her hair, the slight twist that made her gasp. It already felt like it had happened years ago, to someone else.

'Was it his idea? It's always the quiet ones, isn't it?' Lil was chewing something. 'I hope you were using a safe word. We knew ours had to be something we'd never say in real life, so we went for "one-nation Conservatism".'

'It wasn't really like that,' Laura said. 'It was just a lot more ... *more* than normal.'

'More is good! Isn't it?'

'I thought so.' She started working a stone loose from the earth with the toe of her shoe. 'Adam didn't. I mean, he did at the time. But he was being really weird about it this morning.'

'Maybe that's because you called his dad a cunt,' Lil suggested.

'I didn't call him a cunt.' She kicked the stone across the grass. 'I just implied it.'

Lil snorted. 'Look, do you want to come round? We're making Rocky Road. I say we – I'm doing everything while Dora tells me off for eating the raisins. We could go to the park while it chills?'

Laura hesitated. She was right by the bus stop. If she got on the next one she could be at Lil's in half an hour. By the time they'd finished, the window of opportunity for her to do … well, whatever it was she was considering, would have closed. Maybe for good.

'Can I let you know in a bit?' she said. 'I'm really hungover.'

'Suit yourself,' Lil said cheerfully. Laura heard her shutting a door. 'Have some Sprite and a wank – that usually sorts me out.'

'Two lovely visuals in two minutes.' Laura looked over her shoulder; she could see the station across the grass. 'That's a record. Anyway, well done on going for it with Hot Ben.'

'Sometimes you have to, don't you?' Lil said. 'If you don't do it, you won't have done it.'

***

Laura sat on the train as it rattled north, staring at the map running along the top of the carriage. Maybe she could get off at Stockwell, then get the Victoria line, go up into the station and get on a train straight back to Clapham Junction. Or wait at Kennington for a train going in the other direction and do the journey she'd just done in reverse. Nobody would ever know.

The minutes, and the stops, ticked past.

'This is London Bridge,' the automated voice announced. 'Change here for the Jubilee line and National Rail services.'

If she got off here, she thought, watching the doors open, she could do that. She could get the train to Lil's. That would be easy. Or she could catch a bus from outside the station all the way back to Jamie and Whit's. But even if she didn't do any of those things, there were still six whole stops to go. She had plenty of time to make a decision. Plenty of time.

The family opposite her, who between the four of them had six suitcases and a Natural History Museum bag with a cuddly dinosaur poking out of it, started getting their things together. If they stood up as they pulled into Euston, she told herself, it would be a sign that she should too.

They stood up. She didn't.

More minutes. More stops.

'The next station is Camden Town,' the automatic voice said. 'This train will terminate here.'

Everyone in the carriage huffed and puffed. The decision was out of her hands now. But she could just cross the platform, she thought as she zipped up her bag. It wouldn't be a problem to do that. Or, if she did go through the barriers, there was no reason why she couldn't just have a look around Camden, maybe buy some of that ice cream they scraped off a slab in curls, and then get straight back on a train. Nobody would ever know.

***

Camden High Street was just waking up. There weren't any cars on the roads and the air was still nocturnally cool. Laura headed straight for the canal, finding she was speeding up the closer she got to it. By the time she reached the bridge she was practically running. She hurtled over it and careered around the corner – there was Cass's brightly painted boat, exactly where it had been the previous morning. But the main doors were padlocked shut and there was no sign of him anywhere.

She crouched down on the grass at the water's edge so she could look through the open porthole, her heart pounding. There was nobody in there. As she squinted into the darkness the doubts that she'd been wrestling with all the way to Camden solidified into a gut-punch of loss. Why would he have stuck around after what had happened? Why would he want to see her, wherever he was?

Someone coughed behind her.

She spun around and there he was, holding a takeaway cup in each hand, his blue eyes twinkling.

'Of all the towpaths in all of London,' he said slowly, 'you walk onto mine . . .'

'Two coffees?' She stood up, brushing the dirt off her knees; she felt like someone had poured a whole bottle of champagne straight into her veins. 'That's a bold move.'

'I saw you coming out of the station when I was at the hatch.' He put them down on the boat's roof and turned back to her. 'I figured if you changed your mind, I could just drink them both to make myself feel better.'

Laura's heart was knocking against her ribs. She didn't even need to explain, she realised – he already knew. It was so obvious.

'Well,' she said, 'I didn't change my mind. So I guess we're going to have to revert to Plan A.'

He smiled. 'Which is?'

She threw her arms around his neck and kissed him. Within seconds they were tangled up in each other like the teenagers she'd seen the day before and the world had shrunk to just the two of them. He knew everything about her, she thought, pushing herself against him and feeling him press back hard – and he still wanted to be with her. They would find a way. That was all that mattered.

It was cool and quiet inside the boat. Cass shut the door behind them and yanked his t-shirt over his head, his eyes never leaving hers. Where Adam was solid, he was lean and sinewy; she took a step forwards and traced her fingers over his ribs to the grooves that ran from his hips down into his jeans. He reached behind her. There was the other tattoo she'd caught a glimpse of in the cafe: it was a geometric arrow, like something you'd draw onto a map of the night sky. He started unzipping her dress while he kissed her neck.

'Hey, wait, I just remembered . . .' he murmured into her skin. 'You don't have sex until at least the third date, right? That's what you said in Coal Drops Yard. And we haven't even had one official date yet, so . . .'

He ran a finger slowly up and down her spine and she shivered. Nothing had ever felt more right than this.

'I lied,' she said, shimmying the rest of the way out of her dress and reaching down to unbuckle his belt. 'Sorry.'

Chapter 15

bidirectional (adjective): receiving signals from two directions

'Psst! Laura!'

Asha had popped her newly highlighted head up between the barrier that divided their desks and was beckoning her over. Laura, who was bent double in her chair fumbling with her trainers, stopped and glanced up, trying not to let her eyes stray to the huge, marathon-style digital clock looming over the newsroom. It was coming up for one on Wednesday and she was planning – as she had every lunchtime that week – to sneak out to see Cass while pretending to go for a run. It had been ten days since Camden and every time so far had been just as electric as the first.

'Laura! Come on, you'll love this!' Asha's voice jolted her out of her reverie. She got to her feet, grabbing her phone and earbuds, and went over. Asha's desk was a sea of confetti-coloured cards shaped like love-hearts and ringing church bells. This was her last day in the office – she was taking a full week off ahead of her wedding on a Greek island, she'd said, to really nail her skincare regime. She shuffled her chair along so Laura could squeeze in next to her and started working through a series of folders until she reached an InDesign file, which she opened with a triumphant click.

'It's the layout for your piece about the matchmaker!' she announced as the pixelated screen resolved itself into a dummy front page with a note for whoever was working on it, reading: HEADLINE FOR LAURA'S DATING FEATURE HERE PLEASE COPY AND SHOOT PICS TO COME stamped across it. Laura actually gasped in shock – she felt as though she'd just jumped into icy water.

'I found it on the server when I was looking for a template – someone's already started designing it,' Asha went on, using the wheel on her mouse to scroll idly up and down through the pages; she didn't seem to have noticed Laura's horrified reaction. 'It's not scheduled until the end of September, so they must think it's really important if they've already allocated the job to somebody ...'

Laura forced herself to look at the screen as the pages flew past, her stomach churning. The text boxes, obviously, were empty. Bouncy had told her there'd be 2,000 words of space for her feature, which was a lot. She was going to have to fill it with words about her feelings for Adam, the success of their relationship, Cupid's incredible matchmaking model – and all of it would be untrue.

Her desire for Cass was so total that whenever they were together it burned through everything else, like staring straight at the sun. But when they weren't, it wasn't long before them seeing each other secretly started to gnaw at her. If she didn't write the feature, she would definitely lose her job. If she did, she'd have told terrible lies in print that would follow her around the internet for the rest of her life and she might still lose her job anyway. And that, of course, was just the start of it.

Asha had scrolled down onto the second spread of the feature. There, nestled between two more text boxes, was the selfie that Laura had taken of her and Adam on Waterloo Bridge – she'd dutifully emailed it to the *Bugle*'s picture desk the morning after, when she'd woken up glowing with the satisfaction of the evening having gone well and excited about him coming to Jamie and Whit's barbecue. It all felt like it had happened a million years ago, to a completely different person.

'Cute photo,' Asha said, tipping her head back so she could see Laura and giving her a smile – she'd had her teeth bleached for the wedding and they blazed a fierce white. 'How are things with him? Still great?'

Laura nodded; her throat felt tight. Lying to Adam – no, *cheating on* Adam, there was really no sugar-coating it – was easily the worst thing she'd ever done. He'd been a blameless boyfriend, even forgiving her for the scene she'd made during dinner with his parents, and this was how she was repaying him: by sneaking around with the man who'd set them up in the first place. The guilt was almost unbearable – it swamped her whenever they were together and made it hard for her even to look at Adam. He had been badly hurt in love before and soon she was going to hurt him again.

Inge strolled over to them with her lunchbox in her hand.

'All set for your pre-wedding drinks this afternoon?' she asked Asha, who nodded happily. 'Five o'clock in The George still OK? I've told Phil we're not starting until six and Mrs Castle likes him to be home by seven, so with a bit of luck we'll only have to cope with him for about ten minutes.' She gave Laura's leggings and vest an approving nod. 'It's so great that you're getting back into running!' she exclaimed. 'Are you heading out now? Walk with me, will you?'

Laura's eyes darted to the clock again. Inge had a habit of intercepting her when she was going somewhere and using it as an opportunity to download all the things she'd forgotten to tell her during the rest of the day. Normally she didn't mind, but today getting out on time felt like a matter of life or death – it was seven minutes' jog via Coal Drops Yard to Cass's boat and eight minutes back, including getting-dressed time. She quickly stuffed her things into the zip pocket at the back of her leggings and followed Inge out of the newsroom.

As soon as they were away from the desks Inge stopped and lowered her voice.

'I didn't want to say anything in front of Asha, but they've sent me this stupid form to fill in for the Aerodynamica consultation,' she whispered. 'It says I need to "outline the unique value the staff member adds to Bugle Media Group", to persuade them not to make you redundant. What shall I tell them? That you can fit fifteen Mini Cheddars in your mouth at the same time?'

'Sixteen.' Laura realised she'd been in such a hurry to tie her laces that one of them had already come undone. She quickly bent down to re-tie it, mentally filing the form away in the inbox that was stuffed to the point of overflowing right now with everything that wasn't Cass. Her life was starting to remind her of one of those pinboards in police dramas with mad bits of string going all over the place.

'Sorry, Inge, I'd really better go,' she said with forced cheerfulness, straightening up. 'Got to get those kilometres in!'

'Sure, sure – don't let me stop you.' Inge waved her away airily. 'Ah, wait, another thing – Femi wants one of us to help him with his interview prep next week for that permanent role they've got going on the newsdesk. I volunteered you. Sorry.'

'Yup, that's fine,' Laura said distractedly, starting to accelerate away towards the revolving door. Inge was following her, still chatting.

'Oh, and when you get back, I want to pick your brains about shutters,' she was saying – in a couple of weeks, she and Lia were going to be getting the keys to a pink-painted end-of-terrace house in Tottenham with a palm tree growing in the gravel at the front. 'Lia thinks they're one step away from buying shares in John Lewis, but I think privacy is so important in a big city, you know?'

'I agree!' Laura called over her shoulder, speeding up. It was three minutes to one. If she hurried she could be with him by five-past. That left forty-five whole minutes for … She broke into a run.

***

When Laura opened her eyes Cass was sitting on the edge of the bed, pulling his t-shirt on, smiling down at her. She smiled back dozily – then, as the world pieced itself back together, she woke up properly with a start.

'Shit, how long have I been asleep for?' she mumbled.

'Only a couple of minutes – I kept an eye on the time, don't worry. Budge up.' He swung his legs off the floor and got in next to her. His bed, which took up most of the rear cabin, had turned out to be six plastic crates with a camping mattress laid on top of them. It was a startlingly uncomfortable arrangement, full of strange dips and spiky bits, but like everything about the boat, she loved it.

'I read somewhere that you shouldn't sleep on your left side,' he murmured, pulling her towards him.

'Why's that?'

'Something to do with all the blood rushing to your heart and overloading it.' He rested his ear against her

249

chest, pretending to be listening. 'Hmm,' he said eventually, putting his head back on the pillow so their noses were almost touching. 'Everything checks out, but I'll keep an eye on it. Can't be too careful.' She put her arms around him and tangled her legs up with his, enjoying the roughness of his jeans on her bare skin. Cass took her face very gently between his palms.

'Has anyone ever told you ...' he said softly, smoothing her hair off her forehead '... that you snore?'

She punched him on the arm. 'Fuck you, I do *not*. Anyway, at least I don't sleep on a load of boxes from the Big Yellow Storage Company.'

'Hey, don't shoot the messenger.' He leaned down to kiss her, laughing, and she felt her whole body relax into his. After so many years of confusing romantic maybes and disappointing not-quites, the joy of being with him felt like a miracle. All she had to do was turn up and there it was: easy, natural. Perfect.

Cass pulled away, stretched and got to his feet. 'I'm making lunch – come through when you're done. Play your cards right and you might get some hummus that's still within its use-by date.'

She watched him strolling out of the cabin. They'd talked a few times about their situation and she still couldn't get her head around how nonchalant he was. He seemed sublimely unfazed by the fact that his matchmaking model hadn't worked – how could it have, when she was cheating on Adam with him? – and wasn't remotely worried about what was going to happen to either of them when it all came out in less than a month's time.

Here, on the boat, she could talk herself into sharing his blithe optimism that even if she *did* get made redundant, she'd find something else – something better – before long. But each time they said goodbye the anxiety roared back with a vengeance. Of course, nobody at Cupid had actually spelled out that they were looking for a glowing write-up: technically, she could write whatever she wanted as long as she wrote something. But that was clearly what they were expecting – and if she didn't give it to them … She pictured Nush's pointy nails and shivered.

Laura checked the time on her phone and saw that the couple of minutes Cass had said she'd been asleep for had actually been nearly twenty. She groaned and started scooping her clothes off the floor, but couldn't quite work up a real sense of urgency. Without Adam there looking at his watch the whole time, her natural leanings towards being late for everything had nothing to rein them in.

Adam. Dread seeped through her. He'd tried to ring her while she was rushing to the boat and she'd cancelled the call. He'd find someone else, she told herself for the millionth time as she went into her chat with him. He was handsome and sweet – women would be queueing up to be his girlfriend once they stopped seeing each other. He'd be fine.

Laura:

Sorry I missed you!

Was out for a run

Showering now

Everything OK?

Adam:

Hey no worries!

That's great

Just wanted to check what time we're meeting tomo

Laura:

Two I think

At Cupid's office

Will double check and let you know

Adam:
Ok great
It's so cringe we have to make a
  promotional video for them
Can't believe we're being filmed

Laura:
I know
I'd say it won't be that bad, but ...
It will be that bad

Cass was whistling – even though it had only been, at most, about a minute and a half since they'd last touched, she felt a sudden, violent rush of longing for him that vapourised her thoughts about Adam and the awareness that she really needed to get back to the office. She quickly pulled her clothes on and hurried out of the cabin.

She found him leaning against the cooker, eating a family-sized bag of tortilla chips. He was the least health-conscious vegan she'd ever met – he seemed to live off novelty cereals and cheeseless pizza – and she found his imperviousness to nutritional value oddly charming. His computer was on; a window full of code filled the screen.

'We're being filmed tomorrow,' she said, reaching around him to grab a chip out of the bag.

'I saw on the planner.' He put one in her mouth before she could get to them. 'Nush has made a Pinterest board for the promotional video. It's very ... sparkly.'

Laura froze mid-crunch. 'You're joking.'

'I *never* joke about Nush.' He kissed Laura on the cheek, then went and sat down at the computer. 'She's like one of those plants with teeth – it's all fun and games until some-one loses a finger.'

Laura grinned. Her eyes drifted over his shoulder to the screen. It threw her back to the one she'd glimpsed the first time she'd been to Cupid's office – and the first time she'd seen him.

'Does it really not bother you?' she asked tentatively, going over to stand next to him. He looped his arm around her waist.

'What?'

'That it didn't work out with me and Adam. I mean, I know you're not *personally* upset ...' she curled her fingers into his hair '... but professionally, isn't it bad news for you?'

'Not necessarily.' Cass tilted his head back and smiled up at her. 'It's a process. And you were a starting point.'

'Wow, thanks.' She aimed a kick at the base of the chair and he laughed.

'All I mean is, your user experience has thrown up some unexpected bumps in the road, let's say. But that's OK, we'll just refine the model. This stuff happens all the time. Well, maybe not this *exact* stuff ...' He pulled her closer to him. 'But it all turned out fine, didn't it?'

'I ...' Laura hesitated. Cupid had definitely been sold to her as a finished product rather than a work in progress. But maybe these kinds of hiccups were so normal in tech that nobody even thought to mention it. Anyway, did it really matter now? Their time together was so precious, she didn't want to get into anything that might knock it off course.

'Is that about me?' she asked, changing tack and pointing at the screen.

'Hah. No, it definitely isn't.' Cass typed something and she watched as more lines of text sprang up on it. 'It's just something I'm playing around with. A side hustle.'

'What is it?'

'A bot. Someone I know runs a bakery that's really popular – when this is done it'll mean people can just text their order in when they're five minutes away and pick it straight up from the hatch.' He smiled. 'Problem solved. Pretty neat, if I do say so myself.'

'And you do say it.' Laura leaned against him, resting her chin on his head, watching his fingers moving fluently around the keyboard.

'Can you build a bot to go to my meetings this afternoon instead of me?' she asked.

He pulled her onto his lap. 'Would that mean you could stay here?'

'It would.'

'In that case ...' He kissed her and she was flooded with vivid memories from earlier. Him picking her up – he was surprisingly strong – and resting her on the edge of the sink so he could slip her underwear off. Him moving her hands away from his belt buckle when she reached for it. *Not just yet ...* Him looking up at her from between her knees a few minutes later and laughing as she spluttered: *'How did you just DO that???'* The familiar thundering of blood in her ears had started up again.

'Argh, I really have to go, I'm so late.' She stood up reluctantly. 'Inge's going to get suspicious. A newspaper office is a really bad place to be keeping a massive secret.'

'Try a data-based start-up.' Cass kissed her again, long and deep, and she let him.

***

'Just pretend I'm not here, OK?' the young purple-haired cameraman said, giving them what was clearly meant to be a reassuring smile, but which seemed to Laura to be the sort of look you'd give a trailerful of pigs on their way to the abattoir. He'd told them his name when she and Adam had arrived, but she was so on edge about the filming that she'd immediately forgotten it. They were in a glass-walled room at Cupid's office, sitting on adjacent plastic chairs with an empty one in front of them next to the camera. Nush was bustling around like a bee trapped in a bottle.

'I'm going to see if we have a light,' she announced, taking a step back and frowning at them. 'Want to make sure everyone can see your gorgeous faces properly! Two secs, OK?'

They watched her blasting out of the room in her boiler-suit while the cameraman tweaked something on the lens of his camera. The video they were making, Nush had explained in her most syrupy voice, would be used by Cupid on its website and social media channels to promote the business; as its first success story, Laura and Adam would be talking about what it had been like being matched and how their relationship had developed. Nush had told them to be casual, so Adam had changed out of his work clothes into a pair of jeans and a jumper, which he'd brought along in a zip-up suit-carrier. Laura was in the blue gingham dress she'd worn for their first date.

As soon as the glass door clanged shut Adam let his shoulders drop. It had only been three days since they'd last seen each other, but that had just been for a couple of hours. She'd turned up as late as she possibly could for dinner to cut down the amount of time they'd have to spend together. They'd put the light out at ten o'clock – Adam, luckily, had said he was tired. They hadn't had sex in the morning.

'Feels a bit like we're taking a lie-detector test, doesn't it?' he said, staring at the ceiling; he seemed distant and not quite himself today. Laura fiddled with one of her buttons. She felt profoundly uneasy sitting here next to him – it was so much easier to explain away what she was doing when he wasn't actually there.

'What makes you say that?' she asked quickly, following his eyes around the exposed pipes above them and the motivational quotes stencilled on the walls (*GOALS ARE DREAMS WITH DEADLINES*).

'Nothing – I was joking.' He turned back to her and reached for her hand. 'Are you OK?'

'Yeah, totally fine.' She squeezed his fingers; her touch, she thought, was tarnishing them. 'You? You're quiet today.'

'Fine.' He squeezed back. 'Just work stuff.'

'Found one!' Nush was back, carrying an industrial-looking lamp that was almost as tall as her. She plugged it into a socket and flicked a switch on the back – tractor-beam light flooded their corner of the room. Laura and Adam shielded their eyes in unison.

'Oh my god, I just realised, this is the first time I've seen you together!' Nush cried. She put her head on one side and sighed deeply. 'You *guys*.' Then she snapped back into overdrive. 'Cool, shall we get started?'

'Sure.' Laura watched Nush arranging herself in the chair opposite them, her mouth dry. The cameraman was crouching behind the camera, recording diligently.

'OK, let's start with you, babe.' Nush turned to Laura, crossing her denim-clad legs in a businesslike way. 'When you first saw Adam in real life, what went through your mind?'

'I . . .' Nush widened her eyes and gave her a pointed look. 'The first time I saw Adam, I thought . . .' Her palms were damp: he was right, it *did* feel like a lie-detector test. 'He was very tall,' she managed to croak out finally. Nush was still staring at her, urging her to keep talking. 'And nice-looking,' she went on; the laser-gaze didn't let up. 'And you'd bought me flowers, hadn't you?' She turned to Adam in the way she'd seen people do in joint interviews to signal intimacy, *togetherness*, hoping that would do it.

Adam nodded; he suddenly seemed nervous. 'That's right.' He put a slightly stiff arm around her shoulder.

'Ah, that's such a lovely gesture!' Nush trilled and Laura was grateful, for once, to have her crashing in on a train of thought. She leaned in conspiratorially. 'So how did you *feel*, babe?'

Laura shifted uncomfortably in her seat, peeling her legs apart where she'd crossed them. She could see Adam and herself at opposite ends of their London Eye pod, both of them working so hard to keep the conversation going. Then she remembered running into Cass in the casino at Asha's hen – the way she'd *known* that something was going to happen with him. It had had a miraculous momentum of its own.

'I felt like I'd spent so much time rattling the handles of doors that were locked,' she began; the sentence came to her fully formed. 'Then suddenly there was an open one. And I just had to walk through it.'

Adam's arm was heavy across her back. Her breathing was shallow and she didn't want to risk looking at him. Nush, though, looked ecstatic.

'That was *beautiful*!' she sighed. 'Perfect, perfect, got it in one. OK, Adam? What did you think of Laura?'

Adam swallowed. The room suddenly felt suffocatingly close.

'The bathroom's that way, right?' Laura asked Nush, practically jumping to her feet. She had to get out of there, she thought, or something awful was going to happen. 'Sorry, I'm just …'

Away from the blazing light the corridor air was cool on her face; she rested the back of her head against a pillar, wondering how long she could stay away before anyone came looking for her. The girl on reception with the tangerine hair was still wearing her 'Vibe Leader' badge. Laura got her phone out, went into her email and started typing into the body of a new message, words pouring out of her.

I don't know why I'm like this Adam. I'm sorry. I'm so, so sorry

The letters were violently sharp on her screen. She quickly started deleting them, watching the cursor gobble them up until all that was left was a blank, blameless square of nothingness. All gone, she thought. Except it wasn't. None of it was.

'Psst. Over here.'

There, hidden around the corner at the end of the corridor, was Cass, grinning in a pair of jeans and a t-shirt that she'd last seen on his bedroom floor. Her stomach flipped as he beckoned her over.

'What are you doing?' she hissed, caught in a tug of war between dread and desire. 'Are you totally nuts?'

'I've got a meeting with some investors in a bit – and yes.' He started to kiss her, gently at first and then more urgently, nudging a knee between hers and spreading her legs. She automatically ran her hands across his shoulders, suddenly craving the oblivion that being with him always brought. After about thirty seconds he pulled away, exaggeratedly putting a bit of distance between them, like he couldn't trust himself.

'So, how's it going in Room 101?' he asked her, repositioning the straps of her dress. 'Looks very relaxing. Not at all like an interrogation.'

Laura felt tears pricking at her eyes. She turned her head to the side, embarrassed, willing them to stop. Cass put his thumb under her chin and gently turned her face towards him.

'Hey, what's up?' he asked her quietly. 'What's going on? Did something happen?'

'No.' She sighed as quietly as she could, trying to marshal her feelings. 'Well, sort of. I just ...' She hesitated. 'I hate how *dishonest* this all feels and I wish it was you in there. And I feel so guilty for thinking that ...'

'Laura.' Cass lowered his head a little so their eyes were level and she felt her breathing slowing a little, the feeling of being close to him doing its work. 'You worry too much. Just ... relax, OK? It'll work out. Everything does.'

Does it? Laura pictured her parents, and Jamie and Whit, and Lil, all of them weighed down by their own private, unfixable disappointments. 'You're right,' she said, returning his smile.

'I should let you go, shouldn't I? Hey, wait – your lipstick's smudged.' He ran his thumb beneath her lip, neatening the line. She closed her eyes and leaned into him, willing everything else away.

'There,' he said, resting his forehead against hers when he'd finished. 'Perfect.'

***

Two hours later she and Adam left Cupid's office together, blinking as they stepped out into the sunshine. In her mind Laura could still hear him haltingly talking Nush through his hopes for the future – marriage, kids, a move out of London – while she silently died inside.

She was groping around in her bag for her sunglasses when Adam stopped at the bottom of the steps and turned to her.

'So, I need to talk to you about something ...' he said, taking a deep breath. Panic seized her. But no, she'd definitely deleted the email she'd started drafting in the corridor – and anyway, she hadn't even typed his address in.

'Oh?' She located the sunglasses and shoved them on, wanting to hide as much of her face as possible from him. His expression was serious, apprehensive.

'I have to go away for work tomorrow,' he began. 'There's a week-long renewable energy symposium happening in Gothenburg, it's this big annual thing. One of my colleagues was meant to be going but his kid's sick so he's just had to drop out . . .' He looked back at her, cleared his throat, then looked away again. 'We really need to send someone, it's such an important event. Kind of like the Oscars, but for solar power. I've volunteered, anyway.'

Laura's mind was whirring. He was going to be out of the country for maybe an entire week. That meant she might be able to spend six whole evenings with Cass without having to sneak around. They'd be free to act like any other couple.

'Right, right,' she said, stalling, really hoping that he wouldn't pick up on the wobble in her voice – or that if he did, he'd think it was because she was upset about him going away. 'Of course. Um, how long will you be there for?'

'Just until next Saturday. I'll be back in time for us to look after Dora while Lil's off on her date with that guy from Instagram – it's in my diary, don't worry.' He smiled. 'Definitely wouldn't miss that.'

Guilt body-slammed Laura again. He'd clearly been in a funny mood earlier because he was worried about telling her that he was going on this trip, her being upset about not seeing him. And here she was, ecstatic at the prospect of him not being around, while he was reassuring her about the plan they'd made to babysit her best friend's daughter. She was a terrible, terrible person.

Adam reached for her hand and squeezed it. 'Hey now,' he said softly, which made her feel even more awful. 'It's OK, Laura. There's only an hour's time difference, so we can always talk in the evenings if you want to. Right?'

'Right.' She'd never actually done that – called him randomly after work just for the pleasure of hearing him tell her how his day had gone. She'd never felt the urge to. 'You're a good person, you know that?' she said hoarsely; she wanted to give him something nice, a tiny consolation prize. He shook his head.

'Oh, I don't know,' he said quietly. 'I don't know about that at all.' Then he glanced down at his watch. 'I'd better head home and pack,' he said. 'Early start tomorrow, my flight's at nine. Do you mind if we take a raincheck on tonight? I know you were going to come round but I think I just need to crack on, you know?'

'Sure.' If she wasn't going to Adam's tonight, she found herself thinking, she could see Cass. It was incredible how quickly the possibility of getting another fix of him wiped out every other thought in her head. 'I'll see you next week, then?' she said.

'Next week,' Adam confirmed. 'I'll let you know when I've landed, OK? And let's speak tomorrow night.'

He leaned down to give her a quick kiss – their lips brushed for just a second – and then he was gone, striding off towards the river. She waited until he'd turned the corner, then got her phone out and started walking towards the Tube. Her heart leaped; Cass had messaged her.

Cass:
i'm watching your video
'tall'

hahahahahaha
yes, hello
i'd like to report a murder

                                              Laura:
                                    It's not funny!

Cass:
i'll be the judge of that
ooh the open door bit is great
very writerly
maybe you should become a journalist!

                                              Laura:
                                    Go away please

Cass:
do you want me to?

She lost literally hours talking to him like this, messages zipping back and forth between them in a rally that turned minutes into seconds and made anything else she was meant to be doing seem totally irrelevant. It felt like having your hand in a tin of chocolates, promising yourself you were only going to have one and the next time you looked down the whole lot had gone.

                                              Laura:
                                    You know I don't
                          So I'm free tonight, unexpectedly . . .
                                    Can I come round?

Cass:
ah tonight is tricky
sorry!
but already looking forward to your lunchtime visit tomorrow

'Shit!'

She'd walked into someone – a tall, leggy woman in a denim pinafore with white bleached hair, who'd been carrying a large cardboard box. It was on the pavement now with a dent in one of its corners. The woman was standing over it, shaking her head wryly. She looked strangely familiar.

'God, I'm so sorry.' Laura scrambled to pick it up and hand it back to her. 'Nothing breakable in there, I hope?'

The woman raised one of her knees and balanced the box on it as she opened the lid – it was full of neon-bright meringues.

'I mean, this one's pretty fucked …' she said slowly; she had a raspy voice and her face was bare apart from a slash of black lipstick, shot through with a thin silver ring. 'It's totally fine, I'll just tell them it's "deconstructed". People love that.'

The box's lid, Laura saw, had *VEGANISED* stamped on it. As she stared at it a memory floated to the surface of her mind – watching a woman with bleached hair going up the steps to Cupid's office after she'd first talked to Cass all those weeks ago. It was the same person.

'That's the new vegan bakery near Borough Market, isn't it?' she said, pointing at the box. 'I've seen you on this street before, I think …'

The woman smiled as she lifted the dented meringue out of the box and offered it to Laura. 'Yeah, it's my place and I've got a friend who works around here – he loves these, so whenever I've made extras I bring him them. They're made with the water from tins of chickpeas. Why don't you have this one on the house?'

Laura took it from her self-consciously; the woman radiated the kind of effortless cool she'd always found intimidating. She gave her gingham dress a tug, straightening the bodice out. When she got home it was going right in the back of her cupboard.

'I like your lipstick,' she said, not quite able to meet the baker's eye. The woman smiled; her lip-ring twinkled.

'Oh, thanks. I'm a Pisces – we're all about the winter colours. And lie-ins.'

She closed the box's lid and set off again. Laura watched her melting into the crowd, trying to get her bearings back. The whole afternoon was clinging unpleasantly to her – she felt like she needed a shower. She bit into the meringue and it shattered abruptly in her mouth.

Chapter 16

extrapolation (noun): *making predictions based on trends in the data*

She felt it as soon as she opened the door to Stonybrook Street – a kind of thickening of the air that immediately put her on edge, a heaviness warning her that something had happened. She paused on the mat (flashbacks to coming home from school and trying to work out from the way the shoes were arranged in the porch whether her parents had been arguing or not; if there were gaps, that was a bad sign) – Jamie and Whit's keys were both on the hook, but the house was quiet.

'Hello?' she called out. 'Guys?' Nothing. She tiptoed down the hallway. The kitchen door was closed.

She found them on the other side of it, leaning on the worktop in glum silence. Whit had an open beer in front of him and Jamie did as well, which was immediately jarring – Laura had never seen her drinking anything other than wine from a glass. Something else was wrong too, she thought, her heart starting to pound: there was a piece missing from the scene. She did a quick inventory of the room's

265

contents, but everything was where it should be. Then she noticed Harrison's empty bed by the French windows.

'Where is he?' She was trying to keep the panic out of her voice. 'Where's Harrison?'

Whit picked up his beer then put it down again, giving her the sad ghost of a smile.

'He's at the vet's at the end of the road, kid,' he said wearily. 'They took him in as an emergency patient. They're keeping him in overnight. He kind of … collapsed on his walk at lunch. Jamie came straight home as soon as Diane the walker called her.'

Laura looked across at her sister – Jamie's eyes were red-rimmed.

'They asked me if he was on any medication and I said no.' She shook her head and did a clench-unclench with her free hand, like she was feeling around for something that kept slipping out of her grasp; her voice was hoarse. 'Then I remembered those pills Dad gave us – you know, the ones in the plastic bag that we put in Harrison's food every morning. It turns out they're not vitamins at all. They're antibiotics. Very strong ones.'

'Something's up with his heart,' Whit said. 'It's an infection – they think he's had it for a while. Apparently it's just one of those things older dogs can pick up. He's having some more tests done, but they're doing everything they can to get it fixed, OK?'

Laura let the counter take her weight, feeling sick to her stomach. She'd known he was ill and she hadn't done anything about it. This was all her fault. And if anything else happened to him – she felt a tide of nausea rising and quickly backed away from the thought – that would be all her fault too.

'Why didn't Dad say anything to us?' she demanded, desperately avoiding Jamie's eye. There was no way Jamie could know about Cass, but it was so easy to imagine she did and was being judgemental – letting her own guilt take her sister's form. *It's no good you blaming him*, she could hear Jamie saying. *Why can't you take some responsibility for once in your life? This is on you, Laura.*

'He probably thought it was under control.' Whit sounded so helpless – she couldn't bear it. 'I guess he just didn't want you to worry, kid.'

'No, Whit, I'm sorry, but that's absolute crap,' Jamie snapped. 'This is what Dad always does. He ignores things until they get too big to ignore, then he makes them some-one else's problem.' She took a short, angry swig of her beer, then banged the bottle down.

'Sweetheart, come on,' Whit implored her, putting his arm around her shoulders. 'He loves Harrison, we all do. He's just …'

'Just what?' She drained her beer. 'Love isn't this nice, easy thing you can dust off whenever you feel like it – it's hard work! If it wasn't everyone would be doing it all the fucking time, wouldn't they?'

Laura went and kneeled down next to Harrison's bed. The fabric was cool to the touch; it felt horribly unlived in. He napped on top of his treasures like a dragon: his chew-rope, a soggy old tennis ball he'd insisted on carrying home from the Common in his mouth just after he'd arrived, his toy bagel. She picked it up and gave it a squeak, trying not to cry.

Whit crouched next to her, putting a hand on her shoulder.

'Look, why don't you chat to the vet tomorrow morning?' he said gently. 'He's going to drop Harrison off here before work.'

***

267

Laura spent most of the night awake, miserably aware of the cold, empty space at the side of the mattress where Harrison might have been – they were into September now and the nights were getting cooler. At eleven she'd messaged Cass. *Can you talk?* she'd typed. *Shit night, would really like to hear your voice.* He usually replied straight away, but this time there was just one tick for ten minutes, then twenty, then an hour, then two. She tried to get to sleep, but all she succeeded in doing was slipping in and out of a thin, dreamless doze, coming to with a jolt every half hour to check her phone. Finally, at 3.55 a.m., he'd replied.

aargh sorry, just seen this
let's speak tomorrow, ok?

And then, eight minutes later:

i think about you all the time, laura morrison

She fell asleep with her phone gripped in her hand, waking up three hours later with a headache and a numb arm. She flopped onto her front to open the blind, then lay on top of the duvet re-reading Cass's last words, trying to reason her way out of feeling uneasy. He'd probably just been working and hadn't noticed her message. And he'd been so understanding about the fact that she still had to see Adam – the least she could do was be cool about him going offline for a few hours. It really wasn't a big deal.

She checked the time – it was just after seven. Adam, she suddenly remembered, would be at the airport by now; he was definitely the sort of person who factored in the recommended two hours. She guiltily dug around in WhatsApp's GIF library and sent him one of a cartoon plane waving its wings. *BON VOYAGE!!!* she wrote underneath in semi-hysterical capital letters. The animated image flapped at her, reminding her of her mum in her flying days, which then reminded her of her dad. It was no wonder she wasn't accomplishing much at work right now, she thought as she pulled on her tracksuit bottoms: just getting through the days without thinking about any of the things she was trying not to think about was turning into a full-time job.

She left the room and headed downstairs to make the first of several coffees. Jamie was on the landing with her ear pressed against the door of the second bathroom – she and Whit had a gleaming en-suite that she had priority use of – wearing her work suit but with the top half of her hair clipped up and the bottom bit wonky from sleep.

'Whit, can you let me in, please?' she was calling through the wood. 'I left my tongs in here the other day and I really, *really* need them.' She turned to Laura and rolled her eyes. 'He did this on the morning of our wedding, you know,' she said tersely. 'I was banging on the door trying to get my perfume and he was in the bath with a clay facemask on.' She turned back to the bathroom and raised her voice. 'This is ridiculous! Come on, Whit, I can't go to work with my hair like this ...'

'I got shampoo in my eye!' Whit hollered. 'Jeez, give me a break, will you?'

The doorbell chimed. Jamie's head whipped round.

'That'll be the vet with Harrison,' she said and the corners of her eyes crinkled. As soon as she realised Laura was watching her she coughed and her expression snapped back to normal. 'The bill was absolutely ridiculous – that dog's turning into a very expensive houseguest.'

'Good save,' Laura said, giving her sister a wink. 'For a minute there you nearly showed some actual human feeling. Don't worry, I won't tell anyone.'

She raced down the stairs and threw the front door open. There was a dark-haired man in blue scrubs, a rucksack and trainers standing by the gate with a familiar shaggy shape at his heel. Harrison yelped as soon as he saw Laura and barrelled up the path, his tail swooshing joyfully. He collided with her leg and leaned all his weight against it, closing his eyes and panting.

'I'm sorry, I'm sorry, I'm sorry,' she mumbled into his fur, crouching down and trying to blink back the tears. 'I'm so sorry, Harrison.' It felt like waking up from a bad dream. He nuzzled his head against her trousers and made a noise like a beach ball deflating. There was a bandage wound around one of his front paws.

'That's just where the drip was,' the vet said quickly, spotting her looking at it. His voice was north London gruff, but he spoke softly. 'Nothing to worry about.' He was much younger than she'd been expecting him to be – only a year or two older than her, maybe – with kind, watchful brown eyes. His scrubs looked like they'd been ironed in a hurry.

Laura stood up straight, trying to pull herself together. 'It's so nice of you to bring him round,' she said. 'Sorry, I didn't catch your name ...'

'Jem – Jem Osman.' He gave her a smile. 'And it's no trouble, honestly – I've got a house call a couple of roads along after this. Laura, isn't it? Your sister was telling me about you.' He held out his hand then looked at it in puzzlement, like he couldn't remember why he'd done it. 'Er, yes. Right. Anyway, I'll leave you to ...'

'Wait ...' Laura began, keeping hold of Harrison's lead. Everything she'd been wrestling with overnight was bubbling up, threatening to explode out of her. 'I really need to know ... is he going to die?'

She could feel her vision blurring. Jem's eyes widened in alarm.

'Oh, god, no, nothing like that,' he said quickly. He took his rucksack off and kneeled down in front of it, patting the pockets. Eventually he pulled out a little pack of paw-print tissues. 'Have these,' he said, holding it out to her. 'I keep being sent them by a cat food company.'

Laura took the pack and screwed it up in her fist. She was being ridiculous but she couldn't seem to keep a lid on it all. The vet straightened up and gave her another re-assuring smile.

'We've got Harrison rehydrated and we've tweaked his prescription a bit,' he said soothingly. 'I couldn't see anything sinister on the scan, so it doesn't seem to have done him any long-term harm. Honestly, there's no reason to think this'll affect his natural lifespan.'

Natural lifespan. How many more years did that give them with him? Laura wondered. Five? Less than that? She'd been in London for that long and it felt like nothing at all. She scrunched the tissues tighter.

'I'm really sorry about this,' she said to the vet, avoiding his eye. 'I didn't get much sleep last night.'

She could feel him watching her kindly.

'We never have enough time with them, do we?' he said. 'It's the price we pay for loving them so much. But try not to worry about him, OK? Collies are built to last.' He turned to Harrison.

'Right, well, we'll see you in a couple of weeks for a check-up, matey,' he said; Harrison raised his head off the path at the sound of Jem's voice and started whisking his tail. 'You stay out of trouble, alright? No squirrel chasing.'

Cass video-called her on WhatsApp as she was scooping out Harrison's kibble for breakfast. He was still in bed, shirtless with sexy slept-on hair.

'How's the patient?' he asked through a lion-yawn.

'Being brave.' She glanced down at Harrison, sitting at her feet with his ears pricked, and felt a huge swell of love and relief. 'The vet says he's going to be fine.'

'Atta boy!' Cass did a fist-bump to the camera. 'Ah, that's so great. Give him a pat from me, OK?'

'I think he wants to say hi, actually,' Laura lied; Harrison was showing about as much interest in her phone as he did in anything he couldn't eat. She crouched down and held the screen in front of his face. He gave it a cursory sniff, before turning his back on it, lowering his head and licking himself gracelessly. She could hear Cass laughing.

'I guess I'll take that as a compliment.' He propped himself up on an elbow and leaned back against the cabin wall. 'Sorry I couldn't talk last night – something came up.'

'The launch?'

He did another yawn, which turned into a groan of exhaustion. 'I can't wait for it to be over. On a more exciting note, I'm seeing you at lunch, right? If you message me when you're leaving, I'll make sure I'm presentable.' He grinned. 'Unless you want me to stay like this, of course.'

'I want you to stay exactly like that, please.' She was floating on air now, weightless and worry-free. She put her phone on the table and glanced down at Harrison.

'Come on,' she said, giving his bowl a nudge with her foot so its contents rattled. 'Breakfast time.'

He didn't move. He was staring up at her with deep furrows where his eyebrows would have been. He looked – there was no other way of putting it – disappointed. Laura burst out laughing.

Chapter 17

cross-validation (noun): a way of testing how a model will respond to new data

'So, I've been thinking ...' Femi began, picking the straw off the side of his orange-juice carton and poking it through the foil. They were in the *Bugle*'s canteen: Femi had a mountain of hash browns on his tray and Laura had a heap of vegetable matter advertised as 'Chef's Chopped Salad'. She was wearing one of Jamie's work dresses, which her sister had forced her into that morning – they were meeting their mum and her mysterious friend later and Jamie was already so wound up that it had felt easier to go along with her insistence that Laura needed to look 'smart'.

'Dangerous thing to do here ...' Laura muttered as she yanked the dress down; it was at least a size too small. Femi hesitated, clearly not sure if he was allowed to laugh at what she'd said.

'You know the people you're doing your feature on – Cupid?' he said, skewering a hash brown. 'Well, where's their money going to come from?'

Laura tried to keep her face very still. She'd never actually asked Cass that question outright because she was worried he might be offended; their secret relationship felt like something balanced at the top of a wobbling Jenga tower and she didn't want to pull out any of the blocks in case the whole thing came crashing down. At least the subterfuge wasn't for much longer: the three months were up in just under three weeks. And whatever happened afterwards, she told herself, they would get through together.

'Investors, I guess?' She shrugged, attempting to sound nonchalant. 'There's so much capital floating around in tech – people are queueing up to dump cash on the next big thing. I'm sure that's it.'

'But they can't just keep doing fundraising rounds forever, can they?' Femi pressed on, waving his fork around with the hash brown still speared on it. 'At some stage they'll need to be self-sufficient. From what I've read about them, I don't understand how they're going to manage that. Members just pay what they can afford, right? That'll barely cover their costs.'

'Don't you worry, I'm on it!' Laura said, desperately trying to get him off the subject. She took a reluctant bite of her salad, which seemed to be getting soggier and less appetising by the second. 'Look, do you want to do some more interview prep? It's tomorrow, isn't it? We could …'

Femi's eyes had drifted to her phone: Adam was videocalling her. Laura dropped her cutlery onto the table with a clang – she was permanently on edge these days.

'Do you want me to … ?' Femi was hovering out of his seat; Laura shook her head and scraped her chair back. This would be the first time Adam and she had actually spoken while he'd been away and she felt stupidly grateful that she'd be able to tell him she had to go back to her desk soon. The shorter the call, the easier it would be for her to keep up her act – which was now sounding hollow, even to her.

Adam had been in Gothenburg for four days. In his messages he'd told her that the conference was interesting and the city was very clean and well run. They'd been on a boat trip, he'd said, and visited Scandinavia's largest amusement park – but that was as much detail as she'd got. Was he not interested in the daily comings and goings of life in a new city? Or did it simply not occur to him to tell her about any of it? Cass was always sending her funny little vignettes from the Cupid office and the canal.

She hurried over to the living wall in the lobby where the signal was better, leaned against the edge of it and swiped to answer the call. Adam materialised: he was in his hotel room, looking very businesslike sitting at the desk next to the TV.

'Hey!' She smiled, pushing her tongue behind her top teeth in a way she'd read made you look happier. 'Everything OK?'

Adam smiled back at her. The greenery on the living wall tickled the back of her neck. It was the one she'd stood in front of when she and Inge had made her video all those weeks ago, Laura realised. She pressed the tip of her tongue even harder against the inside of her mouth.

'We finished lunch early so I thought I'd give you a quick call.' He cleared his throat and adjusted his tie. 'All set for meeting your mum's . . . friend? It's tonight, right?'

He'd remembered. Of course he had – he was a kind, thoughtful person who'd never dream of going behind her back. Laura wished the fern fronds would come to life and swallow her up.

'You know, I . . .' she began. There was a second's delay, then Adam's screen juddered to a halt. His soft voice came out of the speaker on a time-lag.

'Sorry, Laura, I can't …'

They were out of synch – the signal wasn't strong enough. She shuffled along the wall towards the newsroom to see if that made a difference, secretly hoping it wouldn't. At least then she'd have tried, it wouldn't be her fault.

As the picture came together again something on his desk caught her eye. There was a little memo pad stamped with the hotel's name – and it was covered in pen strokes. She squinted, trying to make them out. It looked like someone's face.

'Have you been drawing?' she asked him. His cheeks flushed.

'Ah, I was just killing some time before breakfast this morning,' he said, quickly turning the piece of paper over. 'It's …'

The lobby clock chimed twice, loudly. It was two o'clock – she and Femi had left for lunch at quarter-past one.

'Argh, sorry, I'd better go,' she fibbed – lying wasn't so much becoming second nature now as first nature, a thing she did constantly with everyone. 'I'm going to be late back …' He smiled and opened his mouth to speak, but the screen froze again before he could. Then the call cut out completely. Laura agonised for a second over whether to ring him back to say goodbye but decided not to – she didn't want to push her luck even more. She messaged him a quick *Sorry! Speak soon xxx* and stuffed her phone as far down into one of the dress's pockets as it would go.

***

The hotel their mum had chosen for the meeting was just behind Oxford Street, a 1970s concrete block concealed behind giant potted palms and fluttering flags. Laura was perched on the wall outside it, swinging her legs against the concrete – for once, her sister was the one running late.

While she'd been waiting for Jamie she'd been re-reading her most recent exchange with Cass.

Cass:
have you ever been to berlin?

Laura:
No
Why?

Cass:
one of my team just got back
he loved it
if you wanted to go some time, we could do that ...

Berlin. She could imagine them there together: waking up late on a futon in a cool loft apartment they'd found on Airbnb, going to galleries, dancing in clubs until the sun came up, laughing over the hypnotic music. The thought fizzed away pleasurably in the pit of her stomach, dissolving everything else.

She heard the rapid clack of stilettos on tarmac and looked up. Jamie was marching towards her, immaculate in a white linen shift dress with piping on the pockets, her nails painted black. She was scowling.

'*There* you are,' she announced, as though Laura was the one who was late. She looked her up and down. 'That dress suits you, you know. You can keep it if you want.'

'I think Ivanka Trump will be missing it by now,' Laura said, grimacing; her feet hurt. (How did Jamie wear heels every day?) Her sister glowered at her, then blasted off towards the hotel like a tornado.

'I know exactly what it's going to be like in here,' she huffed as she tore through the revolving door. 'White plastic champagne flutes and men whose wives supposedly don't understand them. Yuck.' She strode across the lobby like she was going into battle, but she was chewing the inside of her cheek in the way she only ever did when she was nervous.

'Well, there's still another fifteen minutes left of happy hour,' Laura said, reading off the noticeboard next to reception as she tried to keep up.

'That's something.' Jamie snorted. 'Fifteen minutes is probably all I'm going to be able to take.' She stopped and turned to Laura, pivoting on the marble. 'How do I look?'

'Great,' Laura said truthfully. 'Not sure about the funeral manicure, though. I mean, nobody's died.'

'Yet.' Jamie whipped her phone out of her bag. 'Oh my god, look at this,' she said.

Laura took it. There was a message from their mum on the screen.

me n Alan r in the bar, got us a table xxx

'Alan,' Jamie practically spat. 'His name is *Alan*.'

'A-ha,' Laura said, waggling her eyebrows. Jamie scowled at her.

'It's not funny!'

'Come on, it is a bit.'

'You're being infuriatingly fucking Zen about all of this, you know that?'

'I just ...' Laura was about to repeat something that Cass had said to her the other day about change, but Jamie's expression made her think better of it. 'Look, let's get it over with.'

They walked into the bar side by side. It felt as though they were stepping into an aquarium: the curvy walls were made of swirled and dimpled glass; massage-table music was tinkling out of the speakers. Laura's gaze snagged on a couple – her brain put them in that category before she could stop it – on the other side of the room, sitting next to each other on a plump sofa. Her mum was wearing a purple dress and an anxious expression. The late-middle-aged man next to her was wearing a grey suit and some kind of club tie that looked like a stick of rock. Next to her, she felt every muscle in her sister's body tense as Jamie clocked them too.

'How nice of Roger Moore's ghost to join us,' her sister muttered.

Looking at him, Laura thought that wasn't totally fair. What he reminded her of more than anything was one of those chipper British racing drivers in black-and-white photos – something to do with his sandy hair, which he still had most of, and his eyes, which were actually quite a nice china blue. As they approached he got to his feet, smiling at them.

'Welcome!' he said, spreading his arms wide. His voice had a cheery hint of south London, but he was clearly very nervous; he couldn't stay still. 'Now, let's see if I can get you the right way round – it's Jamie, isn't it? And Laura?' Laura nodded. Jamie's face didn't move.

'And you must be Alan,' she said, folding her arms. She regarded the pair of them coolly. 'Well – here we are.'

Their mum had stood up too and was hovering anxiously next to Alan. She looked like she wanted to hug them but was scared to make the first move. It suddenly occurred to Laura that she was actually the least nervous person here. She tried out the feeling of being the one who had it together, testing her weight on it carefully like a twisted ankle.

'Here we are!' she said, trying to make Jamie's words sound slightly less menacing. She sat down on one of the low stools opposite the sofa. Jamie took the other one reluctantly.

'You look very nice, love,' their mum said, reaching over to pat the capped sleeve of Laura's dress, which was digging into her upper arm.

'So do you, Mum.' It was true: the word *glowing* barged into her mind uninvited. Their mum was wearing much less make-up than she normally did and the dark circles that had been under her eyes for as long as Laura could remember had vanished.

'Now, what are you drinking, girls?' Alan asked them as he sat down. He raised his glass jauntily. 'We're on the white port and tonic …'

'Fizzy Porto, we call it!' their mum piped up, rejoining him on the sofa. 'Very summery.' She looked across at him and smiled broadly. 'Alan has a place in the Algarve,' she went on, swivelling her body towards him. 'He goes there every spring, don't you?'

'Oh, it's just a little apartment in Faro Old Town,' Alan said, mirroring her posture; they were already a double act. Watching them interacting like this felt completely surreal. 'But it's got everything you want in a holiday home. I can't wait for you to see it.' He smiled shyly at Shelley.

Their mum laughed and dipped her head gracefully like a swan. It was so strange: you could be sure you knew everything someone's face could do, Laura thought – and then, one day, watch them doing something brand new with it. She didn't know what to feel. No, that wasn't right – she knew exactly how she was feeling, which was … basically fine. Slightly weirded out by the whole situation, but not appalled or devastated or any of the other things she'd been imagining. What she couldn't work out was whether that was normal. Jamie, she knew, wouldn't think it was: her mouth was a furious slash.

'I'll have a sparkling water,' she said icily. 'And before you ask, no, I'm not pregnant,' she went on. 'I'm just not in the mood for an alcoholic drink right now.'

'Well, that's fair enough, isn't it?' Alan said jovially, looking from their mum to Laura, trying to get them all on the same page. He was one of life's peacemakers, she real-ised – she could actually imagine him and Whit getting on.

'Thanks for having Mum to stay, Alan,' she said, trying to fill the silence. 'I hope she hasn't been too much trouble!'

'Oh, no trouble at all!' Alan beamed, giving their mum's knee a quick squeeze. Laura watched Jamie's eyes alight on his hand.

'So – how did you two meet?' she asked them, leaning back in her chair and folding her arms. Alan fished a rice cracker out of the bowl.

'We used to fly the same routes back in the good old days, when your mum was cabin crew,' he said, crunching; Laura found herself really hoping that his teeth were going to hold up. 'Paris, Casablanca, Inverness ... all the big ones. We always had a laugh when we were on the roster together, didn't we, Shel? I had to join the queue to chat to her when we were out, though – your mum was very popular.'

'Alan was a captain,' their mum said, seamlessly taking the baton of the story from him. 'We all used to say his landings were so smooth that you could paint your nails during them!'

Alan's cheeks went pink. 'Well now, I don't know about *that*,' he said, popping another cracker into his mouth. 'Anyway, we lost touch after she had ...' He cleared his throat. Jamie, Laura noticed, had taken one of the paper coasters off the table and was shredding it silently. 'We lost touch. I never had kids myself, but I know what it's like. Your life changes, doesn't it? Then she "friended" me a couple of months ago.' His phone was on the table – he took it out of its mock-leather case and started prodding it with his index finger. 'I have to say, I don't know how I managed without Facebook for all these years. Are either of you girls on there?'

'NO,' Laura and Jamie said in unison. Alan laughed good-naturedly and stood up again.

'I'll just pop over and order the drinks, shall I?' he said. 'Fizzy Porto for you, Laura, yes?' Their mum watched him making his way to the bar with a soft expression on her face.

'So!' she said brightly when she eventually turned back to face them. 'Why don't you tell me all your news, my loves? It feels like we haven't properly chatted for ages, doesn't it?'

Jamie crumpled the coaster into her fist.

'I'm sorry but this is grotesque,' she hissed. 'You're still wearing your wedding ring! Are you ever going to tell Dad you're not coming back? Or are you going to leave us to do it, as usual?'

Laura flinched. Her gaze tracked involuntarily across to the bar – Alan was watching them over his shoulder, his blue eyes wide in horror. Their mum recoiled like she'd been slapped.

'Well, I really think you should apologise, Jamie,' she said unsteadily. 'There's no need for that, is there?'

'I should apologise? Do you have any idea what it's been like – dealing with Dad while you two carry on like a pair of overgrown teenagers, on top of everything else?' She squeezed the fist with the coaster in it. 'Neither of you has ever said sorry, not once,' she said in a low, colourless voice that gave Laura the bad kind of goosebumps. 'Ever. For any of it.'

'Oh, for heaven's sakes, Jamie, not this again. It was such a long time ago! I suppose you've never made a mistake in your life, have you?' Her mum was staring at the ceiling; her accent was slipping back in the way it always did when she was upset. Laura's stomach was in knots.

'I don't think I have, actually. Not like this,' Jamie said defiantly. 'I work incredibly hard, I have a good marriage, I've been bailing Laura out since the spring – sorry, Laura, but it's true – I've coped with a lot of really *painful* shit ...'

'We all have!' their mum cried. She was blinking like she was trying to get something out of her eye. 'You're not the only one who's had a difficult time, you know – I've had my fair share of disappointments, let me tell you.'

'Because of me and Laura, is that what you mean? Us stopping you from having the jet-setting life you wanted?' Jamie snapped at her. 'God, the way you talk about having children ...' Her voice broke. She grimaced and shut her eyes for one, two, three seconds. Then she stood up.

'I'll be outside,' she said to Laura. 'Come and find me when you're done, please.' Her heels rat-tat-tatted on the marble like machine-gun fire as she walked out of the bar.

'Jamie, love, please come back – I didn't mean ...' Their mum hurried after her, wiping her eyes, leaving Laura alone. She heard someone clearing their throat behind her and turned around. Alan was back, sheepishly holding two full glasses. He put them down on the table in silence and sat opposite her on the sofa. She took the one that looked like it contained alcohol.

'How is it?' he asked her tentatively, watching her drink. *You're the together one*, she told herself. *You can handle this.*

'Nice.' She suddenly felt overwhelmingly sorry for him. She gave him what she hoped was a white-flag smile. 'Thanks, Alan.' His shoulders sagged inside his jacket.

'I'm so sorry, Laura.' He leaned forwards and put his head in his hands. 'I never meant for any of it to happen. I was over the moon to hear from Shel, but I thought we'd only email a bit – you know. Then we decided to meet up for a drink and we ...' He shook his head. 'I've been on my own since the divorce, but even before that I hadn't been happy for such a long time.' He looked up at Laura with a kind of fragile astonishment. 'She lights up every room she's in, your mum,' he said, in a choked voice.

'Look, it's OK.' Laura pushed the bowl of crackers across the table towards him as a peace offering. 'I get it.'

Alan's eyes widened in amazement. He looked like he might actually be about to cry.

'You do?'

'I think so.' She saw an opportunity to shoehorn in the little piece of wisdom from Cass that she'd had to shelve earlier. 'I mean, you can't stop life from happening, can you?'

Alan nodded, considering this. 'I used to have dreams about her, you know,' he said. 'After she stopped flying. We'd be walking along a beach and I'd ...'

'I get the picture,' Laura said quickly. 'Shall we talk about something else?'

'Right you are.' He glanced at her empty glass and smiled hopefully at her. 'One for the road?'

Chapter 18

sentiment analysis (noun): *assessing whether a group feels positively or negatively*

'I don't understand why you didn't just go in the hotel,' Jamie muttered. She and Laura were in the queue for a stall in the Selfridges bathroom with half a dozen women ahead of them – Jamie, who apparently had *Mission Impossible*-level knowledge of the floorplans of every department store in London, had stomped them up the escalator in double-quick time, waving away people offering them spritzes of perfume. Now though, Laura thought, she was starting to look deflated.

'I didn't need it then, did I? Anyway, everyone knows fizzy alcohol puts a road through you. I had to have two of those port thingies with Alan while you and Mum were talking.'

Jamie rolled her eyes. The bathroom was hot and air-less, fuggy from the hand dryers and the sloshes of water pooling on the sides of the sinks. Laura's hair was sticking to her forehead. As she pushed it off her face her thumb grazed a mark on her cheek: her mum's lipstick, from where she'd kissed her goodbye in the lobby. *I love you both so much*, she'd said, gripping Laura's shoulders fiercely. Laura had nodded and reached up to squeeze her hand. Her mum had looked so unbearably relieved that she'd had to look away. Alan had made himself scarce – as Laura left she'd spotted him at the other side of the hotel entrance, helping a honeymoon couple heave their suitcases into the lift.

'What did she say to you outside?' she asked Jamie. Her sister shook her head. Her neck was mottled pink – an angry residue.

'She apologised for leaving us to sort out Dad and Harrison. Then there was some stuff about how Alan makes her happy and Dad doesn't. She's sorry if that isn't what we want to hear, but that's the way it is.'

Nearly thirty seconds passed when she didn't say anything at all – Laura counted them, the way you were meant to between seeing a flash of lightning and hearing thunder, to work out how close the storm was.

'I know it sounds totally pathetic,' Jamie went on, looking straight ahead. 'But the whole time she was talking about him I was back in our old kitchen and Dad was telling me Mum had gone away with Mr McManus – except he kept calling him Carlo and for some reason that felt like the worst part of it all. I still have no idea why.' She shook her head. 'You insisted on setting the table every night for four people, do you remember? *Just in case Mum's hungry when she comes back*, you kept saying. I always waited until you'd gone to bed to put the unused knife and fork away. I couldn't bear to do it in front of you.'

Two stalls opened at the same time and the queue inched forward. Laura, though, felt herself being tugged back in time. Whenever she thought about it, that point in their lives felt as implausible as a dream. Had her dad really got lost driving her to school on the first morning because she'd missed the bus and then started sobbing in the layby he'd pulled into? Had she actually run out of socks and, terrified that she'd have to explain to a teacher why nobody had done any laundry for a week, improvised a pair out of tube bandages from their first-aid box at home?

On the seventh day she came home from school to find her mum in the kitchen, red-eyed at the table with a mug of tea, and her dad with his back to her at the window, looking out at the garden. The new overnight bag was in the hallway, looking like a parcel that had been returned to its sender. Laura guessed that Mr McManus had lost the tug of war – and guessing was all she could really do, seeing as nobody seemed to want to tell her what had actually happened. Jamie dropped French and switched to Spanish, but she still had to get through another year of people pointing at her and whispering in the corridors at college. Mr McManus left at the end of that term. The last time Laura had looked him up on Facebook he'd been living with his wife and teenage children in North Wales – his feed was full of pictures he'd taken of puffins. Pembrokeshire was a long way from the Amalfi Coast.

'You're up,' Jamie said, nudging her firmly towards the now-free stall in front of them. 'Be quick, OK? There's a 137 in ten minutes and the next one isn't for nearly half an hour.'

'Alright, Google Maps . . .' Laura pulled a face at her sister, went into the cubicle and bolted the door. She wriggled the too-tight dress up over her hips, grabbed a wodge of toilet paper and sat down on the seat, memories still trailing her like fog. She finished, wiped and noticed that the paper was streaked with pink. She shook her head, dropped it into the bowl and dug in the zipped inside pocket of her bag where she kept everything that she didn't want to fall out. There was nothing there. She leaned forward carefully on the seat, trying not to topple off.

'Jamie?' she whispered. 'Can you come here a second, please?'

There was some testy clacking from the other side of the door and the pointy ends of her sister's stilettos appeared under the gap at the bottom of it.

'What is it?'

'Have you got a tampon?'

'Are you being serious?'

'Well, have you? And keep your voice down, please.'

'Of course I do.' There was a pause – a click of knees and some huffing – and Jamie's hand materialised under the door, holding out a little white bullet.

'That's so like you to use non-applicator ones,' Laura muttered as she took it, trying to resume normal service.

Another click of knees. 'Excuse me, what do you mean by that?'

'You love making life difficult for yourself.'

'Or maybe I just don't need help. Unlike some people ...'

When Laura came out, yanking her dress down, her sister was already holding the bathroom door open, looking pointedly at her watch. *Hurry up*, she mouthed. She'd topped up her make-up – the perfect mask was back in place. Laura washed her hands, went to dry them on the dress, then stopped herself. How many times had Jamie got her period in bathrooms like this? she wondered. How many times had she had to box up all her grief, like something she was returning to a shop, before going out to face the world?

'Check your phone,' her sister said as they walked back out onto the floor. 'We've got a message.'

The week before, Whit had set up a group chat for the three of them, which he'd called THE STONYBROOK SQUAD, and which only he had ever posted in. Laura opened it and saw he'd sent a photo of him and Harrison. They were in the kitchen, posing for a selfie with a muffin tray containing a dozen mysterious brown orbs.

Pupcakes!!! he'd written underneath. *The guy from Pets R Us gave me the recipe. They're made from mince!*

Jamie was looking at it on her phone too. 'My husband is baking for a dog,' she said, shaking her head as they started walking towards the escalator. 'He's lost his mind.' But there was a smile trying to break through. Laura watched her zooming in on the photo, making Harrison's nose enormous, and felt something welling up inside her.

'Look, Jamie ...' she began. Her sister froze by a display of feather-trimmed handbags, giving her a *what-the-hell-are-you-doing* look. 'I know we never talk about it,' Laura pressed on, 'and you can obviously tell me to shut up ...' Jamie was glaring at her now like she'd just mooned the entire shop. 'I mean, I don't even know what you guys have decided to do about the whole thing. But if you are going to ... you know, try and find a way of doing it, I just wanted you to know that I think you'll be a great mum.' She pointed at herself. 'I mean, you've had enough practice, right?'

Jamie was silent, staring at her. They had exactly the same eyes – that was what their mum had always said. Laura could suddenly see everything in her sister's: all the pain that she kept locked away, the constant vigilance it took to keep it inside. How exhausting it was. How isolating.

'I know,' she said eventually, so quietly that Laura almost missed it. She blinked and Laura looked away, back at her phone – Cass had messaged her.

Cass:

in 'words i never thought i'd type' news, i am in clapham
just had a coffee with a developer we want to hire
are there always this many buggies?!?!
it's like the grand prix out here

Laura:
You're behind enemy lines!!!
I'm just heading back now actually

She hesitated.

Laura:
Do you … want to come round in a bit?

Cass:
to your sister's house?
does she know about me?

Laura clicked the screen off and inhaled.

'I need to tell you something else,' she said, talking fast to stop herself backing out of it. 'I'm seeing someone.'

Jamie looked exasperated.

'Yes, I know – we met him, remember?'

'Not Adam.' Laura wondered how long she could feasibly string out the pause between the two parts of the explanation. A year? Five years? The rest of her life? 'Someone else.'

'What? You broke up with Adam?'

'Not exactly …' Jamie's expression was reminding Laura of one she'd seen on a plaster-cast body during the Year 9 coach trip to Pompeii. 'But I'm going to,' she added quickly. 'As soon as I can. I just have to get my feature written. Is it OK if my new … person comes round this evening?'

Jamie's face performed a complicated emotional gymnastics routine – shock into distaste into disappointment, before finally settling on a kind of weary resignation.

'Fine,' she said as they stepped onto the escalator. 'Why not? I don't see how today can get any worse.'

***

Laura intercepted Cass halfway down the path. He was carrying a bunch of flowers.

'You shouldn't have.' Her pulse was fluttery as she glanced around her at the neatly trimmed box hedge, the chessboard tiles and the house's prim white-painted shutters, imagining how it all looked to someone like him.

'I didn't.' He held them teasingly out of reach, leaning in to kiss her. 'They're for your sister. I remember you said she's a tough nut to crack.'

'Creep,' she said, giving the toe of his boot a nudge, but she was secretly pleased. She wanted them to like him and – more ambitiously; it was Jamie they were talking about here after all – him to like them.

Jamie and Whit had arranged themselves in the kitchen, with her leaning against the sink and him sitting at the table. Whit was tapping one of his slippers anxiously against a table leg, clearly terrified that he was going to say the wrong thing. (Which, given his track record, wasn't an unreasonable fear to have; this was the man who up until the age of twenty had thought that drinking and driving meant you couldn't actually drink *anything* before you got behind the wheel, not even water.) Laura had overheard Jamie briefing him in whispers earlier. *Adam doesn't know, no. How on earth should I know what Laura's going to do about it?*

'This is Cass, everyone!' she announced as they walked in, putting on a cheerful voice to set the tone. They both looked up: Laura watched Jamie giving Cass the usual once-over, trying to work out where his hair and tattoos fitted into her own personal scale of Just About OK and Definitely Not OK. Her expression was hard to read, but Laura found it depressingly easy to guess which way her sister was leaning.

Cass raised a hand in greeting.

'Hey, everyone,' he said, giving them a wave. 'These are for you.' He held the flowers out to Jamie.

'That's very kind of you, Cass,' she said stiffly, putting them behind her in the sink. She didn't move to go and get a vase. Laura nudged her hand into his, trying to compensate for her sister's frosty reception. He pressed it and she pressed back; their own private code. She smiled.

There was an open bottle of wine on the table and two half-full glasses. Whit glanced at it, jumped like he'd been poked, then leaped to his feet.

'Get you a glass, buddy?' he asked. 'White OK?' Cass shook his head.

'Ah, thanks, but I'm vegan.' Whit blinked in confusion; Jamie frowned. 'Most wines are filtered through animal products to clarify them. Egg white, gelatin ... sometimes even fish bladders.'

'Yum!' Laura blurted out. Everybody ignored her.

'That must make things very difficult for you,' Jamie said briskly, topping up one of the glasses and taking it back to the sink with her. It was fine, Laura reminded herself: Jamie didn't really warm to anyone at first. Apart from Adam and that had probably only been because Laura hadn't introduced anyone to her for such a long time. Now that the novelty value had worn off, she'd fallen back into her old ways.

Cass shrugged. 'It's OK, you can get pretty decent vegan ones if you know where to look – and I'm not a big drinker anyway.'

'I certainly am after the day we've had,' Jamie said, pointedly raising her glass and maintaining eye contact with Cass while she drank. 'I imagine Laura's told you about the family situation we're dealing with at the moment.' She paused; it was like watching two people play chess, Laura thought, except one of them didn't know they were playing. And half the pieces were on the floor. And any minute now, the board was going to be joining them.

Cass put his arm around Laura. 'She told me a bit about what happened this afternoon – I mean, he's a good guy and your mum's happy, right? It could be a lot worse. I try to think of my folks as people first and parents second. It helps.'

Jamie's jaw was set. The only thing she hated more than someone refusing to take her side in an argument, Laura knew from long and bitter experience, was being talked down to – and although she was sure Cass hadn't meant it like that, it was how Jamie had taken it.

'Laura was telling me that you're from California, Cass,' Jamie said, icily polite. 'It must be nice to be able to put an entire continent between you and your family.'

'It is.' Cass grinned; if he'd registered the dig it clearly hadn't bothered him. 'You should try it.'

There was a clatter of paws on wood coming down the hallway: Harrison, who'd been asleep on the sofa, had woken up. He ambled into the kitchen and greeted everyone in turn: a loopy hand-lick for Whit, a more restrained nuzzle of the knee for Jamie and a long roll on the floor for Laura so she could tickle his stomach. When he came to Cass he put his head on one side, considering the new arrival with narrowed eyes. Cass let go of Laura's hand.

'Hey there, boy,' he said, holding it out to Harrison. 'Remember me from the video call the other day? Feeling better?' Harrison eyed it, sniffed, then took a step backwards. Cass reached forwards – Harrison reversed again, quicker this time. He backed up until he hit Whit's leg.

'What's up, buddy?' Whit bent down so he was at the dog's eye-level; Harrison turned away stubbornly. 'Gosh, I'm really sorry, Cass – he's never this shy normally. No idea what's got into him!' The room had turned into a kind of passive-aggressive daisy chain: Whit was watching Jamie, who was watching Harrison, who was watching Cass.

'He's on some new medication,' Laura said quickly, uncharacteristically annoyed with Harrison. First Jamie, now him – why couldn't they all just be normal? 'It's really strong, maybe that's why he's being funny.' She reached for Cass's hand again.

'Want to watch something next door?' she asked him.

'Are you watching it with me?' She nodded and he kissed her forehead. 'Then yes.' She could sense Jamie suppressing an almighty eye-roll. Whit was going through the cupboard.

'You kids want some snacks for your film?' His deep-rooted need to make everything OK had clearly taken over. 'We've got pretzels, cheese crackers ...'

'Whit ...' Jamie warned. Whit carried on blithely.

'Popcorn? There's salty and sweet! I can't help it, I'm crazy for the stuff. It's like ...'

'*Whit.*'

'Sorry.' He blushed. 'Well, enjoy! It was great meeting you, Cass.'

'And you.' Cass gave the two of them a winning smile, then winked at Jamie. 'Don't worry, we'll leave the door open.'

'Please don't,' Jamie said tartly. The flowers were still in the sink.

Laura hustled them into the hallway, telling herself that it could have gone worse but struggling to think of ways in which it actually could have. She risked a glance across at Cass – he looked more amused than anything else.

'Well, what did you think?' she whispered to him once they were out of earshot, trying to keep the anxiety out of her voice.

'Of them?' He stopped, tilting his head thoughtfully. 'I can see why they're married – I couldn't have done a better job of matching two people if I'd tried.' He did some more thinking. 'Jamie's kind of ...'

'Scratchy?' Laura put her arms around him. 'She's like that with everyone. Sorry.'

'Hey, don't be.' He kissed her lightly. 'She'll come round. We'll work on it next time.' Laura pressed her face into his neck, hugging the words to her like a promise.

***

Cass left after midnight: he'd said he had an early start the next morning. After the way things had gone with Jamie, Laura didn't feel she could try to persuade him to stay over. She lingered at the window that overlooked the street, watching him until he turned the corner and disappeared. Her mouth felt satisfyingly raw. She was pulling a sloppy jumper on over her underwear when she heard the floor-boards creak behind her. Harrison was in the doorway, watching her.

'You could have been a bit friendlier to him, you know,' she said, beckoning him over to scratch his ears. He hopped up onto the air bed and flopped down onto her pillow with a deep, contented sigh. 'Oh, now you want to play nice?

Fine. I'll be back in a minute – I'm just going to grab a drink. Don't bite the mattress, OK?'

There was a light on in the kitchen, casting a halogen glow out into the hall. Jamie was sitting at the table in her dressing down with a water glass in front of her, silent and preoccupied. Her face had been scrubbed clean of make-up and she'd pulled her hair back into a floppy scrunchie that made her look about twelve. Laura hesitated in the doorway. Then she crossed the room, pulled out the chair next to her and sat down.

'Thinking about Mum?' she asked, trying to ring-fence the conversation. She put a hand flat on the tabletop and slid it towards her sister's.

'No, actually.' A beat, then Jamie moved her hand a couple of millimetres to the left, so they were almost touching. 'I was thinking about you.'

'Me?' Laura pulled her hand away; she didn't want to hear this. 'Why?'

Jamie sipped her water. 'Look, I know you haven't asked for it,' she said, 'but honestly, Laura, my advice would be to make sure you're with someone who's really kind.'

Laura stood up and went over to the cupboard where the glasses lived. 'Cass *is* kind,' she said quickly, too wrong-footed to be angry – she and Jamie never talked about this stuff – opening it and reaching to get a tumbler out. For a second her shoulder was level with her face: her skin smelled of him.

'I never said he wasn't.' Jamie went quiet for a moment. 'Although I think you could argue that someone who's prepared to risk both of your jobs like this might be a bit … cavalier, shall we say, however good his intentions are. Anyway, I know kindness doesn't sound exciting, but it's what matters in the long run. I'm not saying that sexual chemistry isn't important – I've been very swayed by it in the past …'

Laura pulled her jumper over her face with her free hand. 'Aargh, please stop talking,' she begged from behind it. 'Please. I'm begging you.'

'I'm being serious.' Jamie drained her glass. 'Adam's a kind person, I think,' she said. She let out a short, sharp laugh. 'Is. Was. I'm not sure what tense to refer to him in, to be honest.'

Eye-rolling, sarcasm, withering put-downs – all of that Laura could handle. But she felt her sister's disappointment like a slap and she hated it.

'I didn't see you worrying about kindness when you were abandoning me to deal with Mum and Dad for all those years,' she muttered. 'That wasn't very kind, was it?'

Jamie looked at her for a long time.

'Look, you're an adult,' she said. 'You have to make your own decisions.' She pushed her chair back and got to her feet. 'Turn the light off when you come up, please.'

Chapter 19

risk (noun): a measure of the potential for loss

'The bad news,' Lil announced as she opened the door to her flat, 'is that Hot Ben cancelled on me. He's had to take his grandmother to a funeral in Eastbourne.'

Laura, who'd been mentally replaying what she thought of as her Cass highlights reel while she climbed the stairs, dragged herself back to the present. Lil was wearing her tied-up pink gingham shirt and the caramel suede skirt with the fringing: her favourite first-date outfit. All week she'd been playing it down, but it was obvious she'd been excited. Laura arranged her face into a configuration that she hoped conveyed the appropriate ratio of empathy and outrage. Once you'd been on the receiving end of it, you never wanted to be the Pity Committee.

'It's totally fine, we're going to reschedule,' Lil went on, waving a hand. 'The good news ...' she raised her voice, as though she was speaking for someone else's benefit '... is that Adam's already here and we're baking!'

'Oh! Wow ...' Laura blinked in shock. Lil had asked them both to come for eleven o'clock. By setting multiple

298

alarms on her phone Laura had actually managed to get to Herne Hill on time. Adam's flight from Gothenburg had landed at eight that morning. He'd told her that he'd been up late the night before discussing a research paper with some other delegates. She'd been secretly hoping that he might have decided to have a nap when he got back to his flat and overslept. But of course he hadn't – he was far too conscientious ever to let something like that happen. She looked at Lil's carefully made-up face, trying to read her expression: the thought of the two of them being alone after their last exchange on Hampstead Heath induced a full-body cringe. 'Has it been ... OK, him being here?'

Lil grinned. 'It's been great, actually – bless him, he turned up with all the ingredients and the cutest present for Dora from Sweden. Come on, she'll want to show you.' She set off down the narrow hallway, pausing in front of the faded Orangina poster she'd bought on a trip they'd made together to the Alexandra Palace antique fair. 'It's really sweet of you both to do this when he's been away for a week,' she whispered with a wink. 'I'm sure you'd much rather be round at his making up for lost time ...'

'Right!' Laura bit the inside of her cheek as she followed her friend past the jam jar of paper peonies Dora had made at school and the bowl of pebbles collected from beaches. Before Lil had bought it, the flat had been owned by an old lady who hadn't done anything to it since the days of glass milk bottles. Lil had painted the walls a bold, sunny yellow, like a Thomas Cook brochure from the 1960s, and there was a frondy palm taking up most of the bathroom with its avocado-coloured fittings. It was all so Lil. Laura wondered if she'd ever get the chance to do the same in her own home – and if she did, with whom. She couldn't actually imagine Cass living anywhere with four walls and a roof.

Dora and Adam were in the turquoise kitchen, rolling up chocolate-filled triangles of pastry to make croissants. Dora was standing on a hop-up stool, wearing a miniature apron, her face furrowed in concentration as she wielded a small plastic knife. Laura coughed; Dora whirled round, squealed, jumped onto the floor and charged over for a hug. Adam dusted off his hands and stepped forward: he was wearing exactly the same outfit he'd had on for the Cupid shoot, except this jumper was red rather than blue.

'Hey! Long time no see!' He pulled Laura into an awkward, slightly stiff embrace. He was taller than Cass, so her hands went instinctively to the wrong places – she quickly course-corrected them, relieved that her face was pressed into his chest. She was finding it even harder to look at him than she had before he'd gone away. Dora made a loud retching noise, then tapped the small of Laura's back.

'Stop *cuddling* and look at what Adam got me!' She held out the apron proudly – it was printed blue and yellow to make it look like the Swedish flag. Laura looked across at Adam; he was blushing.

'They were selling them at the airport ...' He glanced at Lil. 'I remembered you said she likes baking, so I thought I'd pick her one up. My nephew's not even walking yet, let alone cooking. Anyway, I just couldn't resist.' He smiled, then quickly looked at the floor – he seemed almost embarrassed, as though he'd just inadvertently exposed something shameful. He really did want to be a dad, Laura thought, and it was suddenly much too hot in the kitchen. She tried to focus on Dora, who was back on the stool, brandishing a mug of beaten egg with a brush sticking out of it.

'Now, you put this on the tops,' she was explaining to Lil, like a celebrity chef giving a TV demonstration. 'It makes them all shiny. That's what they do in the big tent where people cry.'

'She means *Bake Off*,' Lil whispered. Just then a trilling came from the living room – the landline was connected to a handset shaped like a bunch of bananas, but the ring was exactly the same as the one that Jamie and Whit's phone had. Laura shook her head as she made the connection; she was still angry with her sister. Their conversation in the kitchen had been four days ago and since then they'd been engaged in their own Cold War, with Whit intermittently trying to break the stalemate by suggesting group activities like ten-pin bowling and a trip to the Vauxhall City Farm. (*They've got alpacas called Ben and Jerry!!!* he'd messaged the WhatsApp group; neither of them had replied.) In fact, Jamie had been so focused on being disappointed in her that it actually seemed to have taken her mind off their mum and Alan – which, Laura supposed, was a kind of progress.

Dora's face lit up as she leapt off the stool. 'Is it Dad?' she asked, grabbing Lil's hand. 'Did you send the picture of me to him on his holiday? Did you?'

'You bet I did, peach. Let's go say hi to him, OK?' Lil said, letting herself be towed out of the room. She glanced over her shoulder at Laura and Adam, obviously trying not to grimace. 'We'll only be a second – she wanted me to send Andreas a photo of her in her new apron, but I can't imagine they're allowed to make long calls on the *silent yoga retreat*, can you?'

'Dora's brilliant, isn't she?' Adam said once the living-room door was closed. 'Such a great kid.' He picked up the pastry packet and ran his finger down the chart of cooking times, frowning – he did look exhausted, Laura thought. Drained, actually. Her brain was hijacked by a horrible image of him lying on his pale grey sofa in a couple of weeks' time, looking just like this after she told him she didn't think they should stay together. She picked up the brush and started vigorously egg-washing the last of the croissants, to try and make it go away.

'It was really sweet of you to get her a present,' she said, putting on a bright smile. 'Were you OK getting up for your flight?'

'Hmm? Oh, fine.' He opened the oven door and carefully slid the baking tray in without looking at her.

'And how was the paper?' He blinked, looking confused. 'The one you stayed up talking to people about.'

'Oh, yeah.' He crouched down and started tapping all the oven's dials, checking they were set to the right temperature. 'Really interesting. It turned into a pretty late one though – I'm going to need to turn in early tonight if I don't want to be a zombie at work on Monday.'

Out of nowhere, Laura had a brainwave. It emptied her mind of everything she'd been feeling a second before, in the way anything to do with Cass always seemed to.

'Look, why don't you just head home and put your feet up once we've finished baking?' she volunteered. 'I've got some ... shopping to do in Kings Cross anyway and I think there's a train I can get there from Herne Hill. You can get back to Bermondsey from North Dulwich, right?'

Adam gave her a grateful smile. 'That would be good, actually,' he said. 'Thanks, Laura.'

Dora raced back into the room with Lil behind her. 'We need to do the clock!' she shouted. She pointed imperiously at the kitchen timer on the worktop – Adam picked her up so she could set it. Lil clapped her hands and grabbed her phone off the kitchen table.

'Oh, that's too much – let me get a photo for Instagram. Stay like that, you two.' She held it up, tapping the screen. 'Adam, if you just ...' She stopped abruptly, her face clouding over. 'I don't believe this. It's Ben.'

'Posting from a funeral in Eastbourne?' Laura rinsed her hands under the tap. 'Bold.' Lil shook her head.

'No, he's at . . . a beer festival in Hyde Park. Drinking out of a glass boot.' Her voice was rising. 'I don't get it. Why would he lie like that?'

Dora was staring at Lil, her eyes huge with worry. Adam quickly crouched down so he was her height.

'Hey, Dora? Remember that cool game on the TV you were telling me about? The one with the panda?' Dora nodded, her eyes still on Lil; he put a reassuring hand on her shoulder. 'How about you show me how it works, eh?' He gave them a meaningful look as he stood up, then steered her out of the kitchen, leaving Lil and Laura alone. Lil shut the door behind them.

'That was nice of him,' she said flatly, sitting down at the table and letting her shoulders slump. She shook her head. 'Fucking hell. Honestly, how hard is it just to tell someone you don't want to go on a date with them?'

Laura took the seat next to Lil's and put an arm around her back, then the other one around her front. She leaned in and rested her head on Lil's shoulder. 'I'm really sorry,' she mumbled into the gingham. 'He's not Hot Ben anymore. We'll find another one to give the title to.'

'Will we?' Laura looked up: Lil was biting her lip. She suddenly looked like she might be about to cry.

'I just keep thinking about . . . probability, I suppose.' She pulled away. 'Like, what are the actual odds of me meeting a normal, grown-up guy who makes me laugh, who's great with Dora and doesn't make me secretly hope I'll get thrush so I can get out of having sex with him? When you narrow it down that leaves about seven people in the whole world, doesn't it? And most of them probably live in . . . I don't know . . . *Arizona* or somewhere.'

Laura put her hand over hers and squeezed. 'It only takes one,' she said. Lil snorted.

'Maybe I used up my quota with Andreas. God, I hope not.' She sighed, retying the bow at the bottom of her shirt. 'It's fine, I'll just live vicariously through you and Adam. Come on all your dates, sit between you in the cinema ...'

Laura's eyes darted involuntarily towards the door then back again. Lil noticed.

'What?' she asked. 'What is it?' Laura took a deep breath.

'Have you ever done something that looked like a really bad idea on paper but was actually amazing?' she asked tentatively.

'Sex on a National Express coach,' Lil said instantly. She gave Laura a sideways glance. 'Um, why?' They looked at each other and there was a long pause. 'Oh,' she said slowly. '*Ohhhh.* Wow. OK. Who?'

Laura got her phone out and scrolled through to the last selfie Cass had sent her. Lil shuffled up to her and leaned over it.

'Hmm,' she said, peering at the screen. 'Well, it's a vibe. Very Bay Area. What's he called?'

'Cass,' Laura said, trying to be cool about it but secretly delighted to be able to say his name out loud. 'We met a while ago, but we've only been ... for a couple of weeks.'

Lil digested this. 'So there's been a bit of an overlap,' she said eventually, sitting back in her chair. 'Well, it's not ideal, but it happens. How did you meet?'

'Through ... work.' That wasn't exactly true, but it wasn't a lie either.

'At the *Bugle*? Wow, things have changed – when I started there the best-looking guy in the building was this bloke on Sport who used to pick his teeth in the lift ...'

'Not at work-work.' If Laura broke the sentence down into little chunks the controversial bit might just slip unnoticed between one of the gaps. 'He actually works for Cupid. You know.' She took a deep breath. 'The people I'm writing the feature about. He's their head of data.'

'Wait ... what?' Lil reared back in shock. '*What?* Sorry, let me just get this straight – you're secretly shagging the guy who found you your actual boyfriend?' She stared at Laura for a full five seconds, then shook her head in disbelief. 'Fucking hell. I thought I had problems.'

Laura flinched. Jamie she'd expected it from, but Lil was her most open-minded friend. She could feel resentment starting to bubble up inside her.

'Look, I know it's not ... great, but he's brilliant, honestly – he's clever, and he makes me laugh, and the sex is *incredible*,' she whispered. Lil's eyes were still incredulously wide.

'It would have to be to make up for the shitstorm that's going to hit you when this comes out.' She threw her hands up, sending her bracelets rattling towards her elbows. 'What about his job? What about your job?' Her eyes darted towards the door. 'What are you going to do about *Adam*?'

'We just have to stay together until the feature comes out, then we can break up,' Laura said obstinately, hoping she sounded more confident than she felt. 'It's fine! They do it all the time on *Love Island*.' Lil looked more horrified than Laura had ever seen her; she softened her voice in response. 'I like him so much – please, Lil, I really need you to be in my corner with this one.'

'I am *always* in your corner,' Lil said emphatically. 'But I reserve the right to tell you what I think when you come to me with a really bad idea. And with the greatest respect, Morrison, this is a fucking *terrible* one.'

The door creaked; they both sat bolt upright in their chairs.

'Let's talk about this later, OK?' Lil whispered. Laura didn't trust herself to reply – inside she was boiling. Lil was always going on about how much she hated it when people just followed the script without thinking, wasn't she? Well, she'd thought about it and she wasn't following it anymore. So what was her problem?

Dora's head appeared, followed by Adam's. Laura grabbed her bag and pretended to be looking for something in it. She couldn't look at him, or Lil – she just wanted to get out of there.

'Has the timer gone yet?' Dora asked hopefully.

Lil shook her head. 'Why don't you open the door and see how they're getting on, peach? They smell really great!' Her bright, pulled-together parent-voice tugged at Laura's heartstrings; she tried her hardest to ignore it.

'No, they might go wrong,' Dora said, approaching the oven purposefully. She sat down in front of it, crossing her legs and folding her arms. 'I want them to be *perfect*.'

Chapter 20

deduction (noun): *a technique used to reach a conclusion*

The train from Herne Hill to St Pancras took twenty-one minutes. Laura found a window seat in a nearly empty carriage and wedged herself into it to stew. Why did people think they could just weigh in on her life like this whenever they felt like it? It wasn't like everyone else's decisions were fantastic. How many weddings had she sat through where it had been obvious that the bride and groom were going to get divorced before they'd even opened half of the kitchen appliances on their gift list?

She went onto Instagram and started mindlessly scrolling. Sasha had posted a new story. Against her better judgement, Laura clicked on it. There was Walker in a pair of palm-print trunks, sitting artily on a beach in Ibiza with his back to the camera. Laura snorted at the contrived pose, which Sasha had clearly styled to fit with the rest of her feed, and again at the fact he was even *on* a beach – Walker had skin the colour of semi-skimmed milk and probably got burned in blizzards. The quote Sasha had stuck in the sand at the bottom of the shot was bracketed by heart emojis.

❤ *Be Brave. Love Deeply* ❤

What, Laura thought thunderously, was so brave about getting together with your housemate and moving into a flat with a deli underneath it that sold £4 croissants? But if you went and did something that was actually unconventional – say, falling for someone you shouldn't, like she had – everyone queued up to give you a kicking. She screenshotted the story and was about to send it to Lil with the caption *Some personal news: I am going to be sick*, then remembered she didn't actually want to talk to Lil about anything right now and deleted it. She clicked out of Instagram and messaged Cass.

Laura:
Surprise! I'm in Kings Cross!
Want me to come round?

He was typing. She felt a little tug of pleasure go all the way through her, like someone had pulled on a hidden string.

Cass:
i mean
obviously i do
but the boat's a mess …

Laura:
I don't mind
I'll close my eyes

Cass:
hah
ok
give me half an hour to tidy up?

When she got there he was sunbathing on the roof of the boat in just his jeans, with his eyes closed. She crept up on him, tiptoeing onto the deck and stretching up so she could kiss her way along his side. He smelled of the minty soap he used. He laughed without opening his eyes and let his hand flop down so it was resting on the top of her head.

'How was babysitting?' he asked her, raking his fingers gently across her scalp. 'Peppa and friends all good?' Her entire body buzzed at his touch.

'Oh, fine.' She just wanted to shut the door on all of it. 'Uneventful.' She traced her fingers down his stomach. He laughed, stopping her hand with his.

'Come on, let's get you inside before we're both arrested.' He sat up and swung his legs off the roof. 'My lease has a clause in it about bringing the lock into disrepute ...'

The curtains were still drawn and there were plates in the sink. Laura pulled a wry face.

'This is after the tidying?'

'Ah, come on – I'll wash up when I'm dead.' He kneeled in front of the fridge and started going through it. 'OK, how about a coffee? Or maybe ... something stronger?' He turned around, holding out a short brown bottle. It was the cider they'd been drinking when they went up the canal.

'They had them on special in the place by the station last night, so I thought I'd stock up.' He stood up, tucking it into the pocket of her dress. 'I remembered it was the one you like, so ...'

Laura kissed him, cutting him off. It was a pity Jamie and Lil weren't here, she thought – they'd see how thoughtful he was. And Walker and Sasha and everyone else who'd patronised her about her love life over the years. They could all get lost.

'Will you have one too?' she asked him. 'Keep me company?'

'Why not?' He patted the top of his head; his hair was still slightly damp from the shower. 'Oh, I left my shades on the deck – two seconds, OK?'

He kissed her again, grabbing a t-shirt from the sofa on his way out. Laura watched him as he climbed the steps, enjoying the way the muscles in his back moved as he pulled the shirt over his head, then went to the fridge to find another cider. When she opened the door she saw the six-pack only had one other bottle left in it; she glanced down at the plastic recycling crate next to her feet and spotted the four missing ones were in there, side by side. She smiled to herself.

'Looks like you already started . . .' she called out through the hatch. She stopped.

'What was that?' Cass reappeared, his sunglasses tucked into his belt loop. He saw her expression and stopped in the doorway. 'You OK?'

Something was happening right at the edge of her vision, blooming darkly like the beginning of a migraine.

'Were you having a cider party without me last night?' she asked him, stalling for time, trying to sound normal.

'Oh, it was kind of a last-minute thing.' He smiled and went over to the drawer next to the sink. 'Now, I'm sure I put the opener in here . . .'

Her gaze had snagged on the empty bottles. Two of them were ringed, unmistakably, with black lipstick.

Someone I know runs a bakery, he'd told her right here on the boat. She bent down to pick up the bottle nearest her. Its neck left a dark print on her thumb, and as she stared at it everything suddenly came together. She took a step back-wards, a series of images flashing through her mind one after the other, knocking the breath out of her. The fact he'd had a shower just before she arrived, even though it was the middle of the day. His caginess about making evening plans with her. One tick on WhatsApp for hours, her message unread until four in the morning. The woman carrying the VEGANISED box she'd walked into outside Cupid's office – the one she'd seen there before. The woman with the black lipstick taking the meringues to someone in the building. The woman who'd clearly been here with Cass last night, drinking cider.

Laura could feel him watching her.

'Are you ...' She couldn't get the words out – she'd been wobbling on the edge of a cliff and now the ground was rushing up to meet her. 'Are you seeing someone else, Cass?'

He was meant to be denying it. That was what you did when something wasn't true. But he wasn't. He was just looking at her, his clear blue eyes steady.

'Well, yeah,' he said eventually. 'I am. Kind of.'

Laura sat down mechanically on the sofa, still holding onto the bottle; the hand around it felt numb. She heard someone laugh hollowly and realised it was her. 'Wow. What happened to *radical transparency*?'

'Laura. It's not a big deal. OK? Really.' He sat down next to her and put an arm around her shoulders. She let it stay there, because if she didn't it would mean it was definitely true and she was still hoping he'd yell *'JOKING!'* like he was jumping out from behind a curtain. But he didn't. He just stroked her arm with his thumb in the way you did when you cared about someone. A high-speed train went past behind them, shaking the boat.

'I thought ...' This couldn't be happening, it was impossible. But it was. She could feel the tears pinching at her eyes now, hot and humiliating. How could she have missed it? How had she been such an idiot? 'I thought this was something. A real thing.'

'It is! Laura, it is.' He looked down at the neck of the bottle. 'And that's a different kind of something. We're just friends who sometimes … you know. Hang out. That's all.'

'You don't have a shower after you've seen someone if you've just been *hanging out* – do you think I'm actually stupid?' She shrugged his arm off, then wished she hadn't; being near him was horrible but not being near him was worse. The air on her skin felt cold and there was a sour taste in her mouth; she tried to swallow it down and breathe.

'I talked to her outside your office a while ago. And I saw her going into the building the day we first met. Those meringues were for you, weren't they? And it was her you were making that program for, the one to cut the coffee queue down.' He nodded quite matter-of-factly – Laura wondered if she was actually going to be sick. 'How long have you been … doing this for?'

'A couple of years, on and off. We matched on an app, funnily enough.' He smiled – actually *smiled* – then stood up and walked over to the other side of the cabin. 'Her name's Monica. She worked for a really cool animal welfare campaign group before she opened Veganised. You'd like her.'

'Well, we seem to have lots in common,' Laura said bitterly – the whole boat felt like it was rearranging itself into a nightmarish doppelgänger, stripped of everything good and true. 'Were you ever going to tell me about her?'

'If you'd asked, of course.'

'But you wouldn't have if I hadn't?'

Cass sighed. 'I don't know what you want me to say. This is normal for me – it's just how I do things. There've always been a few people in my life at any one time.'

'A few? Jesus! Are there more?'

He shook his head, maddeningly calm. 'No, it's just the two of you right now. All I mean is, you never said you wanted us to be exclusive. If that's what you want then we can definitely talk about it ...'

'I'd have thought it was pretty fucking obvious!'

He spread his palms – not in an apology, it was more like *well, there you go*. 'I'm really sorry, Laura. I honestly didn't think you'd care this much – last time I checked, your definition of commitment was pretty flexible ...'

Laura flinched. 'No, that's different,' she snapped. 'You always knew about Adam. You made an informed decision. I didn't get to do that.' She stared at him, searching his face for a trace of guilt or regret, but he just looked nonplussed. 'So, what, are you ... polyamorous, is that it? I'm pretty sure you're meant to tell people if you are – I mean, that's the whole point, isn't it? That you're really honest with each other? That you have *rules*?'

'Like I said, I'm not big on rules in general,' Cass said with another shrug. 'I'm a relationship anarchist, I guess.'

There was a horrible voice in her head. *You were wrong*, it hissed, twisting the knife. *Everything you thought, everything you felt, everything you were starting to believe you could actually have – wrong, wrong, wrong.*

She started backing away from him.

'Don't flatter yourself,' she said in a choked voice. 'You tell lies and you hurt people. There's a big difference.'

She grabbed her bag off the floor and hurried out of the cabin, up the steps and onto the bank. He called after her but she didn't stop. The lipstick was still on her thumb, like a bruise.

Chapter 21

loss function (noun): *a way of mathematically mapping the cost of an event*

The mornings were the worst. It was Tuesday now and every day since the terrible afternoon on Cass's boat Laura had woken up before dawn with a sick weight in the pit of her stomach that made it impossible for her to get back to sleep. She'd lie there for a bit as it all flooded back, letting the tears run into her ears, then pull on whatever was within arm's reach, tiptoe downstairs past a snoring Harrison and quietly let herself out of the house. She'd walk slowly across the Common to the bandstand and sit there, hugging her knees in the milky light, watching jogging couples laughing and carefree dogs chasing balls, wondering if she'd ever feel properly human again. They'd known each other for less than three months, she kept reminding herself, and it wasn't like anybody had actually *died*. But it did feel like someone had – the Cass she'd woven her dreams around was gone forever. He was the first thing she thought about when she woke up and the last when she put out the light, only now there was nothing pleasurable about him popping into her head – it was physically painful.

She couldn't focus at work: she kept googling things like 'quick fixes for a broken heart' in a window she'd shrunk to the size of a matchbox and then crying in the bathroom. Inge, who'd assumed her mood was redundancy-related, had suggested the day before that she work from home so she could concentrate. Laura was sitting on her bed now, drowning in emails, staring glassily at one Lil had just sent her.

Lillian Cho
To: Laura Morrison
IMPORTANT REMINDER ...
Tues 18 Sept, 15:16

... that you are amazing. D and I love you THIS much xxx

Laura swallowed the lump in her throat. Lil had been so much nicer to her about everything than she deserved – she'd even offered to take the afternoon off so they could go to Monica's bakery and snoop on her. But she couldn't think about that right now. As well as all of her usual work, her Cupid feature was due soon and she still hadn't started it. Bouncy, though, had already written an introduction, which was lurking sinisterly in another window.

WE JUST CLICKED
Laura Morrison had been dating disastrously for a decade when a new data-driven matchmaking service changed her life forever. Now in a relationship with the man of her dreams, she explains why finding love really *is* a numbers game.

As she read and re-read it, imagining it staring out at her from a newsstand, her insides twisted themselves into vicious knots. Yesterday she'd promised herself she'd call Nush and tell her she wasn't going to be able to write the article after all. Then she'd call Adam, ask him to meet her and confess everything to him. But every time she'd started psyching herself up to do it, she'd been gripped by such terror that she hadn't been able to go through with it. Before, she'd been able to comfort herself with the thought that, however badly everyone took the news about her pulling out of the whole Cupid project, at least she'd have Cass. Now he was gone too.

She picked up her phone and went into their chat. For weeks it had been right at the top of WhatsApp, but she had to swipe down to find it now, which hurt more than she'd ever imagined performing a basic action on her phone could. He hadn't messaged her since Sunday. That wasn't surprising given she hadn't replied to any of his earlier ones asking if they could meet and talk, but there was still a tiny, stupid part of her hoping that he'd pull a rabbit out of the hat that would make it all go away. She scrolled upwards – *i think about you all the time, laura morrison* – and put her thumb over the date so she could pretend, just for a second, that then was now.

'Lunch is served . . .'

Whit, who was also working from home that day – something about the lawn being re-seeded – was hovering in the doorway, holding out a plate with a very large cheese toastie on it.

'Thought you might be hungry,' he said, stepping gingerly into the room and putting it on the end of her bed; he'd spent the past few days tiptoeing around her like she was a cross between someone with a terrible illness and a serial killer. 'It's gone three – you haven't had anything yet . . .'

Laura pushed her phone under the pillow. 'Thanks, Whit,' she said, reaching forward to take it. 'This looks incredible.' He put his head on one side and opened his mouth to speak – she looked away quickly, worried his kind expression would finish her off – then realised his pocket had lit up.

'Ah! That'll be She Who Must Be Obeyed.' He grinned, fishing out his phone and holding it to his ear. 'Hey, sweetheart. Yup, the lawn guy's just gone. All sorted, looks great.' There was a pause; Laura could hear the faint squawk of Jamie's voice. 'She's right here – hang on ...' He passed the phone over. 'Bring it down when you're done, OK?' he stage-whispered, tiptoeing out of the room and closing the door behind him.

'I'm in the supermarket between calls,' Jamie announced. 'They've got a special offer on sea bass. I'm going to get some for dinner – do you want to join us?'

'Ambassador, you're spoiling us with this heavily discounted fish,' Laura said dryly, reaching for the sandwich. Deep down, she was actually finding her sister's predictability very comforting – you always knew where you were with Jamie. She didn't tell lies, or cover up huge parts of her life, or turn out to be a completely different person from the one you thought you were dealing with.

Jamie sighed. 'Well, it's up to you, but you have to eat *something* – you can't just live off coffee the way you have been ...' She went quiet and Laura could feel something taking shape at the other end of the line. Her stomach tensed like she was bracing herself for a punch.

'Is everything else OK?' she asked. Jamie exhaled.

'Mum called me just now,' she said, lowering her voice. 'Apparently *Alan*' – she made it sound like an alias – 'has four tickets to something called the Battle of Britain Airshow and wants to know if we'd like to go with them. It's kind of him to offer but I'm assuming you'd rather not.'

'It's a no from the panel,' Laura confirmed. 'I do think Alan actually is his name, though,' she added. 'He's not, like, Prince. Or David Bowie.'

'The Artist Formerly Known as Alan,' Jamie suggested.

'Alan Stardust. I can imagine him in tinfoil flares.' Laura glanced across at the toastie – the melted cheese was starting to cool and solidify unappealingly. She'd have to force down at least half of it, she told herself as she picked it up: she hated the thought of throwing Whit's kindness back in his face. She'd been doing quite enough of that with other people recently.

'Christ, don't.' There was another ominous pause. 'Dad knows,' Jamie said eventually. 'Mum went round there for a talk yesterday. Apparently he took it pretty well – she's going to start getting her things together when he's away again in a few weeks. They'll sell the house at some point, but they're both OK for money, which is a relief. Anyway, she's not working today and I think she'd really like it if you called her.' Another silence. 'I said you've been having some man trouble.'

Laura choked; so much for always knowing where you were with Jamie. 'Are you joking?' she spluttered. 'Why would you do that?'

'She realised you were blocking her calls and she wanted to know why – what else was I meant to say?' Jamie stopped talking and sighed. 'Look, I know we've both always felt we have to look after them, in our own ways,' she went on in an infuriatingly reasonable voice; now that her outrage had worn off she seemed to have switched into work mode, dealing with their parents' break-up in a logical and busi-nesslike way. 'But maybe you should try letting her look after you for a change. She really misses you, Laura – you've always been her baby. And yes, he's a bit ridiculous, but I actually think Alan's been good for her. You might be pleasantly surprised by how she handles it.'

Laura twizzled the cocktail stick that was holding the remains of the sandwich together left, then right, then left again, too depressed by the idea that anything could ever be a pleasant surprise again to be angry with Jamie. Before Cass, all she'd had was a hunch that she couldn't trust her own feelings, that they might lead her astray and break her heart. Now, she was absolutely sure that was true.

'Right, I'm at the checkout,' Jamie said briskly. 'Oh, can you pick up Harrison's repeat prescription from the vet this afternoon, please? They just texted me to say it's ready.'

She rang off. Laura locked Whit's phone, feeling an unexpected pinch of loss, then reached for hers. She went into her chat with her mum and quickly pressed the video camera symbol before she could find a reason not to. The screen blurred, blipped, then resolved itself into a familiar shape in a pink kaftan, sunglasses and straw hat. Her mum's phone was obviously on her lap: Laura could only see the top half of her face and behind it a stripy sun lounger. Beyond that, right in the corner, was an expanse of painstakingly clipped green grass, like something from a garden catalogue.

'Hello, love! Well, isn't this a treat? Sorry, my hands are covered in Ambre Solaire ...' She was fumbling with the phone – Laura got a shot of the cloudless sky, then the patio with its crazy paving neatly bordered in brick. Now they were back to her face again: she was wearing a coral lipstick that Laura couldn't remember seeing before. It suited her, she thought. The whole outfit did.

'Can you hear me OK?' she went on. 'Alan's kitted me out with a new phone and this is my first video-call, can you believe it!'

Laura nodded. 'Jamie said you were ...' She'd been about to say 'at home', but couldn't quite get the words out. 'Wow, it's so sunny there,' she said instead. 'You look like you're on holiday.'

Her mum tweaked the brim of her hat happily. 'Mmm, life does feel a bit like that at the moment,' she said. 'I ...' She caught herself, her eyes widening with concern as she realised what she'd said. 'Not that before I didn't ...'

'It's OK – I know what you mean,' Laura said quickly. She could hear birds tweeting in the background. 'I'm glad you've got such a nice garden to sit in on your day off.'

'It *is* nice, isn't it?' Her mum beamed. 'Alan's just off watering his strawberries, bless him. We had some of them last night for dessert.'

'How were they?'

'Oh, terrible! Hard as rocks. We've been calling them the Croydon meteorites.' She laughed and then her expression softened. 'Now, Jamie said you've been having a bit of a tough time with a man ...'

Laura flicked her eyes downwards to the keyboard. It had been so long since she'd confided in her mum about anything to do with love. In fact, she could remember exactly when the last time was: she'd been thirteen, crying in the car home from Jenna Molloy's party at Planet Ice because the birthday girl had kissed Jez Butterfield, for whom Laura had pined since primary school, in the queue for slushies. She'd always worried that any emotional burden she added might turn out to be the final straw – a weight that her parents' already shaky marriage couldn't bear. But that was done now, finished now. She didn't need to feel like that. And maybe, she realised, she never actually had.

'Men plural,' she said with a grimace.

Laura told her mum everything. She didn't interrupt or try to change the subject but stayed very still, listening.

'Oh, my poor love,' she said softly when Laura had finished. 'I'm sorry. You've been in the wars, haven't you?'

Laura nodded, too choked up to speak. She swallowed.

'How did you do it, Mum?' she asked. 'Start all over again, I mean. Without being scared you'd get really hurt again.'

Her mum's eyes drifted, just for a second, to where Laura presumed Alan and the strawberries were. She adjusted her hat and smiled. 'Well, everyone gets hurt. I mean, all relationships end eventually, don't they? And even if they end badly, it doesn't mean they were a mistake or that you got nothing out of them. Look at me and your dad. I really mean this, love – neither of us would go back in time and do things differently because we've got you and Jamie to show for it. And I can tell you that for a fact because we talked about it when I went round to see him the other day.' She moved her phone so it was closer to her face. 'You have to make a decision to *try* to be happy.'

A gin and tonic suddenly appeared at the bottom of the screen, held out by an invisible hand.

'Ah!' her mum said; her whole face lit up. 'Sun's past the yard-arm, apparently.'

Laura heard a man's voice speaking in the background: affectionate, solicitous. She'd never heard either of her parents talk to the other one like that.

'Hi, Alan!' she called out. Her mum beamed.

'He says hello!' She turned her head; Alan was talking again. 'He says do you fancy coming down for the day one weekend soon? We could go for a nice walk on the Downs, pop into a pub afterwards ...'

Laura could hear the faint roar of a plane on its way to Gatwick. She imagined she was there too, actually inside the screen, watching her mum and Alan – these two people with a combined age of over a hundred – being sweet with each other like starry-eyed teenagers. There was still so much love in the world, she thought. Maybe not for her – but it was out there. And it could grow and thrive in the strangest places. The feeling shimmered like a bubble for a second, then vanished with a pop.

'Sounds good,' she said, forcing herself to smile. 'As long as there aren't any strawberries.'

Her mum's laughter echoed down the line. They said goodbye and Laura ended the call – Adam had just messaged her, she saw with a queasy lurch of her stomach. She pulled the notification down from the top of the screen so he wouldn't see she'd read it.

> *Hey! Hope your day's going well.*
> *Shall we meet for a drink tonight?*
> *Maybe go out somewhere?*
> *Feels like we haven't talked in a while.*

She just needed time, Laura told herself, stuffing her phone back under the pillow again. Just a bit more time.

***

The Noah's Ark Veterinary Practice was at the bottom of Stonybrook Street. In a past life it had been a music shop and the door still played 'Greensleeves' when it opened. Walker had dragged her in there once to look at an electric organ, Laura remembered as she pushed it; the memory stung like a flick from an elastic band. She'd muted him and Sasha on Sunday after another beach photo, this time of them in a two-person hammock, had popped up on Instagram – it felt like they were deliberately mocking her. Then she'd gone into Words With Friends and deleted the game they'd been playing. She hadn't been able to get rid of their shared scoreboard, though: it was still there on the home page, recording the results of every game they'd played together.

YOU LOST!
YOU LOST!
YOU LOST!

There were three people in the surgery's waiting room: a bald man in a windbreaker with a carry-crate on his knees and two women chatting behind the reception desk.

'Um, hi,' Laura said to them. They both looked up. 'I'm here to collect Harrison's prescription.' They blinked in unison. 'Harrison ... Morrison?'

'Oh!' exclaimed the woman on the left. Her earrings, which were shaped like dolphins, shook as she chuckled. 'Such a funny boy. He made us laugh the last time he came in, didn't he, Dami?'

'He did, Bron,' the other woman, who had chunky cornrows and an identical pair of earrings, agreed. (What had he been doing? Elvis impressions? Press ups? The crossword?) She stood up. 'I just need to package everything up for you,' she called over her shoulder as she disappeared behind a screen. 'Won't be a minute. You just pop yourself down there, OK?'

Laura sat down at the opposite end of the bank of plastic seats from the man with the carry-crate, who'd just opened its lid and tenderly lifted out a huge, floppy-eared rabbit.

Its fur, she noticed, was exactly the same shade of brown as Cass's hair. She screwed her eyes shut as a fresh wave of loss rolled over her.

'Laura Morrison!'

She turned and saw Jem, the vet who'd dropped Harrison off, standing in the doorway of his office, holding a sheaf of pamphlets for puppy classes. He'd done a slightly better job of ironing his scrubs this time, but his hair was still a mess.

'Great to see you!' He smiled at her while slotting the pamphlets into the plastic rack next to the door. 'How have you been? All good?'

Laura opened her mouth to reply and to her horror felt tears flooding her eyes. Before she could do anything to hide them he had crossed the waiting room towards her.

'Would you be alright to wait for just a minute, Mr Evans?' he said, turning to the man with the rabbit as he sat down next to her. 'Laura owns another one of our patients, I just need to have a quick chat with her ...'

'Oh, yes, that's fine,' Mr Evans said mildly, giving the rabbit a pat. 'Marilyn and I aren't in a rush. Tuesdays are our free day.'

Laura wiped her eyes on her sleeve.

'Sorry,' she muttered. 'Every time you see me, I'm crying. I must be the most high-maintenance person you've ever had to deal with.'

Jem's eyes rested on Mr Evans, who'd produced a small hairbrush from his windbreaker and was now attending to Marilyn's fur with it. 'Trust me, you're definitely not,' he said, raising his eyebrows. 'Look, what's up? Is it Harrison? Because if you're worried about him, I can ...'

Laura shook her head. 'No, he's fine, I'm here to pick up his pills. It's ... life stuff. You know.' Jem was watching her calmly, but he was probably coming to the conclusion that she was totally mad. 'You strike me as a pretty sorted person,' she went on. 'You have to be if you want to be a vet, don't you? I imagine you've got your life seriously in order. Unlike me.'

Jem shrugged. 'Oh, I don't know about that,' he said. 'Last night I accidentally threw my oven chips away instead of the foil tray they came in and I had to fish them out of the recycling with tongs. Took me about half an hour. No wonder I'm single.'

He smiled at her, his brown eyes crinkling. Then he got to his feet.

'Well ...' he said '... I should probably get on. But look, you stay here as long as you need to, OK? And remember, at least you didn't eat bin-fries for your dinner.'

Once he'd gone into his consulting room with Mr Evans and Marilyn, Laura ducked outside, got her phone out and brought up Nush's number again.

Do it now, she told herself. *Call her, then call Adam. The longer you leave it, the worse it's going to be.*

Before she could back out Laura jabbed the green circle on the screen. It was ringing – and ringing and ringing. That had never happened before: Nush's phone was glued to her hand and she always picked up straight away. The call cut abruptly to voicemail.

Chapter 22

ground truth (noun): the reality of the situation

'Just so you know,' Lil said, pushing her cat's-eye sunglasses higher on her nose and adjusting her beret, 'I don't condone this behaviour.'

It was 5.30 and Maltby Street was filling up with a Thursday-is-the-new-Friday crowd who'd spilled over from Borough Market and London Bridge. Laura and Lil were sitting at a table outside a wine bar in a railway arch – Lil in striped top and jeans with her trenchcoat over the top, Laura in the same faded and bleach-stained t-shirt dress that she'd been wearing for the past three days with a jumper over it. In front of them, on the other side of the street, was Veganised, Monica's bakery. They'd chosen this table so they'd have a good view of the door – Laura had reluctantly agreed to Lil's suggestion that they scope the place out together and laugh at all the ridiculous Instagram-baiting things it sold. *Think of it like an exorcism*, Lil had urged her on WhatsApp.

'Excuse me, this was your terrible idea,' Laura said, doing an exaggerated eyebrow raise so Lil would know that she was joking; after their disagreement about Cass they were both still being a tiny bit careful with each other. 'Anyway, I'm not the one who's come dressed as a spy from *'Allo 'Allo ...'*

'Excuse-moi!' Lil scrunched up her nose, making her sunglasses bounce. Laura felt her gaze being magnetically drawn back to Veganised again. Its half-moon front was made entirely of glass – she could see a marble slab in the middle, covered in rows of meringues like rainbow kisses, and excited people leaning over it with their phones. It was a beautiful room, she thought sadly. Joking with Lil about this had been morbidly enjoyable, but all that actually being here had done was bring everything that Monica had, and everything Laura didn't, into excruciating focus. She tried to take a breath but it snagged somewhere in her chest.

Lil yawned. 'You know, I've been thinking about what he said to you, and I just can't get my head around how anyone finds the time to be a "relationship anarchist",' she said. 'I mean, it's hard enough finding the time to date one person, right? Do you just not sleep or eat? Do you have to colour-code your Outlook calendar? It must be a logistical nightmare.'

Laura's phone screen lit up: it was Adam, again. He'd already called her twice that afternoon: she'd replied to his message on Tuesday saying she was busy and couldn't talk then, but that she'd call him. She still hadn't done it. Sitting here, barely a mile from his flat, she could feel the pressure building up inside her like water behind a dam.

Lil's eyes followed hers.

'You're going to have to break up with him at some point, you know,' she said firmly. 'What's holding you back?'

Laura looked down at the table. 'I'm just ...'

'... waiting for someone to tell you what to do? Morrison, I love you, but come on! Take action!' Lil leaned back in her chair and folded her arms. 'OK, you really want to know what I think?' she said, looking straight at Laura. 'This isn't really about Adam at all – it's about what the whole Cupid thing meant to you. Ever since Walker you've been worried that there's something wrong with you, that you can't do relationships, right? You were scared you were destined to be single forever and die alone ...'

'I'm struggling to see how this is meant to cheer me up,' Laura muttered. Lil rolled her eyes.

'*I'm* not saying that's what's going to happen, silly – I just know it was something you worried about because I have eyes and ears and I'm your closest friend. Then along comes Cupid and they're telling you that everything's going to be fine if you just do what they say, promising you that happily-ever-after by numbers. And even though it obviously hasn't *actually* worked out like that, that's a really hard thing to let go of. But what's the alternative? Settle down with Adam even though you know it isn't working? Take it from me, that's not something you want to do ...'

Just then a young waiter with his blond hair combed into a quiff and tattoos covering his arms strolled over with a tray holding two glasses – wine for Lil and half a pint of Guinness for Laura, who'd ordered a dark and bitter drink to match her mood.

'Who's having the French red?' he asked them.

'Take a guess,' Lil said, pointing jokily to her beret. 'I actually chose it because the menu said it was fifteen per cent proof – now that's what I call value for money.'

The waiter nodded approvingly. 'An excellent choice,' he said, putting the glasses down on the table. 'Starting your evening strong, I see.'

'My daughter's with her dad tonight, so all bets are off,' Lil said, giving him a wink. She raised her glass. 'Next stop A&E!'

The waiter laughed. 'Well, enjoy,' he said, stepping back. His eyes lingered on her. 'And if you need a lift to the hospital later, I've got a motorbike ...'

Lil swivelled in her chair so she could watch him walking back to the bar. 'He's *cute*,' she whispered, turning back to Laura. 'I mean, probably a decade younger than me, but ... do you think he's like that with everyone?'

'You tell me, Sigmund Freud,' Laura said, raising her eyebrows. She found herself wanting to brush off what Lil had said, but she could feel the words getting to work in her mind, rearranging her mental furniture. Lil stuck out her tongue and was about to reply when her head snapped around towards the street.

'Wait, is that her?' she hissed.

Laura followed her gaze. Monica had come out of the bakery and was leaning against the wall of the tunnel to one side of the arch, her white-blonde bob framing her face like a halo, smoking a cigarette. Laura's stomach lurched.

'I like her hair,' Lil whispered. Laura gave her a pointed look. 'Sorry. I mean, she looks like a real twat.'

'Cass is more of one,' Laura said quietly – all that time she'd spent longing to tell Lil his name, to claim him as hers, and now she could barely bring herself to say it out loud. 'She's not the one who lied to me. He was probably lying to her too.'

'Well, I still think her meringues are stupid,' Lil said loyally. She drank some wine, then picked up her phone from the table. 'Oh! I completely forgot! I know what'll actually cheer you up. Give me a second ...'

Laura glanced across and spotted a familiar collage of white and red at the top of the screen.

'Tinder? I think that's going to do the opposite of cheering me up.'

'I'm not suggesting you go on it, silly.' Lil finished tapping and looked up, her eyes twinkling with mischief. 'Remember Sam, the sales guy from work who was at my birthday last year? Runs loads of marathons? We made him show us his matches when we all went out for karaoke the other night and look who came up ...'

She stopped and handed Laura her phone. There, her eyebrows two perfectly arched sparrow's wings and her septum ring twinkling, was Nush.

'That's her, isn't it?' Lil said, looking over her shoulder at the screen. 'The woman from Cupid who was giving you all that shit about self-sabotage? I remembered her from when we looked at their website together, so I got Sam to send me a screenshot.'

Laura nodded dumbly. 'Wow. She and her boyfriend must have broken up. I guess he didn't move here from America after all ...' She zoomed in on the photo, hearing Nush's sugary voice in her head. *I just want other people to have what I have, you know? To be happy.* Was that why she hadn't been picking up her phone?

'Funny how she joined Tinder rather than making use of her employer's matchmaking services, isn't it?' Lil said archly. 'Honestly, the more I think about it, the shadier the whole thing seems.' She checked her watch. 'OK, it's five-forty-five. We can do the quiz at the Prince Regent later if you want to come back to mine? First prize is a whole box of Frazzles ...'

Laura was still staring at the screen. There was a banner promoting a pair of trainers at the top: Tinder clearly knew that Lil's colleague Sam was a runner and was tailoring the adverts he'd see. She shook her head. Obviously she knew it was happening everywhere, but it was still a depressing thing to be confronted with so explicitly. Plus, Tinder knew hardly anything about Sam compared to what Cupid knew about her, she thought – and they still hadn't managed to find anyone for her. She was about to pull her own phone out when something stopped her in her tracks.

'Oh my god,' she said under her breath. 'That's it. Shit. *Shit.*'

Lil looked at her, frowning. 'What is?'

Laura shut her eyes. In the darkness behind them she found herself picturing the fruit machine at Asha's hen party. The button she'd pressed, the seemingly endless and meaningless blur of colours – and then, finally, the *click, click, click* as everything fell into place. The three tangerines, which she hadn't even noticed while the wheels were turning, but which were now so obvious. The solution to the machine's riddle.

'Nothing,' she said quickly, opening her eyes again. For the first time in a long, long while, she knew exactly what she was going to do. She handed Lil her phone back – the squishy plastic case was covered in half-moon marks where she'd been digging her nails into it. 'Um, what time does the quiz start?'

'Eight.' Lil switched the camera to selfie mode and started using the screen as a mirror, topping up her scarlet lipstick. 'Why?'

'I just need to … pick something up first.' Laura got her phone out. Adam was calling her again – she rejected it and pushed her chair back. 'Can I meet you there?'

'Sure. Bring your A-game, alright? Those Frazzles aren't going to win themselves.' Lil pursed her lips with a *mwah*. 'I might stay here for a while, actually,' she went on, glancing towards the bar – their waiter, who'd been polishing glasses, looked up and caught her eye, flicked the cloth over his shoulder and grinned at her. 'You know. See the sights. Get to know the locals a bit.'

'I think that's an excellent idea,' Laura said, scrambling for her bag. 'I'll see you in a bit, OK? Don't do anything I wouldn't do.'

'That,' Lil said teasingly, 'does not narrow things down much. Can I have your Guinness?'

***

Laura found him on the canal towpath just beyond Kings Cross, next to the shadowy bit under Caledonian Road where anglers unfolded their chairs. Cass was on a bench staring out at the water – the reflected light from the sun setting over it caught his eyes, turning them almost transparent. She felt that if she stared hard enough she might actually be able to see all the way through him.

'Thought you'd be here,' she said. He looked up, his eyes wide with surprise, and her breath caught in her throat. 'I went to the boat first.'

'How did you know I wasn't out painting the town red?' He'd composed himself again and his expression was daring her to join in – a hand held out, an invitation to a dance.

'I have my methods.' She sat down at the other end of the bench from him, at a safe distance. 'Also I could see your wallet on the table. I knew you couldn't have gone far.'

He laughed. 'Very impressive, Sherlock.' She watched him reach down to pick up a pebble from the path. 'I can't believe you remember me telling you about this place.'

'Well, that's what happens when you really like someone,' Laura said pointedly. 'You remember things.'

Cass flicked his wrist, skimming the pebble across the water.

'I told Monica we can't see each other anymore,' he said, looking straight ahead. 'I called her pretty much right after you left – that's what I've been trying to tell you this week. She understood. She was totally fine about it.'

'Oh, well, as long as *Monica's* fine ...' The pebble had sunk.

'Laura ...' He shuffled along the bench so their legs were an inch away from touching. 'Please. Can we just start over?'

She watched the ripples fading out. When they stopped, she told herself, she'd break the spell.

'I can't trust you,' she said when the water was still again. 'Not because you did it, but because you lied about it. No, wait,' she held up her hand as he started to protest, 'you did. Not saying something is lying. The starting point might be different but the result is the same.'

He put his elbows on his knees and rested his chin on his hands.

'I get it,' he said softly. 'I do. And I'm sorry. My whole life ...' He shut his eyes. 'I always had to put myself first, because I knew nobody else was going to. But I'm trying not to be that person anymore.'

They were sitting close to each other. It would have been so easy to rest her head on his shoulder, let him stroke her hair, turn her face to his. For them to kiss. They could walk back to the boat together holding hands and fall into bed. She could pretend, for a couple of hours at least, that nothing had happened. She wanted that so much. She didn't move.

'How did you actually find Adam?' she asked quietly. She waited for Cass to react. If he was surprised by her question, he didn't show it – he calmly picked up another stone. 'He told me on our first date that Nush already knew about his break-up when she got in touch with him,' Laura pressed on. 'If he was the kind of person who spent his life on social media that would make sense, but he isn't – he isn't even on Twitter or Instagram. There has to be some other way they're connected.' She squared her shoulders. 'So, what is it?'

'He's a friend of a friend of someone she used to work with,' Cass said, rolling the stone slowly between his fingers. 'She heard about what happened to him with his fiancée at their cake tasting and thought that he'd be ... open to it. I mean, don't get me wrong, we still put you through the matchmaking model, but do you have any idea how much it would cost to run the kind of people searches we were talking about in that press release you got? Cupid's a start-up, it doesn't have anything like the funding or human resources at the moment. So we had to be a little ... creative to get things off the ground. Fake it until we made it. That's all.'

The hum of the traffic above them and the weeds growing out of the bank and the ducks drifting past looked exactly the same but the world had tilted sickeningly on its axis. She wanted to snatch the stone off him.

'Adam was in a bad place, you were in a bad place – we genuinely thought you two would stick.' Cass dropped the stone and shrugged, smiling. 'That was until I met you and realised you were actually pretty difficult to predict ...'

Just another variable to be factored in. She closed her eyes, forcing herself to stay where she was.

'He doesn't know, obviously,' Cass went on. 'I'm sure Adam's never told a lie in his life.'

'You say that like it's a bad thing.'

Cass wasn't pretending to think this was all fine, she realised. He honestly thought it was. He didn't see a problem with any of it.

'I'm not going to stay with Adam,' she went on flatly. 'I'm going to tell him straight after this. And I'm not going to write the article.'

'Really?' Cass looked genuinely surprised. 'I mean, no offence, but from where I'm sitting it doesn't look like you have a whole lot of other options.'

She couldn't stop her voice from rising in anger. 'Jesus, Cass. That's what everything is to you, isn't it? Nothing's good, nothing's bad, it's just a series of *options*. You can't just shuffle people around like chess pieces whenever you feel like it.' She swallowed. 'They have real lives. Real feelings.'

He just sat there, looking at her, waiting for her to finish. His eyes were clear and cool. She took a deep breath.

'I know how Cupid's making its money too,' she went on. 'Maybe your matchmaking model *is* very clever, but that's not really the core of the business, is it? It's all the "human intuition" stuff that matters, all those questions about what my idea of happiness was. You get members to spell out really personal things so you can sell that information on to advertisers, who'll pay you a fortune for it because it's the key to making people want to buy things. It's all just a giant information grab – you're like one of those data brokers Nush was telling me about, basically.' He was silent, his expression unreadable. 'Do you seriously think people will go along with that? Just sign everything away without reading the small print if they're promised a relationship?'

'Well, people tend to suspend their disbelief when they're looking for love.' He looked right at her. 'I mean, you did, right?'

The blood rushed to her face.

'So just to be clear,' she said slowly. 'Cupid is going to be targeting people who are feeling hopeless about ever meeting anyone, persuading them to open up about their vulnerabilities and then exploiting those to make money. Have I got any of that wrong?'

'Hey, everyone's exploiting something these days,' Cass said, spreading his hands. 'And, you know, vulnerabilities are actually pretty easy to measure.' He leaned closer and lowered his voice. 'Look, I get that morally this kind of stuff is a bit of a grey area. I do. But that's just the world we live in. Show me an industry that's got totally clean hands. Can you honestly say nothing dicey ever goes on at a newspaper?' He raised his eyebrows. 'We're just doing what we have to do.'

He looked like Cass, he sounded like Cass, but this wasn't Cass – not the one she'd gone to sleep dreaming of, whose name on her screen had given her shivers every single time she'd seen it, who'd made her laugh and cry and scream. Maybe he'd never really existed and it had all been in her head. Or maybe he had, but she was the only one who could see him. Either way, she'd heard enough. She stood up, turned on her heels and started walking back the way she'd come.

'Laura.'

She stopped. He was standing up now too, his thumbs hooked into his pockets.

'I wasn't lying,' he said. 'I meant everything I said to you – about you. All of it.'

She took one last look at him.

'Me too,' she said quietly. Then she turned away again.

Once she'd got round the corner she stopped and put her hand on her chest, over her heart. As she felt around for the telltale ridge under her clothes, she could hear a soft whine coming from Inge's wire.

***

Paradise Street was deserted. As Laura hurried along it towards Adam's flat she felt dizzy and disorientated, as though she'd been scooped up by a tornado, spun around at a million miles an hour, then dropped right back where she'd started. It didn't seem possible that barely an hour ago she'd been sitting with Lil just down the road.

Adam, she could see as she got closer to his building, was in: his living-room light was on and he wouldn't have forgotten about something like that. She paused on the front step, weighed down by the thought of what she was about to do. She hovered, her finger over the buzzer for his flat, her confidence faltering, then pressed it with an unsteady finger. She waited, her pulse pounding in her ears. Nothing happened. She jabbed it again, harder this time. A voice came from behind her.

'I've got a blipper, hang on – I can buzz you in.'

She spun around. The woman on the pavement was tall with freckles and long coppery-red hair that she'd twisted over one shoulder of her puffa jacket. She wedged between her feet the Nando's bag she'd been carrying and got something out of her purse.

'Here you go,' she said, handing Laura her keys, which had a black plastic orb dangling from them. 'You just press that on the panel there and everything should be tickety-boo.' Her key-fob was a large, smooth pebble with cartoon eyes painted on it to make it look like a winky face.

'Great, thanks.' Laura took it from her, making a mental note to tell Lil that she'd met an actual real-life person who said *tickety-boo*. She tapped the orb on the entry panel and heard the door click. As she pushed it open she gave the woman's Nando's bag a nod, to be polite. 'You're a traditionalist, I see.'

'I'm sorry?' The woman frowned. She had fair lashes framing eyes that were almost exactly the same shade of green as Laura's and her cheeks were the kind of healthy, windswept pink you couldn't fake.

'Picking up a takeaway,' Laura said, holding the door. The woman blinked. 'Instead of lying on the sofa in your pyjamas waiting for a Deliveroo.'

'Oh! Right! Got you!' She smiled; she had a mischievous gap between her front teeth. 'Well, I was passing so I thought, why not get us a little treat for dinner, you know?'

She lowered her voice. 'I've got some making up to do to be honest – so I thought I'd start with chicken.'

Laura nodded distractedly; in her mind she was already one flight of stairs up, knocking on Adam's door. 'Well, enjoy,' she said. 'And thanks.' The woman picked up the Nando's bag.

'I'll come in with you. Do you know where you're going? The numbering here's a bit all over the place.'

'Flat three,' Laura said, setting off down the hallway. 'First floor. Don't worry, I've been there before.' The woman stopped.

'But that's where I'm …' She took a wary step back, staring hard at Laura. 'Are you …'

Laura stopped too and sniffed. The woman's perfume smelled like morning dew; it was eerily familiar. She was turning her stone key-fob over in her hands – painted on the back of it were the words *GEOLOGISTS ROCK!*

'I'm Laura,' she said. 'And you're …'

'Bella,' said Bella, putting the bag down again. 'I'm Bella.'

Footsteps came from overhead. They both looked up: Adam was charging down the stairs, taking the steps two at a time, running a hand through his still-damp hair.

'Sorry, I heard the door go but I was in the shower …' He turned the corner and froze. 'Laura? What's going on?'

'You tell me,' she said, her brain whirring madly. The world seemed to be turning impossibly fast – everything was crashing into everything else in a way that made no sense. And yet …

Bella folded her arms. 'I thought you were going to tell her today?' she said to Adam, sounding slightly peeved.

'I've been trying to.' His eyes met Laura's; he seemed almost to be pleading with her. 'I called you about five times – you haven't been picking up your phone.'

'Sorry, things kind of ... ran away with me.' She looked from one to the other. 'So are you two ...'

'No!' Adam interjected. 'Hand on my heart, Laura, it's not like that. We've just been ... chatting, that's all. About how things ended. Bella was in Sweden. At the symposium.'

Memories rushed at Laura. The strange mood Adam had been in during their Cupid video shoot, how distracted he'd seemed at Lil's. The drawing she'd spotted on his hotel notepad of a face – Bella's face, it was so obvious. All the things that, now she was actually paying attention, had indicated that something was happening, though she'd been far too focused on Cass to notice at the time.

'And on the last night, when you said you'd stayed up late – it wasn't a paper you were talking about, was it?' she heard herself saying to him. 'You were together. The two of you.'

'Laura, please ...' Adam's voice was hoarse with emotion. He shook his head. 'I am so, so sorry things have turned out like this. You're such a great person and I've loved getting to know you, but ...' He looked at Bella, whose cheeks were even pinker now, then back at Laura. 'My heart's been elsewhere. And I hate myself for not being more honest with you about that. When I think how you ...'

She reached up and put her hands on his shoulders.

'Adam, stop,' she said, squeezing. 'Please just listen, OK? You have nothing to feel bad about. *Nothing*. I ... Look, there's some stuff I need to tell you. About Cupid.'

Bella took a couple of steps towards him protectively – they were standing so close to each other now that their hips were touching. They fitted together so well. Laura could imagine them eating chicken off their laps in front of the TV in his flat later that night, both slightly giddy from the transgression of not having dinner at the table. She felt a pain like a cramp in her chest as she remembered lying on the roof of Cass's boat, laughing as they balanced a pizza box on their knees – she tried to breathe through it, waiting for it to pass.

'But look, your food must be getting cold,' she finished, glancing down at the Nando's bag. She could just about make out the top line of the receipt stapled to it – *Lemon and Herb x 2*. 'I should let you go. It can wait.'

Bella touched her arm.

'Laura …' she began, her eyes wide and solemn. 'Please believe me when I say that neither of us ever wanted to hurt you.'

'I know,' Laura said, giving her what she hoped was a reassuring smile. The world was spinning again – she could feel the wire where she'd coiled it in her pocket, silent now but crackling with everything it held. 'I have to run, but enjoy your evening, OK? And let's speak tomorrow …'

'Laura, wait!' Adam was still frowning. 'What are you going to do about your article? This is going to really mess it up, isn't it?'

She paused in the doorway. This was one of those moments that life gave you so rarely, she thought.

'Oh, don't worry,' she said, and couldn't quite stop herself from smiling as she turned on her heels. 'I'll work something out.'

She headed for the main road, following the route she and Adam had always taken to the station. The streets were still empty and the only noise was the faint breeze rustling the leaves of the oak tree by the church. She wondered if this would be the last time she ever came this way. She couldn't imagine anything bringing her back here. But then again, quite a lot of things she couldn't have imagined had been happening recently – and several of them in the past three hours. She felt lightheaded.

She stopped on the corner to check the train times to Lil's from Bermondsey and saw she had a new message.

> Walker:
> *Hey!*
> *How's tricks?*
> *Me and Sash just got back from holiday*

She started mentally composing a reply. *You were on holiday?!??* she could type sarcastically. *I had no idea! You should have put it on Instagram!!!* Her finger was a millimetre from the screen when she paused. The defensiveness felt reassuring, like an old coat. But, she realised, it was a coat she didn't want to wear anymore. She found herself thinking back to her and Jamie meeting Alan – the way she'd felt, for the first time she could remember, that she was in control of how something turned out, that she could choose a brand new script for herself. From there her mind drifted to the photo of Walker on the beach Sasha had posted. The caption. *Be brave. Love deeply.* The words she'd rolled her eyes over had got into her head now and were putting down roots, weaving themselves in with what Lil had said to her in the bar.

What's the alternative?

If she told Walker how she'd been feeling since they stopped living together, what was the worst that could happen? Really, she had nothing left to lose. She took a deep breath and started typing.

> Laura:
> *I saw!*
> *How was it?*
> *Hope you guys had a great time*

Laura:
Look, I'm sorry things have been weird
It's been a funny couple of months
I've really missed you, Walker
Living with you was great

The messages stared back at her, naked and vulnerable.
She chewed the inside of her cheek as he started typing.

Walker:
I've really missed you too, Laur
Can we hang out properly soon?
I know Hammersmith's a faff to get to
We could meet in the middle?

Laura:
I think that can be arranged ☺

Walker:
☺
Found us a new game to play btw
Eight ball pool on your phone
Absolutely incredible timewaster, Year 9 are all over it

Laura:
Well, if Year 9 say it's good, who am I to argue?

Walker:
Hahaha
I'm going to download it and invite you ok?

Laura:
Perfect

Walker:
See you on the other side …

Chapter 23

solution (noun): the values that produce a true statement

Laura ran through the *Bugle*'s revolving door the next day with a USB stick in one hand and the squashed remains of a bacon roll in the other. Whatever else might have changed in the past twenty-four hours, she thought as she sprinted up the escalator, she still wasn't a morning person. She got her phone out to message Inge – she knew her boss had a day full of meetings and was desperate to catch her before she disappeared to play her the recording of her conversation with Cass – and saw that she had a notification.

Dad has joined WhatsApp!

That couldn't be right. She was about to tap on it when a message came through.

Dad:
dear L hello! just testing out my new What app! Love from dad

She stuffed the last of the roll into her mouth and started typing.

> Laura:
> *Hi Dad*
> *Everything OK?*
> *Didn't know you'd got WhatsApp*

Dad:

dear L thank you! still getting the hang of it as you see but all good so far, love From Dad

Dad:

Dad:

Dear L realised i have never been to the british Museum before and my card gets me and a guest in free! would you like to come today after work it would be good to see you, Love From dad

> Laura:
> *That sounds really nice*
> *Thanks Dad*
> *I'll see you later OK?*

She didn't have time to process the implications of this before the escalator dumped her in front of the security barriers. She scrunched the paper bag the bacon roll had come in into a greasy ball and stuffed it into her pocket, grabbing her pass.

'Hi, Achilles!' she said to the grouchy-looking man with an iron-grey bristle-cut behind the front desk. 'Nearly the weekend!'

'Which means it'll be Monday again before you know it,' Achilles replied grimly. They'd been having the same conversation every Friday for three years – he'd been at the *Bugle* since the days when the office was on Fleet Street, and was widely believed to have actually become embedded in his black leatherette chair, like a torpedoed U-boat merging with the seabed. 'Better be quick,' he went on, waving her through. 'You'll miss French Toast Friday in the canteen if you're not careful.' He did scornful bunny-ears in the air around the words. 'It's a new thing.'

'Since when?'

'Since the management made it their policy to distract us from their attempts at total subjugation with sugary food, that's when.'

'Have you been in?'

He snorted. 'No. I will not be partaking of the opium of the people.' (Achilles wore a pin-badge from the Revolutionary Communist Party of Britain inside his lapel.)

'Sensible.' Laura dropped her pass back into her bag, trying to get her breath back. 'You haven't seen Inge, have you?'

'Oh, she's been in for hours,' Achilles said airily; because he never seemed to move, he was a human log of everybody else's movements. 'I tell you what, there's been a *lot* of coming and going today and I'm not just talking about the canteen.' He beckoned her closer. 'Guess who got the axe yesterday while you were out?'

'Achilles, I'm in a bit of a ...'

'Come on, guess.' He winked at her. 'I'll give you a clue: nobody's going to miss him.'

'Wait ... *Bouncy*?' Laura could feel her mouth hanging open. 'I mean, Phil? Seriously?'

'Yup – went last night. Empty desk, everything. Ah, there's Inge ...'

Inge was waving from outside the canteen, holding an empty paper plate. She was wearing her don't-fuck-with-me wide-leg trousers and brogues combination, which she saved for important meetings and the Christmas Quiz.

'What are you doing out there?' she called. 'Come here, I need to talk to you! I've got some news!' She frowned as Laura rushed over. 'Wait, is that ... *ketchup* on your top?'

'It's part of the design,' Laura said quickly. 'And Achilles just told me what happened – I can't believe he's gone! Listen, Inge, I ...'

Inge put a finger to her lips. 'Wait, there's more. Guess who's stepping into the brand new role of Features Director?' She mimed a drumroll, then pointed to herself. 'Me! I wanted to tell you in person, so ...'

'Inge!' Laura launched herself at her, sending the paper plate flying. 'Wow, this is ...'

'I know! I can drag this place into the twenty-first century!' They both crouched down to pick up the plate and burst out laughing. 'OK, maybe we'll start with the twentieth and see how it goes ...' She put her head on one side. 'Sorry, I interrupted you. What were you saying?'

Laura, her heart pounding, opened her left hand to reveal the USB stick. Inge looked puzzled.

'You've started backing up your work? I mean, that's great, but ...'

With her right hand, Laura wordlessly retrieved the wire from her bag.

'Turns out you were right,' she said, holding it out. 'My days of sneaking around were actually ahead of me after all.'

Inge's face broke into the biggest smile that Laura had ever seen.

'I knew there was a reason I hired you,' she said, sweeping Laura into the newsroom. 'Come on – I'm listening.'

***

The British Museum's outside courtyard was a sea of people. Laura let herself drift through the crowd, reading the email Femi had sent while she was on the Tube.

Just came to find you but Inge said you'd already gone ... I GOT IT!!!!!!! I got the news job!!!! Izzy and I are having drinks in The George later if you want to come? PLEASE COME.

Her dad was sitting on the steps, shielding his eyes with one hand. He was wearing the same clothes that her mum had made him put on when they'd gone to see *Jersey Boys* – with nobody around to tell him what to wear he'd reverted to his last-remembered London outfit. It felt like someone was squeezing Laura's heart. He spotted her and raised the other hand in greeting.

'It's murder in there,' he said as she walked towards him. 'I've just seen two kids biting each other in the queue for the mummies.' She searched his face for signs of existential despair as she sat down next to him – he looked tired and there was a patch of stubble on his neck that he'd missed when he was shaving, but otherwise nothing had changed. Where was he keeping it all?

'That's why you should always go to the cafe first. Never good to go into a museum hungry.' She wedged her bag between her feet. They sat in silence for a while. Her dad was watching a young couple bickering as they unloaded their twins from a pram at the other end of the steps, sunk deep in his thoughts.

'Alan was waiting outside in the car when she came round,' he said eventually, out of nowhere – it was like switching on a TV programme halfway through. 'It's a 2009 Hyundai. Wouldn't have been my choice – they go like sewing machines.'

Laura tried to put a hand on his arm. 'Dad, we've been ...' she began. He waved it away.

'Ah, don't give me that.' The setting sun was directly on them now; he tugged at his tie, then started unknotting it. 'Thing is,' he began – he'd clearly been running through whatever he was about to say in his head, like a child memorising a poem they'd been asked to read in front of the class. 'When I asked your mum to marry me ...' The tie was off now and he'd started trying to roll it up. 'Well, I was sure I was doing the right thing. That we ought to be a family, all live under the same roof, have dinner together every Sunday, all that stuff. I honestly never really thought about whether it was going to make her happy.' The tie was a mess – he squinted down at it, trying to work out where he'd gone wrong, then gave up and stuck it in his jacket pocket. 'Or me. Then when the thing with Carlo happened ... I mean, we patched things up because that was what we thought you were meant to do. When actually ...'

He lapsed into silence again. Laura watched the couple with the twins leading them up the steps, carrying the folded-up buggy between them. They were smiling.

'So what happens now?' she asked him. He shrugged.

'I thought I might go away for a bit – you know, adventure before dementia. Or I could just take myself straight to Switzerland ...'

'Dad.'

'Joking, joking. Costs a fortune to do yourself in there.' He did a wheezy laugh. 'Harrison'll be OK with Jamie and Whit for a bit, won't he? While I'm sorting everything out.'

Laura nodded. She got her phone out and found a picture she'd taken of Harrison with a stick the width of a sofa in his mouth. Her dad's face lit up.

'Good lad,' he said, resting his thumb on the screen right where the tips of the dog's ears started. He smiled in the way he only ever did for Harrison. 'Now, on that subject, how's yours? Still working with windmills, is he?'

Laura looked at her feet. Adam and Bella would be together this evening, cooking in the flat with one of his chill-out compilations on, probably. Cass was out there somewhere too, hidden from her view now. She'd never know the shape of his days again and he'd never know the shape of hers.

'We're not together anymore, actually,' she said. 'I met someone else ... But that didn't work out either. So now I'm back where I started, basically.'

'Oh, I wouldn't say that.' Her dad put an arm around her shoulders and patted her exactly three times. 'Anyway, you're young still. Plenty of time to work it all out.'

'Is there?' She put her hand over his and squeezed. 'You had a child by the time you were my age.'

'And look where that got me.' They both laughed. Then, as if to show that the difficult part of the conversation was officially over, he got a folded exhibit guide out of his jacket pocket and put his reading glasses on.

'I saw something online about these the other day,' he said, running his finger over the illustration of the Elgin Marbles. 'They should give them all back, I reckon. Wipe the slate clean.'

'I wonder what they'd fill it with instead.' Laura looked at the sketch of the huge, echoing room. Imagining it empty gave her a feeling in her stomach like she was at the top of a rollercoaster, momentarily weightless. Her dad refolded the guide and stashed it away again.

'I expect they'd find something,' he said.

TWO AND A BIT MONTHS LATER ...

It was already Christmas on Stonybrook Street, even though it was still only early December. Bauble-decked trees filled the windows, there were bushy wreaths on all the doors and the last of the night's frost twinkled on the pavement in the bright morning sunshine. Someone had put an actual sleigh on their roof, plus a pair of boots poking out of their chimney and, just in case anyone hadn't got the hint, a banner reading *HO HO HO*.

'Wow, they really lean into the festive season around here, don't they?' Lil said as she turned off the main road in her patched-up old Peugeot.

Laura nodded in the passenger seat, peeling the cabin label from the strap of her bag. 'They had this massive tree in Berlin that was made entirely of blown-up condoms,' she said. 'I kept imagining it floating away like a hot air balloon.'

Lil pretended to be shocked. 'Oh, have you just been on an all-expenses-paid work trip to Europe's coolest city? You should have said! I had no idea!' Laura whacked her arm. 'I still can't believe the *Bugle* sent you to cover a robot sex conference. Times have seriously changed.'

'It wasn't a *robot sex* conference – it was a sex tech one,' Laura said, pulling a face at her. 'And it was really interesting, actually. I learned a lot about the future of intimacy.'

'I bet you did.' Lil reversed them into a space, then rolled down the window to read the sign next to the meter. 'Huh, you still have to pay for parking on a Saturday – welcome to Clapham. How long are we going to need? An hour? Two hours?'

'Everything's boxed up and ready to go – I packed before I left,' Laura said, producing a square of paper from her bag with a flourish. 'And I already sorted you out with a permit, don't worry.' Lil took it, shaking her head in wonder. 'Going freelance does wonders for your organisational skills – I've got spreadsheets for everything now. I'm turning into Jamie.'

'I'm not surprised the *Bugle*'s giving you more interesting features to write now you've left. I've sent that clip of you being interviewed on Channel 4 news after your Cupid investigation came out to literally everyone I know,' Lil said as she switched the engine off. 'That bit where Cathy asked the founder guy – what was his name, Jared? – how he felt about trying to get rich by scamming lonely people out of their personal data and he started going on and on about his right to privacy, then *ended the video-call*.' She slapped the steering wheel. 'So good.'

Laura squeezed Lil's hand affectionately. 'You really don't have to drive me all the way to Inge and Lia's in Tottenham, you know. You've already picked me up from the airport, I think that's your helping-me-out quota met for the next five to ten years.'

Lil waved it away. 'Gatwick's easy for me, it's fine. And you're going to take us to that cheese toastie place near their new house once we've unpacked, aren't you?' She turned to face the back, where Dora was buckled into her car seat, wearing a brown corduroy smock, black-and-white striped tights and purple glittery sandals – a combination she'd chosen herself. 'Excited about toasties, peach?'

'STAR BAKER!' Dora yelled. Lil laughed and squeezed her daughter's sparkly foot.

'OK, big smiles, everybody!' She beamed, holding her phone at arm's length and snapping a selfie of the three of them, then turned back to Laura. 'You head on in,' she said, a smile playing on her lips. 'I just need to send this to … someone.'

'Someone, eh?' Laura lowered her voice. 'Would this be a *someone* with tattoos and a motorbike by any chance? Who you were out with last night?'

Lil flicked her eyes towards the back seat and mimed zipping her lips. She and Lucas, the waiter from the Maltby Street bar, had gone for a drink the day before – between his shifts and Lil's weekdays with Dora it had been diffi-cult for them to find a date, but judging by the fact that Lil's last online time on WhatsApp that morning had been 4 a.m., it had been a success.

Laura grinned as she opened the car door, unclipped her seatbelt and swung her legs out. Her feet felt pleasantly sore from all the walking she'd been doing. She'd been alone in Berlin, with time between seminars on virtual-reality headsets and demonstrations of bluetooth-enabled vibrators to wander around the city. She'd got out of bed again at eleven on the night she arrived and put on a dress and walked across the street to a piano bar, where she'd climbed onto a stool and counted out the euros for her first-ever martini. She'd gone all the way up to the top of the Reichstag and bought a photo-book on the separation of the city to read at mealtimes; ordered a second thick hot chocolate straight after her first in a cafe with steamy win-dows just because she wanted to and could. It occurred to her, as she was spooning the cream off the top, that she was happy. Her life wasn't exactly settled – but maybe it never would be. And maybe that was the whole point.

She walked up the chequerboard path to 42 and rang the bell. There was a scrabble of paws on wood from the hallway, before someone unlocked and opened the door an inch. Harrison's nose poked around it, then the rest of him followed. He threw himself at Laura, yelping and rubbing his head against her leg and pinballing off the sides of the porch.

'Harrison, left paw!' Whit's voice called out from some-where inside the house. Harrison stopped what he was doing and obediently offered it to Laura. 'Right paw!' He put it down and swapped it for the other one. Then Whit bounced out from behind the door, grinning from ear to ear.

'Who says you can't teach an old dog new tricks, eh?' He hauled her into a bear hug, with Harrison trying to squeeze himself in between their knees. 'Welcome back, kid! Good trip? We missed you!'

'He's exaggerating,' Jamie said wryly, appearing behind him. Laura hugged her too.

'Got your Christmas twig up?' she asked, craning her neck to see past her sister into the living room. 'Or are you waiting until the twenty-fourth to minimise the amount of peace and goodwill you have to get involved in?'

'Very funny. It's actually a very nice imitation spruce from Habitat,' Jamie said, stepping back. 'And we're decor-ating it right now. Harrison's been a real asset, as you can imagine.'

Lil was coming up the path behind them, holding Dora's hand. 'Season's greetings!' she called out. Jamie quickly straightened up, pulling everything in.

'That's a lovely dress, Lillian,' she said a little stiffly as she got closer. 'Is it vintage?' Lil flicked the Peter Pan collar of her bright blue A-line mini, which she'd paired with white plastic boots, looking pleased.

'Oh, thanks! Yeah, it is – it's Biba, if you can believe that. It starts to smell a bit when it heats up so I can only really wear it in the winter.' Jamie looked slightly terrified. 'And it's Lil, honestly,' she went on warmly. 'The only person who calls me Lillian is my lawyer.'

'Well, I'm a lawyer,' Jamie said, trying to smile. 'So maybe that gives me a free pass.' Dora was looking up at her, chewing her lip thoughtfully; they'd never met before. Jamie crouched down so they were the same height.

'Hello,' she said briskly. 'I'm Jamie. You must be Dora.' Jamie never made concessions for children – she talked to them how she talked to everyone else, at her normal speed and in her normal voice. Children, Laura suspected, strongly preferred this approach.

Dora's cheeks went pink; she looked away shyly, tapping out a pattern on the path with her right shoe. 'Say hello to Laura's big sister, peach,' Lil whispered. She glanced up.

'Hello, Laura's big sister,' she said, giving her a little wave. Jamie waved back and something complicated flashed across her face that made Laura's heart lurch.

'How are you with tinsel, Dora?' Jamie asked.

Dora considered this. 'Good,' she said finally. 'I'm good.' Jamie smiled.

'Well, in that case, maybe you and Mum could help us decorate our tree while Laura sorts her stuff out? What do you think?'

'Yeah!' The next thing she knew Dora had put her hand in Jamie's and was tugging her inside. Jamie was laughing as she allowed herself to be towed, exchanging knowing looks with Lil, who followed them in. Whit took Harrison's lead off the hook behind the door.

'Just taking this one for a quick walk,' he said, scratching him behind the ears as he clipped it on. 'He ate half a pat of butter this morning while I was making the Christmas cake. Don't tell Jamie.'

Laura grinned. 'I'll take him,' she said, tickling Harrison under the collar. 'Honestly. I could do with some air after the flight. I'll bring all my stuff down to the car when I'm back, OK?'

She took Harrison's lead and set off with him towards the Common. He piloted them along his favourite route, up the left-hand side of the street so he could sniff the alley the foxes all pelted along at night and over the zebra crossing. The ice-cream van had migrated to a garage somewhere for the winter – he narrowed his eyes at the empty space where it normally parked, looking around until he'd satisfied himself that it wasn't hiding behind a tree. Once they'd ducked under the railings Laura unclipped his lead and watched him zig-zagging across the grass, slower now than she remembered, with the occasional wobble when his hips clicked, but still alert and absorbed in the smells and the sounds. She chucked him a stick then sat down on the railing, swinging her feet in the air.

As she was waiting for him to bring it back, she spotted a man walking an enormous dog with a lion's mane, a bushy tail and huge paws. Something about his scruffy silhouette was familiar. As he came closer she realised it was Jem the vet.

'I think Narnia's that way,' she called out to him. He wheeled around, blinking in surprise before he realised who she was. He was wearing the kind of mismatched clothes that Laura recognised as having been pulled on at speed due to a slept-through alarm, and his dark hair was sticking up even more than usual.

'Laura!' he exclaimed. 'And Harrison Morrison! No way!' He was smiling as he and the dog ambled towards them. 'Wow, it's been ages – how are you doing?' He tried to flatten his hair down with his free hand, but it sprang up again the second he dropped his arm.

'Good! Really good.' She stood up and looked at the dog panting exuberantly at his feet. 'Who's your friend?'

'Oh, this is Ayi,' he said, reaching down to ruffle her fur. 'It's Turkish for bear. She's turning three today, so we're going for coffee to celebrate. She's a fan of Bean Machine because they pretend not to notice her hoovering up the cake crumbs from under the tables, but I think the house blend at Brew Two is better. What are your thoughts?'

'Bean Machine, definitely,' Laura said, holding out her hand; the dog sniffed it, then gave it a tickly lick with her sandpaper tongue. 'Wow, I can't believe she's only three – she's quite ...'

'Large? She was actually the runt of a litter someone left in a box on the surgery step. When I graduated I swore I'd never take my work home with me but ...' He grimaced. 'She was just so tiny. I know, I know. I'm an idiot.'

They both laughed. Harrison, who was sniffing a half-eaten banana on the grass, looked over his shoulder, checking that he wasn't the butt of the joke. Ayi trotted up to him. He ignored her. She galloped around so she was in front of him, rolled onto her back and stuck her legs in the air, making plaintive yodelling noises.

'Sorry about her,' Jem said. 'She's quite, er, forward. I think she likes him.'

Harrison had given in and was chasing Ayi in circles as she pelted across the grass, yelping with demented joy.

'Well, if she's three, in human years she's twenty-one,' Laura said, raising her eyebrows as they watched them. 'And Harrison's seventy. That's a pretty punchy age gap, isn't it?'

'I'll certainly be having a talk with her when we get home.' Jem tried to sort his hair out again. 'So, are you still living with your sister?'

'Only for the next half an hour,' Laura said. 'I'm moving in with my old boss and her girlfriend in Tottenham today. They've just bought a place with a spare room that they want to let out.'

Something that looked a bit like disappointment passed across his face. 'Ah, my old neck of the woods,' he said. 'I'm from Edmonton originally. Of giant IKEA fame.' He made a valiant attempt to straighten his jumper. 'You know, it's actually not that far from here if you get the Victoria line,' he went on. 'For when you want to visit Harrison. Obviously.'

'Fifty-seven minutes door to door,' Laura said. 'I already checked.' They were still looking at each other. 'I know he'll want me to pop in at least once a week, you see.'

Jem's dark eyes crinkled as he smiled. Kind eyes, she thought. Eyes you could trust.

'Very pleased to hear it,' he said. 'And if you ever want to, you know, find out how he's doing between appointments, you can always email me ...' He got his battered wallet out of his pocket and produced a business card with a Noah's ark printed on it. 'My number's on there too. My actual number, not the surgery one. Please don't give it to Mr Evans – he calls reception about Marilyn the rabbit every single day.'

'I'll guard it with my life.' Laura took it. Jem nodded once, biting his lip like he was trying to stop himself from grinning.

'Well ...' he said. 'We should get going, shouldn't we, Ayi?' He beckoned the dog over. 'I'm really glad we bumped into each other, Laura.'

'Me too,' Laura said, giving him a smile. 'I'm really glad too.'

She kept the card in her hand as she watched him walking away, Ayi plodding along at his heels, looking up at him with an expression of pure devotion. Laura sat down on the railing again and unzipped her bag; Harrison sighed and flopped himself onto her feet, closing his eyes. As she stashed the card away her fingers brushed something round and smooth – a tangerine from her hotel room that she hadn't got around to eating. She lifted it out and looked at it, turning it over and over in her hands, letting the light play on its dips and bumps. Then she pushed her thumb through the soft part at its base and started working it up and up and up in a spiral. The peel came away in a single perfect piece.

Thank you to …

Emma Finn, an agent in a million and the best thing ever to have come out of Twitter. You saw what this book could be, and made me the writer I am – I am so lucky to have someone as kind, patient, clever and hilarious as you in my corner. Here's to many more years of cinnamon buns and dog photos. A big thank you also to Alex Cochran, Jake Smith-Bosanquet, Kate Burton, Matilda Ayris, Laura Gerrard and everyone else at and working with C&W.

Emily Griffin, my extraordinarily brilliant and insightful editor at Century and Arrow. Talking to you about this book for the first time felt like coming home – your warmth, 20/20 vision and boundless enthusiasm have made every step of bringing it to life a total joy. Huge thanks also to Ajebowale Roberts, whose notes always nudge me in the right direction, as well as Lynn Curtis, Amy Musgrave, Klara Zak Claire Bush, Hope Butler, Laura Brooke and everyone at Penguin Random House who's worked so hard on this.

Everyone involved with the Lucy Cavendish Fiction Prize – especially Jo Ryan, Hayley Welch and Nelle Andrew – for taking a chance on the first three chapters. Everything that's happened since then has happened because of you, and I will always be grateful.

Katherine Heiny, my writing hero, for inspiring and encouraging me from the other side of the Atlantic (and for not taking out a restraining order on me; I'd have understood if you had).

Patricia Touton-Victor, for a coat in the rain and so much more. I think you are amazing.

My wonderful friends and colleagues: Adam Coghlan, Alex Peake-Tomkinson, Alex Winter, Alicia Grimshaw, Andrea Poston, Andrew Lister, Andrew Pirrie, Andy McTaggart, Angela Hui, Anna Sulan Masing, Ashleigh Arnott, Ben Cottam, Chris Wood, Charlotte Davies, Claire Strickett, George Reynolds, Ianthe Cox-Wilmott, Izzie Crichton-Stuart, James Hansen, Jenni Moore, Johanna and Joe Derry-Hall, Lale Guralp, Leah Hyslop, Leila Latif, Andrew Lisle and all of Fancy Lunch Club, Leonie Cooper, Lizzy Barber, Vicki, Nick, Bob, Bea and Eddie Rendall, Rach Adams, Signe Johansen, Sion Owen, Sophie Orbaum, Suze Olbrich, Susannah Otter, Tracey Llewellyn and Yassine Senghor. You're the best.

Doris, Bella, Siyah, Nika and Tuuli, for dragging me away from my computer and keeping my feet warm while I typed. 14/10 for all.

James Harlow, tech support, for patiently answering my data questions and stopping me tying myself in knots.

Peter Attard Montalto and Anthony Harte, for pouring wine down me at the end of all the weekends I spent writing this, and for always being at the end of the phone. I'm so fortunate to have you both as my urban family.

Julia Beck, my Lil and my first ever reader, for being the world expert on Adam's mug collection, giving me a place to edit and bringing Nye into my life. Your unstinting love, kindness and care make all the difference.

Edward Williams, my frontal lobe, for always doing the needful, soonest. You make me laugh until I have to lie on the floor, have propped me up more times than I can count, and constantly push me to be a better, braver person. I don't know what I would do without you, Pat.

The Hugheses: Iain, Claudia, Edward and Hannah, for reading everything I've ever written and cheering me on every step of the way. Nobody could have a more devoted and supportive family – I love you all so much.

Finally, the biggest thank you of all goes to you lot, for buying and reading this – you're all absolutely brilliant.